THE
Forever
PLAY

Katy ♡ xoxo
Archer

KATY ARCHER

THE FOREVER PLAY
Nolan U Football #1

© Copyright 2025 Katy Archer
www.katyarcher.com

Cover Design © Designed with Grace

ISBN: 978-1-991138-75-0 (Kindle ebook)
ISBN: 978-1-991138-77-4 (paperback)

Archer Street Romance
www.katyarcher.com

PREQUEL NOVELLA

The Forever Play is the first full-length novel in the Nolan U Football series, but there is also a novella that is well worth reading.

The First Play flashes back in time to Zander & Sienna's romance in high school. You'll get to experience their meet-cute and insta-attraction. You'll see them fall in love for the first time and share all of their "firsts" with them.

It's definitely worth reading before starting this book, and it's only 99c on Amazon or you can read it on Kindle Unlimited.

CHAPTER 1
SIENNA

"Say hi to Grammy, Zoey." I point at my phone screen while my parents wave, their smiles wide and dopey as they try to interact with their granddaughter from miles away.

I miss them.

I want to tell them, but I can't because convincing them to go on this cruise took so much effort. I can't go making them feel bad about finally putting themselves first for once.

They left a month ago and get back in February. Six months cruising the globe. It's pretty epic... and some days I wish I had accepted their offer and gone with them. But I could tell they really needed a break, and the adult-only cruise was the one they wanted the most. They would have compromised for me, but they've been doing that so much over the last few years, and I can't ask them to do it anymore.

So, here I am, with my butt on the couch in the small university town of Nolan and my two-year-old crawling all over my lap while my parents lounge on the upper deck, drinking mimosas and giggling at Zoey's antics.

"Gamee, look!" Zoey shouts, pulling a face that cracks my parents up.

My dad sticks out his tongue and crosses his eyes, making Zoey giggle.

"Me! Me!" she shouts, sticking her fingers in her mouth and stretching her lips wide while growling like a monster and drooling like a bulldog.

Gross.

No one ever warned me how much fluid came out of baby humans.

I swipe my finger under her chin, catching the worst of her saliva and wiping it on her already stained shirt. Seriously. The washing never ends, and now that I'm not living with my parents anymore, I'm *really* noticing it. I had no idea how much they'd been doing for me in the background. Moving in with my old family friend, Russell, has been a huge adjustment. This solo mom life is freaking hard.

"Zoey Moey Pa-Poey, my sweet girl, what are you going to do with Mommy today?" my dad asks.

Zoey shrugs, then starts picking her nose.

I gently pull her hand away from her face and brush her messy curls back while I smile at the screen. "We're thinking maybe the park? It's a nice, sunny day."

"Pak!" Zoey raises her hands in the air and squeals. "Les go!"

I wince against the high-pitched sound and grin at her. "We're just gonna finish talking to Grammy and Papa first, okay?"

"Go now?" Zoey gives me her puppy dog eyes.

I bop her nose with my finger. "Soon."

"Now." Her eyebrows dip together, and I laugh at her. "Soon."

Her lip starts to pull into that cute little pout of hers—manipulation number three. "Now."

I give her a pointed look. "Soon."

"You can get going if you want, sweetie," Mom assures me, but I'm not letting my two-year-old dictate the schedule.

"She's okay." I move my head so I can see around Zoey's curls and smile at my parents. "We'll finish up our call and then get ready."

"Now, Mommy! Now!" Zoey starts to kick her legs, so I lift her off my lap and am about to tell her she can sit and play on the floor until I'm ready, but then Russell breezes in, pushing up his Henley shirt sleeves in that habitual way of his.

"Snacks! Snacks in the kitchen for anyone who needs an energy boost before going to the park!" He's announcing it to the room as if it's filled with people.

Zoey's hand shoots into the air. "Me! Me snacks!"

"Come and get your snacks in the kitchen."

"Me!" Zoey jumps up and toddles toward him, her arms raised. "Me, Unca Russy. Me."

"Well, hello, little lady." He crouches down. "Has somebody got a little hungry in their tummy?" He gives her a light poke in the stomach, and she giggles. "Come on, then." Hoisting her up, he throws her over his shoulder, eliciting more squealing giggles as he dances her out of the room.

I catch his eye, and he winks at me before calling out, "Hey, Al and Beth."

"Hey, Rusty!" They laugh out his nickname in unison, giving me adoring smiles as my new housemate walks away with our little girl.

"Oh, he is the sweetest." Mom pats her chest, giving me that look I've been avoiding every time Russell comes up in conversation.

"Mom, don't start. Please."

"I can't help it. You two would be so perfect together."

"Mom," I whine.

"Well, why not? He's a great guy. He's got a secure job. He's just bought his first home. He's sweet and adores Zoey. He's so good with her."

"You could be the cutest family on the block, Blue," Dad tries to encourage me, but I can't help wincing at them.

Glancing over my shoulder, I turn back and lower my voice. "I don't see him that way, you guys. He's just a friend. If anything, he's more like a brother."

"I know you grew up together, but he's always been sweet on you. It's so obvious."

"No, it's not. Seriously, Mom, we are just friends." I pull a face. "I'm not attracted to him that way. There's no chemistry."

"You could learn to be attracted to him. And chemistry is overrated."

"Are you serious right now?" I shoot her an incredulous look while Dad laughs and nuzzles her neck.

She flushes red, and I roll my eyes while she giggles and tries to keep talking. "Okay, fine. But just think about it. There's never been anyone else since..." Her voice trails off with a pained sigh, and I close my eyes, my chest restricting like it always does when Zoey's father flashes through my mind.

His face is still so crystal clear in my soul. Probably because I can't bring myself to delete the last two selfies on my phone. During my raging I-hate-Zander phase, I got rid of most of them, but then I got to my favorite ones and couldn't move them to my trash. Instead, I stared at our happy faces, laughing at the camera. I was wearing my favorite blue bikini, nestled against his naked torso while a crowd of summer festivalgoers partied behind us. That was one of our best weekends ever.

So yeah, I couldn't get rid of that photo, or the one of him lying next to me on my bed—the loved-up dreamy looks on our faces said it all. Instead, I brushed my thumb over his gorgeous face and bawled my eyes out.

Our year together had been perfect... until it wasn't.

My heart spasms, my chest starting to hurt as my broken soul continues to mourn, even after everything that went down. Even though he doesn't really deserve my tears.

Somedays, I wish I could just stay in that raging inferno of anger and betrayal. It's less painful than the sorrowful ache.

You know what I *really* want? To just feel nothing. To be able to hear his name or think about him and feel absolutely nothing. Now that would be bliss.

"You have to move on at some point, sweetheart." Mom's voice is soft and encouraging. "Don't you think it's time to let go?"

"I want to." I sniff and swallow, putting my brave face on. "Don't you think I've been trying?"

"You haven't been on one date."

"Because I have a daughter who needs me. I don't have time to date or put myself out there. Zoey is my sole focus."

"We get that." Dad nods. "But what happens when she grows up and doesn't need you anymore? What then?"

Sudden tears make my eyes burn, my throat swelling uncomfortably as I try to counter their questions.

Don't make me think about my baby girl growing up and leaving me! She's the best thing in my life!

"Just think about it, Blue. Okay?" Dad's expression is so sweet, I wish I could jump through the phone screen and hide away in one of his big hugs. He always gives the best hugs.

Mom rests her head on his broad shoulder. "Rusty is a good guy. He's seriously the best."

"Mom, stop."

"Okay, fine. If not him, then someone else. Just promise me you'll stay open to the idea of falling in love again. I know you got burned once and you're afraid to move on, but there are good people out there, and one of them is just waiting for you to find him."

How do I even respond to that?

Romance is the last thing on my mind right now.

Don't they get that I've moved to a new town? I know no one except Russell, and simply navigating life is a challenge all its own. I don't have the time or brainpower for romance. Zoey takes most of my attention. When would I even fit a date in?

And just to prove my point, Zoey runs back into the room singing, "Pak, pak, pak!"

Jumping onto my lap, she accidentally digs her knee

into my stomach, and I let out a soft "Oof" before wrapping up the call.

"Love you, girls!" Mom and Dad wave and blow kisses at us.

We do the same and I hang up, trying to shake off my parents' unsettling suggestions.

Romance. Love.

Seriously. They're delusional.

"So, you guys ready to go?" Russell claps his hands together.

I look up from the couch at him, forcing a smile. I didn't realize he wanted to come too. Why am I not jumping all over the idea? It's always handy having two sets of eyes on my little girl.

But Mom's comments have really thrown me.

Is he really sweet on me?

My stomach curls into an uncomfortable knot.

Ugh, Russell crushing on me would be so awkward. I just want to be friends with the guy. He's helping me out while my parents are away. That's it.

When he suggested I move in with him, I figured why not? We've been friends forever. I trust him like a brother. He could help with Zoey. Logically, it works.

But if I'd realized he had a thing for me, I wouldn't have said yes.

Please let my mother be delusional. I so don't want to have to deal with this!

I shake my head and smile at Russell. "You don't have to come. I know you've had a really busy week, and it's only going to get more hectic as the hockey season kicks into full swing. You should take the chance to put your feet up and relax. Why don't you watch one of those documentaries you love?"

His eyes dart to the TV. I knew he'd love my doco suggestion. "Are you sure?"

"Yeah, totally. We'll be about an hour, so you should seriously take the chance to get yourself a little peace and quiet." I bulge my eyes at him while Zoey dances around my feet, still singing the word "pak" and getting louder by the second.

He laughs, brushing his fingers through her curls and smiling at me. "As long as you're sure."

"Yeah, totally. I can handle the park on my own. I totally know the way now and promise not to get lost this time."

He gives me a skeptical smirk. "Just call me if you need anything, okay?"

"Absolutely." Picking up my daughter, I perch her on my hip and walk out of the room to get ready, relieved that Russell didn't insist on coming with us like he did last time.

As soon as Zoey is geared up for the park, smelling like sunscreen and wearing the cute little hat Russell bought her last week, I walk her out to the main living area and start buckling her into the stroller.

Russell helps me carry the stroller down the two front steps and squints against the sunshine as he gazes down at me. "Promise to call me if you need me?"

"Of course." I try to make my smile as broad and believable as possible.

There's no way I'm calling him.

I just need some space right now. I can't have memories of Zander skipping through my head while spending time with the man my parents think is a perfect fit for me.

Honestly. Why would they think that?

Russell is like my big bro. A cousin. I've never once been attracted to him.

I don't want him to be anything more than my buddy.

"Have fun, family." He leans down and kisses my cheek.

Gripping the stroller handles, I force my smile to stay in place as he pecks Zoey's nose, then waves us off.

I can feel his eyes watching me the entire way down the street.

CHAPTER 2
ZANDER

I walk beside Wily as we head to the park, sensing the glances we get from every group of girls we pass. I don't know which of us they're eyeing up. I guess the five Football Frat guys all have different appeal. Wily with his blond waves and bright blue eyes always attracts attention, although it could also be the fact that he's a giant and has the widest Colgate smile in the world. Girls love him. He's a real charmer. I've never known the guy not to have at least three girls vying for his attention anywhere we go.

And then you've got Tyrell, another giant of a man. He's Black and beautiful, according to the girl I sit next to in my health psych class. I guess she's right. I just love that he's intimidating as hell on the field. He's our center and keeps the offensive line in check. And I need those guys. They're my fortress.

"Wily." Grady claps his hands, then opens them for a catch.

Wily passes the ball his way, then jogs after him as we

hit the curb and walk diagonally toward the field at the edge of the playground. The sun is shining brightly, and we'll all be sweating soon, but it's good to get out in the fresh air. Last night's game was brutal, and as much as I should be studying right now, I'm kinda liking this chill start to my day.

Carson grunts when Grady hurls the ball at him. It fires through the air like a bullet and hits Carson just as hard.

"Lil' shit," he complains, throwing the ball back and fighting a grin.

I watch him, repressing a smile as I take in his scarecrow hair and grumpy scowl. The guy likes to play it tough, but I bet there's a marshmallow center underneath all that angst. He's loyal. I know that much. I know he'd bleed for any of us. Shit, he'd probably kill for any of us, which is why we all keep such a close eye on him. The guy's got an explosive temper... and it doesn't help that he likes to put himself in situations where it'll flare up in a second. The number of black eyes and hangovers he's walked in the door with is too high to count.

Coach Jones benched him so many times last season, and it's a pain in the ass. He's the best wide receiver on the team, and I trust him to catch whatever I throw his way.

Lightly slapping his shoulder, I force his hungover ass toward the grass and try to get him running. He lopes along beside me as I pick up the pace and charge onto the field next to the playground.

A bunch of girls out jogging in their Lycra stop to admire us. Wily winks and grins, lifting his chin at them. The blonde blushes and giggles, reminding me of a girl I used to know who did the exact same thing every time I winked at her. Damn, she was perfect. And she's totally haunting me this morning.

I wish I could just forget about her and move on. I've really tried, but I think she'll always be a part of me. My first love. My first time. My first heartbreak.

Trying to get over her tore me to shreds.

And then I went through the "just don't think about her" phase, but I failed around every corner. I think I'm finally accepting that I can never fully shake her, so I'm just enjoying the occasional hookup and focusing on football.

That's why I broke up with her in the first place, so I could throw my everything into this game I love so much. So I have to make it count. I need to play for the NFL. I need to make it big... or losing her was for nothing.

Shaking off my dark memories, I raise my hands, catching the ball Tyrell fires my way before launching a perfect spiral to Grady.

My closest friend in the house grabs it out of the air, diving around Carson, who is failing to tackle him. I laugh as he scores himself a "touchdown" and whoops before doing a backflip. Carson growls and shoves him off his feet, which I know Grady let him do because the guy has eyes like a hawk. That's what makes him such a good running back. I swear he has a sixth sense, because he can always spot the gaps, avoid the tackles, and bounce around the defense like he's got magic feet. It helps that he's fearless. Seriously, I can't fault the guy. He's my best friend and probably will be for life.

Carson gathers up the ball and starts careening down the field, heading straight for me. Wily cuts across his path, barreling into him and lifting him off his feet. He puts him in a quick fireman hold and spins him around while the girls on the sidelines laugh and Carson starts shouting, "Put me down, you fuckin' turd waffle!"

"Turd waffle!" Wily laughs. "That's a good one."

"I mean it, you shit stick!"

He laughs a little harder, spinning Carson around one more time.

"You're such a dick!" he grunts, thumping Wily on the back and trying to kick him in the balls.

"Okay, okay." Tyrell runs over to cool things off before Carson snaps. We can only push the guy so far, and you don't want to be on the receiving end of one of his melt-downs. The guy's got skills with his fists, and he isn't afraid to fight dirty. If anything, he prefers it that way.

Carson lands with a thud when Wily throws him off his shoulder, then immediately scrambles back to his feet and jumps on the guy's back, putting him in a choke hold with one arm while wrestling the ball out of Wily's hands. It bounces wildly, and they scramble after it while I stand there grinning and wishing football could be as untamed as what we're doing right now. There's nothing like scrapping for a ball. Coach never lets us do it for fear of injuries, but he isn't here right now.

Carson snatches the ball and starts running. He's a hell of a lot faster than Wily, and the wide receiver leaves the lineman in the dust.

"Carson!" I shout, raising my hands and trying to warn him about the rocket coming up behind him.

Grady aka Flash is a fuckin' bullet when he wants to be, and Carson doesn't sense his approach until it's too late. With a little yell, he hurls the ball my way, but the pass is made reckless by Grady's side tackle. The ball ends up arcing straight over my head and bouncing into the playground behind me.

I look at Tyrell as the two guys start to tussle and see he's already stepping in to deal with the fight while I retrieve the ball. Running into the playground, I head for the sand pit, where a little girl with blonde ringlets is gathering up the ball.

Aw, cutie.

I crouch down with a smile, ready to get the ball back, when the air is knocked clean from my lungs. The blonde cherub tottering toward me looks exactly like my older sister did as a toddler. Photos of Monica as a baby flash through my head, and I can't believe the similarities. The same open smile and curious gaze. She looked like she wasn't scared to take on the whole world... and neither does this little one.

She stops a few feet away from me and holds up the ball. "Bawl."

I nod and smile down at her. "That's right. Football."

"Foobawl." Her sweet little voice pitches with excitement, and she laughs.

"Do you want to throw it to me?" I beckon with my fingers, then glance around, wondering where her parents are.

She giggles again, then throws the ball with a little grunt, raising her hands in the air with a cheer when it lands a foot away from me, then dribbles to a stop by my feet.

"Good job, kid." I wink at her, then laugh when she claps her hands.

Shit, she's so like Monica it's freaking me out right now.

"Zan-Man, let's go!" Wily calls to me, holding up his hands to catch the ball.

I fire it through the air, then jog back to the edge of the field, turning one more time to look at the little girl. She's crouching down in the sand, gathering handfuls and creating a little mountain.

For reasons I can't even explain, I find myself watching her until my friends are shouting at me again.

"Dude, what's up?" Grady calls across the grass. "Let's go, brother."

"Just give me a sec!" I hold up my finger, pulling out my phone and calling my sister while this little girl is still within my sights.

"'Sup, lil' bro?"

"Do you have a daughter I don't know about?"

"Ew, no. Why would I ever have kids?" Her reaction makes me laugh, and I shake my head.

My sister has taken independent woman to the next level. She's in a relationship now, but who knows if it'll last. She likes to go intense and hard... for short bursts of time. That just seems to be her style. I get why she never wants to bring kids into that kind of lifestyle. She's not exactly the mothering type... although she's had to mother me a time or two.

"Why are you calling to ask me stupid questions? You know I'm at work, right?"

"It's Sunday."

"I have a big case." My sister—the hotshot lawyer.

"Oh, well, sorry. I just..." Shaking my head yet again, I gaze at the blonde cutie and let out a breathy laugh. "You must have a doppelgänger in Nolan, because I am staring at a kid who looks just like you when you were two. You know that picture on Dad's office desk?"

"The one of me playing on the beach in that frilly abomination Mom insisted on dressing me in?"

I laugh. "That's the one. Well, this little girl right here isn't in frills, but man... she looks just like you. It's freaking me out."

Monica snorts. "Well, her mother must be very beautiful, then."

"And look just like you." I start to search the playground for her, but there are so many parents around. A group of moms is standing by the sandpit, watching their kids and talking together. My eyes skim across them, but I don't see any Monica replicas. And the rest of the playground seems clear too. Darting my gaze back to the girl, I shake my head again. "It's seriously incredible."

"You're still staring at her, aren't you?"

"I can't help it."

"Yeah, well, you might want to stop in case her big bad daddy is there and wants to pound on some freaky-ass guy who's staring at his kid."

"Yeah, good point." I turn my back to the playground. "Not the pounding shit, because I can hold my own." I can practically hear her eyes rolling. "But I don't want to be putting creeper vibes out there."

"Good boy."

I grin. "Glad you didn't get knocked up without me knowing."

"I do my best. Love you, bro."

"Love you." I hang up and look over my shoulder again... in time to miss the pass coming right at me. It fires straight past my head and rolls toward the playground again.

"Seriously, Zan! Come on, man." Carson scowls at me. "Get your head in the game."

I snicker at his complaint and turn back toward the playground. It gives me an excuse to take one last look at the little girl who I swear could pass as my niece any day of the week.

CHAPTER 3
SIENNA

I check on Zoey, smiling as I watch her create mountains of sand in the sandpit. She loves doing that. I should be over there playing with her, but my phone keeps buzzing with texts from Russell, and I don't like to be on my screen the whole time I'm with her. I want her to see me present, not distracted on my phone and think that's normal.

She seems content in her own imagination right now, so I glance back down at my screen and read Russell's latest text. I want to wrap up this conversation so I can get back to my daughter, but I can't just go ignoring him because the last time I did that, he got all worried and came to find us, wondering why I wasn't replying to his messages.

Apparently, turning off my phone while I'm out and about is not okay.

. . .

Rusty: David Attenborough is legendary. If I wasn't a hockey coach, I'd totally become a wildlife photographer.

I raise my eyebrows. Two very different jobs, but whatever.

Russell's been playing hockey for as long as I've known him. He's wanted to be a coach since he was fourteen years old. Getting this job at Nolan U was the biggest win for him. It's his first year being an assistant coach of a college team. He spent his first two years out of college coaching a high school team in Nebraska and teaching PE. When this job came up, he couldn't apply fast enough. He's moved his whole life here, even bought a house. I think he's hoping it'll lead to a more senior coaching position.

He's capable, although sometimes I think he acts like he's the senior coach already, and I'm sure the players don't love that. But it's not like I can say anything. What the hell do I know about hockey? I'm more of a football girl, which Russell hassles me about constantly. But I'm not giving up on it.

I fell in love with football my junior year of high school, and I've followed it ever since.

The Broncos are my pro team, but I actually enjoy watching college ball more.

My insides twist as I try not to think about the reasons why. How every time I sit down to watch a college game, I'm not eyeing every player, wondering if it could be Zander.

He plays for Kelsey U, and I'm smart enough never to

watch any games in that division, so why the hell do I think he'll be on some other team?

Yes, I really am insane.

I glance up and spot Zoey, still happily playing, while I try to decide how to tactfully end this text conversation. I don't want to be rude. The guy is letting me live with him, which is saving me bucketloads of money. My parents gifted me my college account when Zoey was born. They could sense how much I wanted to stay home and raise my little girl. I haven't had to use to much of it yet, as they've been generous beyond reason, but they're away right now, and I'm having to dip into that account on the regular. Living rent-free is a huge help, and I have to be nice to my provider, right?

Russell obviously thinks I'm lonely hanging out at the park with my daughter and is trying to keep me entertained.

But I'm at a crowded playground. Why would I be lonely?

My gaze shifts to the group of moms chatting near the swings. Two of them are holding coffees and laughing about something, while the other one pushes her son on the swings and chips into the conversation when her other kid isn't shouting at her to "Watch me, Mom! Watch!"

The mothers all look to be in their late twenties/early thirties. And here's me, only twenty-one, just a baby myself compared to those around me. They probably think I'm a nanny or babysitter.

Shit.

My phone rings and I eye up Zoey, noticing her chatting with a man holding a football.

Crap. She is always talking to strangers. I watch her carefully as I gather our stuff and answer the call.

"Hey, Rusty. What's up?"

"Just checking on my Zoey girl. Does Mommy need backup? I can pause my doco and come join you guys."

"No, that's okay." I try to keep my voice bright and not let it bother me how he always refers to Zoey as his. "I'm just about to head back anyway. Zoey's due for a nap soon, and—"

"You don't want to miss that window. Got it. I'll see you soon, then."

"Okay, see ya." With a little frown, I shove my phone into my back pocket and check on Zoey again.

She's still talking to that guy. Seriously, she's going to be the biggest flirt when she's a teenager. God help me!

"Zoey!" I call, snatching her drink bottle off the bench and shoving it into the stroller.

"Mommy!" she calls back, and my heart smiles like it always does when I hear her voice.

"Hey, baby girl! Time to go!" I try to keep my tone bright. She doesn't need to know that thoughts of Russell and what my parents said and how he behaves are making my skin itch. I should be happy and grateful that Russell loves Zoey so much, that he cares enough to let us live in Nolan with him. The guy is twenty-five. He's a young bachelor and could be living it up, but he's choosing to be Unca Russy to a two-year-old and putting up with restless nights, the odd tantrum, and a chaotic house.

Yeah, you really should be so grateful.

Hitching the diaper bag onto my shoulder, I push the stroller toward my little girl, pulling out my phone one more time and rereading Russell's text, trying to find my happy feels before I get back home to him.

Be grateful, Sienna. Because of him, you don't have to live on your own while your parents are away.

My chest pinches as I send a smiley face emoji back to his "see you soon" GIF, and it hits me yet again that I can be as grateful as I want, but that doesn't change the truth.

Russell's not Zander.

And even though I don't want Zander in our lives... it doesn't change the fact that if I was returning home to a man who owns my heart the way Zander did, I'd be a lot happier to go back there.

But that's never going to happen, now is it?

With a heavy sigh, I slide my phone into my back pocket and walk toward Zoey, but my steps quickly falter.

I jerk to a stop, my lips parting as I take in the man standing next to my daughter.

Shit. *His* daughter.

No.

What the hell is he doing here?

This... no... no!

Zander blinks, staring at me like he's seeing a ghost.

Why is he in Nolan right now?

Why isn't he at Kelsey U where he's supposed to be?

He blinks again, his expression buckling like he can't believe I'm real.

Shit. Shit. Shit!

This is bad.

Zander Donohue is standing six feet away from me.

Six feet!

I never thought I'd see him again, and now he's here. In Nolan.

What the fuck is he doing in Nolan?

My heart starts to thunder, my body frozen as Zoey shouts, "Mommy!" with her usual glee. I can't even smile in response.

Zander's eyes bulge, his skin paling as he watches Zoey run toward me. I scoop her up, perching her on my hip, my eyes still glued to the one person I swore I'd never speak to again.

But there he is.

He looks stronger, more manly somehow.

He's still just as gorgeous as he was back then. Dammit.

Anger flares through me as I gaze at that face I used to trace with my fingers, my lips.

He held my heart in the palm of his hand... and then he closed his fist and squeezed the life right out of it.

"Sparks." He whispers my nickname, and I...

I can't!

I can't do this with him.

I don't want that thrill of desire dancing through me when I hear his voice.

I don't want anything to do with him!

But does he know I'm holding his daughter? The little girl I never told him about? The little girl he didn't *deserve* to know about?

Shit, I have to get out of here.

He shifts toward me, and my head is shaking before I can stop it.

"Nope!" Snatching the stroller handle, I spin in the opposite direction and start running like I'm being chased by a masked gunman.

Zoey giggles, thinking I'm playing a game and

clinging to my shirt while her body jostles against mine. "Fasser, Mommy. Fasser."

"Sienna!" Zander shouts behind me, and I pick up my pace.

"Faster. Mommy's going faster." My voice is trembling, and thank God Zoey doesn't seem to notice. She giggles again, loving this game while I fight a wave of panic.

This can't be happening.

This cannot.

Be.

Happening!

CHAPTER 4
ZANDER

"Sienna!" I try again, picking up my pace and starting to sprint.

Fuck, I should have started running as soon as she did, but I was frozen in place, shock pulsing through my veins like venom.

That little girl said, "Mommy."

Sienna's a mommy to a girl who looks about two years old. I'm wrestling to do the math as I charge after her, desperate for answers.

But by the time I round the corner, she's gone. Vanished... just like she did last time.

"Fuck," I mutter, scraping my hands through my hair and getting a dark scowl from a mother walking past with her babies.

"Sorry," I murmur, my shoulders deflating when I stare down the road, wondering if I just imagined the blue-eyed beauty. She's still a stunner.

I never thought I'd see her again.

But there she was. Holding a toddler. *Her* toddler.

My toddler?

"Double fuck," I mutter under my breath as I spin and look the other way.

Should I just start wandering the streets shouting her name?

What is she even doing in Nolan?

My mind flashes back to the last time I saw her, the way she felt in my arms as we shared our final kiss good-bye. It took everything in me to let her crawl out my bedroom window after the night we'd spent together. I loved her. And it killed me to break up with her, but I knew it was the right thing to do. I'd thought it through, made the sensible decision for both of us. Logically, I was being the better man, not tying her into some long-distance bullshit.

But I'd hated myself for it.

I'd tried to make the most of college, play the best ball I could, fit in with my team. Guilt, shame and disgust all singe me when I think about my first year at Kelsey U and how stupid I was.

I tried to move on with my life, but I became someone I wasn't. I couldn't get over Sienna, it was naive of me to think it was even possible. So, I went back for her...

I had a three-day break for Christmas, and I wasn't about to waste it. I'd been training my ass off, proving to Kelsey U that picking me had been the right decision. I was getting in good with the rest of the team, earning their respect. I didn't love the hoops I had to jump through, but I tried to convince myself it was worth it.

I hated some of the shit I'd been doing. Trying to

meet everyone's expectations was fucking hard, but I had to find a way to still be a valued member of the team... and be with my girl.

I just needed to make some tweaks that would keep me in the team captains' good books, still get me decent field time, plus make sure Dad wouldn't ride me about wasting my talent. I'd do whatever it took so that I could be with the one person I couldn't let go of.

I had to get Sienna back. I'd tried cutting her off, giving us both a clean break so we could spread our wings and learn to fly alone, but I was fucking miserable. I was starving without her, making shitty decisions with unintended consequences. I was lost and I needed her to guide me home again. I didn't care what my parents thought anymore. I had to have her back in my life or I was going to lose my shit and never recover.

Hopefully I wasn't too late to persuade her to get back together with me, to beg her to apply to Kelsey U so I didn't have to live without her anymore.

I'd held out for as long as I could with the no contact thing. According to my parents, I was being merciful, cutting the ties and not teasing her with texts or phone calls the way I'd wanted to.

But I couldn't keep that shit up, so the second I walked through the door, I dumped my bag, hugged my mom, and told her I had someplace important to be.

"Where are you going?" she called after me.

"I'll be back soon. I promise!" I waved to her, and she no doubt assumed I was heading to Noah's house. He was back for Christmas, too, and we'd already arranged to catch up.

But there was someone else I needed to see first.

Sprinting to Sienna's front door, I knocked three times and held my breath as I listened to the shuffle of steps behind the wood.

My heart started to race, my insides jumping as the door creaked open and an unfamiliar face greeted me.

"Yes?" The old man gave me a confused frown. "Can I help you?"

"Oh, uh... hi, sir. You must be Sienna's grandfather?" She'd told me about him, but I couldn't remember his name.

"Who?"

"Sienna." I could feel my forehead wrinkling. "She lives here."

"Sorry, son. You must have the wrong house."

My head jolted back, and I took a few steps away from the house to gaze up at it. "No, this is where she lives. I... I used to come over here all the time."

"Oh." The man nodded, his lips rising into a half smile. "You must mean the people who lived here before I moved in. I never met them. The house was empty when it came on the market."

"What?" I rasped, stumbling back toward him. "You just bought this house?"

"Moved in about three weeks ago."

"But..." I blinked. "She..." Stumbling away from him, I didn't even bother saying goodbye as I ran down the path like a drunk ostrich and wrestled the phone out of my pocket.

Finding Sienna's number, I immediately called her and waited as it rang and rang, then went to voicemail. With an annoyed huff, I texted her.

. . .

Me: You've moved? What's going on? Please call me. We need to talk. It's really important.

She never responded, so I texted every hour until midnight.

And nothing.

Had she changed her number too?

Fuck. I didn't know what the hell was going on.

After a sleepless night, staying up to the early hours, scouring social media and finding all of Sienna's accounts closed, I ducked out of the house before Christmas breakfast and hit up each of my friends. Noah and Emily were stoked to see me but ended up being no help at all.

"She just left. Started the school year a little miserable but nothing red flag-ish, and then one day she just didn't show. I thought she was out sick—there'd been a tummy bug going around and Sienna definitely caught it. But then Olivia told me she'd moved."

"What the fuck?"

"I know." Emily bulged her eyes in agreement with me. "I tried texting her, but she just ghosted me. She didn't say goodbye to any of us."

"Why didn't someone tell me!"

"Why would we, dude?" Noah scoffed. "You made me swear not to mention her name around you. When Emily told me what happened, I wanted to let you know, but you seemed preoccupied with all your stuff, and I didn't want to bother you with it. I thought you were over her, man."

"I'm not." I shook my head, walking out of their living room with more questions than answers.

Trudging home with my shoulders hunched, I fought various waves of pain, annoyance, and confusion. Why the fuck would she just take off without saying anything? It didn't make any sense.

My phone started buzzing as I stepped back into the house.

"There you are!" Mom bustled into the entrance while I shrugged off my jacket and held up my phone. "Okay, but after that call, you're telling me exactly where you've been." She huffed and stormed back into the kitchen while I answered a call from Olivia.

"Hey."

"Emily just texted and told me you're looking for Sienna. Why?"

I sighed, resting my butt on the back of the couch and tucking a hand under my armpit. "I was hoping I could see her. Tell her I missed her." I mumbled out the last part.

"Toy with her, you mean?"

"Hey. No," I grumbled, kicking the heel of my socked foot on the floor. "I genuinely want her back."

"Well, you missed that boat."

"Olivia," I softly pleaded. "Where is she?"

After a sigh that made my stomach hurt, she finally told me. "Truth is, I don't actually know. She moves around a lot and is total shit at staying in touch, even though she promised me she would."

"What the hell happened?"

"I don't know. She wasn't the same after you left, but she was trying and then... one day she didn't turn up to school. She'd thrown up the day before, so I thought she was sick and texted to check on her but she never replied.

A couple days, she came over, perfectly healthy, and told me her parents were hitting the road, and she was going to finish out her senior year via online school. They had some big camper van, road trip adventure thing planned."

I nodded, remembering all the stories she'd told me about tripping around with her parents. "I thought she wanted to graduate here."

"Me too." Olivia popped her lips. "I mean... the day she left, she did seem really upset. She came over to hug me goodbye and was crying and going on about needing a clean break. She wanted to put everything behind her." Her voice dropped to droll and unimpressed. "She was kind of babbling, to be honest, like she didn't know what she was trying to say. In the end, I just hugged her and told her to go have fun. She promised to send me pics and keep me updated but..." Olivia sighed. "She sucks at it. I get the odd text every now and then, but I've had so many messages go without a response that I'm not sure I'm going to bother anymore. It's obvious she wants to be left alone."

"But why?"

"I don't know."

"Well..." I huffed. "Can you tell her I need to speak with her?"

"I doubt it's gonna make any difference."

"Why?"

Olivia groaned like she wished she hadn't called me in the first place. "She was never the same after you broke up. She was obsessed with you, and you tore her heart out."

Ouch. It hurt like a knife through the stomach to hear

that, and I quickly tried to justify my actions. "I was trying to do the right thing. Be sensible."

"Well, she never recovered. If you ask me, you *did* do the right thing. She was way too clingy with you and needed to grow a serious backbone. The fact that she couldn't cope without you tells me she wasn't even ready for you, you know?"

I nodded, not sure I was really following.

"My advice?" Olivia continued. "Leave her alone and let her get on with her life. She's traveling, having fun exploring the country. Don't toy with her heart and make her miss you all over again. You were the one who broke it off, so do the right thing and... keep it off. You need to move on too."

To say I was devastated was the understatement of the year. I couldn't get over the fact that Sienna had just left and not even told me about it. For a second, I worried that she had some serious illness she was keeping secret, but Olivia had said she was perfectly healthy before she left. I couldn't figure out what the fuck had been going through her parents' heads when they just pulled her out of school and hit the road. What the hell was wrong with them?

I spent the rest of the day stewing, which definitely set a pretty morose tone for Christmas. I felt kind of bad about it. It was the first time I'd made it back since starting college, and I was being a grumpy asshole.

Dad and Monica came over for lunch. Even my grandparents were there. It was supposed to be this family celebration, and all I could obsess over was the fact that Sienna hadn't been where I thought she was. That she'd left and not told me.

She'd just up and vanished and was ghosting me, no matter how many texts I sent or voicemails I left.

In the end, my sullen behavior got too much for Dad, and our family lunch ended with a massive argument. I packed my bags and headed back to Kelsey U a day early.

Wincing, I rub the back of my head and fist my hair. Mom's forgiven me since, but it took a hell of a lot of apologizing.

"Zan! What's wrong, man?" Grady runs up to me, resting his hand on my shoulder. "Why are you standing all the way over here? We thought you'd taken off."

"Uh…" I swallow, unable to form a coherent sentence. How the fuck am I supposed to tell him? I just saw the one who got away, and she was carrying a daughter… maybe my daughter.

Fuck, fuck, fuck! What am I supposed to do with that?

"You okay? You look like you're about to pass out."

"Nah, I'm good, bro." I shake him off and start walking back to the field.

He wanders along beside me, not saying anything. He's good like that, never demands shit I don't want to give.

But by the time we reach the grass, I feel like I owe him an explanation.

When Wily walks over to check on me, I spit out a small semblance of truth.

"Just thought I saw someone I used to know."

"Oh yeah?" Wily wiggles his eyebrows. "Was she hot?"

I snicker and can't help tipping my head to the side. "Still gorgeous."

"Ahhh." They start to razz me, and I let them, because I can't tell them everything right now.

They don't know how I broke Sienna's heart.

They don't know how she broke mine.

And they can never know how I returned to Kelsey U and, in an attempt to deal with my personal tragedy, systematically fucked up my freshman year in the worst way possible.

CHAPTER 5
SIENNA

By the time, I get back to Russell's place, I'm ready to throw up. I basically ran the whole way back, pushing the stroller and carrying Zoey until I couldn't breathe. She got sick of being jostled around and soon started squawking until I slowed to a shuffle and panted my way to the front door.

It opens before I can turn the handle, and Russell greets us with a cheerful "Hey, family! How's my little girl?" Reaching for Zoey, he takes her out of my arms, tickling her tummy and making her giggle and squirm.

But her humor doesn't last long. Soon she's grousing and then starts crying.

"What's the matter, lil' bug? You tired?"

"Y-yeah." I find my voice. Having stored the stroller with trembling hands—wrestling it shut with a desperate grunt—I manage to stand and face my roommate.

"Are you okay?" He frowns, concern flashing through his eyes. "Sienna, what's wrong?"

"Nothing." I smooth back my hair. "I'm just not

feeling great. I think my period might be due or something. I'm not sure."

Zander called me Sparks. I haven't heard that nickname in three years. I didn't even realize how much I missed it until he whispered it on the playground. I shouldn't want to miss it!

He destroyed me!

The words in my head are screaming so loud, I miss the first part of Russell's sentence.

Blinking, I try to focus on what he's saying.

"...it sucks, but maybe it's coming early." He gives me a sympathetic smile while my forehead wrinkles.

Does he know my cycle?

You live together. He's not stupid... and he takes out the trash.

I try to talk myself out of the chill that's racing down my spine and shake my head. It's not weird that he knows when I have my period—it's weird that he knows when it's *due*. I've only been here a month, so I would have had at least one. But surely he didn't make some kind of mental note or—

Ugh! Just stop thinking about it. Put Zoey down for a nap and then fold yourself into a corner and cry. You know that's all you're capable of right now.

"Well, do you want to go lie down? I can give Zoey a drink and settle her for you."

"That's really, sweet. Thanks." I force a smile. "But I can put her down. Then I think I'll take a nap as well."

"You sure?"

"Yeah." I reach for my daughter, needing her chubby little arms around my neck, needing her soft hair ticking my exposed skin, needing her weight against my chest.

Cradling her in my arms, I don't even mind when she

wipes her snotty nose on my shirt. She's getting grizzly, so I hurry through her diaper change. I need to start potty training her soon. From everything I've read, she's showing me signs she's ready, but I just wanted to get settled into Russell's place first.

It's been five weeks, Sen. You're settled.

Swallowing back an unexpected sob, I try to ignore the fact that Zander and I have probably been living in the same town for over a month, and I didn't even know it.

Shit, had we passed each other in the street and not even realized?

Picking up Zoey, I rock her in my arms for a minute before laying her down in her crib. She grabs Piggy Watson and Professor Lovebug, squeezing them in her arms before curling onto her side. I rub her back, watching my precious angel fall asleep and still trying to wrap my head around the fact that she was talking to her father less than an hour ago.

Her father.

The man who didn't even know she existed.

I never thought I'd be the type of woman to keep something like that a secret. But I also never expected Zander to change so much when he left for college.

I couldn't bring a baby into his life. After what I saw, I didn't want to bring him back into mine.

But how different would things have been if he'd known the truth?

A shudder runs through me as my mind skips over the last time we were together and straight to the doctor's appointment that changed my life forever...

.   .   .

The doctor's office was cold and sterile. I didn't like it. But if this woman would help me figure out why I kept throwing up all the time, then I was willing to stay in my seat. At first I wondered if it was pure heartache. Zander had been gone for over a month, and I knew that I was supposed to be getting over him and enjoying school, but I missed him so much. Walking the halls knowing I wouldn't be seeing him around the corner... knowing I couldn't wait for him after football practice... knowing he wasn't going to be holding me anytime soon... It was a killer.

I'd been miserable ever since he broke up with me, except for that one perfect night when we said our final goodbye. I wanted that night back. I wanted it back over and over again.

Mom took my hand, giving it a little squeeze and looking as worried as ever while the doctor typed notes and continued asking questions.

"She's been throwing up for about a week and half," Mom explained. "At first I thought it was just a stomach bug, but the fact that she's still so ill makes me wonder if she might have something really nasty, like campylobacter or gastroenteritis. Can she be tested for those, please?"

"If that's what we need to do, we definitely will. Let me just ask a few more questions first." The doctor smiled kindly at me. "Have you had any fever?"

"No," Mom answers for me, obviously mystified by this. "No fever, no rashes, no diarrhea. She just can't seem to hold her food down."

The doctor nodded, then looked at me, her gaze

penetrating my inner core and only exacerbating my anxiety. "When was your last period?"

"Um..." I frowned, confused by the question. What did my period have to do with a stomach bug?

Mom stiffened beside me, her eyes going wide as she turned to hear my answer.

"About three or four weeks ago? My next one's due any day now."

The doctor nodded again, tapping into her computer. "And how was it?"

"I'm sorry?"

"Your last period. Was it normal? Heavy? Light? Anything different about it?"

Mom's breath hitched, and she started blinking really fast.

I frowned at her and started blinking myself. "Um... I guess it was kind of light for me. More kind of spotting for five days or so. Usually, I get this like heavy flood for about two days, and then one day later, it's over, but I guess it just decided to go long and slow last month."

"Okay." The doctor bit her lips together, typed a few more notes, then looked between my mother and me. "Sienna, are you okay with your mother staying in the room with us?"

"Yes, why?"

"I need to ask you some personal questions, and you have the right to confidentiality if you want it."

"Oh, um... no, Mom can stay. She knows everything anyway." The questions were making me even more nervous, and the thought of Mom leaving me alone with this doctor was freaking me out.

Clinging to my mother, I gripped her hand tightly

while the doctor gave us a professional smile, then asked the worst question ever. "Are you sexually active?"

My shoulders slumped, my voice quaking as I shook my head. "No."

"So, you've never once had intercourse?"

"Oh." I frowned, my shoulder hitching. "I mean, I have... had... sex. I just don't anymore." My insides jerked and trembled, sorrow consuming me like it always did when I thought of Zander.

"And when was the last time you had sex?"

I looked at my mother and admitted, "It was the night before he left, so... When was that?"

The color drained from Mom's face, her eyes closing as she rasped, "About six weeks ago."

"Yeah." I sniffed, my chin bunching until Mom huffed and rounded on me.

"You told me you were being safe! You said you used protection!"

Startled by my mother's snappy tone, my slow-ass brain was struggling to keep up.

Wait... what were they implying?

A cold fear shot through me, and I couldn't comprehend that question.

All I could do was argue, "We did use protection. All the time!"

"Did you? That last time? Did you?" Mom's voice pitched and her arms flailed. I hadn't seen her lose it like that before, and it was throwing me.

I opened my mouth to emphatically say, "We did!" but then I remembered. As I sifted through the crazy barrage of emotions that had driven my every move that night, I finally got down to the facts.

"Sienna. Think! Did you—"

"He pulled out," I quickly interrupted her, remembering that moment with sharp clarity, the look on his face as he came all over my stomach, the way I loved him so deeply, so strongly in that moment that I nearly cried. "Yeah, he definitely pulled out."

"Oh my gosh." Mom covered her mouth with her hand and whimpered.

"What?" I looked at the doctor, panic finally blasting through my memories and telling me something I didn't want to hear. The penny was dropping, and it was hitting every raw surface within me. And following in its wake was a tidal wave of pure terror. "No... that, no! Pulling out is a safe method, right? I mean, right?"

The doctor winced, folding her hands together on the desk and giving me a sympathetic smile. "It's one of the least reliable."

My brain seemed to freeze for a second, and I couldn't speak properly. "No... you... I can't... I can't be pr- pregnant."

"We'll have you take a test to be sure." Her voice was so calm.

How could she be so calm? How could she sit there changing my entire life and be so unaffected by it?

"I'm gonna be sick." Lurching out of my chair, I raced to the bathroom, barely getting the toilet lid up before emptying the meager contents of my stomach into the bowl.

As I wiped my mouth with shaking fingers, the truth sank into my very bones. I somehow knew without any tests that the doctor was right.

Resting my hand on my lower abdomen, I struggled

to breathe. I couldn't move my ass off those cold restroom tiles until Mom came and got me.

She'd calmed down by the time the test results were in, and sure enough, the doctor was right.

"Looks like you're pregnant."

Zoey mumbles something soft in her sleep, and I press the back of my hand against my mouth, my eyes filling with tears as I watch her.

She's the most precious, treasured thing in my entire life.

I didn't expect her to be such a gift, but she's been everything I didn't even realize I wanted. She helped heal my pain. Her sweet newborn cries stitched up my heart, her mouth suckling me, her soft fingers resting on my skin, baby laughter and beautiful smiles... every breath she took was a balm for my wounded heart.

But I don't think I realized how bruised and scarred my heart still is.

Until I saw the man who demolished it standing there at the playground today.

CHAPTER 6
ZANDER

I can't stop thinking about Sienna. It's been nearly two days since I saw her and Zoey.

Zoey.

That name will be burned into my brain forever.

"Zoey!" Sienna's voice had rung across the playground, and at first I hadn't recognized it. But now it's on repeat in my brain.

Sienna's voice was always so playful and fun. It was a sweet melody in high school.

It hadn't sounded so light and playful when I heard it on Sunday, but it was still hers.

Mine. My Sparky.

But she's not.

Not the way she looked at me, all bug-eyed and afraid.

All "Nope!" and run.

What the fuck!

I have to find her. I have to know the truth.

Am I Zoey's father?

The thought makes me shudder, twisting my gut into

a painful knot and making it impossible to finish my lunch.

I nudge the tray away from me, too lost in my memories to even hear my teammates around me.

Zoey's a toddler. If she's about two, then there's a really strong chance she's mine. Unless Sienna tried getting over me by immediately sleeping with someone else after I left. The thought fills my mind with a green-red haze, and I shut it off, forcing myself to see this notion through.

Our last night together had been epic. It was a final goodbye.

I can still see her face through my bedroom window, rain running down her skin like tears. I'd pulled her inside and she'd cried against me, mourning the end of our relationship and begging me to hold her one last time.

I couldn't just hold her. I needed her to know that I was hurting too. That I still loved her.

And so we lost ourselves in each other the way we always did.

It came so naturally, our bodies burning with desire, our fingers knowing where to touch, our tongues dancing that familiar tango.

I plunged inside her before putting a condom on. It hadn't even occurred to me until I felt that liquid fire in my veins. I could sense the impending orgasm and suddenly realized how fucking irresponsible I was being.

"I'll pull out before I pop, okay?" I'd barely managed the words. "Or do you want me to suit up?"

She hadn't. She'd shaken her head and whispered, "It's okay. I trust you."

And I had been trustworthy. I hadn't given in to temptation and exploded inside her the way I'd wanted to. I'd forced myself to pull out, to jerk and come all over her perfect stomach. She'd watched me the whole time, her gaze so strong and sure, drenched in adoration. I had to kiss her lips after that. I had to hold her close and not let go.

She spent the entire night in my arms.

And I had no idea one of my swimmers had been left behind.

Fuck. I thought pulling out was a safe method.

One you've never used with any other girl.

I'm all about condoms and safe sex now. There's something almost robotic and mechanical about my occasional hook ups.

I've never lost myself with a girl the way I lost myself in Sienna. She fried my brain, made it that much harder to think about protection when our bodies were doing all the thinking for us. There wasn't logical thought when it came to physical stuff with her. There was only harmony and passion.

Fuck.

I scrape my hand through my hair, reeling at this bombshell that's exploded in my face.

Why didn't she tell me?

If I am the father, why the fuck didn't she tell me!

That's the only thing that's making me doubt Zoey is mine. Because Sienna wouldn't keep something like that from me. It wouldn't matter how hurt she was over the breakup; there's no way she wouldn't have told me I was going to be a dad.

So maybe Zoey's not mine.

Maybe trying to find out will only unearth a shit ton of complications and drama.

But I have to find her.

And I have to see Zoey one more time... to know for sure.

The fact that she looks just like Monica did is a fucking obvious omen, isn't it?

She's yours. You know she's yours.

But I need that shit confirmed.

Clenching my jaw, I keep staring at my half-eaten lunch, the world only coming back into focus when I hear Wily behind me.

"Well, that sucks."

I blink and look over my shoulder. Wily's talking to two of his high school buddies. Ethan Galloway and Liam something. I can't remember. It starts with a C, I think.

Anyway, they're hockey boys and seniors this year, just like Wily and me.

Ethan senses my stare and raises his chin in acknowledgment before rounding up his conversation. "We don't get a say in who coaches us, I guess."

"At least he's only an assistant coach." Liam sighs. "Although he keeps acting like he's the boss."

"The guy's a fuckwit." Casey Pierce glides past, chipping in his two cents as he heads to the hockey table. "I'm just saying it because I know you two pansy-asses don't want to publicly trash-talk the guy, but it's the truth!"

Ethan snickers and shakes his head, then mutters, "It's kind of the truth. He acts more like a drill sergeant than a coach."

"Dude. It's always hard adjusting," Wily says. "I know when Coach Jones started, I kinda hated on the guy."

I tense, ready to defend our head coach to the end. That guy saved my life.

"But I've gotten used to his style now, and I really respect him," Wily finishes, and I relax my elbows back onto the table. "What's the fuckwit's name?"

Liam shakes his head, and Ethan tuts like he doesn't want to say, but Casey pipes up from his end of the table. "That'd be Russell Fisher. Fish Sticks. McDaddy Doo-doo."

What did he just say?

My ears start burning, my back pinging straight.

"Repulsive Russell." Casey lifts his fork in the air.

"Lame!" someone shouts from the hockey table while a few more snort and laugh at their teammate's name-calling rant.

"Fish Fucker." A loud laugh pops out of Casey's mouth, and Ethan raises his hand to shut his teammate up.

"Case, we get it, man."

"Oh, come on, bro. I want to think of at least three more." He clicks his fingers, then grins. "Sheriff Scrotum... Head... Or just Scrotum? Which sounds better? Or should it be Sheriff Ballsack?"

"Casey, shut the fuck up." Asher Bensen throws a grape at his head, and Liam grins when Casey does a dramatic dodge.

Shaking his head with a laugh, Ethan slaps Wily on the arm as if he's about to say goodbye, but I can't let him leave.

My heart is beating so hard my ribs are gonna be permanently bruised.

Russell Fisher.

I know that name!

Snapping to my feet, I spin and face them properly, my expression no doubt doing something crazy because Ethan and Liam both stare at me like I've lost my fucking mind.

I think just have.

"Are you okay?" Wily asks, nudging me with his elbow.

"Did he just say Russell Fisher?" I point between the two hockey players.

"Uh... yeah." Liam nods. "Do you know him or something?"

"I recognize the name." I can barely manage my next sentence. "Is he at the arena?"

"Probably." They nod. "We have practice this afternoon, so..." Ethan's sentence dribbles off as I grab my stuff and bolt away from the table.

"Zan-Man, where the hell are you going?" Wily shouts after me, but like I can stop and answer him.

Russell Fisher.

Well, fuck me.

Sienna used to talk about old family friends they lived next door to in Sacramento. She went and visited them a few times during our year together.

Russell was like an older brother to her, and he used to play hockey. I'm sure she said he played hockey!

Is that the reason Sienna's here?

Because of him?

My flying run slows to a jog as the thought hits me.

She's here because of him.

Is she with him?

Are they a couple?

Do they live together?

Is Zoey his?

Fuck no. He was like four or five years older than her. She wouldn't have... I mean, right?

By the time I can see the arena, I've slowed to a crawl.

The building looms ahead of me in the distance, and I'm wondering if this is the dumbest idea I've ever had. Charging in there to talk to some assistant hockey coach who's never even met me before?

He might not even know Sienna!

There has to be more than one Russell Fisher who lives in the US. It's not that uncommon of a name, right?

But I can't not take this chance.

I have to find her, and he's the closest lead I've got right now.

Squaring my shoulders, I ball my hands into fists and walk toward the arena, steeling myself for whatever this guy is going to tell me.

CHAPTER 7
SIENNA

I sit on the floor, staring at the blocks Zoey's playing with until they're a blur in front of me. My daughter is stacking the colored pieces of wood, then using the toy hammer to smash her tower down. She's having a blast, and usually I'd be laughing along with her, but today... all I seem capable of is vacant stares.

Snap out of it, Sienna! You have a little girl who deserves your attention!

I blink and force myself to sit up straight, reposition myself cross-legged on the floor, and smile down at Zoey.

"Bang! Cash!" She laughs as the blocks tumble into a messy pile.

"Bang. Crash." I grin, hoping my voice is bright enough. Hoping I can hide the angst churning my insides to mulch.

Zander's in Nolan.

Zander saw Zoey.

Zander called me Sparks.

Zander's still the most gorgeous man on the planet.

Zander, Zander, Zander!

Ugh! I wish I could stop thinking about him, but he's haunting my dreams, taking over every square inch of my brain.

I don't know how to shake this.

"Pay squeen?" Zoey looks up at me, rounding her eyes in that puppy dog way she does when she wants something she knows she probably shouldn't have.

My heart melts, and I don't have the energy to steel myself against it today.

"Okay, you can have twenty minutes on the iPad. We'll set a timer, okay?"

"'kay!" She jumps up, her little legs pumping as she runs into my room and grabs my device. I bought an industrial, kid-friendly case as soon as I decided she was old enough to play a few games on it. She's probably still not old enough, but since moving to Nolan and not having my parents around, I've found myself at a loss every now and again... and the iPad has been a lifesaver.

I really need to look into finding some playgroups or toddler classes Zoey and I can participate in. I need some regular things to fill the week. I've been here coming up on six weeks, and I can't use my "settling in" excuse anymore.

And I definitely shouldn't use my "emotional crisis" one. If anything, playgroups might help distract me from this gnawing dread in my stomach.

Zander's in Nolan.

He's in Nolan!

Part of me wants to pack my bags and move. But where the hell would I go?

I don't want to live alone, which is why I moved in

with Russell when he invited me. I'd opened up to his sister, Celeste, about my parents and the cruise and... well, two days later, I got a call from Rusty asking if I wanted to come live with him so my parents could go do their thing. It's just for six months and it felt like the perfect solution. He'd just moved to a new place, he was needing a little company himself, and it felt like all the stars were aligning.

But what the hell, stars? You completely duped me!

They never warned me that my ex would be walking the same streets as I am. No doubt attending the same college Russell is now coaching at. Thank God Zander isn't a hockey man. The thought of him and Russell ever seeing each other makes my skin crawl.

Yeah, I made the mistake of venting in front of Celeste and Russell one afternoon, and they found out the full story. Russell has seriously hated Zander ever since.

Closing my eyes, I start praying that Russell never finds out Zander is at Nolan U.

Unless he already knows and has just been trying to hide it from me.

Did he know Zander was here when he invited me to stay with him?

Surely not. There's no way he would have been okay with this.

My stomach churns and writhes, making me feel ill.

"Here go." Zoey toddles back into the room hugging the iPad to her chest.

"Wait, wait, wait. You have to clean up the blocks first."

Her bottom lip sticks out in a pout.

"Don't give me that look. You know how it goes. We pack away before we do something new."

"But latwer."

"No." I shake my head. "If you want to play with these later, you can get them out again."

Huffing like a bull, Zoey stamps her foot.

I tip my head, feeling calm enough to deal with this right now, but hoping like hell that it doesn't escalate.

"Zoey, there's no iPad until you pack these away. I know you don't like that, but it's just the way it is. Now, I can help you if you like and it'll get done faster, or you can stand there stomping your feet and you'll get less iPad time than you want."

I'm not sure if she followed all of that—two-year-olds aren't exactly known for being reasonable—but I smile at her sweetly, hoping she's picked up enough to understand. Hoping I can avoid a mini meltdown. She's pretty good at those when she wants to be.

Damn, I should have gotten her to pack the blocks away before I even let her get the iPad.

Rookie mistake, Sienna. Up your game, girl, or it's gonna be a tough day.

I snort in my mind. A tough day? It already *is* a tough day.

If I could just shake Zander from my mind, I'd be fine.

I sit there waiting for Zoey to bend, dodging thoughts of my ex and the look on his face when he saw me.

When he no doubt realized that he'd just been gazing at his daughter. Is that why he'd been looking at her, because she was so familiar?

Lightly tucking a curl behind Zoey's ear, I fight a sudden wave of tears. She does look like her daddy. I can see it in her facial expressions sometimes. In the shape of her mouth. She might have my eyes, but she's got his chin.

Sucking in a breath, I start packing away the blocks, needing something to do with my hands or I'm gonna lose it!

Zoey huffs and crouches down, collecting blocks and dumping them into the container.

Thank you, God!

We're done in like two minutes, and I wink at her when she throws the last block in. "Good girl."

She gives me a proud smile, then climbs up onto the couch. "Mommy come."

Banging the cushion beside her, she beckons me while I murmur a soft "Please."

"Peeeease." She grins, and there goes my heart, melting all over again.

I sit down beside her, and she nestles against me. She's so soft and adorable. I love her so much my chest aches. Kissing the top of her head, I unlock the iPad and set the twenty-minute timer, and then she opens her favorite game where she gets to match colors. When she gets one right, the game allows her to dress Juniper the giraffe.

"Red," the iPad says, and Zoey's little finger moves across the screen, putting the two red icons together. "Well done. Now you can put a red sock on Juniper."

"Yay," Zoey squeals and carefully considers which hoof she's going to cover.

I brush my hand over the top of her curls and pull my phone out of my pocket.

Checking the screen, I don't see any new notifications

from my parents, so I open an internet window and stupidly search for Nolan U Football. You know, because I'm trying *not* to think about my ex-boyfriend.

The first thing that pops up is the Nolan U *Sports Digest*: Football Edition. And who should be on the front cover but Zander Donohue himself.

My breath hitches, and I know I have to read the free e-mag whether it kills me or not. The interview comes with a collage of pictures that make me pine for what was lost. He's so handsome it's not fair. I love his little chin dimple. I love how sexy he looks holding a football. I love that smile on his face as he sits next to someone I assume is another football player. Reading his answers, it's obvious this Football Frat place is filled with people he considers family.

I'm glad he's happy.

No, you're not! You wanted him to burn in hell, remember?

I cringe as that familiar wave of anger rides through me. I wish I could hold on to it but as I read the article, it won't cling the way it should. It used to be a black tar that stuck to every surface of my heart, but all I can feel today is a painful, weeping ache. Like my heart is bleeding all over again. My forehead crinkles in confusion as I read his answer about riding the bench his sophomore year just so he could play at Nolan.

Irritation sizzles for a moment. He could have done that at Brighton College, but he chose Kelsey U instead so he'd get more game time. He could have lived thirty minutes down the road from me, but he chose a five-hour drive. He chose to break up with me because long-distance was too hard and... What the hell? He moved to Nolan to ride the bench?

Why!

A growl reverberates in my chest, and I nearly stop reading. But I, of course, can't stop myself, especially when the interviewer asks him if he's ready for some questions from their readers. This should be interesting.

I scan the first one and stop breathing, my eyes rereading his answer to the question about which celebrity he'd like to take out to dinner.

Taylor Swift?

Is he... kidding?

My mind jumps back to the passenger seat of his car as I sat there messing around with the stereo and forcing him to listen to my favorite artist. He tried to deny that he liked her music... at first, but I won him over. No that he'd admit it.

And there he goes, trying to deny it again. The interviewer is teasing him as he says he only listens to her because she's on the radio all the time.

Interviewer (laughing): You are a total Swiftie!

Zander: This girl I knew in high school adored her and forced me to listen to her music all the time. I guess it grew on me a little.

Interviewer: Which girl?

Zander (swallows): No one you'll know. Next question.

. . .

Holy shit, that's me. I was that girl!

The girl he doesn't even want to talk about. The girl who *forced him*.

I tut, skimming through the interview and barely reading the rest of it. The only other answer I take in is the fact that he wants to inject coffee into his veins. I can't help wondering what got him addicted to caffeine. He wasn't a big coffee drinker when we were together.

He wasn't a lot of things he turned out to be.

I shut off my phone before I'm tempted to go back and read the rest of the article properly. I don't want to know what else the readers had to ask. More than that, I don't want to know his answers.

He's moved on. He has a better life now. Living in this frat-style house with all his buddies, playing football, being captain of the team. It's everything he wanted.

And there's no space for me in that life.

There's definitely no space for Zoey.

Shit!

I run a hand through my hair and fist the back of it. I guess all I can hope for is that I never run into him again.

Zoey and I have managed to avoid him since we've been here, right? We can do that again, surely.

Unless he starts looking for you.

He chased you down, called your name.

He's going to want to know why you're a mommy.

He can do the math.

He's not stupid!

Closing my eyes, I sit there fighting off nausea while Zoey plays and cheers herself on... until the timer goes.

"More?" She looks up at me hopefully.

"No, lil' bug. Time's up." Her bottom lip sticks out again, and I'm so close to tears right now, I'm not sure how I'll cope if she decides to get all stubborn and huffy on me.

I can't lose it in front of her.

A wave of unexpected panic surges through me, and I seriously need to burn off this angst or poor Zoey is going to cop it.

"Hey, do you want to go play with Mrs. Ward so Mommy can go for a run?"

"Cookies!" Zoey raises her hands in the air, and I can't help a soft laugh as I grab my phone and call the babysitter Russell helped me find.

She's the mother of one of the other assistant coaches, and she's quickly become Zoey's surrogate grandmother while my parents are away. They clicked within about two seconds, and every time Zoey goes there to play, they end up baking cookies.

"Hello," she answers in a bright voice. "Is this my favorite little chef calling me?"

I laugh. "She's a keen jellybean. Any chance you can do a short babysitting stint so I can go for a run?"

"Oh, I'd love that. Let me get the kitchen ready. I'll see you shortly."

"Thank you. You're an angel."

"It's my total pleasure, darling girl. Believe me." Her laughter is merry and instantly puts me in a better mood.

Within fifteen minutes, I'm unbuckling Zoey from her car seat, and then we're walking up the front path. Mrs. Ward gives out hugs with her effervescent laughter and shoos me away to go have some "me time."

Zoey is so happy to be there, she barely even notices my kiss to the top of her head.

Slipping out the front door, I set my exercise app to go and jog to the sidewalk, then turn left and find my usual ambling pace is much faster today.

And I go with it.

Because maybe if I run fast enough, I can shake off these haunting memories. I can outrun these ugly feelings in my chest and sweat out this pining ache that won't seem to stop plaguing me no matter how hard I try.

CHAPTER 8
ZANDER

I wait outside the arena until someone with a key card happens to walk by. Thankfully, he recognizes me from the latest *Sports Digest* and lets me in with a smile. I explain that I'm just wanting a quick chat with one of the coaching staff.

"Thinking of switching to hockey, huh?" He laughs at me.

I smile. "Not a chance. Just needing some info."

"Okay." He nods. "Who can I get for ya?"

"Uh... I'm looking for Coach Fisher."

"Russell, sure. I'll tell him you're here."

"Thank you."

I wait in the foyer in agitated silence, shoving my fists into my hoodie pockets and wishing the guy would hurry the hell up. Sweat is starting to prickle the back of my neck.

Checking my watch, I calculate how fast I'll have to run to make it to practice on time and wince, knowing already that I'm going to be a few minutes late for the game review video. Hopefully Coach won't notice me slipping into the back.

Of course he'll fucking notice. He notices everything!

Scraping a hand through my hair, I start to pace and am two seconds away from bailing when I hear my name.

"Zander Donohue." The voice behind me is sharp and snappy.

I spin and see this guy walking toward me. He's got a sharp, pointy nose to match his voice, his eyes dark and narrowed, his angular face looking all kinds of pissed off.

"Okay," I murmur under my breath before sticking out my hand. "Coach Fisher?"

He doesn't reciprocate the gesture. Instead, he crosses his arms and keeps glaring at me. "What's a football player doing at the hockey arena?"

"I need to speak with you."

"Obviously."

I frown at his frosty demeanor, but if anything, it's making me more determined to ask my questions. Squaring my shoulders, I force myself to sound more confident than I feel. "Do you know Sienna Erling?"

His eyes flash before he clenches his jaw and looks away from me. "Why do you want to know?"

"I need to speak with her."

There goes that jaw clenching again. He stares at the wall adjacent to me, like he's calculating something, then swears under his breath and mutters, "I knew something was off."

"What?"

He ignores my confusion and fires a death glare straight at me. "Why? Why do you need to speak with her?"

Sighing in frustration, I try to check my tone and stay calm. "We dated for a year in high school. I'd like to see her again. She'll remember me."

"Oh yeah, she remembers you." His eyes glitter, his voice taut and scathing.

I flinch and steel myself. This guy obviously hates me. What the fuck has Sienna said about me? She's the one who took off without a word. She's the one who ghosted *me*... had a kid without even telling me.

Shit, is that little girl mine?

I have to know.

"Yeah, we all know you, Mr. Donohue. Football star. Got your face on the cover of *Sports Digest*." He scoffs. "Should have fucking looked into the football program before I took a job here."

"What?" I frown.

"You're the guy who broke her heart, took off for a new life. Any excuse to get away from your clingy girlfriend, right?"

My heart stops beating for a second, and the air in my lungs feels like toxic ash. Sienna must have been fucking dark on me to say this shit to her family friend. Unless he's more... and that's why he knows the whole fucking story. Well, her version of it anyway.

Sucking in a ragged breath, I force out my next question. "Is Zoey mine?"

The man pales for a second, shaking his head.

I frown. That doesn't feel right.

Stepping a foot closer, I study his face carefully as I say, "But the timing... She's about two, isn't she? And she looks just like my sister at that age."

His nostrils flare and I sense his desperate need to cover the truth, so I keep pushing.

"She's mine. I can feel it in my fucking bones, so just tell me!"

"Watch your mouth," he snaps. "You're a student here, and you don't talk to faculty that way."

I huff, my fingers balling into an even tighter fist in my pocket. It takes everything in me to keep my tone soft and respectful. "Please. Please, tell me the truth."

The assistant coach stares me down like I'm a bug he needs to exterminate before finally sniffing and giving me a stiff nod. "All right, fine. She might have your DNA, but that's it. She's not yours."

A powerful sensation floods my veins. I don't know what it is, but having my suspicions confirmed is making me lightheaded.

I have a daughter.

I'm a... dad!

"She shouldn't have kept that from me." I say it more to myself, but he hears me anyway.

And then he fucking scoffs.

My eyes snap to his face, and I can't help glaring at him.

He glares right back, like he's almost enjoying this somehow. Like my tortured expression—that's gotta be what he's seeing right now, because it's what I'm fucking feeling—is bringing him some sense of satisfaction.

"She was going to tell you, but..."

"But what?"

His jacket rustles as he shrugs and shakes his head. "You don't even deserve her. You don't deserve to be in either of their lives. I'm not telling you shit."

What the fuck? Who is this asshole?

My dread at the idea that he and Sienna might be a couple is sinking in deep, and I'm struggling to reckon with it.

She can't be dating this douchebag.

The idea of his hands on her makes me want to throw up. The idea of him—

"You want to do the best for your kid?" he hisses at me.

My shoulders tense.

"Stay the fuck away from her." He points at me, then turns on his heel and starts striding back toward what I assume are the offices.

I'm so thrown by his venom that it takes me a second to find my voice, but I manage to yell after him just before he disappears from view. "She's my daughter! I have a right to meet her!"

The man jerks to a stop and quickly spins. I can only see the side of his face as he yells back at me. "You forfeited that right when you threw away the best thing you ever had!"

And then he's gone.

And I'm left reeling.

A daughter.

I have a daughter.

And an ex-girlfriend who wouldn't even tell me about her.

Why?

Why did she change her mind?

Why the fuck didn't she tell me!

I would have been there for her. I would have dropped everything.

My parents would have been so pissed, but I don't give a shit.

Why did she think I couldn't handle it?

Sure, I love football, but I would have put her before that.

Except you didn't. You left her for football.

Fuck!

Bile surges in my belly, threatening to rocket right up my throat. Stumbling out of the arena, I start walking for the football stadium, wondering how the fuck I'm going to concentrate this afternoon.

I have a daughter.

Shit!

Sienna had to deal with all that on her own. Although she would have had her parents for support. They would have stepped up for sure. I mean, they pulled her out of school and hit the road her senior year, right? She probably begged them to take her away so she didn't have to walk the halls of high school with a growing belly.

They would have supported her through the pregnancy and Zoey's first couple years.

Shit, shit, shit!

It should have been me. *I* should have been there.

Wait, are they in Nolan with Sienna?

The thought trips me up, my steps faltering as I come to a stop on the sidewalk and glance around as if they're about to pop out from behind the bushes.

They probably want to kill me.

If they hate me as much as Russell Fisher does, then it won't matter how nice they were to me when I was dating their daughter. If they spot me, they'll probably be out for my blood.

My parents are going to fucking lose it when they find out. I did exactly what they didn't want me to do. Or I would have... had I known my girl was pregnant.

But she's not your girl.

You chose to break up with her.

But then I went back for her!

My brain is in chaos as I shuffle to the stadium and end up being so late that I totally miss the game review. Everyone's already in the locker room, getting taped up for practice.

"Where the hell have you been?" Grady asks as soon as I stop beside him.

Yanking off my hoodie, I shake my head, still struggling to talk.

"Dude." He lightly slaps my arm with the back of his hand, looking really worried. "I covered for you with Coach, having no idea why. He was kinda pissed, so you better gimme something."

Pulling off my shirt, I dump it in my locker and give him a pained frown.

And then it all just tumbles out.

"I saw my ex-girlfriend at the park on Sunday, and she had a little girl with her. Her daughter." I wince, my throat burning as I choke out the rest. "*My daughter.*"

Grady's eyes pop wide, his lips parting as he blinks and obviously can't think of anything to say.

"I've just had it confirmed by a guy who knows them, but he won't tell me where they are. He says I don't deserve to know why she didn't tell me and that I should leave them the fuck alone, but..." A ragged breath pops out of me, and I give my friend a pained frown.

"Fuck that." Grady's eyebrows dip together. "That's

your kid. You don't just give up on something that important. I don't give a shit who this douche nugget is that you spoke to. You track that girl down, and you meet your kid."

"Agreed." Wily grips my shoulder.

I spin, not even realizing he was listening in.

He's obviously pretty shook by the news, and I give him a tortured frown.

Squeezing my shoulder again, he responds with a glum smile. "We're here for you, dude. Whatever you need."

"Thanks," I rasp.

"We'll help you find her," Grady assures me before pulling on his protective gear and giving me a stern look. "But right now, you get your head in the game. Can't have our best quarterback getting injured at the start of the season. We need you, man."

"Yeah." I nod, forcing myself to take a breath and focus.

Football first.

Then my kid.

Holy fuck, I have a kid.

An adorable blue-eyed daughter who I am desperate to meet properly.

I've got to find out the truth. What did I do that made Sienna hate me so much?

Dread simmers thick and malignant in my stomach, and my hands start to shake as I wrestle on my protective pads.

CHAPTER 9
SIENNA

It's been nearly a week since I saw Zander at the park, and I've been avoiding it ever since. But today the sun is shining, and I can't resist this cloudless sky. Zoey's been saying "sanpit" repeatedly all morning, and I can't deny her that just because I'm worried about bumping into her father.

Besides, it's a Thursday. He should be in class or at football practice or whatever a college athlete does on a Thursday.

I push the stroller, gazing down the street and playing the game I always try to avoid. The one where I imagine what I'd be doing if I hadn't gotten pregnant.

I would have gone to college. I didn't know what I wanted to study, but the idea of going away to school appealed to me. Dorm life seemed fun. Making friends, hopefully some lifelong connections. But that wasn't my journey. And I wouldn't give up Zoey for anything.

I love being a mother.

This surprised me, because I was giving birth to her when I was only eighteen, but the moment she was placed on my chest, the love I felt overpowered everything. She became my world. She still is my world, and I adore her. She's soothed all my stings and burns. She's made life beautiful again.

"Sanpit!" she squeals, kicking her legs and giggling as I push the stroller to the edge and put on the brakes. "Sanpit!"

"Yes, we're here. Sandpit."

"Sanpit!" She points at it, her blue eyes dancing with excitement.

I can't help laughing at her adorable face as I unbuckle her and lift her out of the stroller. She's wiggling out of my arms and hitting that gritty sand within microseconds. I watch her run across the undulating surface and laugh again when she flops down and starts making angels. My nose wrinkles as I briefly lament the state her clothes and hair are going to be in after this, but like my mom always says, "Everything can be washed."

So, I walk right into the massive sandpit with her and take a seat, helping my daughter make mounds of sand so she can jump on them and destroy them.

I roar and call her Godzilla, which she loves. She doesn't even know what Godzilla is, but she pounds her chest like a gorilla and roars some more, stomping on the newest pile.

"More, Mommy. More."

Quickly pushing more sand together, I create a new mountain for her to demolish, and she roars again. I can't help laughing, and she stops to frown at me.

"Don't laff. Scawee." She points at herself.

"Oh yes." I quickly straighten out my expression and pretend to be afraid. "Don't eat me, Godzilla."

"Goziwa!" She roars and I wail, raising my arms to protect myself, then bursting into laughter as she jumps on me and tips us both over into the sand.

She pretends to eat me, smearing her dirty cheek across mine—gross—so I tickle her, and we tussle in the sand for a minute before she wiggles out of my grasp, then jumps to her feet and yells, "Foobawl!"

She points behind me, her expression pure joy and excitement.

"Fooball?" I try to work out what she means, glancing over my shoulder and feeling my breath disintegrate when I spot Zander standing on the edge of the sandpit with his hands in his jean pockets, watching us with glassy eyes.

The desperate look on his face makes my insides crumple.

My first instinct is to snatch Zoey and make a run for it.

But for some reason, I stand up slowly. I brush the sand off my pants and turn to face him. Crossing my arms, I try to steel myself against the instant desire pulsing through me and keep my stance assertive. I will not let him affect me the way he used to.

"What are you doing here? Aren't you supposed to be in class right now?"

"This is more important," he rasps, staring down at Zoey when she runs over and wraps her arms around my leg. She smiles up at him, and I brush my hand over her curls, wishing my fingers weren't shaking so badly.

I stare down at the sand between us, willing myself to look up and glare at him.

But I can't.

Dammit.

"I've been searching every park in the area looking for you guys. Every day I come out here. I didn't know what else to do. Russell wouldn't tell me where you were."

"Russell?" My head snaps up. "You spoke to him?"

"Yeah, a couple days ago." Zander's eyebrows wrinkle in confusion. "He didn't tell you?"

I shake my head, my stomach curdling. Why wouldn't he say anything?

Biting my lips together, I swallow and can't understand this twinge of guilt pinching at me. I shouldn't feel guilty. Zander didn't deserve to know about Zoey. Not after the way he behaved.

But maybe he did.

I glance back up at his face, and those sad, desperate eyes are doing me in.

"Pay?" Zoey lets me go and toddles over to her spade. Holding it out to him, she gives him her best puppy dog eyes and asks again, "Pay?"

"I'd love to play with you." He smiles down at her, then looks to me, silently pleading for permission.

Oh my gosh, I think he is legit going to cry—something I've never seen him do. My heart buckles without my say-so, and before I can stop myself, I'm nodding.

"Thank you," Zander mouths before crouching in the sand and making my heart bleed.

Zoey hands him the spade and then shows him what to do. He helps her dig some big piles—way bigger than mine—then laughs as she jumps on them, catching her when she topples over and protecting her head. His hands are so big, his arms so strong. Zoey is so safe beside him, and I'm fighting tears as I sit there cross-legged watching the man I swore I never wanted to see again having fun with my daughter.

Our daughter.

I rub my stomach, trying to ease the pain that seems to have lodged itself there.

This is not the Zander I saw at college. This man here is the Zander I fell in love with in high school.

Snapping my eyes shut, I avoid looking, desperately trying to harden my heart against how sweet he's being with my baby girl. Desperately trying to convince myself that not trying a second time to tell him I was pregnant was the right thing to do.

"It's Zoey, right?" he asks. "With a *y*?"

My eyes snap open and I stare at him. His face is so beautiful, his expression so sweet.

Shit.

"Yeah." I clear my throat and nod. "Yeah, with a *y*."

"It's a really pretty name. I like it."

It was the closest girl name I could think to Zander, but I can't admit that to him.

"Does she have a middle name?"

"Uh, yeah... Beth, for my mom."

"Nice." He nods. "Zoey Beth Erling. I like it."

My expression buckles and I look at the ground again, wondering if it's hurting him that his last name isn't attached to her at all.

Zander builds another mound, and Zoey jumps on it

with glee, giggling when she falls over. Zander catches her, propping her back on her feet, and she gives him an adoring smile. "Foobawl."

He laughs. "I'm Zander, but you can call me Football if you want to."

She giggles, then suddenly takes off toward the swings. Used to her erratic shifts at the playground, I get up and automatically follow her. There's another boy on her favorite swing, and I want to make sure she doesn't kick him off. It's been known to happen.

"This one, Zo."

"Dis one." She points to her favorite.

"Someone else is using that one, and you're not allowed to kick him off." I give her a pointed look.

She stares back at me, her little chin going up as she points and repeats, "Dis one."

"It's this one or nothing, lil' bug. Otherwise, you'll just have to be patient and wait for your turn."

As her face scrunches up in that pout of hers, Zander lets out a laugh and shakes his head. "How cute is she?"

"Adorable," I agree with him, fighting my own grin.

Her pout is priceless.

"Why don't you push me while we wait?" Zander tips his head at the vacant swing and walks over to it.

He's ginormous and looks ridiculous trying to fit on the swing. I can't help laughing and quickly cover my mouth so he doesn't know how adorable I think he's being. Zoey giggles and runs over to him, resting her little hands on his knees.

"Too big." She laughs. "Too big." Snatching his wrist, she tries to pull him off, grunting when he won't move.

"But I want to swing." He fake pouts.

"Me sing." She tugs on his arm again, and he stands up so she can climb into the swing seat. He has to help her for the last part, and she lets him while I stand there having open heart surgery.

Moving around behind her, Zander starts to push, and Zoey squeals in delight as she rises up high in the air. He's going way harder and faster than I ever would, and I nearly tell him to stop, but she's having so much fun.

I watch them together. Father and daughter.

Shit. Shit. Shit.

If anyone had asked me last week if not telling Zander about his daughter was the right decision, I would have said yes. The last time I saw him, it was obvious he had absolutely no intention of missing me while he was away at college.

I couldn't interrupt his partying to let him know I was pregnant. What had remained of my tattered heart was completely shredded at the sight of him—

Snapping my eyes closed, I ward off the images while also trying to justify my decision.

But then his quaking voice has me looking at him again.

"She's so beautiful." His eyes glisten as he gazes at me, all the pain I never thought he'd feel shining bright and obvious.

I try to blink away the burn in my eyes and nod. "She is."

He beckons me with his fingers, and I go without protest. I have no idea why. It's like I'm being pulled by a magical force I can't counter.

As soon as I'm standing beside him, watching the

back of Zoey's head as she happily swings, he leans in and murmurs, "She's mine. She's my daughter."

My jaw shakes as I try to clench my chattering teeth together.

And then I make the mistake of looking up at him, and there's no way I can deny it.

CHAPTER 10
ZANDER

"Yes," Sienna whispers. "She's yours."

I knew it already, but finally hearing it from the person who should have told me in the first place makes me feel like I've just been kicked in the balls.

Anger spikes, fast and unexpected. I can't keep the venom from my voice as I whisper-bark, "Why? Why didn't you tell me?"

She steps back, her expression pale and hard. Her jaw's still trembling, and I seriously hate that, but what am I supposed to do here?

She should have told me! And I deserve to know why she didn't.

Crossing her arms, she hunches over on herself while I keep pushing Zoey. Thankfully, the little girl—*my* little girl—is oblivious to the angst going on behind her.

"You just took off." My voice catches, and I have to clear my throat. "I tried to get in touch with you, and you never replied."

Sienna sniffs, raising her chin and looking away from

me. She squints at something in the distance while her long fingers squeeze her bicep. "My parents and I were on the road. We didn't always have good connections. We—"

"Bullshit," I hiss. "You ghosted me. You ghosted everyone. Why?"

She whips around to face me, her blue eyes flashing dangerously when she hisses right back, "You try being pregnant your senior year of high school!"

My gut plummets as I quickly picture the scene. What did she go through when she found out she was pregnant? I can only imagine her shock and fear. And then my mind starts conjuring up images of her cradling a distended belly, growing our baby inside her and me being clueless. Me fucking up my freshman year while she produced our child.

Fuck. Fuck. Fuck!

"Why didn't you tell me?" My voice actually breaks. I have to grit my teeth to keep my emotions in check.

Her headshake is more of a jerky twitch, the grip on her arm only tightening.

"I would have been there for you."

She scoffs and starts to laugh like I just said the stupidest thing ever.

"What?" I frown at her. "You don't believe me? I was missing you like crazy. I would have dropped everything to—"

"Yeah, right. You were missing me?" Her look is so scathing I'm taken aback.

Zoey's swing swoops toward me, and I don't push it this time. I just stand there staring down at my first love and wondering where this hate-fire is coming from.

Her blue gaze is sparkling in all the wrong ways right now. She looks like she wants to burn me alive.

"What?" I whisper. "Why are you looking at me like that?"

She shakes her head, shutting me out with a little sniff and muttering, "No reason."

"Talk to me."

"No!" she shouts, frightening Zoey, who looks over her shoulder with a worried frown. "Zoey, we have to go."

"No," Zoey complains. "Sing! Sing!"

"No, baby. We've got to get home." Sienna pulls her out of the swing, battling the kicking legs and cries of complaint. Securing Zoey against her side like she obviously has a thousand times before, Sienna starts marching back to the sandpit.

I should follow her, keep arguing, but I just stand there, holding the swing chain and staring after them.

Sienna's venom is like nothing I've seen before. I don't know what to do with it. That woman I was just talking to was not the carefree, playful girl I fell in love with in high school.

Yeah, because she's had a kid and has been raising her on her own.

"She wouldn't have had to do that if she'd told me," I mutter under my breath, trying not to seethe as I watch Sienna placate Zoey with a snack from her bag, then buckle her into the stroller.

Zoey distracts herself, sucking on a yogurt pouch while I stand there like the world's biggest douche, watching them walk away from me.

Should I chase them again?

Should I demand answers?

Probably. But I don't know if I can handle that look on Sienna's face again.

I mean, I know I broke up with her, but she eventually said it was the right thing to do. And then we had that final, beautiful night together, and I thought we were okay.

I came back for her.

And she'd taken off with our baby, never wanting to even look at me again.

My watch starts beeping and I check my screen, knowing I can't be late for football practice twice in one week.

With an irritated huff, I jog out of the playground, away from Sienna and Zoey. Away from a problem I know I can't ignore.

I'll be back again.

I'll be waiting on this playground for them, because I have to find out why Sienna hates me so much. And I have to play with Zoey again. Because that little girl is my daughter, and like hell I'm not going to be a part of her life.

CHAPTER 11
SIENNA

I'm fighting major sobs by the time we get home, but I can't let any of it show. Zoey's turned into a total fusspot, no doubt vibing off my torrid emotions, and by the time I fold the stroller away, she's transitioned into a full-blown meltdown. I need to feed her and get her down for a nap, but that's not going to happen when she's in this state, so I do the only thing I can.

I break routine and draw her a bath.

I might pay for it later. Routine seems to be everything to my toddler, but as soon as the bubbles start rising in the tub, Zoey's tears dry up and she gets excited for bathtime.

Helping her in, I kneel beside her, running my hands through the water while she drives her toy boat through the bathtub ocean and I play duck and cover with my memories.

Zander's face as I glared up at him, hating him for what he did to us. Hating him for breaking my heart. Hating him for that day he destroyed everything.

Before I can stop myself, my mind rockets back to Kelsey U and the only time I ever went there...

It had been two weeks since I found out I was pregnant. I'd managed to stop crying but was still throwing up on the regular. Even though I felt like death, I couldn't let that stop me from delivering the news to Zander. And I couldn't do it over the phone.

So, loaded up with travel sick bags, Dad and I hit the road and slowly made our way to Kelsey U. It took six hours, thanks to multiple stops, but I arrived in one piece. It was after eight by the time I got there, and Dad was already on his phone searching for motels we could spend the night in while I sat in his truck, summoning my courage.

I hadn't spoken to Zander since our final night together. It had been two long, painful months, but I'd stuck to my resolve. We both thought a clean break would be better, and I wanted him to be able to focus on his football and studies. This was his chance to really shine. I wouldn't get in the way of that.

So, I kept my distance.

But I couldn't not tell him he was going to be a father.

I wouldn't expect anything from him. Mom, Dad, and I had discussed it at length. They were going to support me, and Zander could be as involved or uninvolved as he wanted to be. I wouldn't make him feel guilty or anything.

I was keeping the baby, and he had a right to access, but I wasn't going to be demanding money or any of that. Thanks to my mom's inheritance, my parents were really well off, and we didn't need the financial support. I just wanted him to know.

Part of me knew that he'd be there for me. Zander was the kind of guy who stepped up, and I wasn't sure how I was supposed to feel about that. I couldn't deny a small fluttering of joy. Would this baby bring us back together?

Oh man, I wanted that.

But only if he did too.

I had to prepare myself for the fact that he might want minimal involvement.

Nausea bubbled inside me, and I was seconds away from reaching for another sick bag.

"Do you want me to come in with you?" Dad softly asked.

I shook my head. "No. It's okay. He probably doesn't want an audience while he processes this bombshell."

Dad's smile was soft with understanding as he tucked the hair behind my ear. "I know this is terrifying, but you're gonna get through this. Mom and I will be there every step of the way." He cradled my cheek. "No matter what's happened in my life, I want you to know that you will forever be my greatest achievement."

Tears lined my lashes before I could stop them.

"And that's how you'll feel when you meet your baby. Being a parent is the best thing in the world. And you're gonna do great, whether Zander's part of it or not."

"Thanks, Dad." My expression buckled and I leaned toward him, resting my head on his shoulder. He kissed my hair and told me everything was going to be fine... and after another minute or so of reassurance, I found the courage to open the passenger door.

Walking away from Dad's truck was hard work, but I made it.

I made it all the way to Zander's dorm, actually. I had to ask a few people if they knew him, and it was a little disconcerting when one of the girls I asked blushed and giggled at the mention of his name. It was unsettling as hell. But then she let me into his building, so I was grateful for that.

By the time I reached the third floor, my stomach was in chaos. Zander was obviously very popular, and I should be happy for him that he'd fit in so easily, but I couldn't shake this sense of foreboding.

And I was right.

That foreboding was trying to warn me of something... and I should have listened.

Forcing my brain back to the present, I refuse to relive what I saw.

But I can't seem to skip past myself tumbling down the stairs, stumbling outside, and throwing up in the closest bush before running to Dad's truck.

I wrenched the door open and jumped in, scaring the crap out of Dad, who had decided to take a quick nap while he waited for me.

"How'd it go?" His voice had been groggy as he blinked and came to.

"Get me out of here," I sobbed.

"Sienna, what happened?"

My stomach convulsed and jerked, making it nearly impossible to talk. "Just d-drive, Dad. Please! Get me out of here!"

The wails I let out after that echo through my mind, and I blink, desperately trying to clear them. Desperately trying to focus on Zoey, who is now making engine sounds with her lips, stealing my heart like she always does with her chubby little cheeks and big blue eyes.

"I love you." I brush the back of my finger down her cherub face and block out the rest.

I block out the ugly feelings bubbling away in my chest and focus on the one shining light in my life.

This little girl, who I will do anything for.

This little girl I have to protect and cherish.

Zander may have torn my heart to shreds, but I guess I should be grateful to him for giving me her.

CHAPTER 12
ZANDER

Football practice sucks.

I try to concentrate, but my mind is a scrambled mess, making it impossible to even participate in the game review discussions. And as for my throwing and drills… I'm total shit.

My coaches aren't blind. They sub me out for the final practice game, and I sit on the sidelines watching Owen send near-perfect spirals down the field while my knee bobs like a jackhammer.

Grady and Carson are on form, catching balls and running plays that prove how good they are. Bobby Fleischer and Mike Braxton run pretty good defense, but my Football Frat brothers are slippery fish today. I'd usually laugh and feel triumphant, but I'll leave the smirking up to Carson, because I can't do anything but sit here like a tortured man.

Fleischer misses yet another tackle, Grady pivoting left to avoid him. He hits the dirt and thumps the grass with a growl.

"They don't call him Flash for nothing, slow ass." Carson jumps away when Bobby tries to swipe his ankle.

Tyrell eyes the exchange like a hawk, ready to run over and intercept. It's no secret that Bobby and Carson are constantly on the edge of an all-out brawl. It's lucky they're never on the field together during game time.

Shit, I should be out there. I should be practicing for the upcoming game, not sitting here shrouded in... whatever the fuck is taking over my brain right now!

And I still have my final training session to go before I can get out of this place, but if I don't stretch and run through those exercises the physical therapists give us, then I'll be screwed for the game this weekend. And I have to be on form for that.

My heart starts pounding all over again as Coach Jones brings us in for his standard pep talk wrap-up.

"Good job today, guys. I'm liking the intensity. We're going to need that kind of focus when we play the Rams this weekend. We have a home game advantage. No travel, so we should be better rested." He sends a few pointed looks around the crew, finishing with Carson, who rolls his eyes and mutters something under his breath. Grady nudges him with a frown, and Carson forces a smile, giving Coach a thumbs-up.

"I'll go to bed on time like a good boy, Coach."

A few snickers and murmuring laughs rustle through the team, and Coach speaks over the top of it all.

"I expect that from all of you. Not just because I want to see you play well, but because I want my men to be healthy. Staying up all hours isn't gonna help your body function to the best of its ability. Now, one final thing before I let you guys go..." He rubs his finger under his nose, and I instantly know that whatever comes next is important and serious. "As some of you may have heard, my daughter is attending Nolan U this year. It's her first time at college, and although I appreciate helpful, friendly students, I do *not* appreciate leering young men who wolf whistle when she passes by the stadium or is waiting for me by my car." His voice takes on a hard, steely edge. "Women are not put on this earth as eye candy or merely for your pleasure. You *will* respect her, you will use your manners, you will not ogle her, and under no circumstances will you date her." He eyes the team. "My daughter is off-limits. Am I making myself abundantly clear here?"

Damn. The look on his face right now.

No way in hell would I be going anywhere near his daughter.

I throw a few glances around the team, eyeing up Watson and Franco. Oh, and there's Wily, although he's a little scared of Coach, so I'm guessing he won't go anywhere near his daughter. And then there's Carson. I throw a side-eye at my housemate. He's smirking like he's gonna do what he wants no matter watch Coach says, but then his smile falters and he nods. I whip my head back to Coach and notice him eyeballing all of the biggest problems on the team. They seem to be shrinking under his glare.

Yeah, I think whoever his daughter is will be safe from the Cougars.

Let's hope she doesn't mind.

But then it hits me.

Oh fuck, it hits me like a rocket.

If my daughter was attending Nolan U and I was in

Coach's position, I'd probably be giving out the same orders. Because I'd do anything to protect my baby girl.

And holy fuck... I actually have one of those now.

Zoey's face pops into my brain with crystal clarity, her cute smile and big blue eyes. The sound of her voice as she asked me to "pay," then told me I was too big for the "sing."

My heart turns to putty in my chest.

The thought of some fuckwit hurting her makes me want to maim something. I've only known her a day, and I already feel an overwhelming protectiveness. Imagine how much stronger that would be if I'd known about her all along.

Shit! Why the fuck didn't Sienna tell me!

Anger travels through me like a tidal wave again, and I don't even notice that Coach has dismissed us until the mass of players around me starts to disperse.

"Donohue!" Coach barks.

I snap to attention and glance at him.

"A word?" He beckons me with his finger.

Fuck.

Clearing my throat, I bang my helmet lightly against my leg as I follow Coach off the field and into his office.

He closes the door—never a good sign—and I stand there jittering in front of his desk.

I'm not usually nervous around Coach, but I'm a wreck today, and it's impossible to hide.

"You feel good about the upcoming game?" Coach closes a few binders, stacking them neatly on the shelf behind him.

"Uh... yeah. I think we've got a good chance for a win.

There are no guarantees, but we played them last season and won, so..." I shrug.

"And you're happy with the gameplay strategy we've put together? The plays I sent you yesterday... you've gone over those?"

"Yes, sir. I spent about an hour last night going through them. It's a solid plan of attack, and I'll make sure my boys execute."

"Good." He nods, eyeing me up like he's waiting for more.

I clear my throat and look to the ground.

After an awkward beat, Coach lets out a soft sigh, fidgeting with the ring on his pinkie finger before looking back at me. "Zander, you know I have faith in you. I recruited you into Kelsey U, and when I left, I brought you here with me. You're one of the best quarterbacks I've ever worked with, and I trust you to see this team through to victory on Saturday."

"Thank you, sir."

"But there's been something really off with you this week, and unless you can clear your head, I don't know how effective you're going to be on that field."

Closing my eyes, I scrape a hand through my sweaty hair.

"Now, you either need to open up and talk to me about it right now, or I'm making an appointment with our team psychologist tomorrow."

With slumped shoulders, I drop into the chair and rest my elbows on my knees. My helmet clunks onto the floor, and I start spilling my guts like I'm unlocking a dam.

"I just found out my high school girlfriend has a daughter. *My* daughter. And she never told me." I glance up with a desperate frown. "Didn't try to call or see me. Nothing. She kept it a secret this whole time, and then I see this girl at the playground who looks exactly like my sister did at that age, and Sienna shows up and the girl calls her Mommy, and I'm reeling. I can't... I..." I shake my head. "And she won't tell me why she kept it a secret. I tried to ask her today, and she got all shitty with me and took off! I'm a dad! I'm a dad to a kid I don't even know!" My breaths are getting short and punchy, my words starting to fall apart.

Coach has moved around the desk, and his hand is now on my shoulder, giving it a gentle squeeze. "It's okay, son. Just breathe. Breathe."

I do as he says, struggling to regulate but knowing I have to. This is all part of my training, right? Find the calm in the middle of the storm. Don't let the stress get the better of you.

"That's a lot to take in." Coach pulls up the chair beside me and takes a seat. "I can understand why you've been off. Can you think of any reason why she might have kept this from you?"

"I don't know." I wince and have to fight the urge to cry.

What the fuck?

I am *not* crying in front of Coach!

Sucking in a breath, I punch it back out and will my voice not to shake too hard. "I broke up with her before I left for college. I wanted to focus on football and making a good impression at Kelsey U." I wince. "And I didn't want to hold her back or hinder her senior year. I didn't want her waiting around for me, you know?"

Coach nods when I look at him, like I need his approval for my shitty decision.

"But I never knew how much I'd miss her. And when I went back to see if we could try long-distance... she was gone. Literally disappeared."

"I see." Coach threads his fingers together. "So, you think she didn't tell you because she wanted to punish you?"

I shrug. That didn't sound like Sienna. She was never vindictive.

"Maybe she assumed you didn't want to know. Or she didn't want to burden you when you were obviously trying to pursue a career in football."

"Maybe," I mumble, gripping the back of my neck.

"Do you think she'll let you see your daughter?"

"She let me play with her during my lunch break today." My lips twitch as I remember Zoey's adorable giggles and how she called me Foobawl.

"So, she invited you to be a part of Zoey's life?"

"No." I let out a weak laugh and am embarrassed to admit, "I've just been going to playgrounds any chance I can get. Just waiting around and looking for them. I got lucky today." I swallow, and my leg starts bobbing again. "Until she yelled at me and took off."

"So, there's obviously some anger and pain lurking there."

"On both sides," I grit out.

"I understand." Coach's voice is so soft and soothing. I glance at his face, waiting for the shame my dad would no doubt make me feel. I impregnated a teenage girl. I did exactly what he told me not to. In Dad's mind, I've probably ruined my life.

Shit, in Dad's mind, he'd probably tell me to forget about it and move on, focus on the game, make something of myself.

But how can I turn my back when I know I have a kid out there? A beautiful baby girl... and her beautiful mother.

Shit, seeing Sienna again was...

I can't even deal with that emotion on top of everything else.

"I know I need to be a part of her life, but Sienna is obviously against it. She fucking hates me." I frown, waiting for Coach to tell me off for my language—the guy talks like a saint—but he doesn't say anything, just sits there quietly while I bob my leg and come up with an idea I detest, but maybe it's one I have to accept. "I mean... should I just leave them alone? They've obviously been doing fine without me. Zoey's a really happy kid. Sienna seems like a great mom. Maybe I should..." My throat swells, and it's a struggle to get the words out. "Bow out. She doesn't want me to be a part of it, and I don't want to cause her any more pain or stress or—"

"Son." Coach stops me with another squeeze to my shoulder. "You have to pursue this. Being a parent is one of life's greatest privileges. I have four kids, so I should know." He grins. "This is your child we're talking about here, and you'll regret it forever if you don't fight for a chance to get to know her. Whatever's going on between you and her mother, you need to resolve it enough that she'll let you be a part of your little girl's life."

My head is bobbing before he's even finished talking. Relief floods me because he's just said everything I needed to hear.

Not that I was waiting for his permission or anything, but I respect the guy, and to have him agree with what I truly want is just the bolster I need.

I turn to him and softly rasp, "Can you help me?"

"Of course. What can I do?"

"Uh, well... I'm pretty sure she's living with a man called Russell Fisher. He's an assistant coach for the—"

"Men's hockey team. Yeah, I've met him."

"Me too. Unfortunately," I mutter.

"Check yourself," Coach softly warns me. "I don't need to know your opinion of another staff member."

I grit my teeth, clenching my fist and tapping it on my knee. "Is there any chance you could give me his address? Or a way of finding him?"

Coach presses his lips together and rises from his chair. "I'll see what I can do. Let me have a talk with him and see if I can get you his address or at least a phone number so you can set up a meeting."

"He doesn't want me anywhere near Sienna and Zoey. He told me to leave them alone."

"Hmmm." Coach scratches his jawline. "Leave it with me. I'll get back to you as soon as I can. Even if we set up some kind of mediation session or something."

"Thank you, Coach." I rise from my chair and end up hugging the guy.

That wasn't my plan, but my arms just wrapped around him before I could stop myself.

He gives me a tight squeeze before pounding my back a couple times and letting me go. Looking up at me with a reassuring smile, he lightly pats my cheek. "It's going to be okay, son."

I nod and dare myself to believe him as I walk out of his office.

CHAPTER 13
SIENNA

My fingers tap on my keyboard as I do a little research on playgroups in the local area. I promised Mom that I would, and I know she's right. Zoey needs to learn to play with children her own age, and I can't keep delaying just because I don't feel like hanging out with a bunch of moms who are older and more mature than I am.

"This isn't about you, Sienna. It's about Zoey."

And of course Mom's right.

I cut everyone off when I was pregnant, too heart-broken and... I don't know, ashamed? Too fragile to have to explain why I was keeping the baby or why I didn't want Zander to be a part of it. Too vulnerable to walk the halls of my high school with a growing belly. I couldn't do it. So, I ran. And my parents sheltered me and kept me safe through it all.

At the time, it felt so right.

But now I'm a single mother with no friends. Except for Russell and his sisters. But do they even count? They're more like cousins.

Crap. If I'm not careful, my daughter will grow up the same way I did—with a total inability to make long-term connections because she's never sure when she'll be leaving, moving on to the next country and big adventure.

That was why my parents wanted to stay in Everett until I graduated. But we hadn't counted on me falling in love, then getting pregnant and having my heart shattered into a thousand tiny pieces.

In that sense, life on the road is a million times safer.

But do I really want that for Zoey?

I had a long chat with my parents last night while I secretly watched the Nolan U Cougars win their home game. I knew it was a bad idea to watch the game, but I couldn't help myself. Seeing Zander in action was a thing of beauty and only amplified my angst and heartache. But do you think I could switch the TV off?

Russell had been out at some hockey coaches' dinner thing. Zoey was asleep, and... I couldn't help myself.

Thankfully, my parents called halfway through the game, and so my concentration was split, which seemed to help.

The game ended before I wrapped up the call, and I managed to keep Zander's existence at Nolan U a secret —which is a miracle, because I usually tell my parents everything.... but I just can't tell them about this.

They went from loving that boy to hating him. And I doubt they'd be too happy about the fact that I let Zander play with Zoey the other day. When I explained why I didn't think Zander should be a part of Zoey's life, they wholeheartedly agreed with me.

But seeing him with Zoey, watching them play

together... I've been plagued by doubts. Maybe Zander isn't the guy he was at Kelsey U. Maybe he's changed. Maybe the boy I fell in love with is still in there somewhere.

And if that's the case... doesn't Zoey deserve to get to know him? Because that boy was—

A knock at the door has me pausing my search.

I glance across the table at Russell, who's been hunched over his computer ever since Zoey went down for a nap. He tired her out on the jungle gym, and she fell asleep on his shoulder as we walked home. It was kinda cute. He's still got stains on his shirt from her messy face.

Glancing over his shoulder, he stares at the front door, obviously confused by who would be intruding on our quiet Sunday afternoon. I look toward the hallway, listening out for Zoey, but the knock hasn't woken her. Thank goodness. She needs the sleep.

"I'll get it," Russell murmurs, rising from his chair and walking to the door while I click on the top search link and try not to eavesdrop.

But it's impossible when Russell's voice rises with a sharp "You were supposed to call first. I only agreed with Coach Jones because he said you were going to be mature about this."

"I have tried calling," a man snaps back, and I tense, my spine pinging straight as I recognize Zander's voice. "It's pretty hard to make an appointment to come here when you won't answer your damn phone."

Russell huffs. "How did you find out where I live?"

"I asked around."

"You shouldn't be here."

"I need to see her."

"She's not yours to see!"

"You know she is! Now stop getting in my way, because I am not giving up, you understand me? This is my daughter, and I won't just walk away because you've told me to."

"I'm the closest thing she's got to a father, and I'm just trying to protect her," Russell thunders back, and I lurch out of my seat, rushing around the table to intercept this disaster. "I don't want you waltzing into her life and fucking it up!"

"And why would I do that?"

"You can't help yourself. I heard all about how you treated Sienna, and I won't—"

"Okay!" I spring up behind Russell, catching Zander's eye and feeling my insides melt and sizzle.

Shit, why does he have to have such beautiful eyes? And that face. He's still so hot and handsome, and my body is igniting just the way it used to in high school. A luscious shiver runs through me as I watch him grip the back of his neck, his bicep curling beneath his T-shirt sleeve.

I attempt to pull myself together and bring a little calm into the situation. "Hi, Zander."

"Hey." His expression softens the second I speak, and it's hard to keep my guard up when he looks at me like that. "I'm sorry to just show up unannounced, but I'm getting kind of desperate here. We need to talk. You know we need to talk."

My head's bobbing before I can stop it. "Yeah, I know."

"What?" Russell barks. "No, you don't." Lightly holding my arm, he stops me from grabbing my shoes. "Sienna, you don't owe this guy anything."

With a soft sigh, I look up at Russell. "I want to talk to him. It's only fair."

"Fair? You want to talk about fair?"

Closing my eyes, I shake free of his hold and softly murmur, "Please. Just... I'm going to take a walk with him. Once around the block. That's it, okay? We'll talk, and then I'll be back. It's going to be fine."

Russell snorts like a bull before muttering, "You chose not to tell him for a reason. Don't forget that."

Wincing, I snatch my Converse off the shoe rack and quickly pull them on.

Russell glares at Zander the entire time, and it's so freaking awkward. My fingers are trembling as I try to tie my shoes, making me slower than normal. I glance up and catch Zander watching me. He gives me a soft smile, and it helps me take a breath.

"Call me when Zoey wakes up?" I glance at Russell, who gives me a stiff nod, then sends another dark glare at Zander, who takes the look with a stoic calm that's all kinds of sexy.

Dammit.

Why does he have to be so gorgeous all the time?

Trying to rustle up my anger is so much harder when he's standing there like that in his baseball cap, fitted jeans, and Nolan U Cougars T-shirt. Even though the cotton is loose around his torso, I can still make out his impressive shape, and my insides are quivering at the idea of just how taut and hot those muscles I can't see are.

God, help me!

Grabbing my shades, I shove them on, grateful that it's sunny. I need the protection as I amble along beside him.

Talk. We're going to talk.

I don't know what the hell we're going to say, but I'm guessing he's still looking for an explanation as to why I shut him out. Can I honestly explain it to him? I don't even want to think about that awful day. Ugly memories taunt me, making my stomach surge as I glance up at Zander's face.

His jaw is clenched, his hands shoved into his jeans pockets as we walk next to each other. I think he's gotten taller. He's definitely gotten musclier. There's a power to him—maybe a confidence?—that he didn't have before, and I can't help being attracted to it.

No wonder the girls all love him.

A bitter spike drives through my chest and I cross my arms, wondering if this walk is the worst idea ever. But I couldn't have Russell and Zander yelling at each other and waking up Zoey.

I huff and glance at him. "So, are we going to talk or not?"

He looks down at me and sighs. "I don't know how to start. I have so many questions, and I don't even know where to begin."

"Just ask, and I'll tell you what I can." My voice is clipped, and I'm sure he can feel the waves of animosity I can't help firing his way.

Argh, these feelings are like whiplash. From attraction to guilt to hate-fire. I wish I could just pick one and hold on to it, but I'm all over the place.

"Okay... um..." He pulls the bill of his ball cap a little lower. "How was your pregnancy?"

I blink, surprised by the question. I thought he was about to start badgering me about why I kept Zoey a secret.

I'm actually kind of relieved that it's an easy enough question to answer. "Uh..." I let out a soft laugh. "It was horrible. I threw up constantly for about twenty weeks."

"No way." He hisses and looks kind of concerned.

I glance away so I can finish the next part. "I felt nauseous for basically the whole pregnancy. Zoey grew well, though. She was healthy."

"But were you okay?" The tender lilt to his voice makes my chest spasm.

Keeping my eyes straight ahead, I shrug and murmur, "I survived, and... it was worth it. The second she was born, I felt so amazing. She lit me up, you know?"

I glance his way, unable to contain my grin.

His lips curve at the edges, like he's about to smile, but his eyes are steeped in sadness. "Did she kick and squirm when she was in your belly? What was she like when she was born? I bet she was so tiny. Did she have any hair? Were her eyes blue like they are now?"

Shit. All these little details I didn't think he cared about.

But look at his face. He wants to know everything.

Guilt hammers me as I nod, then shake my head. "I mean, she kicked a little. She wasn't a big mover. She's making up for that now." I tip my head with a soft laugh. "She's like the Energizer Bunny some days."

"I can imagine."

"And she was tiny when she was born, but her lungs

were definitely strong. She had a little hair, and yes, her eyes were the most brilliant blue."

"Just like yours," he whispers.

I look back at the ground, unable to cope with the wistful look on his face. I deprived him, and he knows it.

Pulling out my phone, I stop on the sidewalk and find some photos from Zoey's first few weeks. His breath catches when I show him the first one, and then he drinks in the rest, flipping through the photos until I can't take it anymore.

"Okay." I grab my phone out of his hand and tuck it away.

He looks bereft, and I want to tell him that I'll send them all to him, but the thought of having his contact details in my phone is freaking me out. I got rid of my last one so he couldn't call me anymore... and now I just want to let him back into my life?

It would be so easy, Sienna. Just give him your number.

I clench my jaw and pick up my pace.

Zander jogs a couple steps to catch up with me. He's looking kind of pale, a muscle working in his jaw before he says in a husky voice, "Those photos are... amazing. She's cute. Always has been. Even on the day she was born."

"Yeah." I nod, my throat feeling thick and gummy.

"And the birth went okay?"

My shoulder hitches. "It was okay, I suppose. She came out in one piece."

"And you?"

A broken laugh shoots out of me. "Worst pain of my life. Thought I was going to die. Screamed the walls down. Nearly broke my dad's hand. Told Mom I couldn't do it and it'd be better if Zoey just stayed in there. You know..." My nose wrinkles as I glance up at him. "It was great."

His laughter is breathy, his expression crumbling. "Damn, Sparks. You're amazing."

I look away from him. I can't see what his eyes are doing right now. It's too dangerous. If he's looking at me the way his voice sounds, I'm going to melt into a puddle at his feet.

And I want to beg him to never call me Sparks again... but I can't, because the idea kills me.

With a loud sniff, I cross my arms and keep staring forward. There's a coffee cart across the street just ahead of us, and I lurch toward it. "Let's get a drink. I read that you're addicted to coffee, so let's get you an afternoon fix."

"You what? When?" He pulls me to a stop before I walk out in front of a car I didn't even see.

I flush, my skin electrified by his touch. His fingers curve around the crook of my elbow, and I can't help glancing down at his hold on me. It's so familiar yet so new at the same time.

"Uh, sorry." He lets me go. "Didn't want you getting run over."

"Thanks," I murmur, then check the street three times before crossing.

Pulling out my phone, I order an iced tea and make sure I pay for myself as well. I don't want him treating me to anything right now. He gives me a sad smile before ordering his coffee, and we wait beside the cart, staring out at the people milling around the park.

"When did you read about me?" he asks again, his

deep, husky voice sending tendrils of pleasure down my spine.

I stiffen my back, trying to counter it. "In the Nolan U *Sports Digest*." I shrug and make the mistake of glancing at him.

His lips are curling up at the corners, like he's stoked that I checked him out.

With a little scowl, I add, "I didn't finish the whole article, but I skimmed to the end and saw your answer about coffee."

"Right."

His disappointment gives me a spike of satisfaction until I start feeling bad and have to mutter, "So, Taylor Swift, huh? Nice choice."

"You still addicted to her music?"

I can hear the smile in his voice and have to glance up at him again. Dammit. I've always loved his grin.

Biting my lips together, I nod, hoping I'm not blushing. "Yep. She's still the best."

"She is."

I snort at his agreement. "But it's not like you're going to admit that to anyone, right?"

"I'll admit it to you." He shrugs. "And only you."

My heart trills, and my stupid body can't help but turn to face him. My mind is being overstuffed with all the times we used to listen to Taylor together. She filled his car and so many spaces we spent time together. She was the soundtrack to our love story, and I've tortured myself with her music over and over again.

And now he's standing right in front of me, gazing down at my face like he's feeling all the same things.

"Remember City of Rocks National Reserve?" he whispers, and I suddenly realize I can't do this.

I can't walk down memory lane.

I can't be here with this man who I loved so freaking much.

This man who will always own the biggest piece of my heart.

CHAPTER 14
ZANDER

I can sense the shift within her, like she's about to turn and bolt back across the road. I reach for her hand, desperate to stop her retreat.

She tenses at my touch, and I squeeze her delicate fingers before letting go and practically begging, "Please, don't go. It's okay. We don't have to talk about anything you don't want to."

"Order for Sienna!" a lady calls.

She jolts and walks to the window, thanking the woman with a forced smile. I eye her carefully as she sips her iced tea and wonder if I'm going to be chasing this gorgeous blonde down the street when she sprints away from me yet again.

But she stays.

My heart pounds, my muscles coiled tight, ready to spring into action.

But she stays.

So I take a breath and reach for my coffee when my name is called.

Sipping the strong brew, I step up on the curb and beckon Sienna with a tip of my head. "Do you want to walk back to your place or go through the park?"

She clears her throat and steps around me, heading for the park. I let her go, walking a few paces behind her. It's impossible not to admire her figure. She's still so hot and beautiful. The jeans she's wearing hug her ass perfectly, and I can still feel the shape of it in my hands. I want to pull her close. It'd be the most natural thing in the world, to wrap my arm around her.

But I lost that chance when I broke up with her, didn't I?

Damn... I lost way more than I counted on. I would do anything to turn back time and change what happened.

Regret always sits heavy in my chest, but this afternoon it's turning my heart into a punching bag. I can feel every fucking blow.

Glancing over her shoulder, Sienna lifts her shades and gives me a pointed look. Her blue eyes are still so sparkly, and I can't help drinking her in. I must look like a drunken idiot as I dribble to a stop and just stand there gazing at her.

"Would you stop walking behind me? It makes me feel like I'm being stalked."

"Sorry." I pick up my pace. "I wasn't sure if you wanted me next to you."

"It's fine." She huffs, making me feel like it's anything but fine.

Shit. This walk is the worst fucking idea ever.

"So... how are your parents?" Sienna asks, although it's obvious she doesn't really want to know. It's not hard to sense the low-lying anger she still has for them. She probably blames them for our breakup. They made no secret about not loving our relationship. They really did put the pressure on me, telling me repeatedly that I was too young for a serious relationship. In the end, I bought into their sales pitch.

Worst decision ever.

I close my eyes and force myself to reply in an even tone. "Yeah, they're still doing that whacked-out 'we're divorced but can't stay away from each other' thing."

She hisses. "Still fighting a lot?"

"Only when I'm there. I think. I don't actually know."

"You're not in touch?"

I open my mouth to respond but nothing comes out. Shit. She can't know everything that went down my freshman year. I was the world's biggest asshole and she'll never forgive me.

In the end, I settle for a lame half-truth. "We still see each other for holidays, and Dad always comes to the big games he can get to."

"I bet they watch every one of them."

"Oh yeah, and I always get texts about those." I nod. "Talking football with them is easy, so I tend to stick with that."

"Okay." She sips her tea, and I miss with an ache how easy it used to be to talk to her. I want that back so fucking badly.

"How are your parents?"

"On a cruise."

"Really?"

"Yeah. When we first left Everett, we traveled around the country in our camper van. I finished school online, and then Zoey was born and we settled in Sacramento for a while, but then they got antsy and we hit the road again."

My stomach curdles, picturing Zoey as a newborn, all wrapped up in Sienna's arms and I'm nowhere to be seen.

"We kept going for another six months or so, but I could tell my parents were ready for more. They wanted to get overseas and were talking cruises. I couldn't imagine dealing with Zoey on a boat, so I encouraged them to go on their own. That's why I moved in with Rusty."

"Rusty?"

"Yeah, Russell." She tucks a lock of hair behind her ear. It still looks as silky as it used to be. My fingers itch to run through those long strands again. I loved it when she let me play with her hair. "That's just his nickname. It pops out sometimes."

A flash of jealousy rips through me with surprising speed and vehemence. I hate that she has anything to do with that fuckwit.

But I can't let it show, right?

So I attempt an unaffected smile. "You guys seem pretty close."

Her eyes dart to mine and she doesn't confirm nor deny, causing this gnawing worry to munch away at my insides. Is there more to their relationship than she's saying?

Shit, shit, shit!

They're a couple.

Didn't Russell say he's the closest thing Zoey has to a father?

Fuck!

But I'm her dad. It's me. I should be the one protecting her!

"How could you keep this a secret from me?" The question spurts out before I can stop it. I promised myself I wouldn't accuse her, that I'd be calm and hear her out. I promised myself that I'd do everything I could to win my way back into Sienna's life so I could have contact with Zoey.

But I can't stop this emotion raging through me, and so I start snapping.

"She's my daughter. I should have been involved. I could have supported you through your shitty pregnancy. I could have been there when she was born! You could have called me. Fuck, you could have texted, Sen!"

Her eyes round, and she steps away from my sudden venom. We've reached the grove of trees on the edge of the park, and she walks into the shade, her blonde hair losing its golden glow. Perching her sunglasses on top of her head, she spins to face me. I've never seen her blue eyes so ice cold before, and it's unnerving. But it doesn't kill the fiery wrath still heating my insides to boiling.

I'm enraged by the injustice of all this.

She didn't even give me a fucking chance!

And I'm about to tell her that when she sucks in a breath, then says, "I wanted to tell you in person."

Her voice is strained and quiet, but that doesn't stop me flicking my arms in the air and barking, "So, why didn't you come to see me?"

"I did come to see you!"

Her shout closes up my throat in a second. Cold dread spreads through my body like a virus as I stand there gaping at her.

She crosses her arms, her voice turning small and shaky. "I came to see you at Kelsey U." Her chin bunches, her eyes glassing over. "But you were otherwise occupied."

My heart starts thundering, ready to beat right out of my fucking chest.

What did she see?

What the fuck was I doing?

I press my hand against my rib cage, wondering if this is what a heart attack feels like. The look on her face right now is killing me.

"I can't do this," she rasps, sucking in a ragged breath and darting out from under the trees.

"Sparks." Instinct has me reaching for her, but I stop midway when she snaps at me.

"No! You don't get to call me that anymore. I'm not your Sparks. I'm not your anything! You made sure of that!"

A bitter ash fills my mind, and all I can do is stand there as she runs away from me, her blonde hair flying.

I have to let her go. I'm too afraid to chase her and find out what she saw me doing.

It must have been pretty fucking bad by the look on her face just now.

Closing my eyes, I dip my head and can only manage a rasping whisper. "Shit."

CHAPTER 15
SIENNA

Tears are streaming down my face as I scurry home. I'm doing this weird walking-jogging thing, like my legs can't decide what to do with themselves. I sniff at the snot dripping out my nostrils and slash at the tears on my cheeks.

He doesn't deserve my tears.

Fuck him!

How dare he get pissed at me when he was the one who—

Snapping my eyes shut, I shudder to a stop and sway on my feet, the memories coming back to me with brutal clarity. Without my say-so, I'm taken off this quiet, sunny Nolan street to a dorm hallway at Kelsey U. I swayed on my feet then, too, shock pulsing through me as I watched the only guy I'd ever loved drive a spike right through my soul...

. . .

I found Zander's room with relative ease. Trying to walk those final few steps was a mission. My insides were wrecked as I experienced everything from excitement at the thought of seeing his beautiful face again to the dread of what I had to tell him.

Nerves scattered through me like loose wires, sending electric spikes up and down my limbs as I came to a stop on the linoleum floor.

Zander's door was only two away. I could see that it was open, and music was pumping out of it.

It was some kind of party mix with a strong beat that thumped and reverberated. It was okay, but not the melodic tunes I always made him listen to when we were driving in his car.

My stomach twisted into a tight ball, and I laid my hand over my belly, an instinctual move, like I was trying to protect my baby's ears... which were already developing, although according to what I'd read, they still couldn't hear anything for a while yet.

But still, I splayed my fingers over my stomach and inched toward Zander's open door.

And then I froze, my eyes rounding to dinner plates as I stared into his room and took in what felt like a scene from a horror movie.

It kind of was.

It was *my* horror movie.

But rather than blood and guts, it was naked breasts and ass cheeks.

My mouth parted, my stomach dropping to my knees while my heart catapulted into my throat and stayed lodged there. I blinked, trying to wrap my brain around what I was seeing.

Zander was on his bed, his shirt off, his sweatpants twisted around his ankles while a girl knelt on the bed beside him. She was sucking him off, practically choking herself while he fisted the duvet and groaned into another girl's mouth.

She was on the other side of him, her large breasts squished against him as they played tonsil hockey.

Breaths started punching out of me.

Or maybe they were sobs.

His hand was splayed on that girl's back. His tongue was inside her mouth. Someone else's lips were wrapped around his dick. His body didn't belong to just me anymore, and it was killing me.

He was oblivious to his audience. He couldn't even sense me watching him, which a few months ago I would have sworn was impossible. We had a silent call between us, could always tell when the other person entered a room. Could find each other across a crowded cafeteria in a heartbeat.

And now he was sitting on a bed, getting it on with two college girls, and I was standing out in the cold, pregnant with his child and completely forgotten about.

Bile surged within me, my stomach convulsing as I slapped a hand over my mouth and ran.

And I haven't stopped running since.

Not really.

Because Zander is trying to find out the truth, and rather than telling him why I didn't want him to be a part of his child's life, I keep taking off.

But what the hell else am I supposed to do?

The guy I fell in love with was not that guy on the bed.

He was someone I didn't know. Someone who left me for football...and obviously a whole lot else. He wanted to spread his wings, and I hadn't realized that meant exploring every other side of himself as well.

How could I interrupt his three-way?

How could I knock on his door and tell him he was going to become a father?

I didn't want that man fathering my child.

And so I ran.

And I thought I'd never have to deal with him again.

But when has life ever played fair, right?

With a hiccupping sob, I wipe my nose with the back of my finger, then wince when my phone starts to ring.

Pulling it out of my pocket, I see Russell's name and suck in a few deep breaths before answering with a cheerful "Hey. How's my favorite girl?"

"She's awake and asking for you."

"Mommy, Mommy, Mommy, Mommy!" Zoey shouts in the background, sounding as happy as a clam.

I force a laugh and singsong, "I'm on my way," hoping like hell that by the time I reach Russell's place, I can stuff all these ugly memories into the back recesses of my mind and get on with being the mother I'm supposed to be.

CHAPTER 16
ZANDER

I walk back to Football Frat in a numb haze. I don't remember throwing out my coffee cup. I don't remember crossing any streets, but eventually I'm walking up our front path and in the door.

The TV's on, but I don't know what's playing. I hear a muffled greeting but can't respond as I haul my sorry ass up the stairs and shut my bedroom door. I even lock it, which is something I don't normally do, but I can't be interrupted right now.

I don't know what the fuck to do with myself.

"What'd you see, Sienna?" I keep whispering, dread bubbling inside of me. "It can't have been..." Shaking my head, I double over, bracing my hands on my knees and moaning, "No. Please. Fuck. No!"

My phone starts ringing and I wrench it out of my pocket, ready to hurl it onto my bed, until I see who's calling me.

Before I can stop myself, I answer in a rush. "Mon." I

whimper her name, and there's a thick beat of silence before she responds.

"Zander?" My sister's voice is sharp and alert as always. "Are you okay?"

"It's bad," I rasp.

"How bad?" Her voice takes on that lawyer quality she uses every time she's facing a crisis. "Talk to me."

"I... she was... pregnant."

"What? Who?"

"Sienna." Plunking down on the end of my bed, I stare at my shoelaces. "She had a kid. A little girl. Zoey."

"Wow, really?" Monica's voice pitches with interest until the ball quickly drops. "Oh shit. No. You're not saying...? She's not the little girl you called me about the other day, is she?"

"Yes," I croak. "The one I saw on the playground who looks just like you."

There's a pause and I can picture my sister's eyes bulging when she whispers, "No, that can't be. You're... She's *yours*? You're a dad?"

"Yeah." It's hard getting the word out, but there it is.

"Holy shit!"

I close my eyes while Monica processes this bombshell. It takes about a minute of sputtering, and then she lets out an irritated huff.

"Why the fuck didn't she tell you?"

"She said she tried, but—"

"Wait, have you told Mom and Dad?"

"Fuck no. Can you imagine how they'll react? I've done exactly what they told me not to." I sigh, flopping back on my mattress and staring up at the ceiling. "I can't tell them."

She lets that hang in the air for a second before softly reasoning with me. "They have a granddaughter. Don't you think they deserve to know about her?"

"It's gonna shock the hell out of them."

"It's definitely shocking the hell out of me."

I let out a gruff laugh and take my cap off, throwing it across the room. "Dad will be beyond pissed. I can't tell anyone until I've sorted out this clusterfuck. I'm trying to talk it through with Sienna, but we keep getting into arguments, and then she takes off."

Monica snorts. "I still can't believe she didn't tell you. I mean, what the actual fuck?"

Clenching my jaw, I try to clamp down the dark dread in my stomach. It hurts, like a viscous tar coating my insides, burning me and reminding me what a shit I used to be.

"It's so out of line, Zander. You have every right to be pissed."

"She said she came to see me," I admit, my voice sounding dead and lifeless. "She wanted to tell me in person."

Monica pauses, and I can picture her lips pursing as she considers this. "Do you think she's lying?"

I wish I could say yes, but—

"No. You should have seen her face, Mon. She said I was... *otherwise occupied*." I can barely get the words out as my mind floods with images of my year at Kelsey U, each one nastier and more brutal than the last.

Monica sighs. "She probably saw you getting it on with another chick."

"God, no!" I bark, sitting up and hating myself. I don't

remember much from that fucked up year, just scattered memories—more like nightmares.

It's not like I wanted to get mixed up in all of that shit, but I was desperately trying to fit in with my team. I wanted them to like me. I wanted to stop missing Sienna. I wanted to stop hurting.

I was too young and naive to realize none of them gave an actual shit about me. People can be pushy and manipulative, and I wasn't strong enough to counter the booze and drugs that kept being shoved in my face. It helped numb the pain. It didn't hurt as much when I was wasted.

Shit! I was such a fucking idiot. Eighteen years old and so out of my depth, I was drowning. I needed Sienna back. She could have kept me grounded. She could have been my lifeline, but I went and fucked that up, didn't I?

I regret so much about my time at Kelsey U. I was a wreck after that first party I attended with the team. I woke up hungover and freaking out because I couldn't remember what I'd gotten up to. There were naked bodies littered around the living room...and one of them was mine. Shit, it was humiliating, but no worse than the time I woke up with *two* half-naked girls draped across my body. We were in my room, and I didn't even know how they got there. It scared the shit out of me, and I swear I tried to get my life back on track, but I kept on getting dragged back into the chaos by my team and my roommate. It was a losing battle and I...

I cringe, scrubbing a hand down my face, hating how weak and pathetic I was back then. Why the fuck didn't I just stand up for myself?

Because you were worried you'd be benched. You

didn't want to get iced out like some of the other guys had been. You didn't want to have to deal with Dad's disappointment. You didn't want to miss Sienna anymore.

There were a lot of fucking reasons I let myself get dragged down, but none of them were good enough.

"Don't be so hard on yourself, bro. You'd broken up. It wasn't like you were cheating on her."

"It doesn't matter. If I'd walked in on her with another guy, I would have fucking lost it. We belonged to each other."

"Zander."

"No! Don't try and fucking justify this. She was still in love with me and carrying my kid... and I was—" My words cut off, I can't bring myself to say it out loud. "I don't know what I was. I was so fucking screwed up that I don't even remember half of what I did. Shit, Monica..." I shake my head, my throat swelling as I struggle to get the words out. "Whatever she saw must have felt like total betrayal."

"You were still in love with her too," Monica murmurs. "In your senior year, when I was telling you that you were getting too intense and you should break up, I kind of didn't realize just how deep the feels were for you two. I thought you were just in the throes of experiencing sex for the first time and all the goodies that come with that. I didn't want you being tied down." Her sigh is even heavier than the one before. "But when you came back at Christmas, and she'd just disappeared... you were so devastated." She tuts. "And you really lost your way after that."

I rub my forehead, muttering, "I was such a shit that year."

"Yeah." She kind of laughs. "Was it the fact that I had to bail you out of jail that gave it away?"

I snort, my tone getting dark and salty. "What did she see, Mon? What the fuck did she see?"

"I don't know. I still think my guess is right."

Squeezing my eyes shut, I fist the front of my hair and give it a light tug. "I'm trying to figure out when she would have come by. That year is such a blur. If she saw —" I shake my head. "Fuck, this is bad."

"Look, bro, maybe you should tell her everything?"

"No way." I shoot off the bed and start pacing. "You're the only one who knows. You and Coach Jones... and even he doesn't know every little detail. I need to keep it that way."

"But telling her the truth might open up some doors for you guys. Really break down the barriers, you know? If you let her in on this, you're showing her that you trust her and—"

"She can't know about the fucked-up shit I got into. She'll never forgive me."

Monica tries to argue, "You weren't responsible for—"

"I was!" I cut her off before she says it out loud. "Sienna can never know. End of discussion. It's a miracle it wasn't publicized."

"No, it was a hell of a lot of hush money from the right people that kept that quiet. The college couldn't afford that kind of scandal, and the donors stepped up big-time. My point is you don't have to be ashamed for—"

"Yes, I do!" I bark, then pinch the bridge of my nose and mumble a string of curses.

My sister goes quiet, letting me pace and huff like a rhino.

My room is too fucking small sometimes! I feel like I'm back in that jail cell again, walking a trench into the floor.

"Do you want her back?" Monica finally asks.

I stop, staring at my reflection in the full-length mirror. "What?"

"Are you just after access to Zoey, or do you want to win Sienna back?"

"I..." I'd given up on that dream a long time ago—when she ghosted me and I thought I'd never see her again. "I don't know. I just... I *have* to be there for my daughter. I can't even explain why I feel so strongly about it, but it's this burning in my chest, Mon. There's a little human on this planet who I helped create, and I have to watch her grow. I just have to."

"Okay." Monica's calm voice takes the panicky edge off mine.

"Okay." I nod.

"Well, you're going to need to find some kind of peace agreement with her mother... the woman who you are probably still a bit in love with."

"Monica." I close my eyes.

"I'm just saying."

"Well, don't *just say* anything. I have to focus on Zoey first. My love life has nothing to do with being a parent. And are you honestly telling me that I should be contemplating a relationship with the girl who totally ghosted me and broke my heart?"

"Sounds like you broke hers first, bro."

A gut-wrenching groan fires out of me, my legs buckling as I crumple to my knees on the floor.

"But let's keep the focus on Zoey, shall we?" Monica's

voice brightens, like she's trying to shine a light into the dark abyss that I'm wallowing in. "Cute name, by the way. Nice that Sienna kind of went for a female Zander."

"What?" I blink, glancing at my surprised reflection in the mirror.

"Zoey, it starts with a Z. Zander starts with a Z. I wonder if she did that intentionally."

My lips part, and now I'm gaping at myself, my insides in chaos as my sister fucks with my brain some more.

"Anyway, the point I'm trying to make is... Sienna is the only thing stopping you from having a relationship with your daughter, which means you might have to compromise and open up a little. Let her in, so she'll let you in? You get me?"

"Monica," I groan. "I can't."

She tuts, her voice getting all clipped and businesslike. "Then you need to be prepared for the fact that you might lose her all over again. And this time will be way worse, because you'll lose your daughter too."

CHAPTER 17
SIENNA

It's been three days since I ran away from Zander, and my emotions have been on a roller coaster ever since. It doesn't help that I currently have my period and I'm feeling bloated, nauseous, and headachy.

I woke up this morning and instantly knew that today was going to be too much for me, but there was nothing I could do about it.

Russell's at the hockey arena all day, Mrs. Ward is away visiting her own grandchildren, and it's not like I can call Zander for help because he's a college athlete with an insane schedule—from what I've researched— and besides, I have no way of getting in touch with him.

And it doesn't help that I've just had the worst phone call with my parents ever. They didn't even say hi when I answered. Mom just launched into an irate diatribe.

"You went for a walk with Zander Donohue?" She was bristling, her cheeks all red.

I bulged my eyes at her and gasped. "Russell told on me?"

"He only called because he cares about you, Blue." Dad's voice was firm. "Which is a lot more than I can say for that jackass who got you pregnant, then went off and tried to pierce every vagina at Kelsey U."

"Ewww, Dad!" Why does he always have to describe stuff in such a gross way?

"I can't believe you spoke with him, let alone went for a walk with him. Sienna, don't you remember what he did to you?"

"Of course I do, Mom." I shut my eyes, not wanting to look at them for this painful conversation. "I just... he found out about Zoey, and he deserved some kind of explanation."

"Well, I hope you gave it to him. In graphic detail!" Dad fumed. "I hope he knows that leaving his door open for his little porn show routine was abhorrent, and he doesn't deserve to even breathe the same air as our sweet little Zoey!"

Thank God my daughter heard her name, because she came running into my bedroom yelling, "Gammy! Papa!"

She distracted them for me, giggling at the phone while they put on happy voices and asked her how Piggy Watson was doing. She held him up to the camera and started babbling incoherently.

They asked her if she took him to the park, and she told them she played with Foobawl.

Thankfully, they thought she meant the ball and not the person. She kept talking so fast that it was basically impossible to understand her, but my parents acted like they totally knew what she was saying.

I got a ten-minute reprieve before she got bored and wanted to go back to her toy zoo animals.

With a smile and nod, I took the phone back from her, dread rolling through me the second she left the room and my parents kicked back into "lecture mode" like there'd been zero break.

I sat there and took it, my anger at Russell simmering deep and hot. I couldn't believe he sold me out. What a fucking putz!

I felt kind of bad thinking about him that way, but come on. He's supposed to be my friend, and he's talking about me to my parents behind my back.

In the end, my simmering anger started to bubble and brew, and I took it out on my parents.

"Okay, you need to stop! Zander knows about Zoey. It's out there. And yes, he made big mistakes, but he deserves to at least see his daughter. He has now. Twice! And he was really sweet with her both times. I love my daughter more than anything, and I'm not about to let her get hurt, so can you guys please just trust me!"

That shut them up... mostly.

In the end, they gave me weak nods and forlorn smiles before Mom plunged the knife in deep and hard. She did it in the softest voice, but I still felt every inch of that blade.

"He had such a hold over you in high school. You don't think straight when you're around him. You need to be careful, Sienna. Don't let yourself get caught in his web again. He'll destroy both you and Zoey if you're not careful."

My ears, eyes, and nose were burning by the time she

was done, and thank God I had the excuse of a playgroup to get to.

I hung up pretty damn quickly after that and got Zoey ready.

And now I'm standing outside this indoor play center I've never been to before and rallying my fraying nerves. Hitching Zoey onto my hip, I open the glass door and hope the other mothers are nice. I don't think I can handle another lecture today.

When I emailed the organizer of this particular playgroup on Monday, she seemed very pleasant, but I'm trying not to get my hopes up. This could be a total disaster, and I need to prep myself for that.

The yell and squeal of kids playing is the first thing that hits me, followed by the laughter of mothers who are clustered together, sipping coffees and watching their toddlers run around like wild animals. I stand and watch them for a moment, observing the mothers who seem oblivious to their children's antics and the ones who are up and down, barely stringing two sentences together before they're racing across the padded floor to break up a fight or rescue their child.

"Pay?" Zoey asks me, blinking her big blue eyes.

"You want to play?"

"Zoey pay." She nods.

"Okay." I walk to the counter and pay before unlatching the secured gate. It's an effort to force my shaking legs inside.

Zoey wiggles out of my arms, and the second she hits the floor, she's off, racing toward a little boy who's diving into the ball pit.

"Watch out for other people!" I call after her before she dives in headfirst.

I wince, ready to go over there and check that she didn't just bash her head, but she pops up a second later, laughing and triumphant. The little boy beside her raises his hands in the air and shouts, "Again!"

"Again!" Zoey mimics him and climbs out of the pit, ready to kamikaze herself back into the sea of balls.

"Looks like fun. Oh, to be a toddler again, right?" A woman beside me laughs, watching the two jump and squeal.

I glance at her and smile, gripping Zoey's diaper bag. "Is he yours?"

"Yes, that's Dayton. Or Dynamite. He'll answer to both."

She winks at me, and I can't help a soft laugh. "My girl's Zoey."

"And she looks to have just as much energy as mine. Hopefully they'll tire each other out and nap for hours." Wiggling her eyebrows, she beckons me over to the table of mothers. "Do you want to come meet everyone?"

"Oh, uh... yeah."

Her smile is kind as she rubs a hand between my shoulder blades. "I'm Fiona. Just call me Fee, and don't worry. None of us will bite."

"Do I really look that nervous?" My laughter is self-deprecating as she drags me across to the table.

"Hey, everyone," Fiona sings. "We've got ourselves a newbie. This is..." She looks at me with an expectant smile.

"Oh, you must be Sienna." A lady with a short bob

stands up and greets me. "I'm so glad you came. Ladies, Sienna's just moved to town. Her daughter is... two?"

"Yes." I nod. "Zoey."

"Oh, I love that name." One of the mothers points at me. "That name was near the top of my list, but then we went and had a boy, didn't we." She rolls her eyes. "*Another* boy."

"Well, you could keep going, Michelle. You might get a girl next time."

"I'm already up to four."

"Perfect. The next one will just pop right out."

The women all start laughing, and I glance around me, feeling so out of place, yet it's kind of where I belong, right?

I'm a mama just like these women. I might be a decade or so younger than most of them, but this is my place in the world right now. Apparently.

Fiona pulls out a chair for me, and I glance across at the ball pit, checking on Zoey before taking a seat.

"She'll be fine. We all watch out for each other's children here, and in about fifteen minutes, we'll round them up for some group time."

"If we don't, they turn feral." Michelle nods. "Unsupervised play has to be in short bursts, don't you find?"

I nod, pretending to know what I'm talking about. Zoey doesn't really have unsupervised play because I'm always there, being her little buddy.

Looking over my shoulder again, I watch her chasing after Dayton and realize that maybe I'm not the little buddy she needs.

Ouch. That hurts.

Turning back to the other women, I try to hide how

Zoey's independence is making me feel. I should be happy for her—being all brave and meeting new friends —but all I can feel is this overwhelming loss. Like if Zoey doesn't need me, where the hell do I fit into the world?

I've never had to ask myself what I want to be, because the choice was taken away from me. And then I realized how much I love being a mother, and... now I have no one to make more babies with.

Russell would make babies with you.

Ew. I can't even go there.

And I want to have babies with someone I love.

Zander whistles through my mind, my heart betraying me by pining for him just the way I used to. I try to harden myself against the fantasy of him slotting back into my life, like no shit has gone down. We could become a happy little family and—

It's not going to happen, so stop imagining it!

"And then Adam goes, 'Well, how hard can it be?'" The woman across from me puts on a voice, and Michelle gasps.

"No. He did not."

"He did! I'm telling you, I nearly kneed him right in the balls."

"What does he think this is, the 1950s?"

"That's what I said to him." The woman flicks her hand in the air, then smirks. "And then I told him that if he didn't think looking after twins all day was such a big deal, then he could do it. So, this week, I'm going away to my mom's place, and he's flying solo. I'm making him use three days of his vacation time. Suck it, Stewy!"

More gasps pop out around me and then a chorus of cheers.

I clap along, forcing a smile and checking on Zoey yet again. She's now crawling through a tunnel that will take her to the steps... that lead to the big slide. Oh man, she's going to love that. I have to make sure I watch her when she comes down.

Swiveling my body in preparation, I nearly miss the question being fired at me.

"What about you, Sienna? Are you married?"

"Uh... no." I shake my head. "No husband problems."

They laugh, but their faces are filled with sympathy.

I turn my back on them and watch Zoey zipping down the slide, loving the way she giggles.

"Good job, Zo!" I shout and hold my thumbs up.

"Fass, Mommy!"

"I know, you went so fast! That's awesome."

"Again, again!"

"Yeah, go again. I'll watch you."

She beams at me, and my heart floods with that familiar sense of love. She's so freaking adorable.

"You're doing so well." Fiona gives my arm a soft squeeze. "I can't imagine raising a child on my own."

"Oh, I'm not completely alone. My parents have been hugely supportive, and I live with a friend now who helps me a lot."

"Still not quite the same." Michelle's smile is sad. "I bet you really miss her father some days."

My smile dies while Fiona softly reprimands her friend.

"Michelle. That's not really our business."

"Sorry. I was trying to be understanding. Dads are such an important part of a child's life, and I don't know what I would do without Jonathan. He's my harbor, you know? And I'm just sad for you that you don't have that. I'm sorry."

"No, it's…" I shake my head, flashing her an awkward smile before turning back to watch Zoey. My eyes are burning as she zips down that slide, and I force an enthusiastic celebration, rising from my seat and going over to play with her.

I don't want to be rude, but I can't sit there listening to stories about husbands and how great or terrible they are. I don't want to be reminded of how important dads are in a child's life.

Zoey has Russell and my father… and Russell's father. She has plenty of men around her.

Just not the one you really, truly want her to have.

Shit. I didn't even know I wanted it until I saw him again.

I'd convinced myself that he was a heartless, soulless, man-whore asshole.

But then he'd seen us, he'd sought us out, he'd played with Zoey in the sandpit and pushed her on the swing. He kept pursuing this thing.

He wants in.

But I'm so afraid to let him.

I fight tears for the rest of the playgroup. The moms are nice enough to "not notice," and Zoey is having too much fun to be aware that Mommy's having a bad day. So, I stay the entire time, even hugging Fiona before I leave. Michelle gives me another abashed smile as I walk out the door and force a little bounce in my step.

Zoey's due for a nap in about an hour. I could just go right home, but I figure we've got enough time to head to the store. Zoey's in high spirits after her fun playing session. She ended up interacting with all the kids during the group activities. She loved the games and songs. I'm going to have to take her again... even though I don't particularly want to go. The harborless freak that I am.

Oh stop, she wasn't trying to be mean.

I struggle to counter my emotions with a little logic, but it's not really working today. Stupid period.

Finding a parking space across the street, I lift Zoey out of the car and use the crosswalk. No more sneaky jaywalking when you've got a kid you have to set an example for. I bounce her on my hip, making her laugh all the way to the grocery store. It's located between the Nolan U campus and Russell's house, and it's my go-to. I'm starting to memorize the aisles and know where things are. It definitely makes shopping quicker, which is always a good thing.

The bell above the door dings as we walk through, and I set Zoey on the floor. Grabbing a basket, I take her hand and remind her, "Stay close to Mommy, please."

She doesn't reply, and I squeeze her hand, glancing down at her. Looking up with an impish grin, she melts my heart, and we walk down the first aisle together, collecting the things I need before heading for the refrigerated section.

Zoey lets go of my hand, holding on to my leg as I try to find her favorite flavor of yogurt. There's no point buying the stuff she doesn't like. I'll just end up throwing those pouches away.

"Blueberry," I murmur. "Come on, where are you? Please have a couple. Even just one will do." Reaching for the back, I move the pouches aside, quickly checking each of them until I come up empty-handed.

Dammit.

"Zoey, you're going to have to have a different flavor this afternoon. Should we try banana?" I glance down for a response, and my heart goes cold. "Zoey?"

Shit. Where did she go?

Glancing around me, I berate myself for not noticing that she'd let go of my leg.

"Zoey!" I call, dashing down the closest aisle and looking around me. "Zoey, come on, baby. Now is not the time for hide-and-seek."

I try to remind myself that she's done this to me before.

She thought it was hilarious.

And thankfully, I heard her giggling and was able to find her quickly.

I pause, straining my ears to hear...

But nothing.

Nothing!

"Zo-ey!" I try to sing her name, seeing if that will coax her out, but it gets me no results.

I start a systematic search, heading from the cold section down toward the cereal aisle. And with each minute that passes, my panic starts to grow until I'm running down the next aisle in a blind rush and barreling straight into a concrete wall.

A hand darts out to catch me, long fingers that I know so well wrapping around my arm to stop me falling.

"Hey. Are you okay?" His husky voice is in full play, and I respond the only way I can...

I burst into tears.

CHAPTER 18
ZANDER

"Sienna?"

"Zander." She blubbers my name, curling her fingers into my hoodie... and I follow my gut. Pulling her into a hug, I rest her head against my shoulder, rubbing circles on her back while Wily stands beside me looking comically confused.

"Who's this?" he mouths, and I give him a desperate *not now.*

Thankfully, he nods while I try to work out how I'm going to help Sienna.

She's seriously distraught right now.

"No, no, no." She shoves me away, brushing hair off her wet face with shaking hands. "I can't find Zoey."

"What?" I'm immediately alert, scanning the store around me. "What happened?"

"I was looking for yogurt and she was standing right beside me, and then she was just... she was gone! And I can't find her!"

"Hey, it's okay. We're gonna find her."

"How old is she?" Wily asks.

"Um, she's, um..." Sienna closes her eyes like she can't even think straight, so I answer for her.

"She's two. Blonde curls. Blue eyes. What's she wearing?"

"Uh... blue overalls with a... a pink T-shirt and purple shoes." Sienna blinks, like she's slowly coming back online.

I rub her arm and keep assuring her. "It's all right. We'll find her."

"I'll check outside." Wily darts away from me, calling Zoey's name, and I wince as the shop bell dings, torturing myself with images of Zoey dashing out into the road and getting hit by a car.

"Oh my G—" Sienna's obviously thinking the same thing, and I quickly snap us out of it.

"Look at me." I lightly shake her. "Whatever it is you're picturing, stop. Now. That's not going to help us."

Sienna's head starts to bob. "Okay. Okay, okay."

"You go let the workers at the front know and then start checking the aisles to the left, and I'm gonna take the right."

"Okay," she squeaks, her voice pitching.

"We'll find her." Kissing her forehead, I dart away from Sienna and try to keep my panic in check as I walk down every aisle, calling my daughter's name—shit, *my* daughter—and praying we'll find her quickly.

I barely know the girl, and I'm fighting a meltdown. I can only imagine what Sienna's going through right now.

But it's all going to be okay.

It has to be.

I used to play hide-and-seek in grocery stores all the

time. Apparently, my mom lost me for a good twenty minutes once when I decided that hiding behind a pile of rolled-up rugs in Target was a brilliant idea.

"Zoey, come on, kid. Mom's freaking out," I call down the next aisle, walking along at a fast clip until I hear a little giggle by my left foot.

Stopping, I tip my head and crouch down, spotting a pair of cute blue eyes sparkling back at me from behind a stack of large tin cans.

"How did you get back there?" I can't help laughing.

She giggles again and shows me by crawling out of her hiding spot, her butt nearly getting wedged by the shelf above until she does a little shimmy and makes it through.

"Wow." I nod. "That's kind of impressive, you little Houdini."

With a playful grin, she bobs on her toes, all proud of herself, and I swear my insides are turning to putty.

"Hi, Foobawl." She brushes her sticky fingers across my cheek.

"Hey." I smile and hold out my hands. "Let's go find your mom."

To my surprise, she steps into my arms without hesitation, and I lift her up and call across the store, "Found her!"

CHAPTER 19
SIENNA

Zander's voice rings across the store, and I come running. I nearly take out the poor man who stopped to help us look and have to shout a quick apology over my shoulder as I tear down the aisle and barrel into Zander for the second time today.

Once again, he catches me with his free hand while I let out a surprised squawk, then blink at my daughter, who is happily clinging to him like a spider monkey.

"Hi, Mommy." She's using her cutest voice, but I'm not having it for a second.

"Zoey Beth Erling," I growl at her, taking her out of Zander's arms and perching her on my hip. "I told you to stay close to me. You know you're not supposed to play hide-and-seek at the store. That's naughty."

Zoey's expression bunches, her lip sticking out in a dramatic pout before her mouth opens and a pitiful wail shoots out of her.

"Zoey." I try to calm her before she gets into that

piercing register that makes my ears bleed. "It's okay. I'm just frustra—"

Her wail increases, cutting me off as Zander's big, blond friend wanders down the aisle, grinning like he can't hear the banshee cry echoing throughout the store.

"Yay." He pumps his fist in the air with a grin. "The lost have been found."

I wince as Zoey's cry pitches to new heights.

"Okay, that's enough, sweetie." I rub her back and go to kiss her cheek, but she lurches away from me.

"No." Stretching out her arms, she throws herself at Zander, who easily catches her and snuggles her against his chest. She buries her face in his neck, crying like the world has ended while I stand there trying not to notice how incredibly sexy Zander looks holding my little daughter in his big, strong arms.

His hand splays across her back, and he starts murmuring something in her ear that soon has her raucous tears under control.

"Are you kidding me right now?" I mutter, gaping up at him while he gives me a triumphant little grin.

I roll my eyes, and he starts to register that yes, seeing my daughter—who I have been raising for over two years now—launching herself into his arms is making me a little salty.

"Sorry," he mouths before going back to his soothing murmurs. "It's okay, baby girl. It's okay."

His husky voice is torturing me all over again, amplifying those feelings that I tried to bury deep under a mountain of hurt and anger and pain.

But there I go, erupting in a matter of seconds, my heart melting and bleeding all at the same time.

Zoey hiccups against Zander's shoulder, and I swallow, not even sure what I'm supposed to do right now. All I seem capable of is gazing up at my daughter being comforted by her father and wishing a thousand times over that things could have gone differently.

"Well." Wily claps his hands together. "I say after a trauma like this, we probably all need ourselves some ice cream."

Zoey's tears dry up instantly, her head shooting off Zander's shoulder so she can look at his friend with a hopeful smile. "Ice ceem?"

I glare up at him, and he gives me an awkward frown. "Uh… yeah, I figure ice cream always makes everything better, right?"

"Me ice ceem?" Zoey points to herself, and he grins at her while the look of pure adoration on Zander's face nearly cripples me on the spot.

He's falling in love with my baby.

His daughter.

The blond man shoots me an awkward look, obviously trying to suss me out. He can tell I'm annoyed with him but probably doesn't realize why. He hasn't thought through the fact that Zoey did something wrong, and now we're rewarding her with ice cream. And he's most definitely not considering the fact that after said ice cream, I have to somehow get her down for a nap.

"Um…" He scratches the back of his head. "Yeah, of course. Ice cream for you. If your… mommy says it's okay." He gives me a hopeful smile. "My treat."

Zoey swivels in Zander's arms to look right at me. "Mommy ice ceem? Zoey ice ceem." She starts tapping her chest as she tries to sell me on the awesomeness of this plan.

I can't help another eye roll as my shoulders slump in defeat. "Great, and now I'll be the Wicked Witch of the West if I say no."

Zander's friend winces and mouths, "Sorry," while I let out a helpless laugh.

"Fine. Whatever. Let's go get ice cream."

"Ice ceem!" Zoey shouts, launching herself at this man she hasn't even been introduced to. He grabs her with a laugh and starts walking out of the store.

I gape after them while Zander leans down and whispers in my ear, "Nothing to worry about. That's Wily. Solid-gold dude. He won't let anything happen to our girl." I spin to blink up at him, and he gives me an awkward smile. "Sorry. Your... your girl. Zoey is, um... she's safe."

My insides spasm, my heart jackknifing as I watch him try to correct his faux pas and a steaming pile of guilt nestles on my shoulders. She is his girl... or she would have been all along if only I'd let him.

But that day at the dorm... That—

I snap my eyes closed and shake my head.

"Here, why don't you let me..." Zander takes the basket from my hand. "I'll get it. You go wait outside with Zoey and Wily."

With a wordless nod, I head for the door, struggling to think straight as I squint up at the sun and hunt for my shades. Zoey is on the ground, bouncing around beside Wily. The giant of a man is crouched on the sidewalk and listing ice cream flavors while she shouts, "Yes!" or "Bluch!" to the different selections.

He starts getting creative. "How about gravy and mashed potato ice cream?"

"Ew!" She sticks out her tongue. "No. No tayto ice ceem."

"No?" He rubs his chin. "Okay, let me think of something else. How about blueberry?"

"Yes! Zoey booberry."

"Good choice, my friend." He holds out his hand, and she slaps it with a giggle.

And there goes my heart again.

Seriously? I'm such a wreck today.

The grocery store door opens, and I turn to find Zander striding out of there with a paper bag.

He hands it to me with a smile. "There you go."

"Thanks," I murmur, about to get out my wallet and pay him back when I notice a box of Nerds at the top of the bag.

Watermelon and cherry.

My favorite flavors.

He remembers.

With a soft gasp, my head jolts up, and I find Zander smiling down at me. And then he gives me a little wink before turning to talk to Zoey. "Who's ready for ice cream?"

"Me!" my toddler roars, making both the boys burst out laughing while I sway on my feet, gazing down at the box of Nerds in my bag and battling a torrent of emotions.

CHAPTER 20
ZANDER

Zoey holds Wily's and my hands the whole way to the ice cream parlor and demands swings the entire way.

"Okay, last one," I tell her for the third time. "One, two, three..."

"Go!" she yells, then starts giggling as Wily and I fire her into the air, her little feet flying high as she swings between us.

The kid is fearless, that's for sure. The higher we go, the harder she giggles.

And the words "more" and "again"—yeah, I think they're her favorites.

Sienna shuffles along behind us, looking kind of dazed. I wish I knew what she was thinking. Losing Zoey really rattled her... or is it the fact that I bought her a box of Nerds? I hadn't planned on it, but when I was waiting at the counter for my turn, I spotted them and my brain shot me back to the first time she tried to woo me with her weird-ass candy.

To me, Nerds are gross, but man, did she try her best to convince me otherwise.

She spent most of our relationship doing it, even coaxing me to suck them out of her belly button.

That's probably the only time I liked them—when I could lick them off her body.

Damn, I miss her body.

Glancing over my shoulder, I quickly skim it, wondering if having a baby has changed it at all. It certainly doesn't look like it.

She's fire.

She always has been.

I imagine she always will be.

Why the fuck did I break up with her again?

It's impossible to remember as I wait in the ice cream parlor line beside her... as I watch her be a mommy.

"One scoop." She holds up her finger. "Your choice is the flavor. That's it."

"Okay." Wily picks Zoey up so she can look at the flavors.

"Chokee, stawbee, nanilla!"

"One scoop, babe," Sienna reminds her, trying not to laugh as she looks at me and shakes her head. "One flavor. How about chocolate?"

Zoey shakes her head, her little face puckering as she scans the selection.

"My favorite is s'mores," I tell her. "Have you tried that one? It's got marshmallows in it."

Her eyes light like a Christmas tree, and she starts squealing. "Mores, mores, mores!"

The guy behind the counter laughs. "Cup or cone?"

"Cone, please," Sienna responds. "And make it like a kiddy size serving, please. I still have to get her down for a nap this afternoon."

"Got it." The man winks at her, and I can't help my frown.

I don't like other guys winking at my woman. That's *my* job.

She's not your woman, Zander.

The reminder is a short, sharp uppercut to the balls, and I step sideways, trying to distance myself from my biggest temptation.

Once we're all loaded up with ice cream, we take a seat in the round booth and neatly lick our cones while Zoey paints her face... and fingers... and shirt with ice cream.

I can't help laughing as I watch her. "I was just the same. I don't think there is one photo of me as a toddler where I don't have some kind of stain or mud or smear across my face and clothes."

"Really?" Sienna whips around to look at me. "I was wondering where she got that from." Her voice dies down to a soft whisper. "She's the messiest kid."

The mood at the table drops by a few degrees as Sienna's brain goes I don't know where, and I sit there shredded by the mere fact that I've been denied my own flesh and blood.

"Hey, who wants to ride the pony over there?" Wily points behind him, and Zoey abandons the last of her ice cream, dumping the soggy cone on the table and scrambling out of the booth.

"Me! Me! Zoey ride it."

"Okay, come on, you messy lil' monster." Wily races her to the pony, and we watch her gleefully prance after the blond giant.

He lets her win, and I shoot a smile at Sienna.

"He's great." She laughs. "Is he one of your roommates?"

"Yeah." I nod. "There are five of us."

"Wow. You must live in a big house."

"Yep. It's an old frat house, but it's all colonial style, you know? I don't know exactly when it was built, but it's gotta be early 1900s."

"That's pretty cool. I'm glad you live with good guys." She nods, her smile genuine, and all I can do is stare at her, drinking in those blue eyes of hers and wishing that I hadn't fucked things up so badly.

Her chin bunches and she looks at the table, giving up on her half-eaten ice cream and pushing it aside.

"You okay?"

"Yeah." She sighs, rubs her forehead, and looks everything but okay. "I think I'm still a little shook. Today's been a really shitty one. I've got my period and was already emotional, and then Zoey goes missing and—" She suddenly stops talking, her swallow thick and audible. "And it makes me wonder if I can cope without my parents the way I said I could." Her expression buckles. "I went to this playgroup today, and I am the youngest by... years. I felt so out of my depth and like I didn't fit at all. But I have to go back, right? Because Zoey needs to play with kids her own age. I never really had that. You know the settled upbringing that you got? I want that for her. I want her to feel secure and safe and be able to make connections. But it's hard, you know? And when I'm feeling this way, I just want... I want..." She sighs. "I don't know what the hell I want."

Her defeated mumble hurts me for reasons I can't explain, and it takes everything in me not to reach across the table and take her hand.

I want that so badly, but I'm worried it'll just make her retreat.

So, I swallow the gravel in my throat and try to make her feel better. "At least you have Russell, right? You like living with him?"

Fuck, I hate that guy's name in my mouth. Asshole.

"Yeah." Her shoulder hitches as her lips curl into a small smile. "Rusty's great."

Acid burns my throat, but I keep asking because I obviously like torturing myself. "So, what's the deal with you and him?"

Her gaze snaps in my direction. "What do you mean?

"I mean, are you guys..." I work my jaw to the side. "Are you guys like *living* together? Or do you just live in the same house?"

She narrows her eyes, and I squirm in my seat while she rests her chin in her hand and tries to read me. "What do you think?"

"I don't know. That's why I'm asking." My voice sharpens with agitation at the idea that she's found a special someone. A someone who's not me.

What the fuck is wrong with you? You should want her to be happy.

I hunch over, staring at the table and trying to ignore the reprimand I'm giving myself.

"Zander, Russell has always been like a brother to me. That hasn't changed." Glancing up, I watch her lips twitch. "He's just been nice enough to let us stay with him while my parents are away. And he's great with Zoey. She seriously adores him."

My chest keeps hurting, but I try not to let it show.

"He wouldn't have lost her today," Sienna mutters, and screw my no hand-holding rule. I reach for her fingers, needing to comfort her even in the smallest way.

"Hey." I give them a gentle squeeze until she's looking at me. "That was not your fault. She took off on you."

Sienna starts blinking, her chin bunching again like she's seconds away from crying. "It scared the shit out of me. Zoey getting kidnapped is my greatest fear. The thought of someone taking her or hurting her, scaring her, holding her against her will... and I can't reach her or help her..." She sucks in a ragged breath, her hand trembling as she rests it against her forehead. "It terrifies me."

"I understand. The thought is harrowing. But I'm around now. Whether you like it or not, I'm staying in my daughter's life, and I will do anything to protect her..." I hold Sienna's chin, encouraging her to look at me. "And you."

She stares at me, her blue eyes so round and beautiful.

I lose all the power from my voice as I track my eyes across her face. "You know you've gotten even prettier, right?"

Her blush is instant, her voice breaking as she leans away from me, pulling her fingers out of my grasp and sniffing. "You look at me like I still mean something to you."

"You do." I'm horrified by the idea that she would ever think otherwise.

With a slow shake of her head, I watch her eyes glass over and feel like dying a little on the inside when she whispers, "But you let me go so easily."

My lips part, and I wish I had something cool to say. Something that would erase all this shit and make it better. But I've got nothing.

And then she goes and keeps talking, driving this spiked ball of regret and pain even deeper into my chest.

"I could never get over you." Her lips form an awkward, watery smile, and I can sense she's about to lose the battle with her tears. "You haunt me every day, because I have this beautiful girl who I love so much, and she looks just like you." The first tears spill out of her eyes as she snivels and rasps, "It's not fair. I had no chance."

Her tears are killing me. I quickly reach for them, brushing them off her cheeks with my thumbs and wanting to promise her that I'll never hurt her again. She needs to know that letting her go *wasn't* easy... and I couldn't even do it in the end. I came back for her!

But I don't get a chance to say any of that, because Zoey comes bounding back to the table and Sienna jerks away from me, quickly wiping her face and putting on a bright smile.

"Hey, lil' lovebug. Was that fun?"

"Yup!" Zoey puts her hands on her hips, her little legs spread wide. "Wywee call me cowgewl."

"He called you a cowgirl? That's so cool." Sienna's face is so animated as she hides all her angst and interacts with her daughter like she hasn't just broken down in front of me.

I sit there staring at her, amazed by how incredible she is, then laughing when Zoey mimics Wily's "Yeehaw!"

The sweet girl with ice cream plastered all over her gives me the cutest grin, and I know without a doubt that I'm going to love her for the rest of my life.

Which is why I have to fix things with her mother.

CHAPTER 21
SIENNA

Zander ends up coming home with Zoey and me. That wasn't the plan, but as we left the ice cream parlor, Zoey wanted him to carry her. Wily had to go, which made her cry, and Zander did his magic thing again where he rubbed her back and said I don't know what, but it calmed her down.

Then it was time for him to say goodbye and she started crying all over again, so he jumped in the back seat with her and talked to her on the drive home. I checked the rearview mirror every chance I could get. Watching my daughter interact with her dad like it was the most natural thing in the world hurt my heart... and made it sing at the same time.

Seriously, this has been the most confusing day ever!

I can't wait for it to be over.

By the time I clean Zoey up and get her down for a nap, I'm exhausted. I might just take a nap myself, except for the fact that Zander is still standing in the living room, patiently waiting to talk to me.

Shit. I can't talk.

I can't handle this right now!

Pulling in a breath, I paste on what I hope is a serene smile and glance at the clock on the wall. "Don't you have to go?"

He checks his watch, an irritated frown whistling over his face before he sighs. "Yeah, but I've got a couple minutes."

"I don't want you to be late. I'm assuming it's football practice, and I know..." I huff, working my jaw to the side and crossing my arms. "You broke up with me for your football career." I swallow and try to ignore that awful jolt in my stomach as I press on with a little more truth. "At least that's the main reason you gave me, so... can't get in the way of that, right?"

Great, now my voice is getting all bitter. I can only imagine what my face is doing. But it's good. I need a little bitter. Zander made me all soft and squishy when he told me I'm prettier than I was before. He made my heart yearn when he comforted my daughter. Dammit, I can't let him tear through my defenses so easily. I have to keep my guard up.

I have to protect myself.

So, I raise my chin toward the front door. "Go on. I don't want you to be late."

He stays put, his feet firmly planted, his hands stubbornly shoved in his pockets while he stares at me and says in a broken whisper, "What'd you see that day you came to tell me you were pregnant? What did I do that made you want to cut me out?"

Oh shit. He looks so wrecked right now.

I don't want to have to repeat my nightmare.

But... he's not going to let this go, is he?

And if I don't tell him, he's probably going to think I was being a vindictive bitch or something, right? Punishing him for breaking up with me?

My eyebrows wrinkle as I force the story out of me. I tell him how Dad drove me up to Kelsey U. How it took so long because I kept having to stop and puke.

"I was so nervous... and I was suffering major morning sickness." I roll my eyes. "All-day sickness."

He winces like the idea of me suffering that way hurts him too.

I dart my eyes back to the shiny wood floor beneath me and keep going, telling him how I asked around campus, trying to find his dorm, and how this blushing girl let me in.

"It was so obvious she liked you and I get that I wasn't your girlfriend anymore, but we'd only been broken up for a couple months, and it really riled me. I was worried that you'd moved on already and I didn't want to believe it, you know?" I clench my jaw, shaking my head and having to force myself to keep going. My fingers dig into my arms until it hurts as I grit out the rest. "And then I found your room, and the door was *open*. I looked inside, and I saw you on the bed." I bite my lips together, unable to continue.

Zander lets out a shuddering breath, his glassy gaze intense, like he's bracing himself for a punch to the face. "What was I doing?"

I blink and fight the boulder forming in my throat. "You were sitting there, half-naked, and one girl was sucking you off while the other was playing tongue twister with you." I shake my head, backing away until I hit the wall behind me. Those images are still so clear, and I hate it. I want to wash them from my mind permanently, but I can't seem to do it.

I cover my eyes with my hand and smash my teeth together, desperate to hold it all in.

"Fuck," Zander rasps. "I don't even remember doing that."

Dropping my hand, I gape at him. "You... what?" My voice gets snappy. "It was you! I saw you!"

"I'm not saying you didn't." He raises his hands to calm me down. "And I remember...waking up and seeing those two girls." His expression crumples like he's in physical pain and his voice turns to a gravely rumble. "I just don't remember how I ended up in that situation. I don't remember going to my room with them or getting naked, I..." He winces, his skin paling to a sick gray. "I... um..." He bites his top lip before finishing in a rough mumble. "It was a bad year for me, and I got into some... things I shouldn't have. I was out of it more often than not."

I shake my head in confusion. "What happened to you?"

"I..." His expression buckles again, and he looks to the floor.

I give him a minute to explain himself, but he doesn't say anything, so I let out a soft sigh and get it over with. "Two girls at the same time. How could you do that?"

He cringes and covers his mouth, squeezing hard and shaking his head.

It's hard to know what to think or believe, but I may as well get out the last of my explanation. "It made me realize that what we had obviously wasn't that special to you."

"Sienna, no. It—"

I raise my hand to shut him up. "I realized in that moment that you weren't the guy I fell in love with... and I didn't want you being a father to our child. You'd moved on while I was back in Everett pining for you. You were living it up and spreading those wings just the way you wanted to." Sudden tears take out my voice, so it ends up turning into a wobbly squeak. "I had to get out of there. And I had to never see you again."

CHAPTER 22
ZANDER

I'm so gutted and ashamed, I can hardly stand up straight. I want to bolt from this conversation so badly. If she knew the whole truth about my freshman year, she'd never speak to me again.

But I can't leave things like this.

"Sienna, I'm sorry. I'm *so* sorry I hurt you." I'm seconds away from dropping to my knees and begging her forgiveness. "I didn't break up with you to spread my wings and get with a bunch of other girls. I swear. That was never my intention. I went to Kesley U to prove myself on the field, but I got caught up in—"

I shake my head, letting out a desperate little huff as I try to explain myself.

But nothing I say can make this better, can it?

What possible words will ever excuse my behavior?

"Things just turned to shit and I messed up. I wasn't over you. I was trying really hard to forget about us and make the most of my college experience, but it was all such bullshit!" I scrape a hand through my hair. "I was wasting my time trying to impress the wrong people and I was fucking miserable. That's why I was drinking. When I was out of it like that, I didn't have to feel anything. But then I'd sober up and hate myself."

I clench my jaw before I spill more of my foul-smelling dirt. I don't want to hurt her anymore than I already have.

Blinking, I sniff and softly admit. "I came back for you."

"What?" Her head snaps in my direction. Her frown is deep with confusion.

"I was missing you so much."

"Obviously." Her dry retort burns me, and I take a step toward her.

"I *was*. I... all that shit left me empty, and I needed you. I was drowning and miserable, so I came back to see you...beg you to forgive me and take me back. But...you were gone. You were..." My words trail off and I shake my head, scuffing the floor with my sneaker and mumbling, "I get why now. It just..." I let out a dry laugh. "You think I let you go so easily, but you left without warning. No goodbye. Nothing."

Her blue gaze is bright and fiery.

"I'm not blaming you. I'm just..." Shaking my head, I look to the floor again, unable to stand her hot glare.

A somber silence fills the room, and then my watch starts beeping. Fuck! I really have to go.

But...

Looking up with a silent apology, I try to think of something to say, but Sienna's still glaring at me.

"You need to go," she mutters.

"Yeah." I nod, hating myself for turning toward the door.

I stop just before reaching for the handle and notice a square notepad and pen on the side table. Reaching for it, I quickly scribble down my number.

"Call me anytime and I'll be there, okay?" Holding out the paper to her, I silently beg her to take it.

After a thick, uncomfortable beat, she pushes off the wall and walks toward me.

The paper shakes in the air between us before she snatches it from my fingers and reads the digits.

"Anything. Small, big, it doesn't matter. I'll be here for you and Zoey."

She doesn't nod, but she does tuck the note into her back pocket.

Her blue eyes graze over me once more, and I whisper a final apology before slipping out the door. "I'm sorry. I'm so fucking sorry."

It's not enough.

It'll never be enough.

What she saw that day...

Fuck. That must have destroyed her.

I was on that bed with two chicks I don't even remember. I was oblivious to the only one who meant anything to me.

If I'd known she was there, I would have dropped everything, chased after her, done all I could to make it right.

But I was such a fucked-up mess that year.

Going to Kelsey U was the biggest mistake I ever made.

That, and breaking up with Sienna.

But maybe if I'd come straight to Nolan… if I hadn't gotten roped in by my reckless roommate and the rest of the team…

Don't blame them. You were the one who gave in to the pressure.

I shake my head, my mind jumping back to that first night I boarded a one-way ticket to my own demise…

I was missing Sienna like crazy, doing everything in my power not to text her every minute of every damn day. But we'd agreed on a clean break. I was here to play football and study hard, to prove myself—and show Coach Watkins from Brighton College that not wanting me was the biggest mistake he'd ever made.

It was my time to shine and be the best. I was only a freshman, but I'd get time on the field. I was determined to get noticed, to fit in with the team and do everything in my power to make my reasons for breaking up with Sienna worth it.

Dad—my entire family, really—had convinced me that I was too young to be tied down in a serious relationship. It was holding me back. We were holding each other back. And I was out to prove that they were right, even though everything inside me was pining for her.

I'd already made the decision that if I was missing her this badly when I went home for my Christmas break, I was going to get in touch with her, see how she was doing. Maybe talk about trying the long-distance thing. Would she be into it?

I may have missed my chance.

Shit, I probably had.

She was the hottest catch in the school. Some other guy had probably swooped in and stolen her from me.

"Fuck." I banged the desk, growling as I pulled my textbook toward me and tried to wrap my head around stuff I didn't even care about.

"Just leave it." Miguel slapped me on the shoulder. "Come on, man. Let's go. Party's started." My roommate opened our door, and I glanced over my shoulder at him.

"I have to get through this shit. The test is next week."

"Fuck that." Miguel laughed. "We're college athletes. We don't have to pass tests to be here."

"But Coach Jones told us—"

"Screw Coach Jones. That guy has his head up his ass."

I frowned. "I don't want to be riding the bench all season. I came here so I could get some field time."

"And you will... as long as you don't isolate yourself from the team."

I swiveled in my seat to face him. "What do you mean?"

Rolling his eyes like I was a clueless loser, my sophomore roommate walked back over to me and rested his hand on my desk. "Coach Jones doesn't run our team. He's not even the head coach."

"He's the offensive coach," I softly argued. "He's pretty damn important."

"Coach Filmore is the only one who really counts. And he likes to give the captains as much responsibility as possible. He's always consulting with the players and making them feel like we're valued members of his team, you know?"

My eyebrows wrinkled, uncertainty swirling through

me. I'd never played on a team like that before. Coaches ruled. That was just the way it went.

"You want field time, you need to get in good with Williams and Hodgkins. They'll be the ones telling Coach to give you a shot. If they don't like you, you'll be riding that bench, dude. I promise you. Just ask any of the guys who are warming that seat every damn week. It took me a while to figure it out last year, but I'm telling you, after one party with Williams, I was in. You have to prove yourself to *those* guys if you want to get on that field."

My stomach sank, twisting uncomfortably as Miguel started flipping my books closed. "So, you get your ass out of that chair and come party with me, man."

I wasn't sure what to do, but the thought of coming all this way only to ride the bench like I would have at Brighton College forced me out of my chair. I was there to impress and get my ass on that field. And if that meant I had to get in good with the senior players... the ones with the most influence... then I guess I had to do it.

It took twenty minutes to walk to the party, and when we got there, it was in full swing. Music was reverberating so loud that I could feel the floor vibrating beneath me. The off-campus house was packed with luscious eye candy that was impossible not to stare at. A couple girls were dancing topless near the couches, and another was in the kitchen, lying on the table, covered in shot glasses and laughing as guys took turns plucking them off her stomach with their mouths.

I'd never been to anything so wild, and I felt instantly on edge. Miguel shoved a beer in my hand and told me to loosen up before taking off after a brunette with long curls and a back tattoo.

I nestled myself into a corner, sipping my beer and wishing for Sienna, second-guessing my decision to leave her.

Fuck, fuck, fuck!

"Hey, tiger." A sultry voice curled around me, and my head snapped to the right.

"Uh... hi." Heat shot down my spine as my eyes traveled the length of this sexy-ass woman dressed in a string bikini and red heels. What the fuck? Did this place even have a pool?

She draped herself against me and whispered, "Wanna dance?"

"Um... I..."

Before I could finish my reply, she dragged me onto the floor, gyrating against me while I tried and failed to get into it.

Was it seriously worth all this?

Partygoers pressed in on me from every angle as I moved my body in a half-hearted dance and fought the urge to bolt for the door... until a cup of beer was launched across the room and I was soon covered in sticky alcohol. The girl dancing with me threw her head back, laughing hysterically, then started licking my face.

Okay, too much. It was too much.

I eased away from her with a polite smile. "Gotta go."

"What?" She frowned at me while I shimmied through the crowd.

I'd nearly made it to the front entrance when a large body stopped in front of me. I jerked back, looking up at Hodgkins and trying for a cool, calm grin. "Hey, man."

"Where you going?" He lightly pushed me back toward the dance floor.

"It's, uh... getting late." I swallowed. "I've got to get some studying done."

"Bullshit." He laughed, nudging me back another step, his eyes glittering with something dangerous that I didn't fully understand. "You're part of this team now, and if you want to stay that way, you play by our rules. It's party time, lil' freshman. So you party."

He flicked his fingers, and a girl holding a tray of shots sashayed over to us. Hodgkins grabbed two of them, handing me one and holding the other up in the air.

"To hot women!" he yelled, throwing back the drink, then looking at me expectantly.

I gazed at the glass in my hand. I'd never had hard liquor like this before.

I'd drunk beer at high school parties, but that was as far as we took it.

Gripping the tiny glass in my hand, I looked around me, feeling every expectant gaze like a laser beam. Glancing up at Hodgkins once more, I caught that hardening in his expression and held up the glass with a weak smile.

"To hot women." Throwing back the liquor, I struggled to hide the fact that it was burning my insides raw.

I let out an awkward cough and Hodgkins started laughing, then pounded me on the back. "That's our boy!" He raised his hands, and the entire party cheered for me as Hodgkins ordered another shot down my throat.

I took it, because what the fuck else was I going to do?

I was all too aware that every eye was on me. The pressure was intense, and as I downed my third shot, I had to remind myself that I wanted to spread my wings. I needed to fit in and become part of this team. I had to prove I belonged there, so I partied it up, acting crazy and winning my way into Hodgkins and Williams's good books.

I don't remember all of that night, but I'm pretty sure I tricked myself into believing I was having a fucking fantastic time.

Until I woke up the next morning, lying naked in a room full of passed-out bodies. I felt like total shit, my head pounding, my brain a fuzzy mess. A girl I didn't even know was draped across me, and my insides turned to ash on the spot.

What the fuck?

Shit, was she the one who'd been licking my face on the dance floor?

Nudging her away from me, I scrambled to find my clothes, humiliation and deep regret burning inside me when I noticed a used condom on the floor. Was that mine?

Fuck, no. I wouldn't do that. I wouldn't have—

Bile surged up my throat as I wrestled to do up my pants, reeling that there was a chance I'd just had sex with a girl I didn't even recognize.

"Please don't let that be true," I muttered to myself over and over again as I tried and failed to remember everything that had gone down the night before.

Sienna's beautiful face whistled through my mind and that bile burned like acid. Had I seriously slept with someone else?

"No." I squeezed my mouth until it hurt. What the fuck was in those drinks I threw back? Why were the details so fuzzy? I remembered the cheering and then we were jumping around a lot and girls were pawing me. I didn't want that and tried to push them away, but they wouldn't leave me alone and then...

"Fuck," I whimpered, sucking in a shaky breath, my mind a complete blank.

I'd never felt like such a shitty human being before. I must have been so out of control. Did that chick seriously take advantage of me when I was obviously wasted? Or had she been wasted too? What the fuck had I let myself get into?

I groaned, stumbling out of the house and getting lost on my way back to my dorm room.

It was the worst hangover of my life, and I didn't know how I was going to perform at practice that afternoon. I fell asleep in one of my classes and was nudged awake as everyone was leaving. I felt like throwing up most of the day, but just before practice, Williams took me aside and gave me a combo of No Doze and Red Bull. Fired up on the energy buzz, I worked my ass off at practice and didn't crash until later than night, when I staggered to my room in a haze. I wanted to close my eyes and never wake up again. But I did... and I was swamped with so much regret that I would have done anything to kill that feeling. So the next time Miguel offered me a drink, I took it. I made him promise not to let me hook up with any random girls —I was here for football. I was doing this to get field time. He laughed in my face, but then told me he'd watch my back, so I downed the drink with him, and then another. He kept passing them to me and the more I drank, the more it helped. It didn't hurt so bad when I was buzzed, so I went along with it. And I attended the parties and smoked the weed and threw back the liquor like they all wanted me to. It got me field time and I played my best despite my shitty lifestyle and before I knew it, I was sucked into a vortex of bad decisions and regret so deep I wasn't sure I'd ever find my way out of the darkness.

Running into the Nolan U stadium, I shed my jacket, slipping into the back of the briefing room as the coaches start up their run-through of our upcoming away game. They talk strategies and tactics most of the time, and guys flip through their playbooks. I scan the backs of heads as I lean against the back wall and wish like anything that I'd started my college career here.

Thank fuck Coach Jones took me with him when he left.

I would have been sunk without him, and I swore I'd never go that low again.

When I came back from Everett that Christmas, I dove headfirst into the party lifestyle. Angry and confused over Sienna's disappearance, I threw myself into becoming a core member of the team... until I found out just how sick their games were getting, and I couldn't play by their rules anymore.

Shit.

Crossing my arms, I try to shove down my past, wishing like hell it'd never happened. Wishing I could bypass that year of my life and pretend that Nolan U is the only college I've ever attended and my Football Frat brothers had my back from the start.

I know they have my back now. Grady was my salvation when I first started here, and I love him like a brother.

Glancing over his shoulder, he can obviously sense my gaze on his back, and he gives me a questioning frown.

Shaking my head, I glance at Wily, who is also silently checking on me.

A big smile spreads across his face, and the second the meeting breaks up, he saunters over with a high five and asks me, "How's papa bear doing? Did you get your little cowgirl down for a nap?"

"What the fuck?" Carson jerks to a stop beside him. "What the hell did you just ask him?"

"Subtle. Thanks, man." I lightly punch the blond giant in the arm and then have to explain his weird-ass question to the only Football Frat guy who didn't know.

We walk to the locker room to get taped up for practice while Carson gapes at me, all bug-eyed, and then hounds me with a constant stream of questions.

By the time I'm running out onto the field, he knows as much as I do... except for the part about Sienna seeing me lost in a threesome and all the shit that followed.

None of the guys can know about that.

They'll never look at me the same, and I'm their captain, dammit. I need them to trust and respect me... and how can they ever do that if they know what an asshole I was?

Shaking it off, I throw myself into practice, giving football everything as I prep for our upcoming away game and try to dodge my undying shame... and the look on Sienna's face this afternoon.

CHAPTER 23
SIENNA

It's Sunday morning. The sun is shining, and I feel like total shit.

Zoey had such a restless night. It didn't help that I was in a foul mood. I think she was vibing off my angst, which stopped her from relaxing into her evening routine, and then she was up and down like a yo-yo half the night.

I hope she's not getting sick.

I checked her temperature this morning just in case, but she seems happy and bright despite her lack of sleep, so it's just me who feels like I've been hit by a bus.

When I shuffled out to the kitchen this morning, Russell took one look at me and sent me back to bed. I took him up on the offer. He's around all day, and I may as well take advantage.

But I can't sleep.

I've tried for nearly an hour, tossing and turning in my bed. My brain won't switch off.

I keep reliving my last conversation with Zander and

that look on his face when he was apologizing. His regret over what happened is obviously so deep. I can't believe he got wasted and ended up with those two girls, but it was almost like he couldn't believe he'd let himself sink so low either.

His first semester at college must have been a total train wreck and I don't understand how he got caught up in all of that shit. He must have been really struggling. The guy I knew wouldn't have gone down that road, but something must have made him snap. He couldn't remember being with those girls at all, so what I saw wasn't him deliberately getting into a threesome because he was some kind of man-whore. He was wasted and not fully conscious of what he was doing.

Are you seriously making excuses for him?

Maybe. Because even though that scenario still sucks, it doesn't hurt as bad. Maybe I can throw a little of my anger at those two girls for taking advantage of him. He was lying back against those pillows, his pants around his ankles and his brain a sloshy mess. Did he even realize at the time what he was allowing to happen to his body?

I bite my lip, playing with the ends of my hair and imagining the man who found Zoey and bought me Nerds allowing that to happen to himself again, and I can't. He's grown up. He's changed.

God, please that be true.

His phone number has been burning a hole in my pocket since Wednesday, but I still haven't put it into my phone. I can't call or text him... can I?

No! You don't need him. He's just...

Just what?

Zoey's father.

The guy who broke my heart.

The one who came back for me.

Shit. Sitting up, I scrape my fingers through my hair and gaze out the window.

"He came back for me," I whisper, struggling to believe it.

The guy I spotted tongue-deep in a three-way didn't seem the kind who would miss me.

But the man who held my daughter on Wednesday and calmed her down? Yeah, he was the one I fell for. And maybe that's who he is now. He must had found a way out of that mess somehow.

Maybe transferring to Nolan U was a fresh start for him or something.

I don't know.

But... can I forgive him?

Can I let him back into my life?

"He came back for me." I flop down, my lips twitching as I stare up at the ceiling and play with the ends of my hair.

Things would have been so different if I'd known that.

I gave him no chance to redeem himself. And a part of me feels bad for that.

Which is probably why I've been obsessing over him. Probably why I secretly watched his away game yesterday. They lost, which put me in a foul mood—don't ask me why.

It's probably why I can't fall asleep right now.

Because he's consuming me.

Throwing back the duvet with a huff, I jump out of

bed and tie my hair up in a messy knot before heading out to the kitchen.

I want to check on Zoey. Her cute little smile will distract me and make me feel better. I'm already running through the day ahead. It's so nice out there, we'll definitely have to get to the park. And maybe I'll take a ball this time. She might like kicking it around. How adorable would that be?

Zipping up my hoodie, I'm about to round the corner into the kitchen when I hear Zoey's voice and go still, leaning my head against the wall and soaking in her sweet sound with a smile.

"Chochos."

"You want more Cheerios?" Russell asks. I love the tone he uses with her. It's always so gentle and sweet.

"Chochos," Zoey confirms her request.

"Can I get some manners?"

"Peeeeeese, Unca Russy."

He laughs, and I can hear the box shaking. "You know, you can just call me Dada if it's easier to say. I don't mind."

I ping away from the wall, frowning when Zoey says, "Dada."

He might not mind, but I sure as hell do!

Whipping around the corner, I paste on a smile and brush my hands through Zoey's curls.

"Mommy!" She grins up at me, a Cheerio perched between her little fingers.

"Hey, cowgirl." I wink at her, and she giggles.

Russell gives me a quizzical frown and I ignore it, wanting to clarify something first.

"It's Uncle Rusty, by the way. Or Uncle Russell. It's not Dada."

He shrugs, a red hue splashing over his cheeks as he lets out a soft laugh. "Uncle Russell is a mouthful."

"Then she can just call you Rusty or Russell."

"Dada's easier to say," he mutters into his coffee cup.

"But you're not her dad."

His gaze snaps to mine, his smile disappearing as he walks toward me and leans in so close, I can feel his hot coffee breath against my cheek. "I'm the closest thing she's got."

I lean away with a forced smile. "I don't want to confuse her."

He growls in his throat and frowns down at me. "She better not be calling that asshole Daddy."

"Russell." I quickly cover Zoey's ears. "Language."

"If I'm not her dad, then he sure as shit isn't." He spits out the words before turning back to the toaster.

My hands shake at his vehemence, my stomach vibrating. I am so not up for this shit today. What the hell?

I know he's annoyed with Zander over the way he treated me, but still. His reaction seems a little extra.

Smiling down at Zoey, who seems to be picking up the awkward vibe and starting to fuss, I get busy wiping her hands and face. She resists me at every turn and is soon squawking. I pull her out of her highchair and pop her on the ground.

She toddles away from me, over to her set of blocks and the zoo animals she was playing with earlier.

Thumping down onto her padded butt, she gets lost

in a world of pretend while I prepare myself some toast and try to avoid Russell's gaze. He keeps checking on me, but I don't really feel like talking to him right now.

After a few awkward moments, he lets out a soft sigh and comes up behind me, wrapping his arms around my waist and resting his chin on my shoulder.

His whiskers scratch my neck, and I tense.

He doesn't seem to notice, his voice dropping to a soft lilt. "I'm sorry. I don't want to fight or anything. I'm just trying to protect you from getting hurt. I really care about you and Zoey."

"I know." I rest my hands on the edge of the counter, leaning forward and trying to subtly pull out of his octopus grasp.

"I can't see you go through that heartache again. And I won't see Zoey dragged into it. She's too important. Too precious. She deserves a stable, trouble-free home."

"I know." I nod and step sideways, wriggling free of his tentacles. I don't like it when he acts and talks like we're a couple.

He's family, sure. But I'm not in love with him, and he will never be Zoey's father.

Moving to the fridge, I take my time making my morning coffee and wait until Russell has basically finished eating before sitting down.

"I was thinking I'd take Zoey to the playground today. Give you a little alone time," he tells me.

Again, I tense. I'm not sure why. He's done it plenty of times before, and I'm usually grateful for it. But him wanting Zoey to call him Dada has really rattled me, and I don't want her alone with him right now.

Skimming my finger around the lip of my coffee mug,

I try to keep my tone casual. "Yeah, I was thinking of taking her as well. I'm happy to do it."

"I can come with." He leans against the counter, grinning at me.

I take in his hopeful smile and force out a laugh. "Cool. I might actually text one of the moms from the playgroup I went to as well. Her son, Dayton, got along great with Zoey. Maybe they can meet us there."

"Oh, uh... sure." Russell doesn't love that. I can tell by the way he pulls back from me and gets busy cleaning up the kitchen. "Hanging out with a bunch of moms. Sounds awesome."

I laugh at his sarcastic quip. "Don't feel like you have to come. I'm happy to take Zoey out for a playdate, and then we can hang later. Maybe after her nap we could build the train set. She always loves playing trains with you."

"Yeah, maybe that's better." He nods, looking disappointed but not saying so.

Rising from my seat, I take my plate over to him. "Thanks." His sudsy hand brushes against mine, and he gazes down at me with an intensity that's kind of unnerving.

He almost looks like he wants to kiss me or something, so I quickly dart out of the kitchen with excuses of getting ready.

He, of course, helps with Zoey, and the stroller is soon fully loaded on the sidewalk.

"Wave to Uncle Rusty," I tell Zoey, and she glances up at the door, grinning and blowing kisses.

"Goodbye, sweet girl. I love you," he calls after us.

"Laloo!" she shouts back.

I push the stroller a little faster, pulling out my phone and quickly texting Fiona.

She gets back to me within a minute, apologizing that they're already busy with a family function today and can't meet up, but she'd love to another time.

I'm not actually that disappointed, although I kind of am for Zoey. She probably would have loved to play with Dayton.

With a little sigh, the thought that maybe I should call Russell and let him know bounces through my brain, but I'm kind of needing a little space from him right now.

Why?

Because he's getting too close.

Because I can't stop thinking about Zander, and being around Russell makes me feel like that's a huge mistake.

Shit. I don't know what to do.

Zander was so sweet with Zoey on Wednesday. He deserves to see her again, doesn't he?

Plus, the Cougars lost yesterday, so he's probably feeling a little salty, and Zoey might cheer him up.

Are you really doing this?

My stomach hitches as I reach for the piece of paper in my back pocket... and quickly realize I'm not wearing the right pair of pants.

"Shit," I mumble under my breath.

"Pak, Mommy?"

"Yeah, I thought we could go to the park. I was hoping I could arrange for your little friend Dayton to join us, but he's busy."

"Aw." Zoey pouts, holding Tony the Pony against her chest. She's been going for that stuffed animal ever since Wily called her a cowgirl. "Wanna pay."

"I know. But I'll be there to play with you."

"Yeah." She sounds so disappointed it's hard not to be offended.

But I laugh it off, knowing she's only two. "So, who do you want to play with, then?"

I'm expecting her to say Uncle Rusty and am already resigning myself to the fact that I'll have to call him and he'll no doubt meet us at the park with a gleeful grin.

Pulling out my phone with a frown, I'm about to unlock it when Zoey surprises me.

"Wywee."

I stop the stroller and peer down at her. "Wily?"

She nods. "Me wanna pay Wywee."

"You want to play with Wily?"

"Yeah." She sits up, looking all enthusiastic as she holds up her horse. "Yeeha!"

I laugh. "You know we're going to the park, though, right? He's not buying you ice cream today. There's no horsey at the park."

"Wywee!" she shouts, hugging her toy horse. "I wanna pay Wywee!"

"Okay, okay." I rub her arm to calm her down, then crouch beside the stroller. "Thing is, I don't know where Wily and Zander live. I think they call it Football Frat, but I'm not sure."

Zoey nods, leaning toward me like I can totally nail this "Find Wily" mission. Touching my cheek with her little hand, she gives me an emphatic nod. "Mommy fine Wywee."

"Okay." I nod. "I'm gonna try." Standing tall, I grab the handles of the stroller and start walking toward the Nolan U campus.

I stop the first person I see and ask if they know where the frat house that some football guys live in is. She doesn't know, but the next guy mutters that it's on Greek Row.

"Where's that?" I call after him.

"Google it!" he shouts over his shoulder, and I try but come up empty-handed.

There's no official street named Greek Row, and I push the stroller forward in frustration, wondering how long I should pursue this thing. The park comes into view, and I think about abandoning my quest and just taking her to the playground.

But my little girl will be so disappointed if we don't find Wily.

She's happily kicking her legs and singing to her horse. It's kind of adorable, so I press on, and two people later, I find someone who is actually helpful.

"Yeah, I know Football Frat." She grins at me, and for a second, I have that ugly flash of Kelsey U and that smiling girl who let me into Zander's dorm. "It's about two doors down from my place."

"And where's that?"

She laughs. "Head down this street and take your first left, opposite the park, then turn right when you hit the Stop sign and it'll be the..." Closing her eyes, she does a quick count in her head. "Sixth house along? Maybe the seventh. It's the one with the Harley Davidson parked out front, and if that's not there, just look for guy trucks. The place is always surrounded by them."

"Okay." I nod, trepidation taking me out as I turn and start pushing Zoey toward Football Frat.

Shit, what am I doing?

I second-guess myself the entire way there and nearly bail when I get to that Stop sign, but then I look down the street and see all those manly trucks the woman was talking about.

With my breath on hold, I push Zoey forward, looking for a Harley Davidson. I don't see it, but I don't have to because the blond giant appears around the side of the house. The second he spots us, his face lights up with a big grin.

"Cowgirl!" He raises his arms in greeting.

"Wywee!" Zoey starts wrestling against her restraints.

I quickly move forward to help her with the buckle.

As soon as she's free, she launches herself out of the stroller, landing in a pile on the front lawn before jumping to her feet and running toward the gentle giant.

"Wywee!" She giggles when he picks her up, throwing her in the air and making her squeal.

I stand there, gripping the stroller and watching with a teary smile.

How cute are they?

"Sienna?" Zander's voice snags my attention, and I glance toward the front door, seeing him standing there in sweats and a hoodie—no shirt underneath. His hair's wet and his feet are bare, and holy sex on a stick. He is so fine.

"Are you okay?" His concern melts me, and I quickly nod and smile up at him.

"Just thought we'd swing by for a visit."

My mouth pools with desire, a hot burn lancing me as I watch him walk down the front steps, a huge smile spreading across his face.

Oh man, he is so happy to see me.

My heart flails dangerously, begging me to run into his arms. Would he pick me up the way he used to? Could I wrap my legs around him? Would his hands grab my ass the way I loved so much? Would he hold me close and kiss me? Make me feel like the only other human on the planet?

Stop it, Sienna.

I force my eyes to the ground, but then have to look back up again when I hear Zander say, "Is that Zoey?"

Zoey turns with a gasp, her face lighting with excitement when she sees him. "Foobawl!" Wriggling out of Wily's hold, she tries to get to Zander.

Wily laughs and launches her through the air. Zander's eyes bulge, and he quickly catches her, then growls at his roommate. "She's not a football, man. Be careful with her."

A smile twitches my lips as Wily gives his captain a bashful apology, then turns to check that I'm not mad.

I smile at him but can't take my eyes off Zander and Zoey for long. She's perched in his arms, playing with the zipper of his hoodie while she chats away. She's talking so fast it's impossible to understand her. She's not even saying proper words, just mimicking what Mom and I do when we see each other and are catching up in fast-forward. The first part of our phone calls are usually spurted out in a rush. I recognize Zoey's intonation and am fighting my laughter as Zander watches her, nodding like he totally gets what she's saying.

"You know?" Zoey tips her head, her words exactly the same as mine.

"Yeah." Zander nods. "Absolutely."

She grins and nods, obviously glad they've cleared that up.

Zander shoots me a look over the top of her head, and I can't contain my laughter anymore.

With a soft snort, I walk around the stroller and stand beside them just as a good-looking Black guy comes strolling out of the house.

He's lean and so obviously strong. His shirtless body hides nothing, and I can see his ripped muscles. Beside him is a willowy woman with long strawberry blonde hair and perfectly applied makeup. She's wearing a miniskirt and tank top that shows off her slim waist and the diamond stud in her belly button. Wow. She is stunning. He links his hand with hers, pulling her down the stairs and stopping beside me.

He grins at Zoey and asks, "So, who do we have here?"

"Grady, Teah." Zander lifts Zoey a little higher and grins. "This is Zoey."

"Hey, cutie." Teah smiles at my daughter, holding up her hand for a high five.

Zoey slaps it with a giggle and points at the woman. "You pity."

"I... what?" The woman looks to me for help.

"Zoey said you're pretty."

"Aw," she croons and tells Zoey the same thing, making my daughter smile, then dip her head, all coy and fake shyness.

I shake my head at her dramatic antics and stretch out my hand. "I'm Sienna."

"Hi." Teah's long fingers wrap around mine, and she gives my hand a swift shake before letting Grady introduce himself properly.

"I've heard a lot about you." He gives me a knowing smile, and a surge of butterflies cascades through me as I glance at Zander.

His gaze is kind of soft and mushy and...

Yeah, I really am in trouble.

I don't think I'm going to be able to stop myself from falling headfirst for this guy all over again.

CHAPTER 24
ZANDER

It takes Zoey all of three seconds to convince me to play with her at the park.

Sienna's bright smile is working some kind of magic on me, and I'm pretty sure I would do just about anything for either of them right now.

Grady and Teah join us, and Zoey refuses to go anywhere without Wily, so he has to tag along too. Thankfully, he doesn't seem to mind.

With a football tucked against his side, he walks in front of the stroller, turning to pull faces at Zoey, which causes fits of giggles.

I can't help laughing or smiling every time that sound pops out of her mouth. It's adorable.

Wily twirls the ball in his hands, which is a habit I'm sure he's had since he was old enough to hold a football. As soon as we're within sight of the park, Grady starts sprinting and calling for a pass. Wily hurls it, but Grady's already outrun him, and I can't help a soft scoff.

"Shut up." Wily laughs. "I'm no quarterback."

Grady throws the ball back and I easily catch it, showing off just a little as I send a perfect spiral across the grass. Grady catches it like the pro he is and gets a whistle from his girlfriend.

"Looking good, baby."

He blows her a kiss, and Wily chases after him.

I linger by the stroller while Sienna unbuckles Zoey and sets her loose. She tries to chase after the big boys, but her little legs aren't fast enough and she soon runs out of steam.

"She's so cute." Teah nudges Sienna with her elbow, and the girls quickly get lost in a conversation.

I run after Zoey, turning back to glance at them and noticing Sienna's smile grow.

Damn, she is so fucking beautiful.

For a second, it takes me back to watching her in high school. Sometimes I'd get to the cafeteria and she was already sitting at our table, laughing and talking with Olivia and Emily. I'd have to stop and watch her for a second... just drink her in.

But then she'd inevitably sense my gaze and—

Sienna's eyes dart to mine, her cheeks turning a pretty pink as she quickly breaks eye contact and tucks her hair behind her ear.

Teah's still talking, and Sienna nods, then says something that makes them both laugh.

This feeling in my chest is overwhelming and I stop running, turning to face her properly just so I can really drink her in.

"Foobawl!" Zoey yells behind me just before two little arms wrap around my leg.

I lift my foot, and she squeals in delight as I start

walking to the playground with her wrapped around my leg.

"Again! Again!" She keeps going until we've made it to the sandpit.

As soon as we're there, she lets me go and takes off for the jungle gym.

I race after her, surprised by her sudden burst of speed. For such little legs, she's pretty damn quick.

Out of the corner of my eye, I can see Sienna moving toward us, and I raise my hand. "I got this!"

She nods and stays put, turning back to keep talking with Teah.

I have no idea what they're discussing, but Sienna's animated expression tells me she's into it. She and Teah are the same age, I think, and it makes me wonder if Sienna has had contact with anyone her age since she got pregnant.

From what I can gather, she's been living with Russell, and before that, she was traveling with her parents and... she cut off everyone from her life in Everett.

Wow.

Checking on Zoey, I spare one last glance in Sienna's direction, smiling as the girls take a seat on the park bench and continue talking like they've been friends for life.

"Wash me," Zoey demands, and I spin back to watch her climb the little ladder and whistle down the slide.

I catch her at the bottom and hoist her back up. Her padded little butt looks so cute waddling up the ladder, and my insides are pure mush by the time she climbs and slides another dozen times.

After that, she's running to the swings, and ten

minutes later, she wants to check out the rope pyramid thing, which she's too short for. But damn if she doesn't give it her best shot.

That determined look on her face reminds me so much of Monica, it knocks the breath out of me for a second.

I'd love to see old photos again. I want to compare what I looked like at that age too.

But all those images are at my parents' two houses, and... I still haven't told them about Zoey yet.

I want to get things cleared up with Sienna first.

And although today is a pretty awesome step in the right direction, we're still on uneven ground. I can sense it.

But having her show up today...

I couldn't believe it when I heard Wily shout, "Cowgirl!" and then my daughter replied.

They'd come to find me. I could have floated out that door.

After a really hard game yesterday afternoon, I was feeling kind of dark this morning, but one look at Sienna's face, one sound of Zoey's giggle, and I was filled to the brim.

I can't stop smiling as I watch Zoey climb and fail.

"Can I help you?" I walk over to steady her, but she shakes her head.

"No help. Zoey do."

"Okay." I raise my hands but hover close by.

She's getting it. Sort of. If her arms and legs were longer, she'd be scrambling up that thing in a heartbeat.

Her little fingers curl around the ropes and she stretches as far as she can go, making it one step higher.

Looking over her shoulder, she gives me a proud grin.

"Good job, kiddo." I give her a thumbs-up and keep cheering her on until she gives up and asks for a rescue. Plucking her off the pyramid, I set her back on her feet, and the second she's free, she charges for the sandpit.

But she doesn't quite make it, because three teenage boys who are obviously fucking blind come barreling through the playground on their way to the basketball court and knock Zoey right off her feet.

She lets out a little wail as she goes flying, and I race toward her.

"Hey!" I bark at the boy whose knee caused my little girl to lose her balance. "Watch it."

He turns to me with a sneer as I crouch down and lift Zoey into my arms. "Whatever, man."

Catching his jacket before he can walk away, I spin him around and eyeball him. "This is a playground for little kids. You don't come charging through here and knocking them off their feet!"

Zoey whimpers, nestling her forehead into the curve of my neck.

The boy scoffs and tries to shake me off him. "Let go, man."

"I will when you apologize to my daughter."

His eyes round, his lips parting as he looks up at whatever's towering behind me.

"We got a problem here?" Wily's got his gruff voice on, and although I know it's all fake, his mean face can be pretty intimidating.

The kid swallows and then jolts when Grady flanks my left side and glares at him too. "What's up?"

"Uh..." The kid spurts. "S-sorry. I didn't see her."

"Now apologize to her." I rest my cheek on top of Zoey's head, and the boy gives me a pained frown before looking at my daughter.

"I'm sorry. Are you okay?"

She sniffs and nods. "Zoey 'kay."

The boy's lips twitch and I let him go, calling out to him and his friends as they run away. "You hurt my daughter again, I will end you!"

"Yeah, we get it!" the boys yell back, running around the fence and passing the basketball between them.

I huff and shake my head, glaring after them before looking down at Zoey.

"You okay?" My voice takes on a soft lilt, and she sits up, her big blue eyes gazing at me—so innocent and pure. "They didn't hurt you, did they?"

She shakes her head, then wipes her face with her dirty little fingers and asks, "Ice ceem?"

"Oh no, you don't, you little manipulator." Sienna appears around Wily. "I know what you're trying to pull, and you are fine."

Zoey starts to pout, and Sienna laughs.

"You've got these three big Cougars protecting you. You don't need ice cream right now."

Zoey pulls a face, which Sienna mimics. It doesn't take the little girl long to figure out that ice cream is off the menu and she gives up with a sigh, wriggling out of my arms and squealing when Wily pretends to chase her to the sandpit.

I glance down at Sienna, resting my hand on her lower back without even thinking about it.

"All good?" I softly ask.

She gazes up at me with a barely there smile and whispers, "Thank you for protecting our girl."

"Always and forever," I assure her before letting her go and walking after Zoey.

Shit, I could have pulled her close right then.

What I wouldn't give for the chance to kiss those luscious lips of hers.

But what right do I have to do that?

CHAPTER 25
SIENNA

It's been nearly a week since I saw Zander. We ended up staying at the playground way longer than I intended, and by the time I got home, Russell was in a snippy mood. I couldn't figure out why, and I wasn't about to add fuel to the fire by telling him I was at the park with the Football Frat guys.

I couldn't admit to the way they melted my heart when Zoey got bowled over by those kids. The way Zander told them off, and his teammates formed an intimidating line in front of that poor boy. He only looked to be around fourteen or so, and as pissed off as I was with him for knocking my daughter down, he looked pretty damn scared by the time Zander finally let him go.

Zoey was safe.

I smile yet again, reliving the scene and then thinking about the daily text messages I've been getting from Zander.

He checks in on Zoey each morning, and I've been sending him pics. He posts back funny photos of him and his teammates. They seem to love putting on a show for my little girl, and I adore them for it.

She's falling hard and fast for these football players, and I'm helpless to stop it.

I mean, I don't need to, right?

Except for the fact that three of them will be graduating at the end of this year, and who knows where they'll end up.

Is Zander hoping to go pro?

What will that mean for Zoey and me?

Shit... am I setting her up for disaster?

She's going to be completely in love with her daddy, and then he's going to take off, not be around while he travels the country playing football and I'm left at home with her. We'll miss him like crazy, and—

Stop it. You're spiraling. Just don't think about it.

It's not like Zander and I are getting back together. He's made it clear that he wants to be a part of Zoey's life, and he's proving himself worthy of being a part of it.

But that has nothing to do with romance.

He wants to be a good father.

That's it.

I swallow, flicking on the TV as a way to distract myself. Zoey fell asleep about an hour ago. Russell's at an away game, and it's just me tonight.

It's the first time Russell's had an away game this season, and he was nervous traveling with his team and leaving me all alone.

I assured him I'm totally fine. If anything, I was looking forward to an evening to myself.

But now that I've got it, I kind of hate being at home all alone with Zoey. It's a lot of responsibility. I can handle it, but this is actually the first time I've spent an entire night with just me and her. All I can hope and pray is that nothing goes wrong.

My mind jumps to images of house fires and masked intruders.

I snap my eyes closed for a second and softly reprimand myself. "Stop it. You're fine. Everything is fine."

And at least Zander is only a phone call away now.

Although he has a big game tomorrow and I have no idea what he's up to tonight, I've got a gut feeling that if I called him, he'd drop everything to be here for Zoey and me.

Picking up my phone, I read through our last couple text chains, smiling to myself as I gaze at the last shot he sent Zoey. It's a smiling thumbs-up. He was praising her for attempting a forward roll. She ended up just rolling on her side, but she thought she was the next Simone Biles. It was pretty cute.

Brushing my thumb over his handsome face, I nearly drop the phone when I get a text message from Russell's sister, Celeste.

Celly: Just checking in. Russell's worried about you.

I roll my eyes and quickly reply.

Me: I'm fine! Seriously. He doesn't have to worry.

Celly: I told him that, but he's a paranoid freak when he wants to be. I'll assure him that you're snuggled up on the couch watching romance movies.

I snicker.

Me: How'd you know?

Celly: Of course I know what you're doing. Have fun!

I send her a few kiss emojis, then glance at the TV. I'm

actually watching an old football game. Or at least the highlights of it.

Denver Broncos versus Seattle Seahawks.

I'm watching with half an eye, playing a game of Puzzle Blocks on my phone and getting increasingly bored. Restless, I rise from the couch and head to the kitchen, opening the pantry and eyeing the candy box on the top shelf.

"You don't need it," I remind myself as I reach for the tin and open the lid, picking out the packet of Nerds Zander bought me and downing a mouthful. I crunch through them, loving the fake watermelon taste, before scoring myself one more mouthful, then flinching when there's a knock at the door.

I go still, my heart rate spiking as I return the candy box to the top shelf of the pantry and shuffle to the entranceway. I'm wearing a Tigger onesie right now. Zoey and I bought matching ones, and she wanted to wear them tonight. Do I quickly whip it off before answering the door? But I'm only wearing skimpy pajamas underneath.

Screw it. Just embarrass yourself and answer the door looking like a Disney character. Who cares what people think as long as you're not standing there half naked.

Alone and half naked.

Twitchy, I inch toward the front door, wondering if I should grab a fry pan first.

It worked for Rapunzel, right?

"Uh... one second."

"Sen, it's me."

Zander's voice stops me mid-step, and I pivot back toward the door and quickly unlock the bolt.

Pulling the door open, I stare at him under the yellow porch light, loving the way the shadows cascade across his face, accentuating his chiseled features. He's so good-looking it hurts. The smile on his face is adorable as he drinks me in.

"Cute." He points at me, and I glance down, cringing at how ridiculous I must look.

"Zoey's got one, too, and…" I shrug.

"I like it."

I can't help a soft laugh and turn so he can check out the tail. Wiggling my butt, I give it a swish, and he snickers but doesn't break into a proper laugh.

Actually, he looks kind of tortured and unsettled standing outside the front door, scuffing his Converse on the concrete.

"Hey, are you okay?" I whisper.

"Yeah. I just…" He winces and looks over his shoulder. "Please don't think I'm a big stalker or anything, but I saw that the hockey team's at an away game, and I figured…" He gives me a helpless shrug. "I just wanted to check that you and Zoey were okay… by yourselves."

My lips curl into a teasing smile. "You don't think I can handle it?"

"I absolutely think you can handle it." He gives me a reassuring nod, then licks his lips before softly confessing, "And maybe I don't just want to check on you."

"What do you mean?"

"Maybe I want to see if you'd like to hang out… without Russell sending me hate vibes and my teammates…" His shoulder hitches. "Being my teammates." A pleading look flashes across his face before he pulls his features into line.

My insides dance, a ticklish thrill racing down the back of my legs. It's pure temptation and zero logical thought.

Which is why I pull the door open wide enough for him to enter. It's why I take a quick sniff of his delicious cologne-plus-man smell, and it's why I shut the door behind me and have to clamp my lips against the giddy giggle that wants to pop out of me.

Zander's here.

It's just me and him.

Alone.

Together.

Goose bumps ripple over my arms, and I'm so glad he can't see them. He can't know how excited I am, because I seriously shouldn't be feeling this excited!

This should be awkward as shit, but somehow it's not. Somehow, watching him slip his shoes off and pad into the living room is the most natural thing in the world.

I trail after him, admiring his fine ass as he sheds his jacket and flicks it over the end of the couch.

"Zoey's asleep." I walk around him, desperate to brush up against him but suddenly nervous that maybe he's not here for that.

He did just say "hang out," right?

Like friends do.

Friends, Sienna!

Zander nods, looking around the living room. He doesn't seem disappointed by the fact that he can't see his daughter right now, and my belly does a little shimmy.

He came to see me. To hang out with me!

"This was a good game." He points to the TV and

takes a seat in my usual spot. I love that his butt is now sitting where mine always goes.

Are you kidding me right now? What is wrong with you?

I clear my throat, trying to lodge the awkward out of it and act like a normal person. You know, in my Tigger outfit. "Yeah, I was just watching highlights and—"

"Eating Nerds." He grins up at me.

"What?" I glance down at my onesie and don't spot any evidence.

"In your hair."

"Oh." My blush must be fire-engine red as I scramble to pull the three little Nerds out of my hair. He turns back to the TV with a soft snicker, and I quickly pop them into my mouth while he's not looking. Sucking them down, I take a seat on the other end of the couch, curling my toes between the cushions while he stretches his arm across the back.

His fingers are close enough to touch my shoulder, and my heart is going wild.

Sienna, seriously. Calm the hell down!

"Can't believe you still like them." Zander's finger twitches, lightly skimming the hair on my shoulder.

"I can't believe you remembered." I nudge his thigh with my big toe.

He glances my way and murmurs, "I remember everything about you."

His gaze is so open, I can't breathe for a second. "Like what?"

His lips twitch and grow into a smile. "Like the fact that you adore Taylor Swift but always get her lyrics wrong when you're singing."

My nose scrunches up. I wish I could argue with him, but that's so freaking accurate.

"And the fact that you hate hot dogs, though very courageously ate one when I took you to that park by the lake."

"Oh my gosh." I cover my face and laugh into my palms. "You knew?"

"You were trying so hard to hide it, but you kept looking like you were about to gag. That's why I told you I was hungry and asked if I could finish your hot dog for you."

I laugh and peek at him between my fingers.

"I never understood why you didn't just say you didn't like them."

"Because you'd already paid for it, and I felt bad."

"Miss Honesty." He shakes his head with a sexy little smirk. "That was the only time I can think of when you didn't tell me the truth."

I shrug, my blush still hot and no doubt obvious.

"I guess I should have asked if you wanted a hot dog before just buying you one." He gives me a little side-eye. "But what true-blooded American doesn't like hot dogs?"

"Oh stop." I lightly whack his arm. "No one even knows what hot dogs are made of. For a guy with a body as perfect as yours, I'm surprised you're willing to put that stuff in your mouth."

He tips his head back with a soft laugh, and I study the line of his throat, wishing I could trail my tongue over his Adam's apple and just keep heading south. I loved exploring his body with my lips and tongue.

Okay, stop it. Be sensible!

Squeezing my legs together, I force my eyes back to the TV. "Are you still eating a super-strict diet?"

"Yeah." He nods. "Gotta be in top shape."

"You're going for the NFL, aren't you?"

He nods. "I'm gonna try."

"Wow." I look back and smile at him, trying to ignore the burning sensation in my eyes. "You're making your dreams come true. Just the way you wanted."

"Not exactly the way I wanted," he murmurs, and I can feel the shift.

He's about to get all serious on me, and as sensible as that would be—you know, to talk about all those things we need to talk about—I just can't do it.

I don't want serious tonight. I want to go back to playful memories and light, fluffy times that don't hurt.

"Wanna play a game?" I quickly ask before he can say anything else.

He gives me an intrigued look, his lips fighting a grin.

"So, I'm gonna say a word, and you have to come up with a song lyric or movie line related to it. For example, if I say sunshine, you might say…"

"I've got sunshiiiine." He sings the first line of "My Girl" by The Temptations, and I bob in my seat, nodding with a happy grin.

"Okay, your turn."

"All right." He tips his head back into the sofa cushions again, and my eyes tracks his perfect lines, scanning down to his collarbone and beyond.

Avert your gaze! Control yourself, woman!

I quickly look at the TV once more and refuse to glance his way, even when he says his word.

"Blue."

I immediately spit out the line Dad always used to sing to me. "Blue eyes. Baby's got blue eyes."

"Yes." He claps. "I was thinking of that old song with all the 'blue da ba dee' bits. You know the one?"

I laugh and sing the chorus of Eiffel 65's song, totally screwing up the lyrics. It came out before we were born, but we both still know it.

"Monica used to play that all the time when we were kids. She loves that song."

Grinning, I resist the urge to ask how his sister is, worried that it might lead to the serious conversations I'm trying to avoid, and instead pick another word.

"Shake."

"Shake it off," he sings, and I laugh, pointing at him.

"You're such a Swiftie."

He goes red while trying to deny it. "I am not. I just knew that *you* would know that song, even though you'd get all the lyrics wrong."

I gasp at his teasing and go to poke him, but he grabs my finger. So I use my big toe, sticking it into his firm abs. Holy shit, he's all muscle.

He snatches my ankle, holding me with ease while that thrill I've been trying to deny races right through me again. Ignoring any sensible warnings, I lunge forward with my free hand and a riotous giggle... and we quickly start a playful tussle that is so familiar, I'm taken back to my junior year of high school.

I'm not twenty-one anymore, I'm a loved-up seventeen-year-old who is laughing as my boyfriend tries to tickle me and I wriggle against him.

Squirming on the couch, I yank at his wrist, yelping when he pulls my leg and tries to tickle my other side.

We flop onto the floor with a raucous thud, both laughing as I land on Zander's chest with a soft "Oof."

The momentum rolls us over, and I'm soon lying beneath him, squished against the coffee table, my giggles fading to oblivion as I gaze up into his beautiful face and feel every inch of him. His washboard abs are resting against my stomach, his hips pinning me to the floor. His arms are on either side of me, encasing me with his strength while his fingers lightly cup the top of my head. It feels so damn good to be under him again, covered by him, owned by his every breath.

His laughter disintegrates, too, his eyes searching mine like he's asking for permission to kiss me.

Oh shit. Yes! Yes, please! Kiss me until I can't breathe!

No, Sienna! He can't kiss you! He'll break your heart again. Don't let him do it!

You'll go falling headfirst, and then he'll leave and you'll be destroyed.

Think of Zoey!

Temptation thrums through me as he lowers his head, his nose gently skimming mine.

I want him so badly it hurts, but then my stupid mouth goes and ruins it.

"Don't," I whisper.

He pauses, his warm breath caressing my skin. "Don't?"

"Don't kiss me," I softly plead, logical thought finally kicking in.

I don't know whether to be relieved or pissed off.

Zander's head jerks back, gazing down at me with a mixture of surprise and hurt. "You don't want me to kiss you?"

"I desperately want you to kiss me." I lick my lips, willing my voice not to shake. "But... you broke my heart, and I barely survived losing you last time. I can't go through that again. If you kiss me, I'm gonna fall so hard and fast, I'll be a broken wreck. I have Zoey to look after now. I can't be nursing a broken heart around her."

"I'm not trying to break you," he whispers.

"Then... don't kiss me unless you mean it." I close my eyes, licking my lips before rasping, "Don't kiss me unless you love me and plan to make Zoey and me a permanent part of your future."

My eyes creep back open in time to see him blinking like I've just slapped him across the face.

And there it is.

That look I needed.

Resting my hands on his shoulders, I try to push him off me. "I get it. I'm asking too much." I push a little harder, grunting to force him up to his knees. Scrambling away from him, I curl my legs to my chest and wrap my arms around them. "I feel like my heart is being held together by sticky tape... really weak sticky tape... and if I'm not careful, it's gonna splinter."

He looks to the floor, all our happy silliness lost as if it never happened. Gripping the back of his neck, he mumbles, "I never meant to hurt you."

Blinking, I try to rein in my tears. Does he have any idea how much he's hurting me now?

All I'm wanting him to do is admit how much I mean to him.

Is it that hard to promise me he'll stay in our lives?

Is it that hard to say, "I love you"?

I thought he came back for me. But maybe he just

said that to appease me, to soften me when I was making him feel so bad over the way he behaved at Kelsey U.

I don't know.

Curling my fingers into my onesie, I start to wonder if I should be grateful for his hesitation. Bringing Zander back into my life will no doubt be a complicated mess... and how do I know he's really changed from the guy he was freshman year?

"Just go, Zander." My voice quakes. "Go, please."

He doesn't move, and I narrow my eyes into a hot glare while pointing toward the front door.

"Leave!" I order him. "I want you to leave. Now."

CHAPTER 26
ZANDER

My body acts like concrete as I get off the floor and stiffly walk toward the door. I slip my shoes on in the awkward silence, avoiding her sad gaze.

How did we go from teasing each other and tussling to me getting kicked out?

I hate leaving her like this.

Shit, should I even be going?

All she's asking for is a little commitment.

A little? She's asking for a lifelong promise.

Can I honestly give that to her?

My future is up in the air as I wait to find out if the pros want me. Coach Jones says I've got a shot, but there are no guarantees.

What if it doesn't come through? I don't even know what I'm going to do with myself.

But what if it does come through?

Can I expect Sienna to drag Zoey around after me? I don't exactly have a say on where I play.

The door clicks shut behind me, and I don't bother looking back.

I clomp down her front path, the cold night air biting at me. I forgot my jacket.

Fuck it. I'll get it another time.

Because I will see her again.

It's just a matter of how.

As a friend?

As Zoey's father?

"Fuck!" I fist the back of my hair, kicking the tire of my SUV and slumping against the driver's door.

She's asking a lot, you know? Considering we've only just reconnected!

Anger fires strong and fierce.

She was the one who left me in the end. She ghosted me! What if I do something to piss her off and she does it again, taking Zoey with her and leaving me high and dry?

Or what if I do something to hurt her?

I can't break her heart again.

Fuck it, she deserves better than that. Better than me.

Beeping the lock, I jump into my SUV and squeeze the steering wheel until my fingers hurt.

"Ahhh!" I yell, slapping the wheel and cursing up a storm before suddenly going still.

Huffing like a rhino, I stare out at the dimly lit street, indecision riding through me like a hurricane.

I have a game tomorrow.

I need to focus on that.

But there's a girl in that house behind me who owns my heart, and am I seriously about to drive away from her?

The game.

The girl.

That's always been my battle, right?

How the fuck am I supposed to handle both?

And which is more important to me?

This is your life we're talking about.

Your future.

Snapping my eyes shut, I clench the wheel and mutter, "Fuck this!"

CHAPTER 27
SIENNA

Unfolding myself from the floor, I slowly stand and stare at the front door. I can just see the edge of it from here. I need to lock it, secure the house, and go to bed. Cry myself to sleep.

He left.

That's what he was supposed to do, I guess.

That's what I told him to do.

To leave so that I won't get my heart broken all over again.

It feels pretty damn bruised right now, so it's probably for the best that I avoid future burns and scarring.

Shuffling to the edge of the couch, I notice his jacket.

Tears burn as I pick it up, pressing it against my nose and inhaling deep. Inhaling him.

The smell is so familiar. I've always loved his cologne.

I want to take this jacket to bed with me, cuddle it like a teddy bear while my tears soak into my pillow.

He left.

I asked too much.

He doesn't love me.

He—

The front door swings open, and I spin with a gasp as it clips shut behind Zander. My heart takes off, spiking uncontrollably as he stares at me with an intensity I've never seen before.

He's back.

He's here.

Does that mean...?

My body starts to yearn with this overpowering pulse that reverberates right down to my soul, and a force I can't counter moves my feet for me when he strides into the room with a purpose that's palpable. I barely have time to breathe before he takes my head in his hands and starts kissing me.

His lips are hot and hungry, his tongue owning mine as he cinches me around the waist and lifts me off the floor.

My legs automatically wrap around him, my Tigger tail swinging as I return home to the one place that could always make me fly.

Zander.

My Zander.

Our tongues meet in a hot tango that's all-consuming. I cling to him, needy and wanting, unabashedly desperate.

Tipping his head, he deepens the kiss while my hands glide around his neck and I whimper into his mouth.

His arm around me tightens, his other hand finding

its place in the back of my hair and lightly fisting my long locks.

Tugging me back, he stares into my eyes and whispers, "I love you." His lips brush against mine before he murmurs, "I never stopped. I couldn't stop."

CHAPTER 28
ZANDER

Walking back through Sienna's front door suddenly seemed like the easiest decision in the world. With her in my arms, everything feels right again—whole, complete, crystal clear.

There is no other reason but her.

No other purpose.

Football is a dream, but she's my soul.

I can't enjoy any of it without her, and so I walked through her door with one intention.

Whether I deserve to be here or not is another question. For now, all I can do is assure her how much I love her. How I'd choose her any day of the week... the way I should have done before I left for Kelsey U.

"I love you," she whimpers back, her words more like soft cries. I can feel the tears skimming down her cheeks. Kissing them away, I nibble my lips across her skin, walking her around the couch in search of a room.

I need her beneath me, splayed out on a bed.

I need to worship her gorgeous body, remind myself

of all her sweet spots, send her over the edge the way I used to.

"Right, right, right," Sienna directs me in desperate whispers.

I veer right, lightly banging into the doorframe. "Sorry. Are you okay?"

She giggles and keeps kissing me, her tongue lashing mine like she can't get enough. I pause in the hallway, pressing her back against the wall so I can take my time, slow down the kiss and soak her in. She's my oxygen right now, and I drink from her, cupping the side of her head and exploring her mouth the way I used to.

Her fingers curl into my T-shirt, fisting the fabric as her hips buck against mine. Her wanton need is a fucking huge turn-on, and I relish it, grinding her against the wall and loving her mewling whimper.

"I want you so bad, baby," she softly cries against my cheek. "Take me to bed or lose me forever."

"*Top Gun*," I whisper before parting her lips with my tongue again.

Her hips buck against me once more, and I obey her silent command, pulling her away from the wall and stumbling down the hallway.

"This one." She tips her head toward an open doorway, and I move through it, licking her neck and nibbling my way to her ear.

I suck her lobe into my mouth, and she lets out a sexy moan just before I drop her onto the bed.

I can't see shit in this dark room, and that's not gonna fly. I want to watch her body writhe and move beneath mine.

Crawling over her, I reach out in search of a little light

and wrestle with the lamp switch until it pops on and the room is bathed in a soft glow.

I take a minute to glance around, loving the row of soft toys along the floor, the clutter of shoes that have yet to be put away. Glancing over my shoulder, I spot a set of drawers, jewelry scattered along the top as well as photos of her parents and Zoey.

I turn back to smile down at her. "Nice room."

She grins. "Just kiss me already."

"Yes, ma'am."

Fisting my shirt, she pulls me back on top of her. I can taste her hunger, that urgent need, but I can't go rushing this. She's in my arms again—something I've wanted for years. I can't go treating her like any other hookup.

"Slow down," I whisper against her neck when she starts tugging at my sweats.

"Slow down?" She leans away with an incredulous look. "I haven't had sex in three years, and you want me to slow down?"

I pause, curling my hand around her frantic fingers to stop her. She hasn't had sex since... me? The idea is humbling and makes me wish upon every star in the fucking sky that I could say the same thing.

She's only ever been mine.

I'm the only guy to ever touch her this way, and...

Brushing my fingers lightly down her cheek, I trace her face and whisper, "I love you."

She swallows, her blue eyes so big and vulnerable right now.

"I want to savor you. This can't be a blind rush to the finish for me. I need... it has to be different."

I don't know if she gets what I'm saying. That every

other girl I've been with has never made me feel the way she does. That any sex I've had since leaving her has either been a robotic release or a drunken mess.

I want to be fully present for this. I want to give her everything.

Her hands drop away from my sweats. She's not tugging at the waistband anymore, and for a second, I worry that she's about to roll away and tell me to go.

But then her teeth skim over her bottom lip and she slowly unzips the front of her onesie. I sit back and watch with a smile as Tigger is sliced down the middle to reveal a skimpy pair of boxer shorts and a shoestring tank that, holy fuck, is the epitome of cute and sexy.

Helping her slide the orange fabric off her arms and down her body, I trail my fingers over the freshly exposed skin, lightly tickling her thighs as I work my way back up her body and nuzzle the cute Tweety Bird who's giving me attitude on the front of her pajama top.

I can't wait to whip this thing off and taste the goodies, but I'm savoring right now. I'm watching, admiring, drinking her in.

Raising her hands above her head, she lightly grips the bedpost above her and purrs, "You want to savor me?"

Holy shit, I love this woman so fucking much.

Her eyes sparkle, but then her teeth are soon pinching her bottom lip, and she's tugging the bottom of her top down with a nervous titter. "My body's changed a little. It's not as... I've got stretch marks and..."

With wrinkled eyebrows, she shifts uncomfortably, her eyes darting to the lamp like she's thinking of turning it off.

"No way, Sparks. The light stays on." Lightly taking

her wrists, I guide her hands back up to grab the bedpost again before trailing my fingers over her exposed arm, then slowly pushing her shirt up. Tweety's face gets wrinkled as I concertina him away so I can gaze down at Sienna's perfect tits. Oh man, I've missed them.

Trailing my fingers lightly around each of them, I run my thumb across her nipples and enjoy her little shudder.

"So beautiful," I whisper, skimming my knuckles down her torso before painting a circle around her belly button. "I need to see your body, baby. I've missed it."

Her eyes start to glisten as she sniffs and nods. "I've missed yours too."

My throat clogs with an emotion so thick I can't speak. All I can do is show her how much I mean what I'm saying.

Reaching behind my head, I grip the back of my shirt and pull it off, throwing it to the side. She reaches for me, her eyes bright with hunger as she trails her fingers down my ridges. It tickles, but I let her explore for a second, loving the look on her face right now.

Talk about feeling admired.

When she licks her lips like a lioness about to pounce, I grab her hands and lift them over her head again. Gently forcing her fingers around that bedpost, I silently tell her to hold on before giving her a playfully wicked grin, then start to work my way down her body.

As much as I want to tear her clothes off, I take it slow. It's a sweet torture as I nudge the straps off her shoulders, licking a path up her neck before sucking her chin and working my way back down between her collarbones.

Her whimper is delicious.

I smile against her skin, nibbling a line between her breasts before pulling the shirt over her head. She flicks her hair out of the way while I push Tweety to the floor, then run the tip of my nose across the curve of her breast before sucking her beaded nipple into my mouth.

Her groan is the sweetest music, and I draw out that luscious sound, teasing her nipple with my tongue while lightly pinching the other between my thumb and fore-finger. She starts to pant, her chest heaving already, and I'm loving every fucking second of this.

She grips the bedpost above her, her arms shaking as I gruffly tell her, "Don't let go, baby."

Undressing her this slowly is the most erotic thing I've ever done. It's taking all my willpower not to pounce and plunge, but I hold out. I fight the animalistic urge inside me, and I trail my tongue down her body, dipping it into her belly button before tracing the faint stretch marks beneath. I don't know what she's worried about. She's still the sexiest woman I know, and I tell her so before cinching the waistband of her pajama bottoms with my teeth.

She groans and starts pleading, "Yes. Please, yes."

I glance up and her eyes are on me, that blue gaze so intense and needy that I let out a soft growl and tug her pants down. She giggles, lifting her hips and letting go of the bedpost to help me out.

"Keep holding on to that, Sparks. It's sexy as fuck."

"I can't," she whimpers. "I need to touch you."

Plunging her fingers into my hair, she fists the back as I tease her clit with the tip of my tongue.

Oh fuck, she tastes good.

Her hips buck and I slip my hands under her perfect

ass, giving it a squeeze as I lick, taste, and explore the oasis between her legs.

My cock is straining for release, and when she starts frantically scrambling to tug my pants off, I kneel back and let her. As soon as my sweats are past my ass cheeks, she dives into my boxer briefs and wraps her fingers around my length.

I tip my head back with a moan, loving her hands on me. She sits up, nudging my boxers down with her free hand.

"I need you naked. Like stat." She starts kicking the pajama bottoms off her feet and I help her out, throwing them over my shoulder before nudging my pants and underwear off.

Gazing down at my erection, she licks her lips before biting her bottom lip and looking sexy as hell. She leans forward to suck me off, but I lightly push her shoulders back.

"No way. It's my turn first."

She lands on her pillow with a light thump, and I wrap her fingers back around that bedpost before parting her legs. I tease her folds open while her eyes slide shut. She tips her head back with the sexiest sound I've ever heard, and I nudge my middle finger inside her.

More sexy-ass groaning ensues, and I suck her erect nipples and finger her, teasing her clit with my thumb before moving back down her body and pressing my tongue against her most sensitive spot.

She jerks and bucks on the bed and I smile against her clit, loving the way she's riding my finger. Sliding my index finger inside her as well, I enjoy her ecstasy—her little pants and squeaks, followed by guttural groans that make my dick even harder.

She's so soft and warm, so open and trusting.

I want to honor that trust. I want to send her over the edge, and I'll dive straight after her, catching her, protecting her, loving her with everything I have.

Sucking her clit between my lips when she arches her back, I enjoy her high-pitched gasps. She's close. She's so fucking close.

"Come for me, baby."

Another groan rockets out of her, and she grips those bedposts like she's about to snap them. Plunging my fingers even deeper, I press my tongue against her clit, licking fast and quick until she's splintering in my arms.

I hold her hips when she bucks and writhes, her hands dropping to my shoulders, her nails digging into my flesh.

Fuck, she's beautiful.

I love her. I love her so fucking much.

Supporting her hips as she glides back down from her high, I smile at her, my lips stretched wide when she opens her eyes. There's a glazed quality to them that makes my dick twitch, and I want to plunge inside her right now. I want to take her hard and fast and... I also want to ride her slow. I want to make this last the whole fucking night.

Her giggle is soft and low as she reaches for my dick. "That was incredible."

Wrapping her fingers around me, I start to make my own music, a groan reverberating in my throat when she pumps me.

"You feel bigger than last time." She skims her thumb

over my head, her nose scrunching in that adorable way I love. "Is that possible?"

"Maybe." I grin down at her, tracing my finger between her breasts. "I think you're bigger too. Don't we keep growing until we're in our early twenties or something?"

Her eyes travel over my chest and torso, her lips curling up at the corners. "You definitely have. Look at you. You're like a Greek god."

A low laugh rumbles in my chest but is soon cut off by her sultry smile and simple words.

"And you're all mine."

"Yeah," I rasp, hoping my expression is serious enough. "I am yours. Only yours."

The smile on her face is the most beautiful one I've ever seen, and that level of trust I'm gazing at right now is so humbling I want to cry.

"I'm sorry I broke us." My voice quakes, and I can't believe I'm going here when her fingers are wrapped around my pulsing dick. What the fuck is wrong with me?

I should be reveling in the pleasure, but all I can see is her glistening gaze. All I can feel is regret that I lost three years with her.

"Shhhh." She rises to her knees, wrapping her fingers around the back of my neck and pulling me close. "Shh-hh," she whispers against my skin before kissing me deep, her tongue sweeping across mine like a slow promise.

My hand automatically curves around her back, pulling her against me until we're nothing but skin on skin. I need to be inside her. I need to join our bodies completely.

Dropping to my butt, I hitch her onto my lap and rub my cock against her folds.

Her teeth lightly brush my shoulder as she shudders in my arms, her fingers digging into my neck and back while I line us up.

My tip is poised at her entrance, my heart thrumming as I squeeze her ass, ready to plunge into her...

But then she breaks my heart and whispers, "Wait, wait, wait. Stop."

CHAPTER 29
SIENNA

My pulse is so strong and invasive I can barely think straight. All I want is that glorious cock of his to spear me. My body is aching for it, screaming at me to get on with it. His tip is right there, that slight pressure a sweet promise of what I've been missing and pining for.

But...

"We can't do this." I pull back, disappointment nearly blinding me, but I've got enough logical brain cells left to know I don't want to get pregnant again.

I can't let one of his little sperm change my life all over again. I'm not ready to take that risk.

Sure, he loves me.

Sure, I'm learning to trust him again, and I want this.

I *really* want this.

But the practical side of me is shouting two things on repeat until they drown out my chaotic heartbeat:

You're not ready to get pregnant again!

Who knows where his dick has been.

The second one makes me shudder, and I slip off his lap entirely, scuttling up the bed.

He looks kind of devastated, and it's only then that I realize I haven't explained myself.

I squeeze my eyes shut, scrunching my nose and shaking my head. "We don't have protection. And I can't risk... I'm sorry, but—"

"I have protection." He scrambles for his pants, giving me a nice shot of his perfect ass as he reaches to the floor and wrestles his wallet out of the pocket.

Pulling a condom out, he gives me a triumphant grin, holding it up, like all our problems have been solved.

My stomach jumps and jitters with anticipation, my sex-crazed hormones doing a happy dance, but now all I'm thinking is... *He carries a condom in his wallet? How often does he have sex?*

His shoulders slump, like he can read my mind, his voice going soft and husky. "The only girl I've ever not worn one of these for is you." He lifts his chin, his gaze holding me still. "You're the only one who's ever truly had me."

My expression buckles as I softly whisper, "But I'm not."

"You're the only one who's had my heart and soul. I may have had sex a time or two."

"Or a hundred," I mutter, then wince at the bitter edge to my tone.

"Not a hundred, Sen. I know I fucked up, and I know what you saw probably makes you think I slept my way through Kelsey U, but I swear I didn't." He sighs. "I can't sit here telling you I haven't had sex with other girls. When I got back to Kelsey U after Christmas, I went a little crazy for a while and partied pretty hard. And since getting to Nolan U, I've had the occasional hook up." He places his finger under my chin, gently guiding me to face him. "I get that you might not be able to move past that. I'd never force you to do anything you don't want to do, but please believe me when I tell you that you're the only girl I've ever made love to."

His face right now.

Shit, he makes it impossible not to believe him.

His regret and shame is so potent, I can practically taste it.

And I know I'll hate myself forever if I end our time together this way. If I kick him out the door right now, I'll be miserable.

So, what are my other options?

You could forgive him.

Licking my bottom lip, I look at the rumpled duvet beneath me, squeezing one of the folds between my fingers and playing with that idea for a minute.

I love him.

I don't want him to go.

I want him inside me, wiping away the last few years with his sweet kisses. I want to be connected with him the way I've never connected with anyone else.

This is my shot to get him back. And I can either take it… or completely ruin it.

Nerves scatter through me like bullets, and I fist the duvet in my fingers.

Zander sighs. "Okay. I get it. And I'm sorry. I'm so fucking sorry I ruined the best thing that ever happened to me. I never meant to break your heart."

He sounds like he's about to cry, and I glance up, snatching his wrist before he can move off the bed.

He stares at me, waiting for my next move.

My heart has catapulted into my throat and it's impossible to say anything, so instead, I slip the condom out of his hand and tear it open.

"Really?" He swivels back to face me properly. His dick, which was starting to soften, quickly springs back into action like it's been injected with a shot of adrenaline.

I smile down at it, my gaze tracking back up his luscious body as my lady parts start to purr in anticipation.

"I want you to make love to me, Zander. I want you stay in this bed for the whole night and hold me and kiss me and come inside me." Rolling the condom over his dick, I then lie back down and beckon him with my fingers. "Make us whole again. It's time to restore what's been broken."

His face is pure beauty as he drinks me in with a reverent look that sends delicious quivers shooting through my belly.

Crawling between my legs, he lies on top of me, his weight bringing instant comfort as I glide my hands around his shoulders and lightly squeeze them.

He gives me an affectionate wink before kissing the end of my nose and then pressing his mouth to mine.

We make out for a minute, just like we used to, his weight pressing me into the bed with just the right amount of pressure.

I moan and wriggle beneath him, the heat inside me

building quickly. His hard length is pressing into my upper thigh, and my pussy is wet and yearning.

"Please, baby," I rasp against his lips. "I need you now."

"You sure?"

"Yes." I breathe the word more than say it.

Reaching between us, he lines himself up, and there's that tip again, pressing against my entrance, promising so much.

Before he makes the plunge, he pulls up on his elbows, gazing down at me and softly checking, "You're really sure?"

I swallow and cup his face, brushing my thumb along his cheekbone. "I'm sure."

And with one smooth thrust he's inside me again, filling all those empty spaces and bringing me home.

The moan that pops out of me is low and guttural, my heart soaring just the way it used to. This is all so familiar yet feels brand-new at the same time. His hard length is all-consuming, filling me, grinding into me one smooth thrust after another.

I match his rhythm, my body remembering this dance like it was yesterday.

"Oh fuck, you feel good, Sen." Zander kisses me below my ear, panting against my neck and grunting as he plunges a little deeper.

I cry out, gripping his arms when he rises up to his elbows and skims his finger around my ear.

"You okay, Sparky?" he puffs.

"I'm amazing."

"Yeah, you are."

I sense the smile in his voice and pop my eyes open to

look at him. He's still moving inside me at a steady pace, but the world seems to go still around us as I gaze up at his beautiful face and am lost in his adoration.

"I love you." I mouth. *I forgive you,* my heart softly says. "You're mine."

"And you're mine." He lowers himself back over me, kissing me slow until I can't concentrate on anything other than the feel of him moving inside me.

Sucking his shoulder, I snap my eyes closed and drown in the physical phenomenon I'm experiencing. I forgot how good this feels. The heat pulsing through me is mind-blowing and addictive.

Wrapping my leg around his hip, I dig my heel into his ass and urge him to thrust a little deeper.

He does my bidding, picking up his pace and hammering into me until he's the only thing to exist in my world.

I can't breathe, my mouth popping open as another orgasm builds inside me. Like a volcano bubbling away, it suddenly explodes with a burst of pleasure, and I can't hold in my lusty cries.

Zander groans along with me, his arms starting to shake as he jerks and plunges three more times—fast and deep and powerful.

I gasp and sink my fingers into his taut biceps when he holds himself over me, his back arched, his hips pinning me to the bed. A shudder runs through him as he lets out a groan and empties himself inside me.

I watch him come, loving the look of ecstasy on his face. He's lost within me, totally consumed by me... and I love him for it.

Splaying my hand over his left pec, I smile at his

thundering heartbeat. His chest is still heaving, like he's just sprinted a hundred meters at the Olympics.

I did that to him.

We did that to each other.

And it feels fucking fantastic!

I can't help my soft giggle.

His eyes pop open and he gazes down at me, lowering himself to one elbow and lightly tracing my hairline with his finger. "I've missed you. I've missed your laugh, your voice, your body. Everything. I've missed you so much."

Tears line my lashes instantly, and I sniffle. "I've missed you too."

Brushing my tears away with his thumb, he kisses me softly, like I'm a fragile bird he wants to protect, before slowly rolling to his side.

I swivel to face him, loving the way he takes my hand and starts playing with my fingers. He wants to say something, I can tell, and I wait him out until he looks at me with a vulnerable frown. "You don't regret what we just did, do you?"

"No." I shake my head.

"For a second there, I thought it might not happen."

I give him a shy smile. "The second you walked back through my door, it was a guarantee. I guess I just got tripped up in the middle there." I wince. "I wish I hadn't seen what I saw in your dorm room. I wish..." I sigh, rolling onto my back and staring up at the ceiling. "I wish I hadn't hated you for so long."

"Hey." He snuggles against my side, resting his arm across my belly and kissing my shoulder. "I deserved to be hated."

"But I wasted so much time and energy on it. And—"

"And what?" He brushes the tip of his nose up my cheek.

"And I'm sorry I didn't tell you I was pregnant." My voice wobbles. "I should have told you about Zoey. Even if it was just an email or something. You had a right to know about your daughter, and I deprived you of that. I told myself it was because you weren't fit to be a father, but..." My lips press together as I fight another wave of tears. "I think I was just trying to punish you for getting over me so easily."

"I didn't get over you." His voice is quaking as I turn to see the tears in his eyes. "You broke my heart, too, you know? I came back for you, and you weren't there." He shuts his eyes, and I quickly catch the one tear that's broken free.

He's crying. He's actually crying.

I've never seen Zander this vulnerable before, and it's busting my heart wide open.

"I know I can never say it enough. But I'm sorry I acted the way I did. I let myself get manipulated and pushed around. I was weak and...and I tried to numb it all with drink and weed." He cringes. "Sometimes it led me into situations that I hated myself for. I didn't even know who I fucking was anymore. So, at Christmas, I came back for you. I was desperate for some kind of anchor. I knew I couldn't find my way back without you. I was going to tell you I was willing to do long-distance until you could join me... but you weren't there. Not even a goodbye."

Guilt shreds me, and I shuffle around so I can drape my leg over his and pull us closer together again. The condom sticks between us and I cringe, reaching behind me to grab a tissue and clean him up.

Yeah, my duvet's going to need washing, too, after the wet mess we made.

But I ignore the problem and focus back on my man.

My man.

He's my man again.

My heart does a little twirl as I press my cheek to his. "We've both made mistakes." I run my fingers through the back of his hair—a gentle caress. "But I'm learning to trust you again."

"And I'm going to give you every reason to."

His promise is so heartfelt and sincere.

Aw, man. I love him so freaking much.

With a soft giggle, I press my lips against his, joy bursting through me like a rainbow as I roll him onto his back and snuggle against his side.

Tugging the blanket out from beneath us, he makes sure we're covered, then curls his arm protectively around me. I draw patterns through his light dusting of chest hair until my eyes drift shut and I fall asleep beside my man, the way I've dreamed of doing a thousand times before.

CHAPTER 30
ZANDER

Falling asleep with Sienna in my arms feels like home. That might be a sappy thing to think, but it's true.

I can't believe I fucking cried in front of her, but that was the most emotional sex I have ever had. It was like our souls were reconnecting or something. I didn't realize how much I needed it. Being inside her was a cleansing ritual.

She let me be a part of her again. Even after everything she saw.

Shit, she can never find out about the other stuff. I won't put her through that.

She's forgiven me, and I need to cherish that.

Fuck, I'm never letting her go again. Even if I don't deserve her, I'm going to selfishly cling, because she's my woman and I can't lose her.

Drifting in and out of sleep, I keep rousing into a semiconscious state and feeling her beside me. Running my hand around her naked body, I reassure myself she's not an illusion before letting my mind float away again.

By the time soft baby cries rouse me, I'm on my side with Sienna tucked perfectly against me. Her ass is nestled into my junk, my knees resting beneath hers. My hand is under her right boob, and I'm in fucking heaven.

Except that someone's crying.

Wait.

My eyes snap open, my body instantly alert as I jerk up straight and hone into Zoey's soft blubbering.

Sienna groans, coming to and pulling back the covers.

"S'okay. Mama's coming," she mumbles, sounding half-drunk as she sits up and flicks on the light.

I squint against the sudden glare and can't help an instant smile as my eyes adjust. Sienna's still gloriously naked, and I skim my fingers down her back as she sits on the edge of the bed and obviously tries to wake herself up enough to attend to our daughter.

"Will it freak her out if I go?" I surprise myself by asking.

Sienna looks over her shoulder and blinks at me.

I blink back, wondering if I should backtrack, but now that the thought is out there, I really want to follow through with it.

Zoey's soft cries increase, and Sienna's forehead wrinkles. "I'm not sure."

"Can I try?" I sit up, already reaching for my boxer briefs.

I've pulled them on before she can reply and move to the door hopefully.

What the hell am I doing?

Why am I so desperate to go and comfort my crying daughter?

I never thought I'd take to fatherhood this easily, but I'm standing in Sienna's doorway like an eager puppy.

"Um... okay. Yeah, I mean, Russell sometimes beats me to it, so having a man walk into her room isn't completely out of the ordinary." She flicks her hand in the air. "She's just never seen you in the middle of the night before. But if she starts screaming, I'll come bail you out."

"Thanks." I grin, darting into the hallway and following Zoey's cries, shaking off the idea that Russell's the closest thing she has to a dad right now.

Well, fuck that!

I'm here, and I'm not planning on going anywhere.

Zoey's room is just down from Sienna's, and I creep in, the soft glow from the nightlight making it easy to find her.

She's standing on the side of her crib, holding the railing and bawling. Her curls are a reckless mess and tears are staining her cheeks, but the second she sees me, she stops crying and gapes, like she doesn't even know who I am.

"Hey, Zoey." I greet her gently, hoping my voice isn't too rough or deep.

Wiping her hand down her cheek, she blinks at me and softly whimpers, "Foobawl."

"Yeah, it's me." Resting my hand on the railing next to her little fingers, I bend down and smile at her.

She eyes me up for a long, thick beat, then whispers, "Mommy."

"You want Mommy?"

"Mommy."

"Okay." I straighten up and hold out my hands. "Is it okay if I pick you up and take you to her?"

She instantly raises her arms, and I pick her up, nestling her against me and cupping the back of her head as I walk her out of the room.

Her cheek falls against my shoulder, and her snuggly warmth fills my chest with a sensation that is off the charts. I've never felt so protective of another human being before. I've never felt this kind of affection.

Splaying my hand across her back, I hold her close and lightly kiss her cheek. This little bundle in my arms is owning me, and I walk back to Sienna's room as slowly as I can, not wanting to let this precious girl go.

CHAPTER 31
SIENNA

It takes all of two seconds to realize that a bare-chested Zander walking into my room with my daughter cradled against his rock-hard pecs is the sexiest thing I have ever seen.

It takes maximum effort not to beg him to fill me with multiple babies so I can watch him be a dad every day for the rest of my life.

"Here we go." Zander's husky sweet voice is in full play, and my ovaries are already tingling.

Screw protection. Make me pregnant now!

Sienna! Stop it.

I quickly pull my sleepy brain into line and gather Zoey against my chest. She snuggles in, rubbing her nose across Tweety before her squishy cheek finds a pillow against my breasts. Her sleepy whimpers make me smile. She's so freaking adorable.

Rocking her against me, I hum her favorite bedtime song while Zander stretches out on the bed beside me. He rubs her back, leaning his head on my shoulder.

I just found my new happy place.

"Foobawl," Zoey murmurs in her sleepy state.

I don't even know if she realizes what she says, but Zander softly laughs. "I love that she calls me that. I can't correct her."

"It's very sweet." I kiss his forehead. "She likes you. It's not hard. Falling for you was the easiest thing I've ever done, and she's gonna be head over heels for you. I can already see it."

"Yeah, I think *Wywee*'s still in top position, but I'm working on it." He snickers.

"You're her daddy. That makes you number one, and she's gonna start to realize that soon enough."

Zander lifts his head off my shoulder to stare at me.

"Stick around and she'll know."

"I'm not going anywhere." He cups the back of Zoey's head and kisses her curls. "I promise. I'm not leaving my girls."

A smile seems to light my entire body, and Zander kisses my grin before snuggling up against me again.

It takes about ten minutes, but Zoey's nighttime grizzles soon dissipate to a gentle snoring. Her little mouth is open and lax, her body completely limp against mine.

"I'll just take her back," I whisper.

"Do you want me to?" He reaches for her, and his hopeful expression is too adorable.

Gently passing our daughter back to him, I support her floppy head until she's resting in the crook of his arm. He gazes down at her with such pure affection that my belly flutters.

And as soon as he leaves the room, I spring out of bed and duck into the hallway. Creeping to the kitchen, I fight my impish giggles as I open the candy box and grab what I need.

I'm biting my bottom lip as I tiptoe back to my room, pausing in the hallway to check on Zoey.

She's lying in her crib, completely out of it, while Zander stands over her, softly rubbing her back and drinking her in.

Hopefully he won't be too long, because I've got plans for that man.

Screw sleep.

I know I'll be smashed tomorrow, but it'll be worth it.

Whipping off my pajamas, I throw them on the floor, the box of Nerds rattling as I jump onto the bed and flip onto my back.

I hear Zander coming, and my stomach jitters as I quickly pour Nerds all over my naked torso and rest on my elbows, waiting for him. With one leg draped over the edge of the bed and the other bent high, I try to look as sexy as I can and hope my man's up for a little late-night fun.

He walks back into the room with a dreamy, sleepy smile but quickly jerks to a stop when he sees me.

I raise my eyebrows and grin at him. "Feel like a midnight snack, Hot Lips?"

"Oh, man." He scrubs a hand down his face. "I fucking love you so much."

A little squeal pops out of me as he growls and lunges for the bed, sucking Nerds off my body like they're lines of cocaine.

He grimaces as he crunches through them. "These are so gross. Why do you eat them?"

"They're delicious," I argue, giggling when he sucks a

few out of my belly button. "And if they're so disgusting, you don't have to keep going."

"Are you kidding?" He glances up with an incredulous frown. "These are on your naked body. I don't care if I hate them, I'm licking every inch of your skin until the only thing left on you is me." His eyes darken with a heated look that has my pussy weeping, and now I'm the one growling, fisting his hair and dragging him up my body so I can kiss that tongue of his.

He tastes like Nerds, and I suck the sugar off his lips. The candy's getting locked between us, melting into a sweaty mess as our lovemaking soon becomes a frantic rush. I yank at his boxer briefs, my nails leaving small scratch marks on him. He kicks them off his foot, completely unfazed by the red welts on his skin.

"Sorry," I murmur, trying to kiss them better, but he nudges me back, sucking my nipples and mumbling in between kisses.

"Never be sorry for marking me like this, baby. I love your nails on me. I love your skin, your tongue, your taste..." He licks another Nerd off his lips. "Well, mostly your taste."

I laugh at his sexy wink, then groan when he shifts on top of me, teasing my clit with a caress of his knuckle before cupping me and sending my body into a frenzy.

His hands and tongue are everywhere, taking me over the edge in a flurry of passion.

I somehow end up with my head hanging over the edge of the bed, the world turning upside down as he leaves a hickey on the top curve of my left breast and teases my clit until I can barely stand it.

As the orgasm rockets up my spine, he plunges into me, thrusting hard and fast.

Just like old times, we get completely lost in each other until he rips out of me and starts muttering about fucking condoms.

I snicker when he scrambles to get another one out of his wallet. My aching needy body is impatient, and I can't keep my legs still as I wait for him.

"Last one." He looks so relieved that I start to giggle, then end up crumpling with laughter that's borderline hysterical when his urgent hands can't open the packet.

"Use your teeth."

"It's the last one! I'm not doing anything to risk breaking the thing." Sucking in a calming breath, he shakes out his hands and tries again, opening the condom with the delicacy of a brain surgeon and carefully rolling it on.

As soon as it's secure, I jump onto his lap, lining him up and sliding straight back over him.

I'm so wet and slippery that I ride him at a fast pace, his fingers digging into my butt as our breath mingles together. We try to kiss, but this pace is too frantic.

Groaning, he pulls me close, then starts working my hips until my boobs are bouncing against his chest. My nipples graze his taut pecs, sending my body into a fresh delirium.

And then he's choking out my name, pulling me down on him with an unbridled force and coming inside me with lusty jerks and moans that are so fucking hot, I follow right after him.

I'm not sure my heart rate will ever return to normal as I rest my forehead against his shoulder and try to breathe. Seriously, I think my heart just detonated. It's now scattered throughout my chest, slowly working its way back into one piece.

A shuddering giggle bursts out of me, and Zander's hand trails down my back.

"What?" he murmurs against my shoulder.

"We have got to use Nerds again sometime."

He snorts and lightly bites my shoulder. "I'd rather use coffee beans."

"Gross." I sit up and pull a face at him.

Cupping my cheeks, he gives me an adoring smile and pulls me in for a slow, luxurious kiss that I would happily stay locked in until morning.

"I'm sure we can think of something else to cover your body with." He nibbles his way to my jawline, then up to my ear. "Maybe I can turn you into my personal s'more. I wouldn't mind licking melted chocolate and marshmallows off this luscious body."

My insides flare with desire as I wrap my arms and legs around this sexy man and start dreaming about all the good times still to come.

CHAPTER 32
ZANDER

I'm used to my alarm going at 5:15 a.m., even on a Saturday. But when I've spent half the night awake with my woman, it feels fucking ungodly having the thing start buzzing.

Sienna moans, squirming beside me and burying her head in the pillow as I scramble to turn it off.

"What time is it?" she mumbles, shuffling her perfect ass against my thigh.

I roll toward her, wrapping my arm around her waist and pulling her back against me. She's such a perfect fit. I fucking love it.

Kissing her shoulder, I then rest my chin on her cheek and whisper, "Just after five. Sorry." I wince. "It's game day. I've got a lot of prep to do."

"Game day," she mumbles.

"But I can come back after the game." I glide my hand down her perfect curves, loving the undulating path I'm taking, traveling her waist and hips, then dipping between her thighs so I can cup her pussy.

She groans, starting to wake up.

"What time is the game?" Her voice becomes more articulate as she rolls over to face me.

I gaze into those sleepy blue eyes. "It starts at twelve thirty."

"Who are you playing?"

"The Kings."

"Ooooo. Are they tough competition?"

I laugh. "Looking at their stats and the game reviews we've done... it should be an easy win."

It's hard not to sound just a little smug. Nolan U has never lost to the Kings, and we're planning on keeping that streak alive today. An electric thrill runs through me as I start to get fired up for the game. I can't wait to get out on that field.

"I hope you do." Sienna smiles, laying her hand on my cheek and kissing me.

"Mmmm." I breathe her in, my arm automatically coming around her waist so I can pull her flush against me.

She giggles into my mouth when I roll us over, finding a home between her legs and already growing hard.

Fuck. I hate that I've run out of condoms. I'm loading up today. I will be returning tonight fully prepared for my woman.

Threading my fingers into her hair, I kiss her soundly, my length getting harder by the second. It's impossible not to.

Her smile grows. I can feel it forming against my lips. I love the playful gleam in her eyes when I lean back and she runs her hands down to my hips, then grabs my ass and gives it a firm squeeze.

I grind against her and her eyes flutter closed, her head tipping back as she lets out a delicious moan. I suck her neck, then kiss my way down to the hickey I marked her with last night. Circling my tongue around it, I then inch a little lower, sucking her right nipple until my alarm starts beeping again.

"Fuck," I growl, moving back up the bed and switching it off. Glaring at my phone screen, I dip my head and do some quick calculations. "I really have to go."

"I know." She gives my ass a light slap. "Get up, Captain."

"Yeah, yeah." I groan, wishing I had time to go down on her. What I wouldn't give to see that sweet body of hers break apart in ecstasy. It'd be the best way to start a day.

So start it that way tomorrow.

The thought makes me grin and I slowly rise, kissing her chin, her lips, the tip of her nose, her forehead, before reluctantly climbing off the bed. She giggles, and I mentally record the sound. I know it by heart already, but this one has a low, husky morning quality to it.

Getting dressed, I fumble around the dimly lit room until the only thing I'm hunting for is my shirt.

Sienna switches on the bedside lamp to help me out, and the second I spot her sitting there with nothing but a sheet draped over her waist, I'm jumping back on the bed. She flops down with a laugh as I kneel over her and kiss her slowly, massaging her breasts, lightly pinching her nipples and making her groan into my mouth.

"Fuck, I really have to go," I murmur between kisses.

"I know." Her fingers wrap around my neck and she

keeps me in place, kissing me deeply before lightly pushing me away.

I get up with an irritated growl and fling clothes and bedding aside until I unearth my shirt.

Pulling it on, I try to stretch out the wrinkles but quickly give up. Who cares if it's a creased mess? Shoving my Converse on, I gaze across the room at the impish look on my girlfriend's face.

Fuck yeah, she's my girlfriend again.

The thought has me diving back for the bed, and she giggles as I kiss her again.

"I really have to go."

"I know." She rises to her knees, squishing her tits against my chest. "I hope..." She trails her tongue along my jawline. "You..." She sucks my earlobe, sending a spike of pleasure straight down to my whining dick. "Have..." Her breath fans across my neck before she starts creating a hickey on my shoulder. "The best..." She lightly scrapes her teeth across my skin. "Day."

My body's in a needy frenzy when she finally pulls away, and I pull her onto my lap, the sheet tangling around her. I hold her close, caressing her naked back and kissing her like I've got all the time in the fucking world.

"You have to go," she reminds me in a breathless whisper.

"I really have to go." I keep kissing her.

"Zander." She singsongs my name, and I laugh against her lips.

"Yeah, I know. I know." Running my hands over her smooth skin one last time, I lift her off me and force myself to stand. "I'll see you later, okay?"

"Yeah." She nods, her bright gaze so sweet it makes my chest tingle. "Have the best game."

"I will." I walk to the door, adjusting my outraged dick and begging it to soften up already.

You're not getting any right now. Deal with it!

Glancing over my shoulder, I notice Sienna pulling on her pajama top. Her ass is still bare, and I linger to admire it while she hunts for a pair of underwear before slipping back into bed.

"I really have to go," I murmur, locked in a trance as I watch my woman arrange the pillows.

"I know." She nods, then points at me. "Go. You can't be late."

"I can't be late," I echo, walking back into the room to kiss her one last time.

She laughs, her tongue gliding against mine. "Zander, you gotta go."

"I gotta go." I cup the back of her head and kiss her deeply before forcing myself away from her.

I'm gonna be so fucking late if I don't walk out the door right now.

"Go." She giggles, pushing me away from her. "I love you. Now go."

Standing beside the bed, I run my fingers gently down her cheek and whisper, "I love you."

The smile she gives me is a light beam that charges me up.

Closing my eyes with a groan, I fight every instinct to jump back into bed and force myself out the door.

I'm just passing Zoey's room when I hear her little squawk.

Wow, that's early. Does she always wake at this time?

I pop my head around the doorframe to spy on her, but she spots me. The nightlight highlights her adorable grin as she stands and starts jumping on her mattress. Her little fingers hold the edge of the crib, and who knew fingers could be so damn cute.

"Foobawl!" She holds out her hands, squeezing her fingers open and shut as she beckons me toward her.

"Hey, cowgirl."

She giggles. "Up?"

"It's not playtime." I tap my watch. "It's still nighttime. See?" I point to the window behind her. "It's still dark outside."

"Zoey wanna pay."

"I know," I whisper, leaning down to lightly kiss her cheek. "I have to go to football now, but I can play with you later."

"You come back?"

"Yeah, I'm coming back." I smile at her.

She grins at me, and my heart is undone.

"Zander Donohue." A firm voice grabs my attention.

I whip around to find Sienna in Zoey's doorway, her arms crossed and a stern look on her face. "You get your butt out that door right now. I will not be responsible for you being late."

"Mommy!" Zoey squeals and starts jumping again.

I laugh, kissing Zoey's cheek before walking for the door and brushing my lips across Sienna's cheek too. "See you later, Sparks."

"Yes, you will." The burning desire in her eyes sets my insides on fire, and I lean down to kiss her one last time before she slaps my ass and orders me out of the house.

I'm running so fucking late by the time I get back to

Football Frat. The guys are already piling out of the house, asking me where the hell I've been.

My smile gives me away, and I then have to put up with some serious razzing. Grady waits for me to grab my shit, and we head to the athletes' food hall together. They always open early on game day and make sure we're eating the exact food we need to get us through. The chefs are world-class, and we sit at those tables while I field a barrage of questions and gibes, shoveling food into my mouth and trying my best to get focused for the game ahead.

CHAPTER 33
SIENNA

Zoey never goes back to sleep, and the morning stretches out in front of me. Russell doesn't get back until really late tonight, and I'm kind of glad about that. I need to talk to him about Zander, and I'm pretty sure it'll go down like a bucket of cold vomit.

I probably shouldn't invite Zander back here tonight. I can only imagine the carnage if he strolls out of my room tomorrow morning and bumps into Russell in the kitchen or something.

No, I have to talk to my roommate first, and I'll do that as soon as I see him in the morning. It's all about the way I sell it. I'll be upbeat and let him know that I've forgiven Zander and I'm deliriously happy. Surely he'll come around, right?

Surely he wants me to be happy.

And how cool is it that I've reunited with Zoey's father?

I mean, it's meant to be, isn't it?

My little girl is finally getting the family she was supposed to have all along.

Memories of last night continue to flitter through me as I go about the day, doing the housework and making sure the place is spotless for Russell's return. Anything to aid my cause, right?

Zoey toddles around after me, chatting away, singing, playing, getting under my feet. But her "help" is also adorable, and I'm in too good a mood to let her antics— even the annoying ones—bother me today.

Zander loves me.

I've forgiven him.

We're back together!

Ahhhh! This is crazy and so freaking right.

Humming to myself, I pull Zoey's sheets out of the dryer and put the next load in. All I have left to do is unload the dishwasher.

Glancing at my watch, my smile falters.

Oh boy. I feel like it should be 3:00 p.m. already, but it's only ten. That's what happens when my daughter wakes at stupid o'clock and our day starts way too early.

Although, watching Zander trying to leave this morning was a thing of beauty. A smile stretches across my face as I relive his failed attempts to go. My chest starts tingling, and I let out a giddy laugh before twirling down the hallway to Zoey's room.

She spots me and starts giggling, following my lead and spinning until she topples over with a little thump.

I laugh. "You okay, lil' bug?"

"Yup." She jumps back to her feet and chases after me.

While I make her bed, she sings me songs and then asks, "Foobawl?"

Turning to gaze down at her, I smile. "You want to see Zander again?"

She nods. "Foobawl."

"You like him, don't you?" I crouch down in front of her, lightly holding her hand.

"Foobawl, Wywee fun."

"They are, aren't they?"

"Go see?" she asks, her eyes rounding hopefully.

My nose wrinkles. "We can't. They're playing a game today. They're gonna be really busy."

She lets out an excited gasp. "Go see! Go see!"

"You wanna watch them play?"

"Go see!" She starts jumping up and down.

"The game will be on the TV later, and we can watch—"

She shakes her head. "Go see! Go see!"

"You want to go to the actual game?"

"Yes!" More jumping ensues, and I stand up, wondering if that's even a possibility. I don't even know if I can get in.

But why not try?

With an excited grin, I jump in on my daughter's enthusiasm, and we start getting ready.

It takes me an hour to gather all our stuff thanks to the earmuffs not being where I thought they were. But we're soon loaded up, and I drive to the stadium.

I'm still not sure I can even get in, but I'm gonna go down there and try my luck anyway.

We arrive with plenty of time to spare, and I find a parking spot on the very edge of the lot. The tailgaters are out in full force, and I lead Zoey through the crowds, buying her a churro before heading for the stadium doors and wondering how I'm ever going to get a ticket.

But then I get lucky.

"Teah?" I spot her strawberry blonde waves and take a risk.

She spins at the sound of her name, her face lighting up when she spots me. "Hey!"

Running over with her arms stretched wide, she pulls me into a hug, then crouches down to greet Zoey.

"Hey, cutie."

Zoey gives her a shy smile, then wraps her arms around my leg.

"I didn't know you guys came to home games."

"Well, we usually don't," I admit. "In fact, I don't even have tickets, so I'm not sure we can get in."

"Oh, well, hang with me. Wily's family always buys a block of tickets every season, and there's usually a spare seat or two for these types of games, so I take advantage."

"These types of games?" I question.

"Oh, you know, not playoffs or the big ones. Just your standard middle-of-the-season games." She grins, then bops Zoey on the nose. "You want to come watch some football?"

Zoey nods, still clinging to me as the crowds around us intensify.

I lift her into my arms and trail Teah through the gate.

We find our seats, and Teah introduces me to Wily's parents. They come to every game apparently, making the hour-and-a-half drive from Denver to support their son.

"I've never missed a game," Mr. Wilson tells me proudly. "I even fly to all his away games too."

"Wow." I nod. "That's commitment."

"Gotta support my boy." The man winks at me. "He's gonna be an NFL starter soon enough. He's got what it takes."

"That's right," Mrs. Wilson agrees with her husband. "Our Wily's going to be the best guard in the NFL."

The couple laugh together, and I share a quick look with Teah, who bulges her eyes at me, then leans forward and whispers, "No pressure, Wily."

I snicker, hiding my laughter in Zoey's hair.

She's sitting on my knee and looking around the crowd. The Nolan U colors are in full force—a sea of blue and red covering the stands. A cougar mascot is down with the cheerleaders, putting on a show while we wait for the players.

A raucous cheer goes up when the mascot flips and spins, giving Zoey a fright. She gapes up at me, and I smile down at her. "Isn't he funny?"

"Loud," Zoey complains, and I hunt out the earmuffs, nestling them on her head.

This seems to calm her a little, and she ends up bobbing on my knee, laughing and pointing when the mascot continues his silly antics.

The dancers are amazing and keep us all entertained. I talk to Teah, enjoying her company. She really is cool.

I find out she's a Sig Be Sister and in her senior year of college. Her friend Bella has become the sorority president, and she's really into the life. But she's also into Grady, so she splits her time between the two.

"The girls aren't really into football, so I only come to a few games a season. Nothing else was on the agenda for today, so I figured why not?"

I nod, understanding completely... although I've grown to love football.

"Do you enjoy the game?" I ask her.

Her nose wrinkles. "Not really. But I enjoy Grady." She winks at me and laughs.

I nudge her with my elbow. "I bet you do."

"Mm-mm. That boy is fiiiine." She sings the word, making me laugh with her eyebrow wiggle and flaring blush. "And so is Zander."

I choke on my laughter, coughing into my hand as I fail to hide my blush and end up just agreeing with her. "He's so hot I can hardly stand it. I can't believe he's mine."

Teah gasps, her voice pitching with excitement. "You guys are back together?"

"Uh-huh." I grin, nodding uncontrollably while she squeals and wraps her arm around my shoulders.

"That is the best news! Grady's been keeping me updated on the saga. I hope you don't mind, but he told me how you were high school sweethearts, then broke up, and how Zander went back for you and you were gone..." She starts talking in rapid-fire sentences, rehashing the drama that has been Zander and me. "And now you're together again, and you can be a family! That makes me so happy!"

"Me too." I jump in on her excitement and we start dancing to the music, watching the marching band with Zoey giggling on my knee.

And then the crowd begins to roar.

We all jump to our feet and I hold Zoey close, making sure her earmuffs are secure as we cheer the Cougars onto the field.

Zander busts through the lineup first, flags waving and pom-poms jostling on either side of him as he lifts his hand and waves at the crowd. Raising his helmet in the air, he grins and does a spin while Zoey starts pointing and shouting.

"Foobawl! Foobawl! Hi, Foobawl!" She waves, but he hasn't seen her. I'm not sure he will, but Zoey keeps waving anyway.

When Wily runs out, she starts to squeal and shout, "Wywee! Wywee!"

Teah laughs and then gives me a "she's so adorable" look. I have to agree with her.

Especially when Wily looks up in the stands, obviously waving for his parents, then spots us beside them. He heads over to Zander and gives him a quick shoulder tap.

My boyfriend spins, his face quickly scanning the stands and then landing on me. The second he spots me, his face lights up, and I start grinning.

My smile's so huge it actually hurts, but I can't stop it.

The look on his face right now.

I blow him a kiss. He blows one right back at me... and our daughter starts yelling as loud as she can.

"Hi, Foobawl! Hi, Foobawl!" Her waves are frantic, and when Zander waves back and blows her a kiss too... I swear I've never felt this level of joy before in my life.

This could work.

Me, Zander, Zoey... football.

This could actually work.

CHAPTER 34
ZANDER

Seeing my girls waving at me from the stands is the best fucking thing in the world.

I stand on that sideline grinning up at them while the rest of the team piles onto the field.

"Zander." Carson slaps me on the back. "Focus, dude." He frowns, glaring over my shoulder. "Who the fuck are you blowing kisses to anyway?"

"Uh... no one." I shove my helmet on, turning my back on Sienna and Zoey.

Not everyone on the team knows about the fact that I'm a father, and I'd like to keep it that way. Carson knows, but that's only because Wily's got a big mouth. He hasn't met Zoey and Sienna yet, and that's probably for the best.

Shit, my teammate's right, though.

I need to focus.

But holy shit, they came to the game! They're here!

Zoey with her little earmuffs is plain adorable. Damn, I want a pair of binoculars so I can get a closer look, study her cute little curls and those chubby cheeks. Then I want to home in on my Sparky, study every contour of her perfect face and—

"Let's go, Donohue." Coach points to the middle of the field, and I run in for the coin toss.

"Heads," I call, eyeballing the tight end captain while the coin flips through the air.

"Heads it is." The referee points at me. "Your call."

"We'll receive." I nod.

"We'll defend this goal." The Kings' captain points over my shoulder before we both run back to our respective teams.

I grin up into the stands because I can't fucking help myself.

"Donohue!" My eyes snap to our offensive coach, and I force myself to concentrate as Coach Jones gives us a quick pep talk, then sends the receiving team onto the field.

I hold my breath the way I always do, waiting for Mathers to catch the ball and make some ground.

"Yes!" Wily shouts as Mathers snatches the ball and starts running. "Go, go, go!"

Thanks to a key block from Michelson, Mathers makes a good thirty yards before being tackled, positioning us beautifully for the first play.

"Just like we planned." Coach Jones slaps me on the back, pushing me out for the first offensive play.

I glance over my shoulder, quickly finding Sienna. She's talking to Teah, smiling and laughing, and fuck... it's so good to see her here.

Memories from last night flood me as I form a quick

huddle with my team and remind them of the first play strategy we've been practicing all week.

"Okay, Carson, Flash, we're doing a hook and ladder. Watch their cornerback, he was fucking fast in his last game."

"We're good," Grady assures me, sharing a quick glance with Carson before we break and get into position.

My heart is thrumming the way it always does when I set up for the first play, but it's so much louder today because Sienna is crowding out my game space. Her sweet moans are filling my ears, the feel of her body sliding against mine. Her perfect tits. Shit, I love her body. And those eyes.

I force myself not to look into the stands, but it's taking maximum effort.

Eyeing up the defensive line, I check their set position and am confident we're in the clear to pull off our play without adjustments. The crowd is roaring for us, eager for points on the board, and I do my best to block them out.

"Hut hut," I call to Tyrell, who fires the ball back to me.

I catch it and take a few steps, tracking Carson until he's in the perfect position, then throwing the ball to him.

He snatches it out of the air, then spins and snaps it to Grady, who takes the pass and ducks through the gap we predicted would be there. He gains a sweet twenty yards or so before being taken down, and I start clapping as I move up the field.

"Yes! Good job. Good job!"

I'm so stoked with the execution. I want to play well for my girls. I want to show Sienna how fucking hard I've been working. She needs to know that I didn't just give her up for nothing.

Except you did freshman year.

But I'm making up for it now.

Glancing over my shoulder, I scan the stands for her yet again, spotting her blue sweater and waving at Zoey. Sienna points my way, and Zoey starts waving. I want to blow them another kiss, but someone's barking at me.

"Zander!" I spin and spot Tyrell beckoning me with his hands. "Let's go, man."

He looks mildly annoyed, and I shake my head and give myself a quick reprimand.

Dude! Focus the fuck up!

I wince, slapping my helmet and running over for the next play... which I completely fuck up because just before the ball is snapped to me, I'm flooded with an image of Sienna naked on her bed and covered in Nerds. It was the sexiest fucking thing, and my body ignites in all the wrong places as I nearly drop the fucking ball, then mistime my step back and make the worst fucking throw of my life.

Grady scrambles to rectify my mistake, but he can't jump high enough to reach the ball, and it ends up landing right in the hands of the Kings' cornerback.

"Fuck!" I yell as Wily and another guard haul ass to bring him down.

They manage to tackle him, but the ball now belongs to the Kings.

I have not fucked up that badly in a game before, and holy shit!

I can't even look at the stands as I run to the sidelines and get bawled out by my offensive coach.

"I'm sorry," I mutter, whipping off my helmet and cringing at Coach Jones.

He just shakes his head, sending out the defensive team, then turning back to me and barking, "Shake it off, Donohue. We'll need you when we get the ball back."

I nod and bury my head in my hands as the humiliation rides through me.

What the actual fuck!

Tyrell plunks down beside me. "What the hell was that, man?" He leans his elbows on his knees.

"It was a mistake." Grady stands up for me. "They happen. Get over it."

"Zander doesn't make mistakes like that," Tyrell argues. "He was distracted."

"Probably wanting to blow more kisses into the stands," Carson mutters darkly.

I tense, refusing to admit how fucking right he is.

Shit! I so want my girls here, but it *is* distracting. Fuck, if I can't play with Sienna around, then this is never going to work.

Get your head in the game, you asshole. Win it for them.

Clenching my jaw, I bob my leg and give myself one final look. Turning around, I scan the stands and notice Teah sitting by herself.

What?

My eyes dart around the area as I try to spot Sienna and Zoey. I manage to catch a glimpse of them as she heads up the stairs... toward the exit.

With a sinking gut, I turn back to face the field.

Fuck. She's leaving already? One fumbled play and she can't watch anymore.

Shit, shit, shit!

We have to win this game. I have to play the best football I ever have and demolish the Kings.

Which is exactly what we do.

Fired up and ready to rectify my dismal start, I pace the sidelines, waiting for our turn on offense, and then I have my best game all season. I've never wanted a win more. Every time Sienna tries to sneak into my brain space, I block her out. Zoey's adorable smiles will have to wait until later.

I zone in on the game and play like the quarterback Coach Jones believes I am.

Perfect passes, a flea-flicker that sends the crowd wild, and three touchdowns that are fucking textbook quality. I manage to call last-minute changes that are spot-on, and all I wish as our team celebrates a dominating win is that Sienna had been here to see it.

I don't know why she left.

Maybe it was because of me, I'm not sure, but it got me fired up. I wanted to play well for her. I just wish I could have done that when she was actually here to see it.

As soon as we're back in the locker room and Coach has given us his final words, I pull out my phone and notice a text from Sienna.

Hey. It's Sienna here. Yay! You won! Sorry I couldn't see it in person. Two plays in and Zoey was already losing it. I had to get her out of there before she ruined the game for everyone around us. I think the crowd was a little too much for her. Anyway, she's down for a nap, and I got to watch the last quarter of the game. So proud of you.

. . .

My chest fills with something glorious. I have no idea what this feeling is, but I could get high on that shit.

She's proud of me.

And she was kind enough not to mention my humiliating fuckup just before she left.

Fuck, I love her.

Closing my eyes, I pull in a breath and quickly call her back.

"Hey!" Her bright greeting amplifies that fantastic buzz in my chest, and I grin.

"Hey, beautiful. Thanks for your text."

"You're welcome. I'm glad I got to use your number for something so positive. How are you feeling?"

"Yeah, pretty good. I'm stoked with the win, especially after my epic fuckup at the beginning."

Why are you bringing that up, you douche?

I wince and scratch the back of my sweaty head.

She laughs. "It was just one mistake. The way the commentators were talking, you played like an American all-star. Seriously, they couldn't say enough good things about you in that last quarter."

Thank fuck for that.

"Yeah, I just took a minute to get my head in the game, I guess."

"I hope I wasn't a distraction."

Yes, you totally were!

But I'm not about to tell her that. I'm desperate for this to work, so I just need to figure out a way of dividing my focus when she's around. I have to be able to tune her out... just like I did after she left.

I can do it.

I *will* fucking do it.

Because I can't go screwing up my NFL chances now that she's back in my life.

Dad always said Sienna cost me my best shot with Brighton College, and like fuck I'm going to let him prove me right on this.

Sienna and I can be together, and I can still play the best football I ever have.

This will work.

I'll make it work.

"...and then I was practically screaming at the TV. It's lucky I didn't wake Zoey." Sienna laughs, and I only just register that she's talking to me.

I press my finger into my ear, trying to hear her better as the guys in the locker room talk and laugh behind me. They're in celebration mode, and it's getting a touch wild.

"I missed some of that, sorry."

"No, that's okay. I can hear the noise in the background. I should let you go."

"Can I come over later?"

"Uh..."

That buzz in my chest quickly dies. Why the hesitation?

"I want to say yes, but Russell gets home tonight, and I'm not sure how it will go down if you're here."

Anger spikes through me thick and fast. That assface better not get in the way of me and Sienna.

"I just need to talk to him about us first. Give him a heads-up. It's all going to be okay. He just has a bit of a thing about you, and I need to talk him around."

"Do you need me to be there for support or anything?"

"That's really sweet, but no... I think I better field this

one on my own. Maybe Zoey and I can see you tomorrow, though?"

"Yeah, definitely. I'll try and get all my studying out of the way first thing in the morning, and then we can spend the rest of the day together. Would that work?"

"Yes." I can hear the smile in her voice, and it makes my lips twitch. "Zoey can always have her afternoon nap in her stroller. We can go for a walk or something."

"Sounds perfect."

"Looking forward to it already."

"Me too. Last night was…" I grin down at my sweaty uniform and shake my head with a no doubt dreamy smile.

"It was everything," she finishes for me, and I can picture her blue eyes sparkling the way I love so much.

"I love you, Sparks."

"I love you, Hot Lips."

I'm laughing as we say our final goodbyes and hang up. And then I must be blushing, because Wily walks past me at just the wrong second, and I am toast.

The number of hassles and jeers I have to put up with for the next ten minutes is ridiculous, and I end up giving them all the finger before stripping off my uniform and showering up.

The rest of the afternoon and evening is lost in celebration, but I don't stay up too late, because I have myself a pretty perfect afternoon lined up for tomorrow, and I want to make sure I'm ready for it.

CHAPTER 35
SIENNA

Dreams of Zander kept me entertained through the night, and I was already buzzing to see him by the time Zoey woke me. I couldn't wait for the afternoon to roll around so we could visit him again.

Getting up with a yawn and a stretch, I pull my pajama shorts down so I'm not exposing the curve of my butt and head into the hallway. Russell has already collected Zoey from her crib and is dancing around the kitchen singing with her in his arms.

She's giggling, resting her head on his shoulder and looking all kinds of cute with her messy bed hair. Her pink-and-purple dinosaur pajamas just add to the whole effect, and my heart blooms with affection.

Until Russell murmurs, "Dada's gonna make you pancakes, okay?"

"Pancakes!"

"Hey, nicely said. You're getting so good with your words, honey. Dada's proud of you."

Zoey smiles at him while my stomach twists into a tight knot.

"Morning, Uncle Rusty." I enunciate his name with more clarity than I ever have, giving him a tight smile as I breeze into the kitchen and speak to my daughter. "Is Uncle Rusty going to make you pancakes?"

"Yeah. Unca Russy." She rests her head on his shoulder again, and now my stomach is trembling.

At least she got his name right, though.

I'm really not loving his Dada bullshit, and I need to shut that down.

But that might naturally happen now that her *real* father is becoming a part of her life again.

"Pancakes, pancakes!" Zoey bobs in Russell's arms.

My roommate winks at me, passing Zoey over before pulling ingredients out of the pantry.

"How was the game last night?" I ask as Zoey wriggles out of my arms.

I place her on the ground, and she runs to the toys she was playing with before bedtime. The plastic dolls and animals bump together as she pulls them out of the toy box and sets up an imaginary scene.

Keeping my eyes on her, I half listen to his rundown of the hockey team's away game.

They lost, unfortunately, and his recount gets a little snippy.

"If they'd done it like I told them to at practice..." He shakes his head.

I flash him a quick grin. "That's not always possible. You never know what the other team is going to do, and they have to respond in the moment."

"Yeah, but I still think Bergeron is too soft on them. If I was head coach, I'd run a much tighter ship."

I raise my eyebrows, wondering what the players think of that. He probably hasn't said anything, but I can imagine he doesn't mind acting like head coach sometimes, and for a guy who's only a few years older than the senior players, I can't see that going over too well.

"If the players would just respect what I have to say a little more, then we wouldn't have had those screwups yesterday." He tuts. "I'll be having a word with them at practice tomorrow."

I nod and figure changing the subject to something more upbeat is a better way to lead into my news.

Cracking an egg into the bowl, I wait for him to add the milk, then start whisking them together. He sifts the flour, sugar, salt, and baking powder into a separate bowl while I worry my lip.

"So, what did you guys get up to while I was away? You cope okay without me?"

I laugh at his little wink and assure him. "We were fine."

"Foobawl!" Zoey calls from her spot on the floor.

Whipping my head to look at her, I bulge my eyes with a silent "be quiet!" but she's two! It's not like she can read my mind.

"You played football?" Russell laughs. "How? We don't even own one." Then he glances at me, his eyebrows dipping together. "You didn't buy her a football, did you? You know I want her to play hockey."

There goes my stomach, twisting all over again.

"That'd be up to her." I give him a firm look. "She can play whatever sport she wants."

"Yeah, just not football." His frown deepens. "Thank God she's a girl."

I can't help a soft scoff. "Girls can play football if they want to."

He snickers and shakes his head. "You're so cute."

Oh yeah? Well, I'm quickly feeling very un-cute and starting to get pissed at your sexist ass!

I wish I could say that to him, but I bite my lips together and hold it all in. I'm trying to keep things calm and light so I can tell him I'm back together with a man he hates for hurting me.

And yes, I appreciate that. But Zander and I have worked it out now, and he's not going to hurt me again. Just like I won't hurt him.

We're moving forward, and it'd be unfair not to let Russell know.

"So, um..." I push my big toe into the kitchen floor and gaze down at my purple nail polish while butter sizzles in the frying pan and Russell gets ready to pour the pancake mixture.

"So, um, what?" He forms a beautifully round pancake before turning to me with an affectionate smile. "You missed me, didn't you?"

"I..." Before I can even reply, he moves into my space, wrapping his arm around my waist and pulling me close. To say I feel kind of vulnerable in my skimpy shoestring pajama top is an understatement. I pull the neckline up to cover my boobs a little better and rest my hand on his chest, lightly pushing him away.

He doesn't seem to notice. He's too busy staring down at my face while I try to avoid direct eye contact. "I really missed you too. I know I'm going to hate every away game. I mean, I was even wondering if I can arrange for you guys to come next time, you know?"

"I... um... I wouldn't want to disrupt your routine. Or Zoey's," I quickly add, lightly nudging him back. "Is the pancake ready to flip?"

He glances over his shoulder. "Not quite yet."

My subtle attempts to get him off me aren't working, and I force another smile, wishing he'd let me go but not wanting to hurt his feelings either.

Ugh. The look on his face right now.

He seriously did miss me, and I'm suddenly super worried that it's in a very different way than I will ever miss him.

"Russell..." I let out a breath.

"Sienna," he whispers, leaning in like he's going to kiss me.

"Pancake!" I jerk away from him, lurching out of his arms and grabbing the spatula off the bench. "It's ready for flipping." My voice is high, my laughter deranged as I shove the spatula under the pancake and totally break it.

"It's not quite ready." Russell leans in behind me, wrapping his fingers around mine and helping me flip it.

Shit. This is bad.

You need to say something!

His breath skims my neck, and I lean away from him, glancing over my shoulder and inwardly shuddering at the affectionate glint in his eye. Until his eyebrows pucker and he reaches for my pajama top.

I slap my hand over the neckline, but he flicks my fingers away, hooking his finger into the fabric and pulling it to the side.

"What's that?" He slowly spins me around so he can

look at my skin. "Is that...?" His lips flatline, his eyes hardening as he stares at the top of my breast, obviously confused. "Is that a hickey?"

"Um." I glance down at Zander's mark and quickly cover it back up.

"Who gave you a hickey?"

"What's hickee?" Zoey wanders into the room with a plastic elephant in one hand and a curious look on her face.

"Uh... nothing." I jerk my eyes to Russell, who glares right back at me. "Does Mr. Elephant need a friend?" I point at the toy in her hand. "Why don't you see if you can line up five animals for me?" I hold up my hand, wiggling my fingers and desperately trying to buy myself some time.

Zoey looks at her fingers and wiggles them, then nods. "Five amimals. 'Kay." With a little skip, she hurries back to her toys and gets to work.

She's still only just learning to count, so it might take her a minute. That's all I can hope.

"Russell." I turn to my roommate.

He's standing at the stove, smacking the first pancake onto the plate with a growl. "Who gave you that, Sienna?"

"Look, I planned to talk to you about this today."

"Sienna, who?" He spins, his agitated glare making me shrink away from him.

I look to the floor and softly mumble, "Zander."

There's an awful, ugly pause that makes my skin prickle before he seethes, "What?"

Clearing my throat, I lift my chin and try to appear braver than I feel. I knew he was going to hate this, but his expression right now is making me queasy. "Zander and I worked things out."

"What the fuck?" His anger is being overridden by this horrified confusion. "You can't be serious."

"He came over on Friday, and we had a long talk. We managed to clear the air on a lot of things, and..." My lips twitch as my insides turn just a little mushy. "And now we're back together."

"Here?" Russell points to the floor. "He came here? To *my* house?"

"Well, I mean—"

"He gave you that in my house!" He points at my chest.

I place my hand over my cotton shirt, pressing it close to my skin.

"You had sex with him, didn't you?" Throwing the spatula into the sink, Russell leans against the counter like he needs support.

I swallow and struggle to figure out how I'm going to smooth things over.

Spinning back around, he gives me an incredulous glare and raises his voice a little higher. "I can't believe you had sex with that prick in my house!"

"Russell, please." I raise my hand, glancing into the living room to make sure Zoey's okay. She's looking our way, obviously confused by the fact that one of her favorite people is so angry. I spin back to try and placate him. "This is a good thing. I know you're mad about the way he treated me, but he's apologized. We've talked it through. He's explained what a mess he was and how out of control things got. He was missing me and—"

"Whatever," Russell scoffs. "Missing you? Are you fucking kidding me?"

I close my eyes with a sigh. "He wants to make up for the lost time, and... I want that too. He's the love of my life."

"Why?" Russell looks disgusted by the very idea. "The guy completely betrayed you. I can't believe you're even willing to trust him again. He's gonna hurt you. He'll cheat on you or he'll leave you, or something will happen that will break your heart all over again, and I can't watch that happen."

"He's not going to hurt me like that again. He loves me. He loves Zoey. He's her father."

"Well he shouldn't be!" Russell's eyes flash. "He doesn't deserve her. He doesn't deserve you!" His voice breaks as he snatches the pan off the stovetop and throws that in the sink as well.

It makes a noisy clatter and I flinch, crossing my arms, resisting the urge to bolt from the room.

"I'm the closest thing to a father Zoey's ever had. It should be me! Not him. Me!" He slaps his chest, then throws his arms wide. "God, how could you do that, Sienna?"

He looks completely wrecked, and I don't know what to say.

An uncomfortable minute ticks by that feels more like a millennium as I stand in the kitchen, curling my toes on the cold kitchen floor while he clenches his jaw and keeps shaking his head.

Zoey patters in, raising her arms for me to pick her up.

I hold her close, drawing comfort from her soft cheek

against mine. She plays with my hair at the nape of my neck, and I stare across the room at Russell.

He lets out a huff, gripping the counter behind him and muttering, "Look, this is my house. And I know you live here, too, but I should get a say in what goes on under my roof, and that guy is not spending any more nights here. In fact, you're not seeing him again."

"What?" I can't stop a surprised laugh popping out of me. "Russell, you can't..." I laugh a second time, shaking my head. "You can't say that to me. I can see whoever I want."

His nostrils flare as he gives me more headshaking and huffing.

I stand up a little straighter, a sudden spike of anger making my voice terse. "You're not the boss of me, and... I can't believe you're acting this way. You're treating me like a naughty teenager or something. I mean, I know you don't like him, but—"

"That's right." He moves like a snake, darting across the room, getting up in my face. Zoey clings to my neck, hiding her face while Russell spurts a little venom on me. "I don't like him. I despise him for the way he treated you. I mean, what the hell? Who the fuck leaves you?"

"Russell." I bulge my eyes at him. I don't like him talking this way around Zoey, so I cover her ears, giving him an urgent "Shh."

"You're making a huge mistake." He waves his finger at me. "And Zoey will end up paying the price for your selfish, sex-crazed, emotional behavior!"

Emotional? He thinks I'm *being emotional?*

I have never seen this side of Russell before, and I seriously do not like it.

Flashing my eyes at him, I start rubbing Zoey's back. She's whimpering against my shoulder. I hate that Russell is scaring her. She can feel the angry tension in the room, and I need to get her out of here.

"I'm gonna... go." I move to leave the kitchen. "Give you time to cool off."

He snatches my arm before I can leave.

I gasp in fright, his strong fingers digging into my skin.

"Great, so you're just going to walk out on this conversation? Real mature, Sienna."

The way he spits my name makes me want to slap him, and it takes everything in me not to bite back. By some miracle, I keep my tone calm and even. It helps that Zoey is quietly crying against my neck. I refuse to raise my voice around her and scare her even more than Russell has.

Licking my lips, I softly reply, "This isn't a conversation. This is you getting annoyed at me for no good reason. I haven't done anything wrong, and you can't control me like this. Now let me go."

"I'm just trying to protect you from your own idiocy and keep Zoey safe. You're not thinking straight. You're not thinking about her well-being!"

"I know what I'm doing, Russell. And she's *my* daughter. Not yours."

My words are an obvious blow, and he reels away from me like I just slapped him.

His chest heaves as he glares back at me and hisses, "You're gonna regret this."

I sigh and shake his hand off my arm.

"You will. And then you'll be back on my doorstep, crying and looking for help." Tapping his forehead, he looks like a slightly crazed version of the boy I grew up with. The one I always looked up to like an older brother. The guy who has helped me out so many times in the past.

But this version?

I don't know him... at all.

"You need to start using your head and stop following your emotional, brainless heart. You're wasting your time with him."

"That's my decision to make," I hiss, hating how much this is rattling me.

Spinning out of the kitchen, I storm to Zoey's room, but Russell follows me, bleating on about what a loser Zander is. Zoey starts to cry harder, and I decide to bail on getting us changed. Instead, I push past Russell to the front door, snatching the stroller and wrestling Zoey into it.

I don't even know where the car keys are right now. I just want to get out of this house!

Zoey's wailing incoherently, and Russell's still shouting.

I shove my sneakers on and unbolt the front door.

"No," Russell barks, snatching the stroller handle. "She's hungry. Leave her here."

"What?" I throw him a horrified glare.

"If you're making stupid decisions like this, she's better off with me."

"You're insane." I throw the door open and yank the stroller out of his grasp before wrestling it down the front steps and hitting the curb with a bump.

Zoey gets jostled and cries a little louder while Russell stands at the front door yelling at me.

"You can't just take her away from this safe haven. Where the hell are you gonna go? To him? To that football frat?" He spits out the words with such derision, and now I'm fighting my own tears as I push the stroller away from him.

"How could you be so selfish, Sienna? You're a shitty mother!"

Zoey lets out another loud wail and starts sobbing about elephants and "amimals."

"Amimals!" she screams and kicks her legs while I lose the battle with my tears and start running with the stroller, trying to get as much distance between me and Russell as possible.

Shit, I must look insane, running down the street in my Tweety Bird pajamas with a wailing baby.

As soon as I round the corner, I slow to a shuffle and try to pull myself together.

I don't want to be a shitty mother.

I want to do what's right for Zoey, and Russell's venom and accusations have completely thrown me.

Jerking the stroller to a stop, I crouch down and unearth a Vitamin C lollipop from Zoey's diaper bag. Hardly a healthy breakfast, but it might stop her crying. Unwrapping it with shaking fingers, I hand it over, and she pops it into her mouth with a soft whimper.

I clean up her face with a tissue and find the blanket I was supposed to wash. It's got a big stain on the front, but I wrap it around her legs, making sure she's warm enough as a breeze whistles through my skimpy pajamas.

Shit, it's cold this morning, but like hell I'm going back.

Reaching under the stroller, I rustle through the diaper bag and realize I left the better stocked one at Russell's. It's got everything in it, including my wallet and phone... and probably my car keys.

"Shit," I whisper under my breath, running my fingers through Zoey's curls and stressing over what to do.

It's still kind of early. Will Zander mind if I just show up unannounced?

He didn't seem to the other day.

Just do it, Sen. You need him... and so does Zoey.

I glance down at my daughter. She's stopped crying now, her big blue eyes staring up at me with all the trust in the world.

"Hey, should we go see Daddy?"

She blinks and doesn't say anything.

"Football. Football's your daddy."

It's a lot for the poor little thing to take in, but she pulls the lollipop out of her mouth and softly murmurs, "Foobawl."

"You wanna go see him and Wily?"

She nods, sticking the lollipop back into her mouth and resting her head on the edge of the stroller.

I kiss the top of her head, reminding her how much I love her before pushing her toward Football Frat and hoping I'm not making as big a mistake as Russell is convinced I am.

CHAPTER 36
ZANDER

I got up early, motivated to get through my workload so I could call Sienna as soon as I was done.

Loaded up with caffeine and nibbling on a bagel, I managed to get through two hours before the text on my screen and the pages started to blur.

I need a proper breakfast, but if I can power through, then I'll be free for the rest of the day. And I want to spend every second I can with Sienna and Zoey.

I'm stoked with my progress this morning and glad I skipped my one sleep-in this week.

The essay I have to get written for my sports psychology class is almost finished. I just need to proof it and make any final tweaks.

I'm now free to jot down some game analysis notes. I don't normally do this, but I want to impress Coach Jones after my serious fuckup on the field. Yes, we won. Yes, I dominated for most of the game, but that first pass... he saw right through that shit, and I need to prove to him that I can be in a relationship and still focus on the game.

My plan is to have a meeting with him next week, update him on my personal life—because the guy has always had my back, and he cares about his players that way—and then talk through strategies of how to make the most of my season.

He's been going the extra mile and helping any players who are keen to take this to the next level prepare for the scouting combine in February. It's going to be the week of our lives. This is what we've been working for all along. Wily's going to ace it. He was born to play ball, and I guarantee there will be teams vying for him.

Me?

I've got a decent shot—according to Coach—but there are no guarantees.

I can't go screwing things up.

But I can't turn my back on Sienna and Zoey either.

I have to find a way to have both.

And I can.

I will.

My parents might say otherwise, but...

I shake my head and glance at my phone. I turned it off last night before I went to bed. Dad will be calling today. It's inevitable. He always loves to do our own little postgame analysis, and it's painful. He'd already told me he couldn't watch the game yesterday due to work commitments, but he will have recorded it and watched it last night, no doubt taking notes so he can have a long string of criticism to load me down with.

Brushing my thumb over my black phone screen, I shake my head.

I sit through that damn conversation every week, doing

my best to keep the peace. Occasionally what he says is really helpful. Most of the time it's nitpicky, and more often than not, he has my muscles tensing with irritation.

He's going to be all over me after that awful pass, and he'll want to know why.

I can't tell him.

Not yet.

Shit, he's going to hit the fucking roof.

I clench my jaw, tapping my thumb on the phone screen. I'm hoping Sienna isn't trying to call me, but it's first thing in the morning, and she might not even be up yet. If she is, she's probably padding around the house in those Tweety pajamas with a sleepy smile while Zoey plays at her feet.

I gaze out the window, loving the image in my mind's eye. Shit, how can something be so sexy and adorable at the same time? My woman.

I grin, but my smile fades when I think ahead to the conversation she's going to have with Russell today. I hope that jackass doesn't make it hard for her. If he's got a problem, he can speak with me.

The thought sends a spike of unease shooting through me, and I nearly switch my phone on, but...

Dad might call.

And I have to get this done.

"Focus. One thing at a time."

I'll give this one more hour, and then Sienna can have the rest of my day. I'll call her as soon as I'm done and do whatever she needs me to.

If I can just get some notes down on yesterday's game, I might be able to speed up my call with Dad. He'll be able to see that I thought it through, and I can hopefully counter some of his points.

Typing everything I can remember, I take full ownership of my shitty pass and list some possible ways not to make that mistake again. I pull up old seminar notes and videos I've watched on mental conditioning. I should have put some of those strategies into practice yesterday, and I didn't. I'll spend more time on it before the next game.

Pulling up the schedule, I scan ahead to the upcoming teams we're facing, and my gut sinks when I spot the Kelsey U Titans. We're playing them in early November, and I'm already dreading the game. Last year was total shit. They were out to demolish me, and I got bashed around so badly that Coach pulled me for the second half of the game. He was furious. They played dirty and mean, and they were obviously targeting me. The offensive line was spent trying to protect me, and Coach wanted me off the field to give everyone a break.

"Their tactics are underhanded. It's why I chose to leave the first chance I got. Don't lower yourselves to their level," he warned the rest of the team at halftime. "You go out there, and you beat them fair and square."

We didn't.

It was our biggest loss of the season.

But that's not going to happen this year.

We're going to face those fuckers, and we're going to win.

My nostrils flare as I keep pounding my keyboard and making sure I'm doing everything in my power to be in perfect form for that November game.

I get so absorbed in what I'm doing that I'm only

vaguely aware of the knock at the front door. One of the other guys will get it.

It's no doubt some chick here to see Carson... or Carson himself because he forgot his key again and no one's been downstairs to unlock the door yet.

I roll my eyes, shaking my head and focusing back on the screen in front of me.

CHAPTER 37
SIENNA

It takes ages for someone to answer the door, and for a second, I worry that I got the wrong house.

But there's a Harley Davidson parked in the drive, so I knock again and cross my fingers.

Zoey's stopped crying now. Her lollipop is all gone and she's probably still hungry, but she's distracted by what I'm doing. I've left the stroller at the bottom of the stairs, and she's in my arms.

It's frickin' freezing out here, and I'm wearing next to nothing. Thank God the streets were basically empty as I hurried here. Even so, I'm shivering while trying to wrap the dirty blanket more securely around my daughter.

I can't believe I let Russell drive me out like that. I should have used my brain and taken the time to at least get dressed and grab a coat, my wallet, and keys. I just mindlessly walked out the door because I couldn't stand another second of him.

And now my insides are turning blue and my skin is covered in goose bumps.

We're at that time of year where you almost need thermals in the morning and shorts and T-shirts in the afternoon. I love and hate fall weather.

At least the leaves are pretty, though.

I glance at the lawn behind us, scattered with browns, reds, and yellows. Idyllic. Like a painting with this villa in the background.

But that doesn't change the fact that I'm freezing my ass off out here.

Knocking on the door for the third time, I finally hear someone shout, "Would someone get the damn door!"

"All right!" someone else shouts, and Zoey tenses in my arms as the door swings open and we're staring up at grumpy-looking scarecrow.

His hair is a wild mess, his refined face made even more angular by the blurry-eyed scowl he's wearing. His jeans hang low on his hips, ripped and scrappy, while the open shirt he's wearing looks—and smells—like it could use a decent wash.

I take a small step away from the door and wonder if I'm about to start running down a second lot of front steps today.

"What do you want?" His voice is husky, but not in the sweet sexy way Zander's is. It's more like a gravelly growl, and the way his eyes are traveling down my body puts me on edge.

"Oh, um... I'm... uh... I'm looking for Zander. Zander Donohue."

The man gives me a quizzical frown, shooting his gaze to Zoey before narrowing his eyes on me again.

Tears quickly start to burn my senses and I blink, begging them not to fall as I take another step back and start babbling. "I'm sorry, do I have the wrong house? I thought this was Football Frat. I was here not long ago, and it looks familiar, and the—"

A large body appears behind Mr. Scarecrow, and I deflate with relief the second I spot Wily's smile.

"Hey, Sienna." I could just about kiss that wide grin of his. *Oh, thank God.* "And my lil' cowgirl."

Zoey giggles.

"Come to Uncle Wily, kid!"

He reaches for my daughter, and she goes to him willingly, smiling when he hands her his football, then starts complimenting her dinosaur pajamas.

"I wish I had a pair of those. They look super comfy." He turns back to wink at me, but his smile drops away when he notices that I'm in my pajamas, too, and my teeth are chattering. "Carson, move." He shoulders the guy aside and beckons me to come in. "You're freezing. Here." Leading me into a living room area, he grabs a blanket off the back of the couch and wraps it around me.

Carson's now standing in the archway, leaning against the oak frame and studying me like I'm a big problem. His eyes dart to Zoey again, and his frown only deepens. I bite my bottom lip, wrapping the blanket a little tighter around myself, then sending a silent SOS to Wily.

He rolls his eyes and pulls me into a side hug. "Don't mind him. He's going for the Prick of the Year Award."

"Dick," the scarecrow scoffs and saunters out of the room, shouting up the stairs. "Zan, you've got company!"

I tense against Wily's side until I hear Zander's faint reply. "Cool. Down in a sec."

Wily gives my shoulder a light squeeze before letting me go. "Have you guys had breakfast yet? Grady's making pancakes if you want some. I'll tell him to make some extra if you're staying."

"Are you sure that's okay if we do?" I dart my eyes to Carson's retreating back.

"Of course it is." Wily rubs my arm, obviously trying to warm me up while smiling at Zoey. "Inviting two pretty ladies to stay for breakfast is most definitely okay. You like pancakes, cowgirl?"

She nods, hugging his football like a teddy bear, then giggling when he starts making silly faces.

I let out a watery laugh, so incredibly grateful for Wily right now.

He gives me a worried smile, his hand slowing to soft circles on my back. "You okay?"

Forcing a nod and a smile that feels anything but genuine, I softly murmur, "Yeah, I'm fine."

"Little liar." He winks at me and then glances toward the archway as footsteps sound on the stairwell.

"Foobawl!" Zoey points at Zander the second he appears.

His face lights with a grin as she wiggles out of Wily's arms and runs over to him. She's still holding Wily's football, and Zander picks them both up with a laugh. "Hey, pretty girl. I didn't know you were coming to see me this morning. This is the best surprise."

My insides get all mushy as I watch this man with our daughter and know I've done the right thing by coming here.

He looks at me, all lit up like a Christmas tree until he spots my face. Then his eyes skim down my body, and he suddenly registers what I'm wearing.

His smile slips away in an instant and he's walking

across the room, his steps quick, deep concern making his voice thick. "What happened?"

"I..." I shake my head, tears getting the better of me. Now that he's here, now that I'm safe and I can lean against him and let it all out, my body shudders and a pitiful whimper pops out of my mouth.

The second I rest my head against his shoulder, his arm comes around me and I'm cocooned to his side.

"Hey, cowgirl, let's go see how Grady's getting on with those pancakes." Wily reaches out to take her.

"Mommy." She sounds worried.

"It's okay, Zoey. I've got Mommy. I'll bring her through to the kitchen in just a minute, okay?" Zander's voice is so soft and sweet it sends a wave of fresh tears coursing through me. "Do you think you can make a pancake for her? If I remember right, Mommy loves lots of butter and maple syrup."

I smile and nod against his shoulder.

"Come on, let's go." Wily takes Zoey, and the second Zander's arms are free, he's pulling me flush against him and cradling the back of my head.

"Talk to me, Sparks. What happened?"

I suck in a breath that sounds more like a sob, and he holds me that much tighter, his strength and powerful body bringing me instant comfort.

He brushes his lips across my head. "It must have been bad if you left the house in nothing but your pajamas. Did you have a fight with Russell or something?"

I nod. "It's never happened before. We've always gotten along so great, you know? But I tried to tell him about you and me, and he just lost it." My voice pitches. "He was so pissed that we'd done it in his house."

"You told him we had sex?" Zander sounds surprised. "Please tell me you didn't lead with that."

I let out a whimpering laugh at his teasing and lightly slap his side. "He saw the hickey, and it all just kind of spilled out."

"Saw your hickey how?" He pulls back, checking the positioning and then looking ready to throttle something.

I swallow, worried I'm gonna be facing another meltdown if I don't word this carefully. Stepping back from Zander, I wrap the blanket tightly around myself and whisper, "We were making pancakes in the kitchen, and..."

He was standing too close.

He was thinking we were something that we're not!

How do I say that to Zander right now? His eyes are bright with this intensity that I don't feel strong enough to handle.

My expression buckles, my chin trembling as Zander closes his eyes with a soft sigh. "Just tell me he didn't do anything totally inappropriate. Give me a reason not to go over there and slay his ass for touching you."

I bite my lips together and sniff. "He just spotted the edge of it under my shirt. These pajamas don't exactly hide much."

Zander looks pained as he opens his eyes and stares at me. "Do you have to wear them around him?" He cringes. "And I know I'm a total dick for saying that. You should be able to wear whatever the fuck you want, but the idea of that asshole looking at you makes me see red, baby. I'm sorry."

"It's okay." I shake my head, the right side of my

mouth curling up. "I'd never let him touch me that way. I've only ever been yours."

He grunts, reaching out to tug the edge of the blanket and pull me against him again. "I don't want him making you uncomfortable. He drove you out of the house wearing only this, and you look completely wrecked. And freezing."

Tucking me even tighter against him, he rubs my back vigorously, pressing his warm cheek against my cold one. I snuggle into his cocoon and murmur against his shoulder, "I knew it was going to be hard to tell him about us, but he was..." I sniff and rest my head into the crook of his neck. "I've never seen him like that before. He was so *angry*."

"He didn't hurt you, did he?"

"No, he wasn't physical. He was just vile with his words, telling me that I was making a huge mistake and that you weren't allowed in his house ever again. He doesn't want me seeing you." My voice starts to flail. "And that I'm a terrible mother because you're going to hurt me and Zoey." The words break apart as I let out another sob.

"That's bullshit." Zander leans away so he can look me in the eye and swipe my tears with his thumbs. "You're not a terrible mother. You're amazing. That's got nothing to do with me and everything to do with you."

His voice is so assertive. So sure.

"And as for me... I'm not going to hurt you, and I'd rather die than do anything to hurt Zoey. I love you. I love her. I know I haven't known her that long, but seriously, Sen. I love her, because she's part of you and part of me. And I mean, she's adorable. It took her all of two seconds to steal my heart. I thought she was the cutest kid I'd ever met, and that was before I knew she was ours."

I sniff, smiling at his sweet words. "Thank you."

His swallow is thick as he gazes down at me like I matter. "Russell's wrong. And I'm..." He clenches his jaw. "I'm so fucking riled that he treated you that way."

"It's o—"

"No, it's not okay, Sen. He yelled at you. He bossed you around. He disrespected you. He scared you enough that you felt you had to rush out the door. And that is *not* okay. No one treats my woman like that."

My heart gives a happy little squeeze until worry starts to override the pleasant sensation.

"I just don't want you getting into it with him. I... that's..." I shake my head. "Please promise me you won't. I can't worry about that too. He's a staff member and you're still a student, and you've got your career to think about and..."

"I won't do anything stupid," he assures me. "I'm just telling you I want to."

Closing my eyes with a relieved smile, I nod and then get a pleasant surprise when his lips land on mine.

"Mmm." I lean into the kiss, the blanket dropping off my shoulders as I wrap my arms around him and let myself get lost for just a moment.

My tears melt away as he brushes his tongue along mine and holds me close.

I love this man.

I love him so much.

"Pancakes!" someone shouts in the entryway.

It gives me a fright and I jump in Zander's arms, then

start laughing when Grady walks out in sweats and an apron.

"Stop making out and come eat!" He uses the spatula to whack Zander on the ass, then jumps away with a grin when Zander chases after him.

I wrap the blanket back around me and follow them into the kitchen, smiling at Wily, who has Zoey on his knee. He's feeding her small pieces of pancake while explaining the rules of football.

She has no idea what he's saying, but she's too happy filling her little belly to care.

"Mommy." She points at me, then laughs at the two guys laughing and tussling behind me. "Siwwy."

"That's right, Zo. Those boys are silly." I wink and then laugh as Zander pings up straight, shoving Grady away from him and winking at our daughter.

She grins and holds her hands up to be taken.

"One sec, beautiful." He holds up his finger, taking off his hoodie and swapping out the blanket. He even does up the zipper like I'm a toddler who can't. It's adorably sweet.

I'm now swamped by this warm, soft fabric. Pulling it up to my nose, I take a whiff of his delectable scent and grin at him. He gives me a quick kiss before turning to take Zoey off Wily's lap.

"Did you make Mommy a pancake?"

"Uh-huh." She points down at her plate, which has about three mouthfuls of pancake left.

"You made Mommy's pancake, then ate it?" Zander starts tickling her belly, and she giggles and squirms, tipping her head back with glee.

I laugh and pull out a chair, smiling up at Grady as he

places a fresh pancake on the plate in front of me. "Thank you."

"My pleasure." His friendly wink makes me warm, and I spin back to find Wily grinning at me across the table.

Yeah, I think my day has just gotten a million times better.

Shoving up Zander's ginormous sleeves, I wrestle to reach stuff without dragging his hoodie through sticky maple syrup or melting butter.

Zoey keeps sitting on his knee, poking holes in his pancake with her finger, then licking the maple syrup off her sticky digits.

Zander doesn't seem to mind, and I can't help tipping my head and murmuring, "You like Daddy's knee, don't you?"

Zoey looks at me, resting her head against Zander's chest. "Daadee."

Zander goes still, his fork poised in midair, his eyes rounding to dinner plates as he looks at me. They start to glisten, and I smile back at him, biting my bottom lip and feeling my own eyes burn.

I'm still not sure if Zoey knows exactly what she's saying, and there's a strong chance he's going to be Foobawl again next time she wants to get his attention, but... holy shit.

She just said Daddy.

And it was to the right man.

The only man.

CHAPTER 38
ZANDER

I'm pretty sure I stopped breathing the second my little girl leaned her head on my chest and said, "Daadee," in the sweetest voice known to man.

I think I'm about to fucking cry, and it's taking everything in me to swallow this boulder in my throat.

Cupping the back of my daughter's head, I give her a little kiss and murmur into her curls, "Love you, Zoey."

I'm not sure she hears me, because she starts humming and resumes her pancake-poking routine, but I will eat Swiss cheese pancakes for the rest of my life if I get to hear her call me Daddy again.

Holy shit.

Sienna brushes her fingers across the back of my hand, her smile on full beam. When she goes to pull away, I grab her hand and kiss her knuckles.

She smiles and sucks in a shaky breath. "Hey, is there any chance we could stay here tonight?" The second she asks the question, she blanches, cringing and looking down at the table. "I'm sorry. I didn't mean to blurt it like that. There's no pressure. I just—"

"Of course you can." I stop her before she gets too worked up. "You can stay for as long as you want."

Her eyebrows rise, and she looks around the kitchen. "You guys won't mind?"

Grady shrugs. "Teah sleeps over all the time."

"Teah doesn't have a two-year-old." Sienna cringes again, and I laugh and shake my head.

"Okay, so this will be the first time we've had a kid staying here, but..." I look down at my little girl. "You melt hearts, don't you, sweetie?"

"Uh-huh." She nods, obviously not knowing what I'm asking, and it makes Sienna laugh.

Zoey glances at her mom, sees her laughing, and quickly joins in, which in turn makes me and the guys start laughing too.

She really is the cutest kid.

Wily stands from his chair, towering over us as he carries his plate to the sink. "If you're gonna stay, you'll probably want to get some more stuff, right?"

Sienna slumps back in her seat, looking worried.

"I can go," I offer.

"No way." Her eyes bulge. "I don't want you anywhere near that place. If he's home, it'll be a nightmare. I'll just walk back and get some stuff."

"Why didn't you drive here?" I spear another mouthful of pancake with my fork.

"I couldn't find my keys," she murmurs. "I think they're in Zoey's other diaper bag along with my wallet and phone." She covers her face with a groan. "I wasn't thinking straight, and I didn't want to start looking for it. Plus..." She makes a face. "It's actually Russell's car I've been using. I was supposed to get my parents' when they left on their trip, but it was acting up, and in the end Russell told me I could just use his, and..." She shakes her head and finishes with a mumbled "You don't need to know all of this."

"I can drive you back there." Wily smiles down at Sienna.

I spin in my seat, eyeing him up. "You'll look after her?"

"Of course I will." He shoots me an incredulous frown. "I'll even take Tyrell. A little bulk flanking her might not be a bad idea."

"He's not going to hurt me," Sienna assures us, but none of my teammates give a fuck. The guy is on our shit list now, and she's not going back to that house without serious backup.

"He made you walk out in the cold in nothing but your pajamas." Grady crosses his arms, making his defined biceps look even bigger and stronger. Good. I want her to see how safe she is here.

Sienna dips her eyes and softly murmurs, "I chose to walk out that way."

"He must have done something to make you leave in such a hurry." Wily flicks his hand in the air. "Plus, he made you cry. What a dou—" His eyes dart to Zoey, and he clears his throat. "What a dingleberry."

Sienna lets out a weak laugh and rubs her arm, massaging her bicep for a second. A hot flash burns through me as I worry that Russell grabbed her, tried to intimidate her even more. I don't want her going back there, but like fuck I'm gonna order her around the way he did this morning.

That shithead!

Resting my hand lightly over hers, I catch her eye and hide all my angst with a soft question. "What do you want to do, Sparks?"

She sucks in a shaky breath and lets it out slowly, bobbing her head and answering with a slight quaver that has me riled all over again. "I'll go back and get some things. It'll be okay. But..." She glances at Wily. "Are you sure you don't mind coming with me?"

Wily wipes his hands on a dish towel, his smile growing big and confident. "It would be my pleasure. Let me go get Tyrell too." His face lights with glee. "Ooo, this is gonna be fun!"

"I don't want..." Sienna's words trail off as Wily dashes out of the kitchen, and I give her hand a reassuring squeeze.

"Don't worry. They'll be good."

She lets out an edgy laugh, then asks, "Do you mind if I leave Zoey here?"

Oh shit, really? She wants me to watch Zoey... without her?

The thought makes me instantly nervous, but like hell I'm saying no. I've got to prove myself to this woman, and Zoey seems to like me. She called me Daadee, didn't she? I can do this without any harm coming to her. Right?

"Yeah, of course." I try to sound more confident than I feel, and this seems to ease Sienna's worry.

"Thank you so much."

Taking Zoey's hand, she blows a raspberry into our

daughter's palm, making her giggle before telling her the plan.

"I have to go and get some clothes from Uncle Rusty's place. And I'll get some toys and your pack-n-play." She leans forward, her eyes dancing playfully. "We're gonna have a sleepover with Daddy. Does that sound like fun?"

It takes a moment for that to sink in, but then she starts to nod and point at me. "Pay Foobawl?"

"Yeah, he'll play with you." Sienna nods. "He's going to watch you while I go get some of our things."

Glancing up at me, Zoey studies my face before giving me a cheesy smile.

I smile right back, kissing the tip of her nose and making her giggle again.

Holding her hand up, she squeezes her fingers open and shut. "Bye-bye, Mommy."

"Bye, my lil' lovebug. I'll be back soon." Sienna kisses Zoey's cheek, wiping sticky syrup off her lips before giving me a nervous smile.

"Do I get a kiss too?"

"Always." She grins, brushing her lips against mine in a chaste kiss. Even that's enough to keep me going until she gets back.

I watch her rise from her seat, tugging down my hoodie. I love the way it shrouds her. Her beautiful legs are still very much on display, but at least she'll be a little warmer. I would offer her some pants, but I don't think anything in this house will fit her slight frame.

Picking up Zoey, we walk Sienna to the door, and I watch her pile into Wily's truck with Tyrell in the back seat. The guy has obviously just woken up, but I'm grateful that he's going without question, ready to protect my woman.

Holding Zoey in my arms, we wave them off. Then I look down at the sticky-faced toddler and wonder what the heck I'm supposed to do with her until Mommy gets back.

She gives me a sweet, innocent smile, then lets one rip... and I'm pretty sure that wasn't just a fart.

Sniffing the air, I grimace and put on a brave smile.

"Let's hope there are some diapers in your stroller, huh?"

"Poos." Zoey wrinkles her nose.

"Yep. Pretty sure that's what I'm smelling." Shaking my head, I walk down to the stroller, grabbing the diaper bag out of the bottom and muttering to myself.

Welcome to fatherhood, dude.

CHAPTER 39
SIENNA

My heart is racing as we drive toward Russell's house. I can't believe he spoke to me that way this morning. His venom was frightening, and I'm kind of glad I'll have these two big football players to protect me. But I'm also worried.

They're students.

Russell's faculty.

I don't want them getting into trouble for me.

Which is why after I direct Wily to the closest parking spot, I say, "You guys can wait here if you want. I'll be as fast as I can."

They both snicker like I just said something funny and then open their respective doors.

I frown, worry taking huge chunks out of my stomach as I shuffle to the front door on stiff legs.

Walking up the two front steps, I knock on the door, then let myself in.

"Russell?" I call, creeping slowly into the house. "It's me."

"Thank God," I hear muttered from the hallway, and then he appears, pushing up his shirt sleeves with a smile, until he notices the two big guys behind me. "Where's Zoey?"

I swallow, fidgeting with my fingers as I reply in barely a whisper. "She's with Zander."

"What!" His bark is fierce, and I flinch in spite of the fact that I'm trying to be brave. I don't want to get into another argument with him.

I hate feeling this fragile, but this morning has totally thrown me.

"Sienna, how could you leave our girl with that jackass?"

Closing my eyes, I hold fast to the anger spiking through me. "He's her father, and he's really good with her. I trust him."

He scoffs like I'm insane, then flicks his hand at the muscle standing behind me. "And who the fuck are these guys? I didn't invite you into my house. Get the hell out of here!"

"Russell." I raise my hands to try and calm him. "They're just here to help me carry some stuff, okay?"

"Carry stuff?" His incredulous expression would be funny if I didn't know there was a volcanic eruption brewing.

God, help me!

Licking my lips, I shuffle back until I can feel Wily's hand lightly steady my lower back.

"She's staying the night at our place," a low voice rumbles behind me.

I glance over my shoulder and look up at Tyrell. His steely expression leaves no room for argument, and I practically shudder with relief until Russell starts barking.

"The fuck she is! Zoey is not spending the night at some football frat house. Sienna, are you out of your fucking mind?" He starts tapping the side of his head and thunders toward me. "You can't do this. She belongs here. With me. Are you seriously saying you're going to make her spend the night with a bunch of idiot football players?"

"She's safe. And they're not idiots."

"You don't even know them!"

"I feel like I don't know you right now!" I bite back and go to move around him, but he cinches my arm and tugs me toward him.

"Just listen to me. I—"

"Don't touch her." Tyrell's soft growl is about as chilling as the death glare on Wily's face right now.

I didn't even know the friendly blond was capable of such an expression, but my eyes round as he moves toward us like lightning and quickly wrenches Russell off me.

"Hey," Russell snaps. "Watch it. I'll report you to campus police if you're not careful. Or better yet, I'll call the fucking cops. You two are trespassing right now. I didn't invite you into my home, so get the fuck out."

"We're not leaving her alone with you, and if the cops show up, I can tell them exactly how you're manhandling this woman and scaring her," Wily argues.

Russell lifts his chin, his nostrils flaring as he points between the two of them. "This is none of your business."

He looks so short next to them it almost makes me laugh. Almost.

Inching farther away, I cross my arms and watch his eyes flash bright with anger.

"You don't even know what's going on here, so stay the fuck out of it! This is between me and Sienna."

Tyrell crosses his arms and moves in, his deep voice rumbling. "We're not going to stop you from talking to her, but you don't touch her, and you sure as shit don't insult her."

"Or us," Wily adds with a growl before glancing at me, his expression softening, his voice a sweet lilt. "Why don't you grab your stuff? We'll help you carry it to the truck."

"This is insane," Russell mutters, his sharp gaze landing back on me. "You're moving out?"

"I'm staying the night with my boyfriend." I give him a pointed look. "And so is Zoey."

"Why?" He trails me to my bedroom. "Seriously, Sen, I don't understand what's going on here. Zander Donohue is no more than a sperm donor. He's not worthy of you."

I roll my eyes, snatching a pair of baggy sweats off my bedroom floor and pulling them on. "I've already told you, we worked things out."

"He's gonna hurt you again," he snaps. "And Zoey will get caught in the crossfire. I'm more worried about her than anything."

Gritting my teeth, I snatch an empty bag out of my closet and start loading it up.

"Come on." Russell's voice takes on a whiny edge while Wily walks into my room and stands guard like a watchdog.

Tyrell hovers in my doorway, ready to pounce into action.

Their presence riles my housemate, but I don't want to ask them to move. I kind of like having them close by. It makes me feel safe. Which is weird, because mere weeks ago, I would have said Russell was my safety net. But he can't hold a candle to these big football players.

My hands start to shake as I snap my underwear drawer open and snatch out handfuls of socks and panties. I'm definitely packing for more than one night. I know I shouldn't, but I can't help it. The thought of coming back here and having to listen to more of Russell's shit is abhorrent.

"I can't believe you're not willing to see reason on this. That guy nearly destroyed you. He stomped all over your heart. I would never do something like that. I've been there since day one. I was there when Zoey was born!"

"No, you weren't." I spin to face him. "My parents were, and you popped by a few days later to meet her. You're not her father, Russell!"

"I'm the closest thing she has to one!" His arms flick up, then slap back against his thighs as he huffs and obviously wants to pace but can't. My room isn't big enough with two burly football players as well. "You can't just take her away from me."

"I'm not." My voice pitches as exasperation gets the better of me. "I'm spending the night with Zander, okay? And I'm doing that because you are being completely unreasonable about this entire thing. I'm not a child, and you can't boss me around like one. I really appreciate that you let me move in with you while my parents are away, but that doesn't make you an authority over me or Zoey!"

Pushing past him, I hand my bag to Tyrell and head down the hall to Zoey's room.

Russell huffs after me, snatching her suitcase out of my hands when I go to place it on the bed.

"Hey!" Wily barks, grabbing it off him and carefully laying down the pink unicorn case like it's a rare, ancient artifact.

Russell growls in his throat, his look lethal as he glares at Wily, then turns back to me.

I ignore his stare and quickly pack Zoey's things. She needs so much freaking stuff, it's going to take longer than my room, but like hell I'm forgetting anything.

Grabbing her favorite books and stuffed animals, I throw those on top of her clothes, then bend down to wrestle the portable crib out of the closest.

"Here, let me help." Wily takes over, and I brush the hair off my face with a grateful smile.

Russell scoffs and shakes his head. "You're making a mistake."

"I've stopped listening to you. This is happening whether you want it to or not."

My words seem to finally hit home, because his shoulders deflate and his vibrant anger is replaced with a sorrowful desperation. "Look, I'm sorry, okay? I'm just worried about you and Zoey. I want you to be happy and safe."

"I will be both of those things where I'm going," I assure him, catching his eye and hoping he can see how much I mean it.

"Please, please don't leave." He blocks my way when I try to get back to Zoey's closet.

"Russell."

"I'm sorry." His voice cracks. "I'm just going a little crazy here, because I've only ever heard you talk shit about Zander."

"That's not true."

"After he hurt you, you made him seem like the devil incarnate."

Guilt pinches me for a second, but I justify it with the truth. "I always loved him. Even through all my pain. Even when I *wanted* to hate him, I couldn't stop loving him. And now we've worked it out, and we're back together. Why can't you just be happy for me?"

"Because I don't trust him." His eyes wash with concern and... is he fighting tears right now? "Please, please, don't take Zoey away from me."

"I'm not doing that. We're spending a night or two with Zander. You're still going to see her, okay? But if you won't let Zander come here, then I'm going to go to him."

Russell's expression hardens, giving me a serious case of whiplash.

I have never seen him like this before, and I don't like it.

I mean, sure, he used to lose his shit on the ice in college, and Celeste told me he'd have mega meltdowns at home sometimes, but I always thought she was exaggerating. Maybe she wasn't. All I know for sure is that his anger has never been directed at me before, and it freaks me out.

With a sad sigh, I zip up Zoey's suitcase and start for the door.

He tries to block my path, but a gentle nudge back from Tyrell gets me through unscathed.

Russell stays in Zoey's room while I collect some of

her toys from the living area and find her diaper bag under the coffee table. My phone, wallet, and keys are tucked into it, and I nearly ask Russell if I can please take his car. But I value my life, so it looks like Zoey and I will be walking everywhere for the next few days.

I pass Tyrell the last of Zoey's things to put in the truck, then turn back to call out, "See ya, Rusty. Give me a call when you've calmed down and I'll bring Zoey over for a playdate."

He appears in the doorway, his eyes glistening as he gives me a silent nod.

Then I walk out the door on quaking limbs.

I don't know what to feel as I slip into Wily's truck.

Russell's always been an older brother to me, but he obviously saw me differently, and now I'm tearing holes in his world. I don't know whether to feel guilty or relieved that I've left.

Ugh. This is all just sitting so bleak and ugly in my chest.

Why couldn't he just be happy for me?

Why did he have to treat Zander like some kind of supervillain?

Shit, how badly did I really talk about him as I was processing what I saw in that dorm at Kelsey U?

He's not going to do that to me again, though, right?

He's changed. He regrets what happened. He wants me back.

Curling my fingers into two tight fists on my lap, I keep my gaze focused out the window and am grateful Wily and Tyrell aren't saying a thing to try and make me feel better.

I need this silence so I can stew... and convince myself that I'm right and Russell is 100 percent wrong.

CHAPTER 40
ZANDER

Zoey's stench permeated the entire upper floor. It didn't help that it took me forever to change her diaper. It was the foulest thing I've ever done, and I ended up breaking the first diaper by ripping the tabs too hard. Then she got all wriggly on me, and I had to chase her naked little butt around my room before I could snag her and get her giggling ass into a fresh diaper.

I was exhausted by the end of it all, and Carson was livid.

He left the house in a huge huff, complaining about the smell. I managed to cut his rant short with a few gruff words. I didn't want him scaring Zoey or making her feel bad.

"Just get that shit out of here!" he whisper-barked in my face before thundering down the stairs and slamming the front door shut.

Zoey flinched and her bottom lip began to wobble, but I quickly distracted her by dancing her down the stairs and outside. We played in the backyard for a bit, running through leaves and then trying to find the biggest one we could. I turned it into a fan, and Zoey jumped and giggled at my feet, reaching up for it and wanting to fan me back.

I crouched low and grinned at her as she fanned me with the leaf, then managed to smear my face with dirt.

I was just wiping it off when my phone started buzzing. Assuming it was Sienna, I answered it without taking my eyes off Zoey.

"How's it going, Mommy?" I wanted to keep my voice bright and upbeat despite the tension in my chest. I sure as shit hoped Wily and Tyrell were protecting her.

"It's your father, and this is a video chat. Why am I staring at your cheek right now?"

Oh shit!

Pulling the phone away, I pop to my feet, blinking at my father on the screen and quickly trying to cover my faux pas. "Oh... uh... hi. Hi, Dad. How's it going?"

His eyes narrow, and I put on my best smile before stealing a glance at Zoey, who is now collecting leaves like a bouquet.

She is seriously the cutest.

"I wanted to go over your game yesterday."

"Yeah, I know." I wince. "It's just not a great time right now."

"Why?"

"Well, I'm... busy."

"You look like you're standing in your backyard. Why, I have no idea, but I'm guessing you've got time."

"Yeah, I just, uh—"

"Now, the game." Dad gets right down to business while I scratch the back of my neck and wait for the hammer to fall. "Thankfully, your second half was golden, but what the fuck was up with that pass in the first quarter? Zander, it was just plain embarrassing, and I—"

"Foobawl, look!" Zoey yells, running over to me with a bouquet of leaves. Her expression is so triumphant, I can't help an adoring grin...

And my father sees it all.

"Zander, what's going on? What the hell is foobawl?"

"I am." I let out a soft laugh, then swallow, my insides turning to cooked spaghetti when I look at my phone screen. Dad's stern face has always been intimidating. Even as an adult I find it unnerving, but he's miles away, and fuck it... I'm just gonna have to tell him the truth.

Why delay the inevitable, right?

With a swallow, I explain. "Zoey calls me football."

I wink down at her and she grins, her nose scrunching just the way Sienna's does.

"Who the hell is Zoey?" There's a dangerous edge to Dad's tone, but I try not to let it rattle me.

Licking my bottom lip, I face the one person in my life who I know will hate this the most and just say it. "Zoey's my daughter."

Dad goes instantly pale. I can practically see the blood draining from his face as I get out all the details he probably doesn't want to hear.

"Sienna had a kid. I didn't know she was pregnant. I only found out a few weeks ago, and—"

"Wait," Dad snaps.

I cringe, holding my breath even though I hate myself for feeling like a little kid about to get bawled out by his old man.

"Let me dial your mother in."

Shit. Well, this just keeps getting better, doesn't it?

Clenching my jaw, I crouch down when Zoey starts tugging on my pant leg and try to hide my angst with a broad smile. "Those are so pretty."

"Fowers!" She holds them out.

"Leaves," I correct her. "Yellow and red leaves."

"Lellow."

"That's right." Rubbing her back with a proud grin, I then point behind her. "Do you think you can find me some more yellow leaves?"

"Lellow?"

"Yeah, yellow."

She nods and skips off, tripping over and landing on her hands and knees. I dash over to help her, but she just giggles and gets back to her feet, skipping off again to collect yellow leaves for me.

I love the way she talks. *Lellow*. Seriously. Too cute.

"What's going on? Why are you calling me into your football debrief?" Mom's face appears on the screen.

I wave to her. "Hey, Mom."

"Hi, sweetheart. Your father's not riding you too hard about that pass, is he?"

"Of course I'm not." Dad stands up for himself, and I don't say a damn thing.

My heart's racing too hard as I wait for the impending meltdown.

"It's not even about that, Elise. Our son has some important news to share, and I think you better sit down."

"Well, that's never a good sign," Mom murmurs as she pulls out a kitchen stool. "Zander, what's going on?"

"I have some big news."

"That you found out weeks ago and didn't bother to tell us," Dad snips.

Working my jaw to the side, I let out a dry laugh. "It's not like it's the easiest news to share, Dad."

"I can't believe you didn't say anything. Something this big?"

"What is it!" Mom ends up barking. "I'm dying here. What? Tell me what's going on."

Pulling in a short breath, I let it out and rush to say, "Sienna got pregnant just before I left for Kelsey U."

"What?" Now Mom's the one who's going pale.

"She didn't tell me about it, but a few weeks ago, I found out that... I have a daughter. Her name's Zoey, and she's—"

"You have a daughter?" Mom interrupts me. "You're a father? You're a... you're a..." She lets out a little screech, her face going instantly red. "You did exactly what we warned you against doing!"

I close my eyes, then force them back open so I can check on Zoey.

She's crouched down, singing to herself while hugging a pile of leaves to her chest.

"I can't believe you got Sienna pregnant."

"I didn't do it on purpose," I mutter.

"I can't believe she didn't tell you," Dad seethes. "Why would she keep something like that from you?"

"Was breaking your heart not enough?"

"Mom, I broke her heart, too, okay?"

She huffs like that shouldn't matter.

"Listen, you guys, I know this is a lot to process, which is why I hadn't told you yet. I've been trying to figure out the best time... and what to say. I know I did exactly what you didn't want me to do, but it's happened. And now I want to step up and do the right thing."

"Don't you dare give up football." Dad points at me.

"I'm not planning on it," I reply with forced calm. "Sienna and I are going to figure out a way to make this work."

Mom's lips part with horror. "You're getting back together with her?"

"I love her." I give the screen a pointed look. "I always have. And we're in the process of mending everything. Just trust me, okay? No history is being repeated, I swear."

"I can't believe this." Dad pinches his nose. "You have a kid now. Responsibilities. How are you going to make it all work?"

"I don't know yet. I just know that I have to try. I can have both. Sienna and I are going to work it out so I can still be a pro football player and a father... and—"

"Your game better not slip like it did in high school," Dad interrupts me. "She totally distracted you, and you can't afford to let that happen again." His expression bunches into an even sharper frown. "Wait, is that why you played so badly in the first quarter last game? Was she there? Was she—"

"Dad! Stop it!"

My parents both blink as I raise my voice at them. I haven't done that in a long time, but enough of this bullshit!

"You have to trust me. I'm older now, and I can figure this out. I don't need your judgment and constant 'words of advice.'"

They both frown at me like I've just offended them,

and I sigh, my shoulders sinking as I let my parents process this shitty conversation.

"Foobawl." Zoey comes running back. "Lellow!" She's waving the leaf in the air like she's just found gold.

I crouch down with a grin. "That one is really yellow. Good job." I hold my hand up for a high five, and she slaps me some skin before leaning against my leg.

"Can we see her?" Mom's voice is suddenly soft, almost vulnerable.

I hesitate, wondering how Sienna will feel about that.

But it's not like we can hide Zoey forever, right?

I give my parents a stern look and murmur, "Be nice," before turning the camera to face my little girl.

Dad's grumblings of "I'll course I'll be nice" fade to dust as the camera lands on Zoey's cute face.

She stares back at my parents, then waves. "Hi. Me Zoey."

"Oh my gosh, she looks exactly like Monica did." Mom's voice is all breathy before she lets out a watery laugh and waves back. "Hi, Zoey. I'm Zander's mommy."

Zoey stares back at the screen while my dad starts blubbering. "She's beautiful."

"I know, right?" I kiss Zoey's curls and smile down at her.

"Just like Monica." Dad's voice catches, and he starts blinking.

What the hell?

Is he about to cry?

I've never seen my dad this emotional before, and it's freaking me out.

"Uh... guys, are you—"

"How old are you, Zoey, sweetheart?" Mom's smiling

at my daughter, tinkling her fingers and giggling when Zoey holds up her fingers.

I correct the amount she's showing. "Two. You're two."

"Me two." She nods, then holds up the leaves she's been collecting. "Lellow!"

"You've been collecting yellow leaves?" Mom is fully engaged now, and it's kind of funny listening to her high-pitched voice and expressive demeanor. "Aren't you a clever girl."

Zoey grins at the phone, then looks at me with a worried frown. "Why cwying?"

Glancing at my dad, I let out a soft laugh and explain, "Those are happy tears. My dad's just really happy to meet you."

Dad blinks and sniffs, swiping a finger under his nose. "Does she know you're her father?" He's asking me but using the same tone my mother just was. Keeping this all light and playful.

"She's getting there." I kiss the top of her curls again, and Mom lets out this soft whimper.

"She's so cute."

"Yeah, I know. You'll have to come meet her in person sometime."

"When?" Mom jumps off her stool, running over to the calendar on the wall. "Can we come one weekend?"

"That's a long way to go for just the weekend, Elise."

"Oh, Brett, stop. It's just a two-hour flight and a ninety-minute car ride."

"And the first forty minutes to even get to the airport."

"It's not too far!"

"And he's got football. We can't get in the way of that."

"Oh!" Mom lets out a little growl, and I quickly cut through the brewing argument.

"Why don't you guys come for Thanksgiving? I'm playing on the Friday, but we could see you on Thursday maybe. I'll need to check with Sienna first. And if you come, you have to promise me you'll be nice to her."

"Of course we'll be nice to her." Mom looks offended.

I shoot a dry look at the phone. "Yeah, because you were always so warm and inviting when we dated in high school."

Mom opens her mouth to counter me, but she's got nothing.

They were just plain mean to my girl back then, and I can only imagine how she'll react if they show up in Nolan for a weekend.

"Let me just talk to her and I'll get back to you. If it's not Thanksgiving, then we'll try to find another time, okay?"

"You're not going to deny us access to our grand-daughter, are you?" Dad asks.

"I just introduced you to her." I bulge my eyes at him and am already dreading their visit.

But then Dad catches Zoey's eye and blows her a kiss. She giggles and blows one right back. Then Mom gets in on the action, and I crouch there until my knees start aching while Zoey attempts to catch wayward kisses.

"Zan-Man, where you at?" Tyrell calls through the house, and I quickly stand, bringing Zoey with me.

"Coming!" Looking at the screen, I'm not about to go into the details of Sienna's morning, so I cut the call short. "Guys, we've gotta go."

"Byeeee!" Zoey starts waving.

My parents wave back and blow more kisses, and I have to hang up on them because they won't end the call.

Racing back into the house, I place Zoey and her handful of leaves on the dining room floor and open my arms for Sienna.

She rushes into them, resting her head in the crook my neck while I share a look with Wily and Tyrell.

Tyrell shakes his head, looking pissed as he trudges up the stairs with Zoey's portable crib. At least I think that's what that is.

Wily appears with an armload of toys and gives me a sad smile that quickly morphs into a playful grin when Zoey bounds toward him yelling, "Amimals!"

"Are these yours?" Wily sounds so surprised it makes Sienna laugh, and I ease away from her, smoothing back her hair.

"How bad was it?"

"It sucked." Her smile is tumultuous, and I brush my lips across hers and pull her back into a hug.

"It's over now. We can just switch off and enjoy the rest of the day together." I nibble my way along her jawline and lightly suck her neck. "And we've got the whole night too."

Sienna tightens her hold on me, then starts to softly giggle as I kiss and tease her neck until I find that ticklish spot I discovered when she was seventeen.

CHAPTER 41
SIENNA

The rest of the day goes by in a happy blur. Zander helps me get the crib set up. We squish it into the corner of his room, and I can't help glancing at his bed, knowing I'll be snuggling up beside him tonight.

Is it too soon? I know it's only a night or two, but it feels like we're moving in together. It's so fast and unexpected. Logic keeps hounding me to see reason, but...

It's where you belong, a soft voice in my head reminds me, and this warm tingly sensation in my heart is louder than Mr. Logic and his judgments.

I've loved Zander for years, so in that sense, it's not rushed at all. It's more a case of "about damn time!"

"You good?" Zander takes my fingers, lightly playing with them and kissing each tip.

I smile up at him and nod, loving the way his arm sweeps around me and pulls me close.

"Mommy! Mommy! Mommy!" Zoey calls from downstairs, and I reluctantly let my man go and head down to see what our daughter wants.

And that's pretty much my day.

Zander making me all mushy, and Zoey demanding my attention.

Teah and Grady show up around lunchtime and we eat together, laughing over Zoey's antics as she puts on a show for her adoring crowd. Teah's laughter is so sweet and amps Zoey up even more until she's practically a performing monkey.

It's an effort to settle her after that, and even quiet play isn't enough. I know if Zoey doesn't go down for a nap soon, she's going to go full-blown Hulk on everyone.

She doesn't settle easily, because she's not used to Zander's room and all these big people around. There's been so much conversation and laughter, her poor little senses are on overload. It's not a bad thing, it's just an adjustment, and it's one I hope she can make because I seriously *love* being at Football Frat.

I rock Zoey until my arms just about drop off. She battles me the entire time. In the end, Zander comes up to help me, but that just wakes her up all over again.

After a tearful meltdown, she finally drifts off to sleep, and I lay her down, holding my breath and praying she doesn't wake up as I creep out of the room.

The door creaks when I open it and I freeze still, glancing over my shoulder, but finally my little girl is out for the count.

Thank God.

I creep downstairs and notice how still the house feels.

"Zander?" My call is so soft he probably can't hear it, so I go in search of my man and find him in a small den tucked away at the back of the house. It's set up like a library with a wall of books, a desk, and two armchairs on either side of a coffee table. In the middle is a chess set. This room feels so out of place compared to the rest of the house, but I kind of love how cozy it is.

My man is sitting at the desk, a laptop open in front of him.

"Hey." I say it softly, not wanting to startle him.

Spinning around to face me, his eyes are bright with hope. "She asleep?"

"Yes." My voice and smile are filled with relief, I can tell.

"You're amazing." He tips his head to admire me.

I brush my hand through the air. "She always falls asleep eventually. Sometimes it just takes longer than others. And it's a new environment, so..." I shrug and look around the den. "Hey, where's everyone else?"

"I sent them off. I wanted the house to be quiet for our girl, and they were all happy to go and do their own thing. Wily's no doubt flirting with some chick at Java Jeans. Grady and Teah will be doing something romantic. Who the fuck knows what Carson's doing, and I'm pretty sure Tyrell went to the library."

"Thank you." I smile at him. "That's really thoughtful."

"That's okay." He rises from his chair and saunters over to me. "Got to look after my girls."

A giddy giggle bubbles in my belly. His girls. I didn't realize how desperately I love those two little words until just now.

Curling my fingers into the back of his hair, I pull him toward me and kiss him full and slow. He's got to know how much sentiments like that mean to me.

"Mmmm." Zander gets into the kiss, his hands gliding around my body, then smoothly moving south to cup my ass.

He gives my cheeks a squeeze, and I nudge my hips toward him, silently letting him know that "Yes, he's the sexiest man on the planet" and "No, I will never get enough of him."

"You're so fucking sexy, Sen. You always have been."

I grin against his lips, licking a soft trail along his tongue before sucking the tip into my mouth.

"I don't suppose we have time for..." He pulls back with a hopeful grin, and I laugh at his eyebrow wiggle before mimicking his expression.

"Unless you're studying." My voice has a teasing lilt. "I wouldn't want to get in the way of that. I can just go and—"

Zander cuts me off with a searing kiss, lifting me off the ground and walking us over to the armchair.

"Here?" I murmur against his lips.

"It's not like we can do it in my room," he says between kisses. "And no one's home. I told them to be gone for at least an hour or two, so we're good, baby. We are so good."

Sinking against him, I let myself get lost in the moment. The temperature of our kissing increases by a few degrees—or a hundred—as the thought of having this man inside me again sets my blood to boiling.

"I love you so much," I pant against his cheek before sucking his earlobe between my lips and working my way down his neck.

His hands are everywhere, gliding all over me, squeezing, teasing, igniting.

By the time I reach his collarbone, he's lifting his hoodie off me, and I'm soon tugging at his T-shirt. Our naked torsos slap together, and I let out a satisfied groan. Sitting on his lap like this, straddling his powerful thighs, breathing in his intoxicating scent... I'm practically orgasming already and he's barely touched me.

"You feel so good, baby," I whimper against his shoulder as he unhooks my bra and makes quick work of nudging me back so he can suck my nipples and send me orbiting the moon.

Craning my head back, I moan and grind against him, the friction skyrocketing my heart rate as need and desire pulse through me in blinding waves.

"Gotta have you," I whisper, jerking away from him and scrambling for the tie on his sweats.

He helps me out and lifts his hips so I can undress him. He's soon bare-ass naked on the armchair, and the chess set is rattling behind me as I drop to my knees and go down on him.

The groans rumbling in his throat make me triumphant, and I love the way his fingers curl into my hair at the nape of my neck, his other hand cupping my head tenderly like I'm precious.

Sliding my mouth up and down his impressive cock, I do my best to make him feel good.

"Oh fuck. Oh fuck," he's soon whispering and pulling me off him. "Wait, wait, wait. I want to be inside you. Please. Is that okay?"

I wipe my glistening lips and grin. "Of course it is."

"Condom," he rasps, pointing to his sweats on the floor. "I've been carrying a few on me ever since our night together."

I laugh and crawl over to his pants. Scrambling in his pocket, I pull out that lifesaving square and get myself a little love tap on the butt.

Zander's soft slap makes me laugh, and I glance over my shoulder at him, hoping I'm looking sexy enough as I pinch the packet between my teeth and slowly crawl back to him.

CHAPTER 42
ZANDER

I'm totally right. Sienna is the sexiest woman on this planet.

She's prowling toward me like a sex kitten, and I'm helpless to do anything but watch her. She's so fucking fine I can hardly stand it. Her lips and tongue working my cock over was pure bliss, but I know this next part will be even better, because there's something about being inside her that makes me feel so zoned in and connected.

We'll be joined in the most intimate way possible, and I can't get enough of it.

Ripping the packet with her teeth, she quickly sheathes me while my frantic hands work to get her yoga pants off. They're like Fort Knox, and I grunt and wrestle those damn things while she gets the giggles, making it that much harder.

"Stop laughing, woman." My growl is playful and completely ineffective, but she does me the courtesy of yanking her pants off and flashing me her sweet pussy.

Diving out of the armchair, I pin her to the floor

before she can get up, devouring her sweet tits before working my way down her body and making sure she's wet and ready for me.

"Ah!" she cries out, then starts to moan and gyrate on the floor.

I hold her legs down, sucking and licking her clit until she's undone.

She bucks and whimpers as the orgasm takes her out, and I sit back on my heels and watch her, grazing the tips of my fingers down her body until she clamps my hand between her legs.

"No more touching," she gasps. "I just need..." She's struggling to speak, her perfect tits jiggling as she sits up. "I just need you. In me. Right now."

"Yes, ma'am." I wink at her and get lost in her smile as she nudges me back up in the armchair and climbs onto my lap again.

I only just have time to check that the condom is still in place before she's grabbing my cock and lining us up. As she sinks onto me, stars scatter in the corners of my vision. I let out a guttural moan.

Her warm oasis is heaven, utopia, fantasy land. My dick is singing happy tunes as she slides all the way to my hilt, then slowly rises again.

"Is that good?" Her blue eyes scan my expression, and all I can give her is a jerky nod.

"Good," I rasp. "So fucking good."

This makes her laugh, and the sound wraps around me. Gently guiding her hips, I help us find a rhythm, and her giggles have now changed to moans of pleasure, which are a different kind of symphony that I love just as much.

Massaging her tits, I squeeze them, rubbing my thumbs over her nipples while she rides me, her blonde locks catching sunlight when she tips back into the ray shining through the window.

She's so hot.

She's fire.

And she's mine.

It's hard to believe I've got her back. After everything went down, I thought I'd lost her forever. But here she is, loving me the way I don't deserve to be.

Threading my fingers through hers, I open my eyes and look right at her. "I love you."

She smiles back at me, her eyes sparkling before she closes them and leans back even more, changing the angle and making those chess pieces wobble.

Rising from the armchair, I go with her, enjoying her surprise as I shove the chessboard aside and lay her back on that coffee table.

It's awkward as hell and I end up popping out of her, but as the chess pieces scatter across the floor, I drop to my knees and plunge back into her. The new angle is fucking fantastic, and she lets me know it with a high-pitched wail that is all things beautiful. That just might be my new favorite sound.

"Oh." She huffs and pants, her chest heaving as I lift her legs and take her deeper. "That's good. That's so..." I pound into her, disrupting her words. "Good."

Squeezing her thighs, I push them back toward her belly, driving us home in a heady rush.

Her toes curl, pointing right at me as I pick up my pace.

Blood pounds through my brain, making me dizzy.

Trailing my hands down her body, I hook my fingers around her hips and hold on tight as I hammer into her.

And then white fire is spreading through my body, licking every muscle and nerve until I can't hold it anymore.

"I'm coming." I sputter out the words, plunging deep two more times before gripping her ass and convulsing inside her.

She groans, her hot pleasure gushing over my cock as she arches her back on the coffee table.

I run my hands across her body, caressing her smooth skin and loving every inch of her.

I'm not sure I'll ever catch my breath.

I don't know if I even want to.

My heart pounds for this woman. All those wasted times with girls who meant nothing to me. That rush I was chasing was with her all along. I was just too stupid to see it.

But now I know.

Sienna owned my heart back then.

And she stills owns it.

Always and forever.

CHAPTER 43
SIENNA

So, it turns out one night was not enough.

Zoey and I have been here for three days now, and I don't see myself ever wanting to leave. My little girl adores these big football players, and they're so sweet with her. Well, most of them are. Carson treats her like she's an infectious disease. He's one grumpy bastard, that's for sure. I can't imagine him ever smiling, and the way he stomps around the house makes me wonder why they put up with him.

The others are all great, and they're honestly so busy.

Every morning, they leave pretty early. I get kisses and neck nuzzles at around five in the morning, and then Zander creeps downstairs to have something to eat before his strength and conditioning workout. I can hear the guys downstairs, trying to be quiet for my sake, and usually drift off after the front door closes.

Yesterday, I hung out with that playgroup again and found it easier this time around. Zoey loved it and came home exhausted. While she napped, I read a book in the den and tried not to relive every second of the sexy times Zander and I shared on the coffee table. He's so freaking hot I can hardly stand it.

I can't wait until we get another session together. It's hard with Zoey sleeping in the same room as us, but we did have a shower together before we went to bed last night and got each other off while soap suds ran down our bodies.

His fingers are magic. His lips are divine, and I feel slightly sex-crazed every time he walks into the room, but I figure we have some making up to do, so that's probably why my hormones are acting like little beasts at the moment.

Zoey slept for a good long while, and since she woke up, we've done some laundry, cleaned the kitchen, and I'm now in the throes of making her dinner.

The front door pops open just as I'm frying up her chicken tenders.

"Foobawl! Wywee!" Zoey runs out of the kitchen, and my heart gets all warm and mushy when I hear them greet her.

A few moments later, Zander walks in with our girl in his arms, and I'm undone.

"Hey, Sparky." He kisses my lips, his hand resting on my lower back, and I know I'm home. "That smells good."

"Mine." Zoey points at herself.

"Yeah, I know. Deeeelicious."

Zoey giggles. "Deewish."

"That's right. Delicious." Zander makes a big show of licking his lips, then pretends to eat Zoey, munching on her hand and up her arm to raspberry her neck. She gets the giggles, her little squeals echoing throughout the kitchen as Carson stomps in, yanking the fridge open and pulling out a can of beer.

He spins, glaring at me before snapping the beer open and guzzling it like it's water.

I try for a polite smile and ask him, "How was practice?"

After a baleful glare, he lets out a ripper of a burp, which is his only reply.

I wrinkle my nose, turning back to Zoey's meal prep while he crushes the can and throws it toward the recycle box. It misses, pinging off the floor, and it takes everything in me not to demand he pick it up and throw it away properly. But I don't really want to interact with that douchebag right now.

"Dude," Zander softly warns him.

"What?" Carson bites back.

My boyfriend raises his hand. "Just chill."

Turning off the stove, I quickly pile chicken and veggie sticks onto Zoey's plate. I can feel the tension in the air, and my little girl has gone quiet, too, her big eyes looking between Carson and Zander.

The scarecrow scowls at his roommate, his defined nostrils flaring, a muscle in his jaw working as he looks on the verge of eruption.

My first instinct is to grab Zoey and run, but Zander's got her securely in his arms, and I'm not sure what to do.

"Chill?" Carson finally says, his tone icy.

I dart my eyes to Zander, but he's not looking at me. His firm, steady gaze is on Carson, and I'm just gonna hold my breath for a lil' minute.

"How am I supposed to do that? This is my own fucking house, and I can't chill because you've turned it into a nursery with your little girl and missus walking around here acting like they own the place."

"Carson—"

"No! This can't stand, man. And you know it!" Carson points at the ground. "It was supposed to be one night. But as far as I can tell, they're not going anywhere, and that's a real problem."

"Come on. They're just here for a few days. No one seems to mind."

"I mind! How the fuck are we supposed to party or have chicks over when these two are here? I can't even walk around naked in my own fucking home!"

I flinch. They have parties and chicks here all the time?

I didn't know that.

Gripping the counter behind me, I dip my eyes to the floor while Carson keeps ranting.

"This is not a daycare center, it's a football frat! You feel me? And I'm not okay with your little family moving in. This should have been a house discussion, but as usual, you just made the call without consulting anybody."

"That's bullshit. I asked, and everyone agreed."

"Not me!"

"Yeah, well, you weren't there."

"How am I supposed to stick around when this stink bomb here keeps making our house smell like a dumpster!" He points to Zoey, and my hackles go up.

I shift to block my girl from his view, but Zander steps forward before I can, getting up in Carson's face and hissing, "She's my daughter. Show some respect."

"I don't care who the fuck she is! She doesn't belong

here!" His eyes swing to me. "Neither of them do. It's not fair to the rest of us," Carson thunders.

And now my eyes are burning.

I don't want to leave, but I don't think we should stay if this is the kind of angst we're causing. The thought of going back to Russell's is like a boulder in my stomach, but—

Zander growls and starts complaining that he has to put up with Carson's shit all the time. Carson counters his shouting with some growls and complaints of his own, and I think they've totally forgotten that my sweet two-year-old is caught between them.

Until she lets out an ear-piercing scream, then yells, "Ba-da-ba-da-ba!"

We all freeze still, every eye in the room bulging as we look at her indignant expression.

"Excuse me?" Carson frowns at her.

She holds up her little finger. "No souting." Her face puckers. "Too loud."

Carson rolls his eyes and gives Zander a pointed look. My boyfriend stares down at his daughter, mumbling a soft apology, but Zoey doesn't hear him. She's too busy reaching out toward Carson.

"What are you doing?" Mr. Scarecrow frowns. "I don't want to hold yo—okay, so this is happening." He catches her before she starts to fall, pulling her against his chest and staring down at her like she's a mystery he doesn't want to solve.

She touches his cheeks, squishing them together as she softly demands, "Nice voice, pease."

I cover my mouth, trying not to laugh as Carson talks through squished lips.

"You want a nice voice?" His tone dances over the words like he's a happy camp counselor. Pulling away from Zoey, he stares down at her, still talking in that singsong way. "Okay, well, your daddy is being a complete dick right now."

My mouth opens and I frown at him while Zoey's nose scrunches up.

"What's dick?"

"Something your daddy isn't very good at wrapping."

"Okay, that's enough." I step around Zander with a little growl and pull Zoey out of Carson's arms. "We're going to eat this up in Zander's room, and you two can shout at each other as much as you like." Snatching Zoey's dinner, I walk out of the room and hear Carson's voice drifting down the hallway as I go.

"All right, fine, she's adorable."

I grin.

"But she still can't stay here. This is not a place to raise a toddler, and you know it."

My smile fades.

Shit, he's right. And Zander knows it too.

I hear his reply as I reach the stairwell, "It's just a few nights until we can sort something else out for them."

"Make it quick" Carson snaps before stomping out of the kitchen.

I hurry up the stairs so I don't have to interact with him again.

Placing Zoey on Zander's bedroom floor, I set her up with a picnic dinner. She's eating so much later than usual, and it's going to throw off her bedtime routine. Oh man, I hope she doesn't have a rough night. That's the last thing we need right now. It'll be the nail in the coffin from Carson's perspective.

A motorcycle engine roars to life outside, and I get up, walking to the window and staring down at the driveway. Carson revs the engine and squeals away from the house.

And my gut sinks.

He has a really fair point.

This isn't a daycare center, and I've just muscled my way in here.

Glancing back over my shoulder, I watch my little girl happily eating her dinner and wonder if I just have to lump it and move back in with Russell. It's not fair to stay here. It's not—

The door pops open, and Zander appears.

"Hey." He smiles at me, looking completely unfazed by the argument downstairs. Brushing his hand through the air, he wanders over to me, wrapping his arms around my waist and resting his chin on my shoulder. "Don't let him get to you. He's a grumpy asshole, and there's always a problem." He sighs. "He's the most challenging roommate."

"Have you ever thought of voting him out of the house?"

Zander's hand brushes my hip before he stands tall and turns to check on Zoey. "We can't." Dropping to the floor, he awkwardly crosses his legs and holds up a carrot stick, encouraging Zoey to eat her veggies. "This will make you strong, and carrots help you see better in the dark."

Zoey perks up, snatching the carrot stick and munching on it while I sink to the floor beside them.

"What is it with Carson? Why can't you ask him to

leave? I mean, is this really a big party house? I don't want to squash anybody's style."

Zander tips his head with a soft laugh. "We have parties sometimes, but not during football season. We're too busy. He's just pissed off because he doesn't know how to act around little kids or girlfriends. He's awkward as shit when Teah comes over."

"Why doesn't he like us?"

"It's not that. He just..." Zander sighs and gives me a sad smile. "He's had it rough, you know? And he doesn't have a lot of support. He's never had a girlfriend. He screws around a lot, but he can't handle relationships. It's like he's wired to push people away or fuck it up before they can get too close."

"But he's let you guys in?"

"Sort of. I guess we kind of tolerate each other. He can be a real pain in the ass, but he doesn't have anyone looking out for him, and none of us have the heart to kick him out. He obviously can't leave either, which tells me he secretly likes being here." Zander shrugs. "So, we put up with his bullshit and figure at least if he's here, we can keep an eye on him. Stop him from self-destructing."

Running my hand up his arm, I give his shoulder a squeeze and whisper, "You're a really good man, you know that?"

He lets out a soft laugh and shakes his head, focusing back on Zoey and getting her to finish her dinner.

I don't know why he won't agree with me.

He *is* a good man.

And that's why I don't want to leave this place. I want to keep living with him and being a family the way we were always supposed to be.

But it's not going to be as easy as I thought it would.

Carson seems determined to put a stop to this, and he was here first. I just wish I could think of an easy solution.

My daughter is currently living with a bunch of college football players. That's not normal.

But I don't want to be anywhere else.

Glancing at her crib in the corner of the room, I worry my lip as practical logic and emotion go to war in my chest.

CHAPTER 44
ZANDER

So, much to Carson's annoyance, Zoey and Sienna have been living at Football Frat for three weeks now. It's pissing him off big-time... and there's nothing I want to do about it, because I fucking love having my girls here.

Living with Sienna is the easiest thing in the world.

And sure, having a toddler has its moments. Zoey is small, but she can be loud and demanding when she wants to be. But she's also a total charmer and has turned every heart in this house to putty.

Well, except for Carson's, but I think he's faking it when he does his grumpy asshole routine whenever my girls are around. Needless to say, he's spending less and less time at home. It worries me. That guy can get up to some nasty shit when he's angsty, but so far I haven't had to pick his drunken ass up from any parties or bail him out of jail.

Although, he did show up to practice hungover the other day. Dammit.

Coach was pissed and made him stay late after practice to do some extra work. It didn't help that Carson got all mouthy and turned fifteen minutes into forty-five. Ever since then, he's been even more agitated. He's barely home, and I know I can't keep expecting him to be cool with the living arrangements.

I hate that he's probably right.

It's unfair to expect everyone to accommodate Sienna and Zoey for my sake. We really need to figure out a different living situation, but I hate the thought of leaving Football Frat. I love these guys. They're my family.

But so are Zoey and Sienna.

So for now, I'll just keep ignoring the problem and pretend like this is all working out the way it's supposed to.

I love coming home to my woman. She's so fucking amazing. I don't always have that much time to give her. Between practices and school, I feel like I'm always working, but she never complains, and we stay up late, whispering together in the darkness on those days we haven't spent much time together.

She's so easy to talk to.

We've literally spent *hours* talking—dreaming about the future the way we used to, making up wild plans that aren't always realistic, but it doesn't matter. We've caught up on the years we've been apart. She's shown me every photo and video on her phone, so I've been able to watch Zoey grow up from birth. Damn, I wish I could have been there. She's apologized for keeping me in the dark so many times now, just like I've apologized for giving her a reason to.

Thankfully, she'll never find out the worst of it.

The thought of losing her again kills me, so I'm clinging like a fucking limpet.

I try to avoid any conversations to do with Kelsey U, and each time she brings it up, I subtly change the subject. Or not so subtly. The look she gets on her face sometimes is like a punch in the chest. But how can I ever tell her?

The things I did that year are…

My insides twist and writhe as I pull on my pads and get ready for the game ahead.

I've been dreading this one all season, and people only think they know why. Last year was bad enough, but playing the Kelsey U Titans this year makes me feel like I'm a flaming torch about to run straight into a powder keg.

Sure, Hodgkins and Williams are long gone. They graduated a few years ago, but Morales and Coplin are still there. Biggs and Whitman are gonna be all over me.

This is my last game against these guys—hopefully they don't make the playoffs, and hopefully none of them go pro—and I have to make it count.

We lost to them last year, but like hell that's happening again.

I'm going out there, and I'm going to play some of the best football I ever have.

I have to.

Because I can't let those demons from my past haunt me anymore.

I'm desperate for a clean slate. I want to be everything Sienna needs me to be. I want to be the kind of father Zoey deserves.

And I'm going to prove myself on this field.

I have to.

Wrestling on my jersey, I try to keep my head on straight as we run through pregame drills, then get our final pep talk from Coach.

It's a good one, firing us all up until our knees are bobbing and we're ready to run onto that field like a bunch of warriors.

Busting through the sign, I raise my arms at the home crowd. They're going wild, jumping to their feet and cheering for us as we run, jump, and acknowledge them.

I scan the stands, wondering if Sienna made it the way she wanted to. I spot Wily's parents first and then track left, and my stomach sinks.

Shit. She did make it.

I didn't have the heart to tell her I didn't want her here.

She seemed so determined to come and support me… if she could line up a babysitter. All I can hope is that it's not Russell. He's been calling every day to interact with Zoey, and it riles me so fucking much. But my daughter adores the guy and Sienna feels bad, so she lets it happen. She's even taken Zoey around for a few play-dates, and I hate that Russell's so great with my kid. I hate that Zoey loves Uncle Rusty, but it's not like I can deny her, right?

What kind of asshole would that make me?

Swallowing down my angst, I point into the crowd. Sienna starts jumping and laughing, blowing me kisses, so excited to be here.

Fuck.

I wish I could tell her to go.

I don't want her seeing this shit.

And I don't want her anywhere near those Kelsey U fuckers.

God, please don't let my worlds collide. I'm begging you.

CHAPTER 45
SIENNA

I will be forever grateful to Mrs. Ward. She's watching Zoey for me so I can come to this game. It'll be past Zoey's bedtime by the time I go back to collect her, but so worth it. Hopefully Zoey won't turn feral. If I'm lucky, she might even fall asleep on Mrs. Ward's couch, and I can just bundle up her sleepy little body and take her home to Football Frat.

Man, I love living there.

It's been awkward some of the time, I guess. The house isn't really set up for a toddler, but Zander's been doing little things to make it safer. He even bought a car seat for his SUV. It was the sweetest thing. Zoey was stoked, excitedly climbing into it and demanding a drive.

She loves Zander so much. She loves all the guys, even Carson, who tries to avoid her like the plague. If he's ever home, she'll always try to interact with him. I should put a stop to it, but it's so funny watching Carson squirm.

Oh man, he wants us gone so badly. I cringe and try to

flick the thought from my mind. Darting my eyes away from his helmet, I focus back on my man.

I'm so freaking proud of him right now, leading his team onto the field like the champion he is.

He's told me about his dreams to play pro ball, and I'm going to support him all the way. I don't care where we live next year, as long as we can be together. If he gets drafted, I'll just follow him. I've got no ties to any place in particular, but I'm tied to him, and I'm happy to stay that way for life.

Russell doesn't know about any of this.

I'm pretty sure he'd blow a gasket if he found out. He's still annoyed with me for staying away for so long. One night has turned into three weeks, and he is riled.

Thankfully, he hides that whenever I take Zoey over to play or catch up with him at the park, but the rest of the time, I'm getting a steady stream of texts that constantly question my sanity. He loves to complain about my choices. But after each rant, I then get a thread of apologies and begging not to cut him out of Zoey's life.

Honestly, he's infuriating.

But Zoey loves him.

He is really sweet with her, and I can't forget the fact that he and his family have been my longest friends. Growing up the way I did, I struggled to make connections that would last. But the Fishers have always been an anchor point, and even though Russell drives me bonkers sometimes, he'll always be a part of my life.

My parents have been kind of pissed about my latest decisions, but I'm slowly trying to talk them around. They understand that Zander and I have worked things out, and they're cautiously optimistic, but they're really unhappy about the rift in my relationship with Russell, which is probably why I've been trying to appease everyone and keep Russell in my life.

Which annoys Zander, so I still can't keep everybody happy.

I internally roll my eyes and try to focus back on the game.

Zander seemed nervous about this one. I get that it's his old school, and I'm assuming that's the main problem, although he won't confirm nor deny.

He gets so hedgy whenever I mention Kelsey U. He has yet to share any details of his time there. I think he worries that it'll just bring up that ugly memory of what I saw. But I've forgiven him for that. I want to move past it and just forget, which is why I probably let it slide whenever he changes the topic off Kelsey U.

But man, he was agitated this morning. He wouldn't say he was, and he put on a smile whenever he was interacting with Zoey, but I could feel the tension pulsing out of him, which is why I was determined to find a babysitter and be here to support my man.

"Woohoo! Go get 'em, baby!" Teah cups her hands around her mouth and cheers on Grady.

Some of her sorority sisters are with her tonight. She's introduced me to Bella and Trinity. They seem nice enough, although I thought they weren't into football, so I'm surprised they're here. Unless one of them is making a play for one of the football guys. Yeah, that makes sense.

I dart my eyes to them, trying to figure out who they're swooning over, but I'm distracted by Wily's mom. She's still talking, telling me all about how amazing both her children are. Wily's sister, Blake, is a freshman at a college in Chicago this year. She was valedictorian at her high school, and apparently she's going to cure cancer and be the first woman to walk on the moon. Okay, so Mrs. Wilson didn't *actually* say that, but she may as well have. She is one proud mama. As for Wily, well, the sun shines out of his ass, and her "little" boy is going to play pro and one day make it to the Super Bowl, where he'll make game-changing tackles and blocks and be instrumental in winning the team that trophy.

Phew! Talk about pressure.

I'm sure glad I'm not a Wilson.

And I'm sure glad Wily doesn't seem to wear that pressure at all. He's so smiley and laid-back that it makes me wonder how he came from two such intense people.

"Okay, let's go, let's go." Mr. Wilson claps, watching the kickoff like it's a life-and-death situation.

I swallow and turn my attention to the game, cheering when a Cougar's receiver dodges two tackles before being brought down.

"Yes! Good positioning! Well done! Well done!" Mr. Wilson is clapping and shouting like the team can actually hear him.

I hide my smile and watch the game without a word, pride bursting through me when Zander steps out onto the field.

There's my man.

He clips his helmet and bends into the huddle. I can imagine what he's saying, calling the perfect play. He's been studying his playbook like a freaking Bible, and his intensity around this particular game has been way more potent. He's been staying late to review game videos with

Coach. It's like they're on a mission to take down the Titans. They don't want to just beat this team—they want to annihilate them.

Biting my lips together, I watch them set up for the play, tracking my man as he prepares for the snap.

He yells out a final direction before the ball is snapped into his hands. Taking a few steps back, he does a spin, then passes the ball off for a running play. He's quick and efficient, but he doesn't see the guy coming in from behind and gets completely slammed.

I can practically hear his bones crunching as he hits the turf. Damn, that was rough. Was it even legal?

The referees don't seem to be doing anything about it, and all I can do is watch Zander as the guy who tackled him gets up, pushing Zander's helmet with a rough shunt before walking away.

That asshole!

I growl, rising to my feet and feeling that fire race through me. How dare he treat Zander that way!

Zander gets up, looking a little worse for wear before jogging up the field to get set for the next play. The Cougars managed twelve yards, but I can sense that this is going to be a really tough game. The Titans seem to be out for blood, and I can't help wondering if this is why Zander was so nervous about this game.

He knew this was coming.

What I want to know is why.

CHAPTER 46
ZANDER

I knew this game was going to be tough, but holy fuck!

By halftime, I feel like I've been run over by a steam-roller. The Titans want to break every bone in my body. And you'd have to be blind not to notice it.

"I'm pulling you," Coach tells me as soon as we get to the locker room.

"No way," I growl. "You promised me you wouldn't."

"They are trying to demolish you!" Coach argues back, pointing toward the field while the rest of the team goes quiet around us. "This isn't just about football to them. The entire team hates you. You've got a target on your back that you can see from space, Zander! And I don't want you to get hurt."

"I'm not hurt," I mutter.

Coach shakes his head. "You are going to be black and blue tomorrow, and you know it. We've still got the rest of the season to get through. The playoffs are more impor-tant than this game."

"We won't get to the playoffs if we don't win this game," I hiss.

"Yes, we will!" His clipboard slaps against his leg as he lowers his arms, then looks around the locker room. Everyone is staring at us, and I can't hold their gazes.

"Dude, what the fuck happened at Kelsey U?" Grady quietly asks me.

I shake my head. We went through this last year, and I refused to tell them then. I'm not about to open up that ugly-ass can of worms right now. They'll never respect me again.

"Zander," Coach sighs. "I know you want to win this game. I get it. And I understand that you want to be the guy on the field when you do it, but our team is about more than tonight. It's about more than one game, and I won't see you get injured over this. They're playing mean and dirty, but just clean enough not to get penalized."

"Yeah, I'm pretty sure their gameplay is to kill you, bruh." Tyrell shakes his head. "We're doing everything we can to protect you, but…" He hisses. "It's getting rough out there."

I close my eyes, hating how right they are.

Hating that history is repeating itself, just like it did last year.

I don't want to be on the sidelines. I want to be in the action, throwing perfect passes and running those plays that make me so fucking good on the field.

"Please, Coach," I try one last time.

He huffs, resting his hands on his hips and looking at Tyrell.

My friend gives me a doubtful frown but eventually gives in with a resigned huff. "We'll keep him safe."

"One more hard hit and you're off." Coach points the clipboard at me. "I mean it, Zander."

"Got it." I nod, lifting my chin at Tyrell as a silent thank-you.

He just shakes his head and turns to check on his offensive line while I mentally gear up for a second half that I know will be brutal.

Carson and Grady flank me as we run out of that tunnel. Carson is fired up, ready to dish out a little hellfire of his own. One thing I love about the guy—he's loyal and will bust his knuckles for anyone in our house if he has to.

And that's exactly what he does the minute we step back onto the field.

"Thought Coach would have benched your sorry ass," Biggs sneers as I run out for our first offensive play. "You obviously like my kind of punishment, Donohue. Does it get you off, having your ass handed to you?"

"Get the fuck away from him." Carson shoves the guy back with a growl.

Biggs immediately springs back, ready to pummel my friend. I move into the defensive, Grady right beside me as we protect our own, and a quick scuffle ensues.

The crowd roars as I shove and push back where I can, desperate to throw a punch but smart enough not to.

"That's it! Break it up!" The referees and coaches are yelling at us, tugging us away from one another, and we end up getting into position like irate bulls. My chest is heaving, my heart thundering as I eye up the Titans' defensive line.

They're glaring back at me. I'm a piece of trash that's about to get scrunched into a ball and thrown away.

"Fuck you, Donohue!" some guy calls from the end of the line.

I don't even know who he fucking is.

It's clear the rumors about me are still rife. It kills me that the only version they'll hear is the one about how I broke the captain's jaw and ended up in jail for the night. They only know the twisted version of why I left Kelsey U and escaped to Nolan for a fresh start.

They have no idea how desperate and ashamed I was.

All they see is a traitor.

And they're out for my execution.

We've gotta win this game.

Scanning the haters opposite me, I prep for Play 29, then suddenly notice one of the Titans shift position at the end of the line. They've figured out our play.

Shit.

"Add one! Add one!" I shout down the line, and my boys quickly scramble, resetting for Play 30 as I yell, "Hut! Hut!" and collect the ball.

Our last-minute change confuses the Titans for a second, and I'm able to set up the next play perfectly, launching the ball downfield to Carson, who's sprinting into position. He's covered by Grady and two other players and easily snatches the ball out of the air, hugging it to his body and charging for the end zone.

"Yes! Yes! Yes!" I shout, running after him and jumping in the air when he crosses the line and slams the ball down.

Starting the second half with such a sweet touchdown is giving the Titans the proverbial finger, and I relish every second of it.

I get shoved and jostled by the opposing team as we

run off the field, but I ignore their sneering insults and walk past Coach with a grin.

"Attaboy." He slaps me on the butt as I pass him, and I take a jittery seat on the bench.

This is far from over, but it's a fucking good start.

"We're gonna win." Grady takes a seat beside me.

"Fuck yeah, we are." I nod and slap his hand with a grin.

He doesn't smile back, just nods, keeping himself centered like he does in every game, and starts talking about our next play. Coach probably has it lined up already, but Grady's a strategy guy and I indulge him, nodding as he runs through the next scenario.

And as usual, he's right on the money.

We're up next, and Coach is instructing us with the play Grady predicted. We run onto the field fired up and ready to go.

And damn if we don't execute the shit out of that play.

By the end of the game, the Titans are walking off the field with an eighteen-point defeat. It's fucking satisfying, but judging by the looks I'm getting, they'd rather shoot me dead than shake my hand.

"Fucking traitor," Morales mutters as I pass him on the field.

I clench my jaw and keep walking, refusing to engage with that asshole.

He doesn't know shit.

He wasn't there that night.

And all I can hope is that he didn't get caught up in that sick game Hodgkins and Williams were playing when I was at Kelsey U.

But I guess he was a freshman at the same time I was,

so there's no way he didn't know what the fuck was going on.

Shit, he was probably part of it too.

CHAPTER 47
SIENNA

Wow. That game was intense.

Thank God Zander made it out in one piece.

I stood in those stands, sick with worry as I watched the aggression on the field. The Titans were brutal, but the Cougars fought hard, and I couldn't be prouder.

Checking my watch, I know I should probably go and pick up Zoey, but I want to see Zander first, so I pace outside the stadium, rubbing my arms and trying to stay warm as I wait for my man.

Teah and her sorority girls have gone to Offside—the local sports bar—to celebrate with the team there, but I can't do that, so I'll kiss and hug my man now, then take his car and head off to collect our daughter. He can catch a ride with his buddies, and I'll be waiting at Football Frat when he gets there.

Some might say that I'm missing out, that becoming a mother at eighteen robbed me of a college education and this freedom to party, but...

I love being a mom.

I seriously think this is what I was born to do, and skipping a party so I can care for my daughter does not feel like a big loss for me.

Sure, I'd love it if Zander would come with me, but I'm not going to deny him a few drinks with his buddies. He deserves to celebrate this win, and I'll be reminding him of that... as soon as he gets out here. We mapped it all out before he left for his pregame ritual, and we're sticking to that plan whether he wants to or not. He needs to celebrate with his teammates...,and then we can celebrate in our own special way when he gets home.

A thrill races through me, a smile curling my lips as I check my watch again. My smile turns to a wince, and I pull out my phone to text Mrs. Ward, letting her know that I'm going to be running late.

She texts back after a few minutes with a photo of Zoey, who's asleep on the couch, snuggled up with three of her favorite stuffed animals.

Mrs. Ward: Take all the time you need, sweetie.

I send back a string of grateful emojis before tucking my phone away and glancing up to see Zander walking toward me.

"Hey!" I run over to him, ready to launch myself into his arms, but stop short when I notice how gingerly he's moving. "Oh, baby." I slow my approach, gently wrapping him in a hug when he's close enough.

"I'm okay." He squeezes me against him, breathing in my hair before nuzzling his lips into my neck.

"I'm so proud of you," I whisper. "That was a rough game."

"I knew it would be." He keeps me close, even when I go to pull away.

With a soft giggle, I nestle back against him, letting him hold me because he obviously needs to. "Thank God you're okay."

"Yeah, I'll be a bit stiff tomorrow, but I'll head to the gym for a therapy session and will be back to normal in a few days."

"I couldn't believe how brutal that team was. It felt like they were playing dirty and getting away with it."

"Yeah, they were just within the rules."

"And when that fight nearly broke out..." I pull back to study his face. "I was worried Carson would get penalized and—"

"Yeah, thankfully that didn't happen. He was instrumental tonight."

"He was." I nod, almost loath to admit how talented he is, but... credit where credit's due, I guess. "He's a... you know, he's, um... a great player."

"Yep." He smiles at me like he knows I'm struggling.

I can feel the blush rising in my cheeks and let out a self-deprecating laugh. "Okay, fine. He was amazing! You guys make a great team." I put on a fake pout. "I just wish he wasn't such a grumpy ass at home. I wish he liked me."

"He probably does like you. He just doesn't know how to show it."

"Yeah, whatever. He wants to see me and Zoey out of the house." I cringe. "And it makes me feel bad that we haven't left yet, but—"

"You're not going anywhere," Zander growls, tightening his hold on me. "I like living with my woman. I don't want you to go."

My smile turns mushy. "I like living with you too. I love the fact that even though I'm about to say goodbye to you, when you get home after Offside, you're going to be climbing into bed beside me and keeping me warm. I'll get to wake up with you in the morning and do this." Rising to my tiptoes, I give him a light kiss, which quickly deepens. I wrap my arms around his neck, relishing the feel of his tongue sliding against mine.

I couldn't love this man more if I tried.

His hand glides up my back, splaying between my shoulder blades as he drops his bag and wraps both arms around me. He's in no rush to end this kiss, and so we linger in that freezing parking lot like we're the only two people on the planet.

Except that we're not.

"Well, well, well. Ain't this sweet."

Zander stiffens, ripping his mouth from mine and drawing me even tighter against him. I glance over my shoulder, my insides jittering as a bunch of supporters dressed in yellow and black quickly surround us.

Titans fans.

And they look pissed.

I swallow, my fingers curling into Zander's jacket as he shifts me to his side and starts walking forward. But we don't get very far.

Our steps are quickly blocked as the line converges in front of us.

My eyes dart across the wall of yellow and black before I glance up at Zander.

His jaw is clenched, his expression pulled into a tight glare. "Move," he growls.

"Aw, come on, man. We just want to say hi," the guy mocks him.

He's tall and blond with a preppy-boy haircut. Although it looks as though he's older, obviously graduated a few years ago. His gaze glints dangerously as he stares my boyfriend down, and then his eyes brush over me.

I shudder but try not to let it show.

"Who's this?" He goes to reach for me, but Zander slaps his hand away, shoving him back.

"Ooooo!" The guy raises his hands in surrender, but his mocking laughter is grating. "So, you've got yourself a serious lady, huh?"

The group around us laugh and jostle one another like this is the funniest thing in the world.

"Got yourself a little *girlfriend*." The way he says that last word makes my insides crawl.

"Back the fuck off," Zander growls. "Just leave us alone."

He tries walking us forward again but gets pushed back.

I jostle against him, and he catches me before I lose my balance. His arm is a protective shield, and I lean into his chest. I seriously don't know how we're going to get out of this, and fear is spiking through me as my imagination plays out various scenarios.

None of them are good.

Are they about to beat up my man?

I can't let that happen.

I can't—

"Does she know?" the guy asks. "Does she know what a traitor you are?"

My eyes dart to him in confusion before tracking back to Zander, who is practically vibrating. I spread my hand across his stomach, trying to calm him, but he's zoned in on the nasty D-bag right now, and...

"Shut the fuck up."

"Oh, so she doesn't." The man grins, turning his nasty smile on me. "You don't know that Zander here spent a night in jail?"

My heart stops beating for a second. That can't be right.

"Yeah, he broke our team captain's jaw. Can you believe that?"

"No," I bite back. "He wouldn't do that."

"Oh, he did." The man's eyes glint at me, and I quickly look to Zander for reassurance, but I'm not getting it.

Zander's glaring at the guy, his body shaking just a little harder as he avoids my gaze.

"You know he was her boyfriend, right?" the guy spits at Zander. "You're lucky he never pressed charges."

"You know why he didn't," Zander seethes. "He deserved jail time as much I did. Fuck, we all deserved it!"

What?

What is he talking about?

My heart slams against my rib cage as I try to wrap my brain around this. What is Zander saying? That he *did* break someone's jaw? That he ended up in jail?

That doesn't sit right for me. Zander would never do that.

"Always such a good boy." The guy's eyes narrow. "But you're not so innocent."

Zander's hold on me loosens, and I can't understand why.

"I know that, okay?" His rasping reply jolts me.

"Does she?" The line in front of us starts to snicker when the D-bag points at me.

My boyfriend's jaw clenches as he moves me around him, shielding me behind his back while the guy in front of us starts yelling at me.

"Do you know about the roofies and the girls? Do you know what your precious boyfriend did to Williams's girl?"

CHAPTER 48
ZANDER

The second those questions are out of his mouth, I know I'm done.

Fuck!

He just sold me out, and I don't know how the hell I'm supposed to explain any of this to Sienna.

I can feel the shift behind me. A second ago, she was clinging to my jacket, but her hold has loosened. She's now shuffling away from me, moving back into my line of sight and looking hella confused.

Fuck. Fuck. Fuck!

"Zander?"

I look at the ground, unable to maintain eye contact. I want to kill Boyle right now. He was in that fucking room. He knew exactly what went down, and he's flipping the story to make me look like the ultimate villain.

Fuck, maybe I am.

"Well, have yourself a good night, Donohue." Boyle slaps my arm.

I growl, flicking him off me as he laughs and tips his head, beckoning his yellow-and-black crew to split.

Glaring after them, I watch them saunter off and wish it wasn't illegal to shoot people dead. I fucking swear, I've only ever wanted to kill someone once—that night when I saw what those assholes were doing—but the anger pulsing through me right now is making me want to kill again.

"Zander." Sienna shakes my arm. "What was he talking about?"

I glance at her, unable to form any words. She looks so horrified right now... and she has every right to be.

"Roofies?" she questions me, and I feel sick. "What did you do to that guy's girlfriend?"

Closing my eyes, I can't answer her. The shame is too thick and strong. It's riding over me, pulsing through me in these nauseating waves that I can't counter.

"Oh my go—" She slaps a hand over her mouth, staring at me like she doesn't even know who I am.

Her blue eyes fill with instant tears.

Swallowing, I look back to the ground.

"Please tell me none of that was true," Sienna blubbers.

I can't respond.

"Zander!" She slaps my arm. "Tell me they were lying!"

But I can't.

The one thing I never wanted her to know is now out there. And there's nothing I can do to stop it.

I mean, I could try to explain, I guess.

The story isn't exactly how it's been construed just now, but what's the fucking point?

I'm guilty as hell.

And I hate myself for what happened.

"I fucked up," I manage, but that barely skims the surface.

"No." Sienna starts shaking her head and backing away from me, no doubt thinking about those girls she saw me with, then hearing "roofies" and jumping to conclusions.

I want to snatch her back, beg her to forget the past and just move on from here.

I'll never *ever* be the total shit I was my freshman year.

But she's not going to let me promise that. I can sense I've already lost her as she stumbles back a few more steps, then spins on her heel and takes off running.

My insides buckle, crying out, raging for her to stop and let me explain.

But I can't.

What fucking right do I have to do that?

I don't deserve her in the first place.

I don't deserve Zoey.

My sins will haunt me for the rest of my fucking life.

And that's exactly what I deserve.

CHAPTER 49
SIENNA

Instead of driving to Mrs. Ward's place, I delay my pickup by a few more minutes in order to rush back to Football Frat and grab my stuff. I'm an emotional wreck as I race up the stairs and pack a bag for me and Zoey.

The thought of leaving kills me.

But I can't stay.

I can't share a bed with Zander tonight.

I mean, what the fuck!

I don't even know that man.

I'm reeling as I shakily shove clothes and diapers into bags.

I thought I had forgiven Zander for everything, but he didn't tell me he was a rapist! That he broke a guy's jaw and ended up in *jail*!

My brain is struggling to compute all I heard.

I wanted to deny every syllable, but then Zander wouldn't talk to me. He just stood there confirming it all with his silence. His shame-faced frown was a sword right through my heart.

How can I be with him now?

He's kept that part of himself from me, and even though he acted as though he'd changed since Kelsey U, how do I really know it for sure?

How do I let him be around Zoey when I know what he's capable of?

I feel sick.

Laying a hand over my stomach, I sway on my feet, wondering if I'm about to hurl chunks, but the nausea passes as I fist Zander's hoodie, then let out a feral wail and pull it off me.

Throwing it down on his bed, I scream at the duvet, pounding my fists on the mattress until the raging anguish has passed through me.

Resting my forehead on the edge of the bed, I suck in a few whimpering breaths and force myself to pull it together. I have to go and collect my daughter now.

I have to find a place to stay tonight.

Russell's. You know you have to go back there.

I whimper again but force myself to stand.

Wiping my face, I square my shoulders and grab my things. I walk down the stairs like a zombie. My chest hurts. I seriously feel like my heart is crumbling. Zander shattered it once before, and I managed to glue it back together. I thought it'd been fully restored, but the way it's turning to ash in my chest right now tells me I was dreaming.

A broken heart can never be fully whole again, and mine's just been decimated.

With hiccupping sobs, I climb into Zander's SUV and drive to Mrs. Ward's place. I'll have to get it back to him somehow, but I can't think about that right now. I just need to focus on picking up my little girl and making sure she feels safe and secure.

When I get there, I have to sit in the car for a minute, parked on the curb outside Mrs. Ward's house and desperately wiping my face dry. Putting on a bright smile for her is nearly impossible, but somehow I manage a whispered conversation.

She waxes eloquent about my perfect daughter and what a sweetheart she is. Gathering my little bundle against me, I cradle her, sniffing in her sweet smell and willing myself not to cry. Gently buckling her into her car seat, I'm desperate not to wake her. One whisper of her little voice and I'll be undone.

"Thank you, Mrs. Ward." I give the woman a hug goodbye and jump behind the wheel before I start blubbering again.

She waves me off, a flash of concern crossing her face just before I drive away.

The trip to Russell's house only takes four minutes, and by the time I arrive, I'm a wreck all over again. I knock and then use my key to open the door. He's just rising from the couch as I walk in, and the second he sees my face, he's across the room, pulling me into his arms and checking if I'm okay.

"I don't want to talk about it," I cry against his shoulder. "I just need to get Zoey to bed."

"I'll go get her." He presses a quick kiss against the side of my head before dashing around me.

I collect the bags while he carries Zoey to her crib. She looks so warm and secure in his arms.

Shit! I don't want him to be the better father for Zoey. I want that to be Zander.

But it's not, is it?

My insides wail again, this silent scream rising inside me.

Russell lays Zoey down like an expert. She doesn't even wake, her floppy limbs splaying open on the mattress. Placing the stuffed animals around her, I fight more tears when she curls onto her side, murmuring in her sleep, completely oblivious to the storm brewing around her.

How am I supposed to explain this to her tomorrow?

How do I tell her that she can't ever see Foobawl again?

Seriously? Never again?

This is over for good?

"It has to be," I blubber softly as I leave the room.

The second I'm in the hallway, Russell is stepping in my path, cradling me against him. "What happened?"

But how do I respond?

I can't tell him the truth.

All I can blubber is "It's over."

Russell sighs, rubbing my back. "I knew he was going to fuck up."

I tut and shove him off me. "I don't want to talk about it."

"Hey, I'm sorry." He lightly grabs my wrist as I try to storm away. "I'm just glad you're home."

I shake my head, crossing my arms when he pulls me in for another hug. My body is stiff and wooden as he rubs my back again, trying and failing to comfort me.

"I want to go to bed."

"Shhh, it's okay."

"Russell, let me go!" I snap, wrestling out of his grasp.

He looks hurt by my venom, but I'm too wrecked to care about his feelings right now.

"I'll see you in the morning," I mutter, padding down the hallway to my room.

Crawling into bed, I don't even bother getting changed. Instead, I pull the covers over my head, curling into the fetal position and squeezing my eyes shut.

Images flood me—cruel, taunting memories of Zander on his bed with two girls plastered against him.

How many girls were there?

How many girls were willing?

How many weren't?

Bile surges in my stomach, but I clamp my teeth, holding it in as I'm tortured by one horrific image after another.

It can't be true, right?

But that look on Zander's face.

That shame.

Closing my eyes with a whimper, I bury my face in the pillow and cry myself to sleep.

CHAPTER 50
ZANDER

I stand in that parking lot like a fucking statue until someone slaps me on the shoulder.

"Hey, Zan. You okay, man?" Wily's grinning down at me, oblivious to the nightmare I'm living.

Forcing a nod, I try to smile, but who the fuck knows what my lips are doing.

I just lost everything.

But all I can see is a girl lying on a bed, her dress ripped open, her limp legs spread wide. She was so fucking spaced out. Her body was loose rubber, so easily manipulated. She would have had no chance. The way Hodgkins was staring down at her like she was a tasty steak ready to be devoured. Boyle was lined up behind him, already unzipping his pants, and Williams—the guy who was supposed to protect her—was ripping off his condom and laughing. "Enjoy the ride, boys."

I wanted to fucking kill them all.

"Zander?" Wily gives me a little shake. "You ready to

go?" He points to his truck, and I gaze across the parking lot in a muddled daze. "Dude. Are you concussed?"

Wily bends down, and I blink at his worried frown, then shake my head.

"Nah, man, just... exhausted."

"Yeah, I get it. You got yourself a beating tonight." He slaps my shoulder, his laughter loud and grating. "You're one tough little shit, though, aren't ya? Come on, let's go celebrate at Offside."

"Not tonight, man." I shove my hands into my jacket pockets, balling them into fists.

"Aw, I get it. Gotta get home to your girls." He shakes his head with a grin. "How life changes, right? You're a papa bear now. Gots to go look after your family." He nudges me like this is the cutest thing ever.

And I can't even crack a smile.

My family?

What family?

I just lost them.

Clenching my jaw, I nod and walk toward my car, only to realize that it's not there. Sienna took it.

My shoulders slump as I start my walk home. The cold air hits my exposed skin, but I clench my jaw and ignore the urge to order an Uber. I just keep walking, not looking back when I hear Grady shouting after me, not even lifting my hand to wave my teammates goodbye.

How can I, when my mind is back at Kelsey U...

"You fuckers," I growled, launching myself into the room and snatching Hodgkins's shirt before he could bury himself in that girl.

He wasn't going to take it easy—I could tell by the gleam in his eye, by the way he roughly parted her legs even wider, pushing her knees into the mattress.

I couldn't let him do it.

I didn't care that I was just a freshman and he was my captain. Like fuck he was going to rape that girl.

"Hey!" Hodgkins rounded on me, his glare hot and dangerous. "You better wait your fucking turn, Donohue!"

"You're not touching that girl!" I shouted back before throwing an accusing glare at Williams. "What the fuck is wrong with you? She's your girlfriend!"

Williams fired a warning scowl my way, but I wasn't about to back down.

"What the hell did you give her, man!" I tried to push past Hodgkins to reach the girl before Boyle got his filthy cock inside her.

Shit, I couldn't even remember her name. But I knew she had a sweet smile. She always looked at Williams like he hung the moon. He didn't fucking deserve her. The poor girl probably thought she'd scored big, dating the captain of the football team. They'd only been together a few weeks. Was this his plan all along?

Fuck. How many other girls had he done this to?

"Stay out of it, man. If you don't want to share the way we do, then that's fine. But you mind your business and get back downstairs."

"You sick fucks!" I shouted, launching myself at Williams like a feral dog.

I hadn't even planned on coming upstairs, but I'd had way too much to drink and needed to piss. The downstairs bathroom was a cloudy weed den, and I could hear people screwing in the tub. So I came upstairs and passed the doorway, glancing through the crack and jolting to a stop. When I saw what was going down, I sobered up in an instant.

My knuckles caught Williams off guard, and he stumbled back.

Hodgkins tried to grab me, but I fought him off with a snarl, pouncing back on Williams, who was the biggest culprit in my eyes.

Who the fuck treats his girlfriend that way?

My insides raged as I managed to pin Williams down. He was the bigger man, but I was running on pure fury, and my fist became a powerful piston, driving into his face one blow after another.

Hodgkins eventually ripped me off and held me down while Boyle kicked the shit out of my thighs and stomach. Williams was out of it, lying prone on the floor while his loyal teammates hammered me until the police showed up.

The second the cops crowded into the room, Boyle started yelling that I was trying to rape Williams's girlfriend.

"He roofied her!" Boyle shouted. "That asshole was raping her! Look!" He'd pointed at the unconscious girl, still fully exposed. "When her boyfriend tried to stop him, he went feral and knocked him out!"

Williams was just coming to, groaning in agony as I was rolled onto my stomach, my hands roughly cuffed behind me.

"You're under arrest for assault and battery. You have the right to remain silent..." The rest of my rights faded into a hot fuzz as my face was smooshed against the carpet and Boyle kept spouting off heinous lies about what had gone down.

As I walk into Football Frat and climb the stairs, I realize that I will never get over this.

I may not have touched Williams's girlfriend, but how many other girls had I touched my freshman year? Had all of them been willing? I was so fucking out of it at some of those parties, how would I really know?

I sat in that jail cell and hated myself with every fiber of my being.

I yearned for Sienna but knew I didn't deserve her. I still didn't know why she'd ghosted me at that point, but I knew as I rested my head back against that concrete wall that I couldn't stay at Kelsey U. My path to self-destruction was about to drop me off a fucking cliff.

If I was accused of the lies they said about me, I was toast.

It was my word against theirs.

Pulling out my phone, I slump onto the end of my bed, my fingers shaking as I call Monica.

She was the one who paid my bail. She was my legal counsel.

She saved my ass.

"Hey, bro. Heard it was a tough game tonight. You doing okay?"

"She knows," I rasp. "She knows the truth now."

There's a horrible pause and I sniff, waiting it out as my eyes burn. Resting my head in my hands, I fight the urge to start fucking weeping.

"How'd she take it?" Monica's tone is soft and calm, the way it always is.

I usually find it soothing, but not tonight.

Shaking my head, my voice breaks when I say, "She looked at me like I was the scum of the earth and then took off."

"What?" Monica's voice gets sharp. "Did you tell her everything? What parts does she know?"

"It doesn't matter, Mon." My voice sounds old and rusty. "It's over."

"No, no, no," she snaps. "Tell me exactly what you said to her."

"I've lost her again."

"Did you tell her about the part where you protected that girl? How you broke that motherfucker's jaw for treating his girlfriend that way?"

"I never deserved her. Not after what I let happen."

"You didn't let anything happen!" Monica argues. "You saved her."

"And how many didn't I save?" I stare at the carpet. "How many times did I turn a blind eye, not wanting to believe the rumors? How many girls got raped because I didn't—"

"Stop it," Monica cuts me off. "You're not doing this to yourself again, do you hear me? You were cleared of all charges. You didn't do anything wrong. And you are not responsible for not knowing what was going on."

I sniff and shake my head. I should have known. I should never have cared about what those fuckwits thought of me. I spent most of that year trying to impress them, and for what?

They turned on me the second I tried to do the right thing.

They tried to destroy my life.

"We got you out. You've had a fresh start. You're a new man. And you are not going to let those fuckwits screw you over again, you hear me?"

"Monica—"

"No, you shut up and listen. You do not give up on Sienna. She's the one for you. She always has been. You have a daughter together, and like hell I'm letting you walk away from that because you feel like you don't deserve them. That's bullshit! Now, you call her and you tell her the truth, the *whole* truth, and nothing but the truth."

I scrub a hand over my mouth before mumbling, "She's gonna hate me."

"She'll hate you more if you don't paint a really clear picture of what went down. You're not guilty, Zander. Stop acting like the villain and start being the hero I know you are." She huffs and mutters, "Shit, that sounds so fucking cheesy, but you know what I mean."

Closing my eyes, I swallow down the vomit surging in my throat.

"Call her. Promise me you'll call her."

Knowing she won't let up, I eventually nod and murmur, "Yeah, I'll call her."

"And be honest. She deserves it."

A shudder runs through me, but I nod, then sniff and mutter a goodbye.

Hanging up, I stare at my phone screen, hovering my thumb over Sienna's name.

One phone call. You can do it, man. Just explain and then apologize. Apologize a million times over.

Gritting my teeth, I tap Sparky on my phone screen, my hand shaking as I raise the device to my ear.

But she never answers.

I try three more times before I finally give up.

Kicking off my shoes, I lie down on my bed, that loathing that used to eat me alive taking over again, devouring my insides one greedy bite after another.

I eventually drift into a restless sleep... and dream about the girl I let slip through my fingers once again.

CHAPTER 51
SIENNA

I spent most of Sunday ignoring Zander's calls and crying in my bed. Russell didn't have any prior commitments, so he stepped up and played Daddy for the day. He told Zoey that Mommy was sick and left me alone as much as possible.

Zoey didn't love it, but she was relatively accepting, and if she got too fussy, Russell managed to distract her.

I was grateful for his help, although the fact that he was *so* helpful just made me cry all the more, because Zander should have been doing that job.

I wanted Zander.

But I also didn't.

Because he did something completely abhorrent and hid it from me.

Of course he hid it from you! Would you want to admit to raping someone?

I couldn't get past it. The thought that he would do that to some helpless, drugged-up girl made me sick. I never actually threw up, but my nausea was over-powering.

And I still feel ill as I sit on the floor, watching Zoey play.

My insides are numb.

It's hard to crack a smile and play happy families with my girl when I'm feeling this destroyed. It's like losing him all over again... but so much worse.

"Okay, I'm off. I have a meeting." Russell swans into the room. He's been in such a chipper mood this morning, and it's grating.

He cooked Zoey breakfast while I sat at the counter sipping coffee.

He sang as he loaded the dishwasher. He laughed as he chased Zoey around the living room, trying to make her brush her teeth.

And now he's leaving, and I can't fucking wait.

Am I the worst? I should be grateful for Russell. But his joy over filling a slot that belongs to another man drives me crazy.

I guess I should just get over myself. Mom told me I should fall for Russell, but—

"I'll drop off the asshole's car on my way to the arena, and you can have mine for the rest of today, okay?" Russell crouches down, kissing the top of Zoey's head while my chest starts to hurt again. "See you lovely girls later." He grins, then leans forward and kisses me.

Right on the mouth.

I pull back, blinking at him like he just slapped my face, but he's already on his feet and walking for the door.

Scrubbing my lips with my hand, I try to wipe him away as a fresh bubble of tears starts brewing.

I don't want to have to deal with this shit too!

How am I supposed to tell the guy who's helping me out that I don't love him that way and he needs to stop forcing his agenda?

I don't have anywhere else to go right now, and I just... I can't handle this!

Pulling in a shaky breath, I wipe my lips again, rubbing off the last of Russell and yearning for Zander in a way that's just plain mean and unfair.

I shouldn't want him at all after what he did!

But still my heart calls for him.

"Lellyfant." Zoey holds up her plastic animal.

"Yep." I nod and give her a weak smile.

"Mon...chee."

"Monkey," I correct her, my voice wooden.

"Lilon."

"Lion."

She grins. "Rhino."

"That's good."

Her proud smile is adorable. I should be laughing like I normally do, praising her amazing talking, but instead my eyes flood with tears. Looking away before Zoey spots them, I rise to grab a tissue, then get distracted by my phone.

It's vibrating on the coffee table, so I pick it up. I don't recognize the number, but it could be one of the moms from the playgroup, and as loath as I am to be around other people right now, Zoey definitely deserves better company than me.

Maybe I should let it ring, and the caller can leave a message.

I bite my lip, quickly scanning my brain and

concluding that everyone at Football Frat is no doubt at school, and if it's not my parents, then it must be a play-group mom.

Shit! Just answer it. Think of what's best for Zoey!

With a huff, I swipe my thumb across the screen. "Hello?"

"Sienna? Hi. It's Monica."

It takes me a split second to register who that is, and then my insides run cold.

"Please don't hang up." She rushes out the words.

I huff. "Did Zander tell you to call me?"

"Of course not. He feels fully deserving of your ghost-ing, but... he shouldn't. He's not a bad guy!" Monica's voice pitches. "Look, I know it's probably not my place to intervene, but my brother is infuriatingly stubborn, and I know he hasn't told you the whole truth yet."

I close my eyes, feeling slightly dizzy. "I know the truth. I found out about the girl and how he roofied her and... and—"

"He never roofied anyone. I don't know what you've heard, but I can assure you that if it wasn't for Zander, that girl would have been raped multiple times that night. He saved her."

"What?" I plunk down on the couch. "But he said..." My brain struggles to recall exactly what he said, until it suddenly dawns on me...

He didn't say anything.

He just stood there while I jumped to all the wrong conclusions.

Oh shit. He's been trying to call me. To tell me the truth and—

"Why didn't he tell me the other night?" I whisper.

"Why did he let those Kelsey U guys lie about everything?"

Monica sighs. "By the sounds of it, they didn't lie about *everything.*"

I stiffen.

"Zander did break the captain's jaw. He was running on white-hot rage when he saw what was happening. He couldn't believe someone would treat their girlfriend that way, and he pounced without thinking... thumped that jackass until he was an unconscious blob on the floor."

I hiss, picturing the scene. I've never seen Zander that angry before. It's kind of hard to imagine. But then maybe I *can* see it, Zander's face puckered in anger while his arm worked like a piston.

The image scares me a little, and I glance at Zoey, so innocent and sweet on the floor.

So vulnerable.

"So, yes, he got arrested and accused of a bunch of bullshit, but with help from me and Coach Jones and a few eyewitnesses, he was cleared of all charges." Monica snaps me back to attention. "Unfortunately, he scored himself the eternal wrath of the team because he told the police everything he knew. He had to get away from Kelsey U after that. Thankfully, Coach Jones's new job coincided with all of this, and he took Zander with him."

Not sure what to say, I slump back on the couch, trying to absorb everything.

"I'm not saying he didn't have a really bad year and get caught up in a bunch of stuff he regrets. He was trying to impress the wrong people. He thought he needed to act like them to be accepted by them, so he got into drinking big-time, smoked a little weed, slept around."

I squeeze my eyes shut, not wanting to hear any of this.

"Shit, sorry. I know that's probably hard to hear." Monica huffs. "But you need to know that when push came to shove, he did the right thing. And there are witnesses to prove it. Believe me, I went into full-blown PI mode to find out the truth. I interviewed everyone at that party, and enough people were saying the same thing. Those assholes had roofied girls before. They were big on sharing their girlfriends whether the girls wanted that or not. Zander was oblivious to all of it. But when he saw what was happening... he totally saved that girl. A few of his team-mates got reprimanded, and things got ugly for a while."

"What happened to the main culprits?"

"Much to my complete aggravation, it became a case of 'he said, she said,' and the boys got off with warnings. They tried to kick Hodgkins and Williams off the team, but then the school board stepped in and did everything in their power to avoid a big scandal. Hush money was paid out, and the whole thing got swept under the rug. It was a total shit show and handled so badly, but the team blames Zander for exposing what was really going on. I'm pretty sure he put a major dent in their partying lifestyle, and I imagine a lot of girls started avoiding the Titans."

My mind is reeling as I try to absorb all of this. I can't believe Zander had to play with those assholes, and their hatred toward him has definitely endured judging by Saturday's game.

"So..." I lick my bottom lip. "Zander never had nonconsensual sex?"

"No! Don't think that for one second. I mean,

according to what he's told me, any sex he had at Kelsey U was a drunken mindless mess. He'd wake up beside some girl and only have vague, fuzzy memories of the night before. I know he's paranoid that on one of those occasions, he might have slept with someone who was just as out of it as he was... But I'd argue that no one was asking for his consent either. I swear, too much alcohol and sex is a really bad idea. I hate that he had to learn that the hard way."

I let out a shuddering sigh, slashing a tear off my cheek.

"Since moving to Nolan U, he hasn't gotten wasted once. He's really big on only drinking a beer or two, then stopping, and he hasn't touched drugs since his night in jail. He never wants to be that out of control again. I swear to you, Sienna, he's a changed man. You can trust him."

My chin bunches as I try to talk through my tears. "I really want to, but it made me feel like I don't know him at all. He never talks to me about his time at Kelsey U, and it was so shocking to hear all that stuff."

"You do know him." Monica's voice is soft and soothing. "He's an inherently good man. He just lost his way for a while. And he blames himself that he didn't figure things out sooner. He carries the guilt of what happened to those girls before he found out what was going down. I'm not sure he'll ever forgive himself."

That sounds more like my man. No wonder he didn't want to tell me.

"I think your forgiveness would really help, and I've been bugging him for weeks to open up and tell you the truth. He was just so ashamed and worried that you'd never speak to him again."

I bolt upright, blinking at the wall.

Shit, that's exactly what I did. I wouldn't take his calls. I completely shut him out!

He'll never tell you anything if you don't give him a reason to trust that you'll stick around through thick and thin. Shit, Sienna, stop bolting like a scared rabbit.

I have to see him.

I have to make this right.

Jumping off the couch, I hurry into Zoey's room, grabbing her day bag and quickly filling it as I rush to say, "Thank you, Monica. You've been a huge help."

"Anytime. You gonna go see my bro?"

"I'm going to try."

"That's what I wanted to hear. Good luck, chick. Let me know how it goes."

"Sure." I hang up and shove the last of Zoey's things into a bag before running to get dressed.

Armed with the truth, I'm now desperate to see Zander and make things right again.

Because I hate doing this life without him.

He's a good man, and Zoey deserves to have her father in her life.

Just like I deserve to be with the only man I've ever loved, dammit!

CHAPTER 52
SIENNA

Thank God Mrs. Ward is home and available to watch Zoey. As soon as I pull up beside her house, she opens the door and comes down the path to greet us. Zoey kicks her legs in excitement and yells, "Baking!"

"That's right, my sweet. You ready to for The Great Nolan Bake-Off?"

I laugh and Zoey looks confused for a moment, then giggles just because we're grinning at her.

Kissing her cheek, I wave goodbye and nervously jump back into the car. I have no idea where Zander is, which is why I park near the main admin building, then wander through campus asking for directions.

I'm now loitering near Athletes Hall and wondering how I'm supposed to get in.

When I asked at the admin building if they could please check Zander Donohue's schedule so I could find out where he might be, they looked at me like I was crazy.

As I was leaving, kind of dejected, some girl with bright red curls said, "A lot of the athletes have lunch in

Athletes Hall at this time of day." Pulling out her phone, she showed me a map of campus, and I could have kissed her.

"Thank you so much."

"You're welcome. Hope you find him." She trotted down the stairs next to me, then wandered off, shouting, "Lani!" and waving as she ran off toward a gorgeous woman with long black hair and a stunning smile.

Threading her arm through hers, I watched as the two of them walked along, laughing with each other.

For a second, it made me think of Olivia and how I just ditched that friendship like it meant nothing to me.

I cringe.

How many times in my life have I just run away when things got too hard?

Ever since I was a baby, I've been on the move and shifting. It's like my first instinct is to pack up and run when things get uncomfortable.

But I can't run from this.

Wringing my hands together, I glance at various people passing by, hoping one of them will turn for Athletes Hall and let me in. I can see I need a key card, but I don't want to stand right next to the door.

So, I'm waiting in a patch of sunshine, and the first person to come in or out of that place, I'm chasing down and—

"Sienna?" I whip around at the sound of my name, and my insides deflate as I watch Russell walking toward me with a big smile. "What are you doing here? Where's Zoey?"

"Uh, she's with Mrs. Ward." I tuck a lock of hair behind my ear and look to the pavement.

"You came to see me?" He glides his hand along my lower back and tries to pull me in, but I quickly jump to the side and shake my head. And that's when his smile disappears, his expression hardening. "Then why are you here?"

"Because I need to speak with Zander, and I—"

"What?" His tone gets sharp and snappy.

I internally cringe but stand my ground. "Do you know if he's in there? Could you please check for me?" I point to the building behind Russell and swallow when I catch a glimpse of his thunderous expression.

"Are you getting back together with him?" His voice is low and strained, and part of me wants to just lie.

But I can't keep trying to soften this truth for him. I just have to say it straight and clear.

Keeping my eyes off his face, I nod. "I hope so. We just need to work out a few things and—"

He snatches my arm. "Why are you doing this?"

"Because I love him and need to make things right between us."

I try to shake him off, but his hold on me tightens. "You are insane, you know that? He's a complete asshole. You can't keep going back to him like this. It's not fair to Zoey. I won't let you break up our family this way."

My eyes flash as I find the courage to look right at him. "Russell, we're *not* a family. You're not Zoey's father. Zander is. And I want to be with him, and I want her to have the privilege of being raised by him."

I may as well have kicked him in the balls. His face is practically ashen as he lets me go and whispers, "How could you do this to me? Have I not taken good enough care of you guys?"

"It's not that. You're great." I close my eyes, rubbing my forehead and mumbling, "I just don't love you in a romantic way. We can't be a family like that, Russell. Even if Zander wasn't in the picture, I'd be saying this to you."

It takes every ounce of willpower to open my eyes and check his expression. His jaw is clenched and he's shaking his head, looking beyond me like it's taking everything to hold himself together.

"I'm sorry," I whisper. "I don't want to hurt you, but I should have made this clearer a long time ago. You can't just kiss me goodbye like I'm your wife or something, and you can't keep making Zoey call you Dada. You're her Uncle Rusty, and she loves you so much. But we need to make sure those roles are clearly defined."

His nostrils flare as he stands there saying nothing.

"Russell, please, just—"

He turns his back to me, stalking off, his shoulders hunched as he walks away.

Now is probably not the best time to ask if he could please come back and swipe me into Athletes Hall. Dammit.

Crossing my arms, I pinch my biceps, feeling completely awful. I hate that I've just hurt Russell after everything he's done for us. But I had to tell him the truth, right? He obviously wasn't getting it, and... I've done the right thing.

I just wish it didn't hurt so much to do it.

Shuffling a little closer to Athletes Hall, I try to look through the glass doors to see if I can spot Zander, but they're tinted and it's impossible to—

I gasp as the doors slide open and a broad, muscly

man steps out of the building. He jolts back, moving to the side before crashing into me.

"Sorry," I murmur, biting my lip and looking to the ground.

"That's okay." His smile is kind, his brown gaze looking me over like he's trying to figure out why I'm here. "Can I help you?"

I suck in a breath, then quickly blurt, "I'm looking for Zander Donohue. And I swear I'm not some stalker-ish fangirl, and I know I could just call or text him, but I have to *see* him, you know? It's really important. This conversation can't happen over the phone. I need to be able to look into his eyes." Okay, so now I'm rambling. "And it's been the worst weekend, and we have to make things right, and I just need to find him and see him."

He takes all that in with a slow nod, then tips his head and asks, "You couldn't just call and get him to meet you somewhere?" The man's low voice is soft and easy, and now I feel like a total idiot. "Or are you worried he won't answer? I take it you guys had a fight or something?"

I nod, figuring I'll just go with his assumptions rather than having to explain that I've actually been ghosting Zander and not the other way around.

Shit.

Rubbing my forehead, I look up with a desperate frown. "Do you know if he's in there?"

The door pops open again, and a man with messy blond hair and tattoos rising up his neck saunters out. He gives me a friendly smile before looking at the kind man I'm talking to. "'Sup, bro?"

"Do you know if Zander Donohue's in there?" he asks for me.

"Yeah, he's at the football table by the window." Mr. Tats gives me a curious look before darting a glance at his buddy.

"Think we should let her in?"

He smirks, checking me over one more time. "Oh, why not. Athletes Hall could use a little drama every now and then." He raises his chin at the swipe pad. "Go on, Padre. Let her in."

"Oh, really?" I perk up as the shorter man pulls out his card and swipes it. The doors pop open, and I dance through them, spinning back to smile and wave. "Thank you!" I put my hands together. "Thank you, thank you, thank you."

Mr. Tats laughs while the Padre guy gives me a kind smile. "Good luck."

They turn and walk off while I nod and mumble to myself, "I'm gonna need it."

CHAPTER 53
ZANDER

My phone clatters onto the table as I drop it next to my lunch tray. Still no reply from Sienna. I left my final message last night, and all I can do now is wait. I won't hound her. She needs time to process, right?

But then Fuckwit Russell dropped my car off this morning. Found me just before I was about to walk into class and dumped the keys in my hand with a punchable smirk. "It's in the lot behind Athletes Hall. Have a nice life."

He didn't mean that last part, and all I could do was stand there, gripping my keys and hating myself some more. Part of me wanted to chase him down and ask how Sienna was doing, but he wouldn't have told me anything anyway.

Fuck. I've lost her for good.

With a soft groan, I bury my head in my hands, forgetting that I'm surrounded by my teammates. A hand lands on my shoulder, giving it a light squeeze.

"I'm sorry, man. It sucks." Grady tries to commiserate with me, but what does he know? His relationship with Teah is fucking perfect.

A foot nudges me under the table. "Snap out of it, dude. Focus on football."

Because that's Carson's answer to everything. And girls and parties and booze.

Yeah, well, I'm not going down that road again.

Not that any of them understand why I'm so uptight about that shit.

Fuck. I would do anything to erase my past. Not all of it, just that shitty-ass year where I became someone I didn't even know and—

"Zander."

My head pops up, the last voice I expected to hear cutting through my internal wailing.

"Sienna?" I blink, wondering for a second if she's an apparition.

She's standing on the other side of the table, her eyes bright and fiery, her mouth set in a determined line.

"We need to talk. Whatever you have going on, cancel it. I don't care if it's class or practice or what. Get out of it now, because this is really important."

Holy shit.

She has never spoken to me like this before. It's sexy as fuck.

It makes me want to jump up from the table and follow her like a well-trained police dog.

But why is she here?

To kick me in the nuts or forgive me?

To torture the truth out of me or tell me it's okay?

Would you fucking man up and go with her! She deserves the truth.

With a thick swallow, I nod and stand, my tray rattling when I accidentally kick the table with my knee.

Grady and Carson watch me like hawks as I stand and straighten my shirt. I glance at my best friend, who gives me a short nod and mutters, "Got you covered, bruh."

"Thanks," I croak, my eyes darting past Carson, who's shaking his head and looking annoyed.

Ignoring him, I walk down the line of tables, Sienna parallel to me on the other side. Her gaze is like a laser beam, and I'm seriously fried by the time we reach the door.

"Let's go to my car," I murmur, my insides writhing as we walk in silence to the parking lot.

I open the door for her, and she slips into the passenger seat while I walk around to the driver's door. My heart is pounding. I'm not sure where to go. She probably doesn't want to head back to my place, and I don't really want to sit here talking while curious students walk past, so I start the engine and drive to the other side of campus, heading behind the hockey arena to a wooded area that hardly anyone comes to.

Pulling the car to a stop near a grove of trees, I glance around and notice we're the only ones here. It actually kind of feels like we're the only people on Earth right now, and that's a good thing. Because what Sienna wants to say is going to weigh a fucking ton, and I don't need an audience.

As soon as the engine stops, I unclip my seat belt and start fidgeting with my watch strap. We haven't said a fucking word to each other since she appeared in the hall, and I'm dying.

Sienna's always got something to say.

And now she's quiet.

And I can't handle it, so I softly croak, "Did you get my messages?"

She shakes her head. "I haven't checked them."

"Oh." I work my jaw to the side. "So... uh... what are you—"

"Monica called." She sniffs, and then her eyes land right on me.

Damn, she's so beautiful I can hardly breathe sometimes. Those eyes are so bright and blue, staring at me with this addictive fire.

I can't let her go.

I can't lose her.

Clenching my jaw, I nod and run my fingers across the top of the steering wheel before gripping it tightly. "I'm guessing she told you... everything."

"Yeah." Sienna clears her throat and sniffs again. "My big question is... why didn't you? Why didn't you stop me on Saturday and explain everything? I walked away believing you were a rapist."

My face buckles and I wish I had something eloquent to say, but all I've got left is the raw, ugly truth. There's no more hiding right now. I just have to let her in and suffer the consequences. "I was so ashamed."

"But why? You saved that girl."

I wince, my throat swelling up tight, making my words quiet and thin. "She was probably just one of many. What if I knew and just didn't want to see it? How many girls got roofied and raped because I didn't want to rock the boat? Because I was angry and hurting and just wanted to get lost? I used the excuse of partying and fitting in and 'this is the way it's done... this is what I have to do if I want to get game time.' But what fucking bullshit!"

I slam the wheel, tortured in a way that's almost physical.

My chest hurts.

My knuckles feel like they're about to pop through my skin.

"I gave you up." My voice cracks. "I lost you. And I turned into a total shit. I spiraled, and I'm so ashamed of the person I became. I'd do anything to erase that year of my life. I deserved so much worse than a night in jail and a few broken ribs."

"They broke your ribs?" Sienna reaches for me like the injuries are fresh.

I lean away from her, not wanting her to touch me. I don't deserve her touch. I don't deserve fucking anything!

"They were just fractured," I mutter.

"Assholes," she hisses and shakes her head. "They were the ones who deserved to be in jail. You didn't do anything wrong. You saved her!"

A cold bleakness travels through me as I repeat my point. "But who didn't I save?"

"Zander." She tips her head. "You can't torture your-self that way. If you'd figured it out earlier, you would have acted earlier."

I shake my head, wanting to believe her but not sure if I can. So many parties. So much booze. I got wasted so many times.

"Hey." Sienna's hand is soft as she cups my cheek and guides me to look at her. "You need to forgive yourself."

Her eyes, so blue and kind.

God, I love her so much.

"Sure, you were a train wreck that year. But you're not anymore. And even back then, when you were making shitty decisions, the real you was still buried underneath, and it shone through when it needed to. Zander, you are good. You're a good man, and you need let yourself off the hook."

"How?" I rasp. "I've got a daughter now, and if anything like that ever happened to her..." Fear chokes me blind, and the tears I was holding back suddenly spring forth.

Sweet Zoey, my precious girl.

The thought of someone abusing her, scaring her, taking advantage of her body... a broken jaw would be the least of their worries.

"It won't happen to her." Sienna shifts in her seat, leaning over the handbrake and practically sitting on my lap. "Zander, listen to me." She holds either side of me face, her eyes bright with conviction. "You won't let anything like that happen to her."

"But it could. So easily. Those girls... *that* girl. She's someone's daughter."

"And I bet her father is really grateful for you."

Her words stop me short. I gaze back at her beautiful face and can't breathe.

"You saved his daughter. And you'll keep your own safe." Her smile is watery as she brushes her thumbs across my cheeks, wiping my tears away. "You're a good father, Zander. And I'm sorry that I denied you the first few years of her life. I'm sorry I didn't try harder to let you know."

And now her voice is wobbling, tears lining her lashes.

We can't both be crying. My heart's completely slain already. This will end me.

"Don't cry," I whisper, practically begging her. "I forgive you, okay? I get it. After what you saw me doing... I... get it."

"I'm sorry," she mouths, and I shake my head again.

"You don't have to be sorry. I'm the one who's sorry. I gave you the best reason to walk away, and I'll regret that forever."

"Please don't," she whispers. "You're here now."

"And I'm not leaving you again," I promise. "I really want to be the best dad I can for Zoey. The best man I can for you. I just wish I hadn't..." I let out a shaky sigh. "I want to change the past so bad. If I hadn't left you... If we'd just stayed together..."

Her sniff is delicate as she nods and sucks in a shaky breath. "We can't change any of that. All we can do is take what we have now and do the best we can with it." Lifting her leg, she straddles me.

I push the chair back as far as it will go, settling her on my lap and running my hand up to her neck. I need to touch her soft skin, feel her closeness.

"Let's make a deal." She licks her lips, and I nod, willing to agree to anything. "I'll stop running away every time I get hurt or scared. I'll stay. I'll talk it through. I'll answer your calls."

I smile at her.

"But you have to promise that you'll be honest with

me. *Every* time. No matter how shitty the truth is. You have to talk to me, Zander. Let me in."

"I will," I croak, cupping the back of her head and looking her right in the eye. "I love you, and I promise I won't hold back anymore."

Her eyes glisten as she smiles. "And I won't run. I'll stay. Forever."

CHAPTER 54
SIENNA

Forever.

The word resonates in my head as I fist his shirt and drag him toward me. Our lips connect with perfect pressure—a melding of souls, a promise of the years to come. My heart starts to flutter like a bird released from its cage, and all I can think right now is...

"I want you," I murmur against his lips.

He pauses, his breath skimming my cheek as he looks into my eyes. "You want me? Like..."

"Yes." I nod. "I really need you right now."

"Right now?"

I nod, struggling to explain how vitally important this connection is to me. I need him inside me. I want our bodies bonded together in the closest way possible, and it has to be right fucking now.

Desperation surges through me as I wrap my arms around his neck, squishing our bodies together while heat pumps through me in needy waves that are making me lightheaded.

"Sparks," he whispers against my skin, his arms looping behind my back, his fingers wriggling under my clothes and tracing patterns on my bare skin.

I whimper, wishing we could strip each other fully naked, but although we have privacy right now, I'm still aware that this is going to have to be a clothed quickie. Intense and real and just as meaningful as anything else we've done, but still... if a car drives past...

Zander seems to get this as well, his hand trailing around to my front so he can squeeze my boob, teasing my nipple through the lacy fabric of my bra.

"You sure?" he murmurs between kisses.

"Uh-huh." I fist the back of his hair, changing angles and kissing him deep and slow.

He moans into my mouth, and I can feel him growing hard beneath me.

Yes, yes, yes!

Urgency fires through me as I scramble for his pants. The top button pops open, and I rise up so I can yank down his zipper and set him free. Lifting his hips, he helps me shimmy his pants down to his thighs, and I smile down at his glorious manhood.

He's definitely bigger than he used to be. I wrap my fingers around his warm, hard cock, and we moan in unison when I give him a slow pump, then wipe the bead of liquid with my thumb.

"Sparks." His voice is low and guttural, sexy as all get-out, and my pussy is already weeping.

My entire body is vibrating, desperately needing this, and when his hands glide up my thighs, rounding my butt cheeks and giving them a firm squeeze, I whimper again.

A thick pulse of yearning beats through me as I pump him a little harder and he tucks his fingers into my waist-band, tugging my yoga pants down.

It's awkward as hell in this cramped space, but we manage this game of Twister, giggling into each other's mouths as he tugs my pants off, letting them dangle from one ankle. As soon as my pussy is free, he's sliding his fingers between my folds.

I'm still pumping his cock, and he's struggling to talk but manages a rasping "You're so wet."

"I need you, baby."

I gasp as his finger slips inside me, my inner walls clenching around him. His thumb teases my clit, and I moan against his cheek. He feels so good I can hardly take it.

His lips nibble my neck, then suck my earlobe while I start riding his fingers, gyrating against them but knowing I want something else.

"I need this"—I squeeze his cock—"inside me. Please tell me you've got—"

"Yes, yes, yes," he murmurs. "And well done for remembering." He grins at me, reaching into the back seat for his bag. "You make me forget. You're so addictive I can't think straight."

I keep stroking him, loving the way his hands shake while he's trying to pull a condom out of the box. At one point, he stops to tip his head back and groan, "You better stop or I'm gonna come before I even get inside you."

I immediately let him go and help him rip a condom free, then open the packet. Rolling it on for him, I check that it's secure and stop to smile at him.

Cupping his cheek, I brush my teeth over my bottom lip, then whisper, "I love you, Zander Donohue."

"I love you." His kiss is sweet and delicate, enough to make my heart fly right out of my chest and start fluttering around the car as I line us up and sink onto him.

His fingers dig into my thighs as he releases a sexy-ass moan. I love that sound so freaking much. Rising, I slowly lower myself again, watching his face as he tips his head back and groans again. His eyes are closed and he's lost in me, lost inside me, lost within us.

Caressing his cheek, I stare down at him, smiling when he kisses my palm. I run my thumb across his bottom lip, rising and sinking in a languid rhythm that's just for us. His eyes creep open, and he catches me watching him. The smile he gives me lights my soul. I can feel it burning within me, an orb of light that seems to shine brighter and brighter the longer we're connected this way.

His hands run up my thighs, the pads of his fingers teasing my skin as they travel to my sweet spot. His thumb starts working my clit, and I can't help a gasping moan. It's the weirdest sound, but holy hell. He's taking me over, filling and stretching my core until I'm consumed by him and his fingers... his magic fingers are...

My breathing turns ragged, my chest starting to heave as I pick up my pace.

The world around me fades.

There's no car.

There are no trees.

The birds aren't chirping outside.

There's just him and me.

There's only rising and falling.

There's nothing but this sense of fulfillment.

"I love you," I whisper. "I love you, I love you." My voice pitches as the orgasm builds within me.

I'm riding him faster now, my body pumping in time with his thumb on my clit until I feel like my heart's about to explode.

"Zander!" I cry out just before it takes me, flooding through my body in a wave so strong and pure I'm not sure I can handle it.

"Oh fuck." Zander snatches my hips, his strong fingers digging into me as he pumps me a little harder. "Fuck, Sparks. Fuck, I love you." He's basically groaning his words at this point, and I'm reveling in the delicious sounds coming out of him... coming out of us.

We're a wet, hot mess—a slip-and-slide of ecstasy. A joy ride of epic proportions.

"I'm coming," he groans. "Oh fuck, I'm coming."

Digging my fingers into his shoulders, I bite my lip, smiling at his reckless urgency when he thrusts his hips up and pulls me down on top of him. And again. And again. And...

"Ahhhh." He moans into my neck, licking and kissing my skin while he jerks inside me.

I pull him close, struggling to breathe, my hands shaking as I squeeze my thighs against his perfect ass cheeks and hold on tight.

Zander's heart is thundering against my chest, and he's gulping air as if he's just been underwater, holding his breath for too long.

"That was...," I barely manage.

He nods. "Yeah. Yeah, it was..."

"I know, right?" A delirious laugh pops out of me. I kiss the side of his face, loving the way his arms tighten, holding me as close as possible while we recover from that heady rush.

"Move back in with me?" His voice is so quiet, it takes me a second to catch what he just said. But as soon as it registers, I lean back to make sure he's serious.

His face is so beautiful, his eyes deep with sincerity.

"I need you with me. I want to come home to you and Zoey. I want to wake up beside you. Please, Sparks. Move in with me."

My heart burns for this, the very idea making me giddy, but...

"What about Carson? And the rest of the guys?"

Brushing my hair over my shoulder, he gazes up at me with a reassuring smile. "We'll make it work. We'll find a way, a compromise so we can be together."

"Carson has a point about Football Frat not being the best environment for a toddler."

"The guys love her."

"Yeah, but for how long? The novelty will wear off soon enough, and—"

"I feel like you're making excuses to—"

"No." I laugh at the way we keep interrupting each other as I grab his face and quickly assure him, "I *want* to move in with you. Of course I want us to be a family together. I love living at Football Frat. I'm just trying to be considerate of everybody else. I don't want to get in the way of college life, you know?"

His expression softens, his eyes glowing with affection. "We'll figure something out, Sen. There's bound to be a solution, we just have to find it. But for now... for tonight... be with me."

His tone has a gentle vulnerability to it that touches my heart, and I'm saying yes before I can think better of it.

"Really?"

Oh, that hopeful grin. He's adorable.

"Yes." I laugh, kissing him. "I'll go back to Russell's and collect our stuff, then pick up Zoey from Mrs. Ward's place. I'll be there by the time you finish practice."

"Okay." A broad smile takes over his face as he holds my neck and pulls me in for a slow kiss that curls my toes.

"We're gonna make this work, Sparks. It's gonna work."

"Yeah." I nod. "It is."

CHAPTER 55
ZANDER

It took a little minute to clean up after our hot, sticky hookup.

Shit, that was intense and so fucking good.

I wish we could have been fully naked, but being inside her that way was like signing a contract or something. I don't know if that sounds dumb, but after everything I'd confessed and we'd promised each other, it felt so fucking right to finish our conversation that way.

I'm now running late for practice, but I'll explain everything to Coach as soon as I get the chance. If he's pissed, he's pissed. I did the right thing this afternoon... and there's one more thing I gotta do before I can finally make peace with myself.

Walking into the locker room, I seek out my friends. Thankfully, they're all taping up and getting dressed in the same area, and I rush over to them before I lose my nerve.

"I have to tell you something," I blurt.

They all turn to face me, and I glance over my shoulder, lowering my voice so the rest of the team can't hear me.

"It's important."

"Aw shit, you just had sex, didn't you?" Carson shakes his head, narrowing his eyes at me. "Are we gonna have to start living with a toddler again?"

"Yes, but that's not what I need to say." I swallow, my insides buckling as I check their faces.

Carson's grumpy demeanor drops for a second, genuine concern flashing across his face. "What is it?"

Grady rests his hand on my shoulder. "Are you about to hurl chunks? You look green."

I swallow, clenching my jaw and wondering how I'm gonna get through this.

If Sienna can forgive you, these guys will too.

"Okay, gentlemen, let's go!" Coach calls from the door.

I spin and catch his eye.

He frowns at me. "You better hurry up and get your ass ready for practice."

"I just have to talk to these guys first." I point at them with a flick of my thumb as the last of the team trails out. Shit, I hope Coach Jones can read minds. I throw him a desperate, pleading look.

His eyes narrow into two thin slits, and then realization slowly dawns. He knows what I'm about to do, and without a word, he gives me a quick nod and mumbles, "See you out there soon."

Eyeing my housemates, a look of mild concern washes over his expression before he turns and leaves.

"What the fuck was that about?" Carson points after Coach.

I close my eyes with a shuddering sigh and tell them,

"He knows everything. He knows exactly why I transferred to Nolan U. He helped me do it."

"O-kay." Grady frowns. "What aren't you telling us?"

He almost looks offended, and I shake my head and glance at Wily.

He gives me an encouraging smile, nodding and silently telling me to get on with it.

My legs buckle and I plunk down on the closest bench seat, resting my elbows on my knees and letting it all out.

I don't hold back and tell them every ugly, dirty detail of my life at Kelsey U. I can't look up at their reactions, so I keep my eyes trained on the floor, confessing my darkest sins and hoping they won't kick me out of the house.

"So, when Coach offered to let me go with him, I jumped at the chance." I sigh. "I know I don't deserve it or anything, but... I just had to get away from the Titans."

I finally stop talking, smashing my teeth together as I wait for them to respond.

The silence that follows is painful, and my knee starts bobbing as I wait it out.

"Well, fuck me," Grady mutters, taking a seat beside me and shaking his head. "How did we not know about this? I'm surprised it wasn't splashed all over the media. That's a huge scandal."

"The school managed to keep it quiet. To be honest, I was really grateful for that, although..." I shrug. "Maybe it would have been better if it was publicized. Maybe that's exactly what we all deserved."

"I would have killed those motherfuckers," Carson hisses. "That asswipe is lucky you only broke his jaw."

"We should have tackled harder at Saturday's game." Tyrell's tone is just as dark as Carson's.

Wily takes a seat on my other side, nudging me with his elbow. "No wonder you're so paranoid about drinks and drugs at our parties."

I glance at him and nearly can't believe his smile.

He's smiling? At me? After everything I just told him.

He laughs at my expression. I don't know what my face is doing, but he elbows me again. "Dude, what? Are we supposed to hate you now or something?"

I blink and shake my head. "I... maybe?"

"Oh, please." Carson rolls his eyes. "So you were a little shit for a year. I'm a shit all the time, and you guys still let me live with you." He shrugs, throwing on his practice shirt. "You could have told us this ages ago, man. It's not like we would have kicked you out of the house."

"I just... hate myself for what I let happen. What I did. What I became." I cringe, running a hand through my hair.

Tyrell shrugs. "We all make fucked-up choices we regret. That's life. When it came to the crunch, you did the right thing."

"Yeah, man." Grady squeezes my shoulder. "Don't waste your time beating yourself up. It's done. It's over. You gotta live in the now."

I let out a surprised laugh, shaking my head. "You guys are..." I huff out another laugh, then swallow and look around at them all. "Thank you."

"Don't worry about it." Wily slaps my back, then stands tall. "Come on, let's go play some ball."

With a nod, I stand and give each of them another

silent thank-you before letting them know, "Sienna and Zoey will be back tonight."

"What?" Carson whines. "Are you fucking kidding me? They're not moving back in for good, are they?"

I clench my jaw and give him a nod. "I want them with me, man. Sienna's my woman, and Zoey's my daughter. They belong with me."

"They can't live at Football Frat. It won't work."

"Well, I'll just have to figure out some new living arrangements, then." I shrug, hating that idea, but—

"Are you kidding me?" Wily argues, lightly shoving Caron's shoulder. "We're not breaking up the crew."

Carson shoves him back. "We can't add to it with some chick and a toddler!"

"Fine, it'll be a temporary solution."

"It better be," Carson warns, grabbing his helmet and pointing it at me with a warning frown. "I want to be able to walk around my house butt-ass naked. I want to be able to bring chicks home and bang them as loud as I fucking want. I can't do that with a toddler in the room next door."

I raise my hands. "That's fair. We'll figure something out. If you just give me a little time, I'd appreciate it."

"Make it quick," he mutters before stalking out of the locker room.

I wince at the rest of my teammates and get various slaps on the back.

"We'll figure it out. Don't worry man."

"I don't mind having them around."

"Yeehaw!" Wily makes a coyote call and puts on a thick Southern drawl. "My little cowgirl's coming home."

CHAPTER 56
SIENNA

I sing my way back to Russell's place. Taylor Swift keeps me company, and I belt out the lyrics to her most romantic songs, my body still buzzing after what went down in Zander's car.

Mmmm-hmmm. I love that man so much I could burst.

Seriously, I feel like I'm flying, giddy laughter bubbling inside me as I pull up beside Russell's house.

But the light emotion quickly dies when I pull his keys out of the ignition and realize that I'm about to piss him off... or hurt him... all over again.

Shit.

Closing my eyes, I rest my head on the steering wheel and take the chicken's way out, praying that he's not home and I can just call him later to tell him what I've done, and that Zoey and I will be moving back in with Zander.

I swallow. I wonder what the Football Frat guys will think of that.

Worrying my lip, I try not to let reality spoil what has been an epic afternoon.

Zander and I are back together, for good this time. No more secrets. No more ghosting. We're making this work. I'm determined.

And that's what gets me out of the car.

That's what has me walking up the front steps.

Determination to be with the person I was born to be with.

I've only ever loved him, and now he's mine forever.

A smile tugs at my lips, then grows to full beam when I walk into the house and quickly realize it's empty.

"Thank you, God," I murmur to the ceiling as I rush to Zoey's room, gathering her stuff as quickly as I can.

Reaching under the changing table, I go to grab her diaper bag and am surprised to find it missing. I thought I'd dropped off the small bag at Mrs. Ward's, but I must have given her the bigger one. My brain wasn't functioning at full capacity this morning. The small one is probably in the stroller, which is in the back of Russell's car still.

"Okay, fine. So, I'll just..." Reaching under Zoey's crib, I pull out her little pink suitcase and fill it with three days' worth of clothes. I'll need to come back again, but I don't want to clear everything out of Russell's place until Zander and I have come up with a more permanent solution. Living at the Football Frat won't work. I'm not sure what we're going to do, but Zoey's crib and changing table can stay here until we definitely know.

Skipping down to my room, I pull out my suitcase and start filling it with the essentials when my phone starts ringing.

I glance at the screen, my stomach twisting uncomfortably, but I answer the video call anyway.

"Hey, Mom."

"Hey, Blue!" Dad pops up behind my mother before she can even say hi.

I laugh. "Hey, Dad."

"We just wanted to call and check in," Mom explains. "We know you had a rough weekend. How are you doing today?"

"I'm great, actually." I smile at the screen and just decide to say it. "Zander and I have worked it out. For good this time. We're back together, and... I know you guys probably don't love that idea, but he is Zoey's father, and I love him. I *really* love him."

They take a second to absorb that, blinking and opening their mouths like goldfish, until Mom manages to sputter, "B-but what about—"

"He's told me everything, and he wasn't in the wrong the way I thought he was. He was being way too hard on himself. Anyway, I've forgiven him. He screwed up big-time that year, but I can't hold that against him forever. He's a good man... and I love him."

"Yeah, so you've said." Dad's tone is dry, his concern obvious as he squishes next to Mom so I can see his face.

Mom worries her lip just the way I do, then lets out a sigh. "How's Russell taking this?"

"Not well," I admit. "I bumped into him on campus when I was looking for Zander, and he was... *pissed*."

"Aw, sweetie."

"Look, I'm sorry." My expression buckles. "I know you wanted me to fall in love with him. You had this perfect

435

plan for me, but... I've never felt that way about him, and he was trying so hard to force the issue."

"What do you mean?" Dad frowns.

"He just..." I rub my forehead. "I didn't mention it to you guys, but he's been trying to get Zoey to call him Dada, and this morning when he left for work, he... he kissed me right on the mouth." I frown. "It made me so uncomfortable."

Dad's frown is morphing from concern to anger. "He shouldn't have done that."

"I know, right?" I nod, relieved that my parents are agreeing with me on this.

Mom winces. "That must have been awkward."

"Yeah, when it first happened, I didn't even know what to say, but then when I found my head a little later, I told him that I wasn't comfortable with it." My lips turn into a soft pout. "I think I really hurt his feelings."

"Well, he's obviously not taking yours into consideration." Mom shakes her head. "And I'm sad that he has feelings for you that you can't reciprocate, but he still needs to respect you and your boundaries."

I nod, but still feel kind of bad. Not guilty, just... sad that things aren't easier.

"I don't want to hurt him, but..." I shrug. "I'm in love with someone else."

"Are you sure?" Dad asks. "You really want Zander?"

"Yes." I say it so emphatically that I start to laugh... and then emotion gets the better of me, and I perch on the end of my bed and tell them everything. My feelings, my misunderstanding, his truth, our forgiveness. It all spills out in a torrent, and finally they understand it all.

"Wow." Mom's in shock.

Dad's nodding and tipping his head. "Well, he sure screwed up pretty badly, but at the end of the day... he did the right thing."

"He's a good man, Dad. I never should have cut him out the way I did."

His smile is glum. "Maybe we all made the wrong call there. But at the time, it felt right."

"It did." I nod. "But it was still wrong of us. We shouldn't have kept him in the dark like that. He's actually a really good father. You should see him with Zoey. It's seriously adorable."

Mom starts to smile. "Is she still calling him Foobawl?"

"Yeah." I laugh, slashing the last of my tears away. "I'm not sure she'll ever call him Daddy. Well, she did one time, but... I'm not sure when it will happen again."

"It'll happen," Dad assures me, his eyes starting to glisten as he stares through the phone at me. "I know this has been a tough ride, but I'm proud of you, Blue. You're a good mom. You're a good daughter."

"Aw, thanks, Dad."

"You've always known your heart," Mom continues. "From the youngest age, you've always been so determined to go after the things you want. And ever since you met Zander, you've wanted him. He lit you up like no one else could."

My smile grows wide. "He still does."

"I can see that." Mom laughs, then leans her head against Dad's cheek.

He shifts to kiss her forehead, and then they snuggle close again.

"I love you guys." I blow a kiss to the camera. "I better go pick up Zoey."

"Okay." Mom nods. "Let us know how it goes with telling Russell."

"Yeah." I wince. "I'll call you in a couple days."

Dad gives me a thumbs-up. "Give my grandbaby a kiss from me."

"Will do. I'll make sure she's around for the next call."

"That'll be lovely." Mom blows a few kisses back to me, and then I hang up and quickly pack the rest of my stuff.

Russell could be home at any minute, although he's most likely at hockey practice. Glancing at my watch, I hurry anyway, hauling my stuff out to the car and loading it up. I'll have to return it tomorrow. I'll talk to him then and hope he won't be too angry with me. Maybe I should bring Wily and Tyrell along for protection detail. They seemed to work pretty well last time.

With a nervous laugh, I pull away from the curb and head to Mrs. Ward's house. I still have the spare key to Football Frat, so I'm going to collect Zoey, take her back there for dinner and a bath, and make sure we're all unpacked before the guys get home.

Checking the time, I wince. Man, I am so late to pick up my baby girl. The call with my parents took over an hour, but it was an important one. Knowing I have their support means so much to me.

I should call Mrs. Ward and let her know I'm coming, but I'm almost there, so I drive just a touch faster and pull into her driveway at a quick clip. Jumping out, I run to the front door and do a friendly knock, bouncing on my toes while I wait.

An excited buzz is vibrating through me, and I'm grinning like a circus performer when Mrs. Ward finally opens the door.

"Hey." I greet her cheerfully. "I'm so sorry I'm late. The day got away from me, but... is Zoey... here?" My chatter trails off as I take in Mrs. Ward's confused expression.

"Well, no, dear."

A sharp jolt shoots through my chest. "I'm sorry?"

"Russell came to pick her up. He said you'd called to let him know you were running late."

What!

My insides flail, my hand trembling as I place it against my surging stomach. "When did he come?"

"About an hour ago. I thought you knew." Mrs. Ward steps toward me, worry creasing her expression, border-line panic filling her eyes.

Oh shit. I don't want to make her feel bad. Or worry her.

Putting on a bright smile I'm far from feeling, I nod. "You know what? Of course. I remember now." Tapping my forehead, I put on the show of a lifetime. "My brain is so muddled today. This is what running late does to me." My laughter is high and pitchy as I back away from her front door and start heading for the car. Raising my hand, I call over my shoulder, "Thanks again for looking after my girl."

"Anytime, sweetheart. You take care now."

I don't think she's convinced by my performance, as she stays in the doorway, looking at me with a worried frown as I pull back onto the road and squeal off.

Punching my phone screen, I call Russell.

439

"Hello, Sienna." His voice is sounding eerily strange. It sets my teeth on edge.

Panic starts to get the better of me and I end up shouting, "Where's my daughter?"

"She's safe."

"What the hell does that mean?" I slam on the brakes, my chest heaving at the intersection while I stare at my phone screen. "Where is Zoey!"

"She's safe with me. If you want to see her, all you have to do is agree to never see Zander again. You come and stay with me, and we can be a family. Just the way it should be."

My blood runs cold.

Is he serious?

This can't be happening right now.

I feel like I've just been transported into some sick psychological thriller.

A horn blasts behind me and I jolt, moving through the intersection blindly before pulling to the side of the road and gripping the wheel.

"Russell, you tell me where you are right now."

"You leave Zander right now."

"I'm not going to do that! Now stop acting like a crazy psycho or I'm calling the police."

He lets out a soft laugh. "If I hear one siren, I will disappear with her for good, and you'll never see her again."

What the fuck?

My eyes bulge, my heart catapulting into my throat.

"Have you completely lost your mind!" I shout. "You give me back my daughter!"

"I've told you how to get access to our girl. It's up to

you now, Sienna. Say yes and I'll tell you exactly where we are."

"What?" I breathe out the word, shock stealing all my volume.

"I'll give you a minute to decide." He hangs up, and I gape at my phone, his words swirling around me before I let out a rage-filled, panic-induced scream.

CHAPTER 57
ZANDER

Practice was intense, but it was exactly what I needed.

Sweat is pouring off me as I jog down the ramp to the locker room. I ran so many fucking drills today, but I was focused and on form. Knowing things are right with Sienna again was the energy injection I needed.

The Cougars are going to see out this season and win our conference. I can feel it.

Stripping off my damp gear, I stow my pads away and throw my practice jersey at the hamper. The fact that our football laundry gets done for us is fucking epic. I feel sorry for the guy who washes that stink pile each day, but I'm grateful.

I must thank him the next time I spot him. If only I could remember his name.

Shit. I hate that I suck so bad with names.

"Good job out there." Grady puffs, stripping off his clothes while walking over to me. "You were on fire, man."

"Yeah, I'm feeling it today."

"I wonder why." He wriggles his eyebrows, and we laugh together, pounding fists before Wily muscles in on our conversation.

"What's the haps tonight? We going to Offside?"

"I'm out." Carson, who has the ability to get changed like the fucking Flash, is already heading for the door.

"What, you not gonna shower, you disgusting douchenozzle?" Grady calls after him.

He turns with a smirk and raises both middle fingers. "Chicks like me sweaty."

I roll my eyes while Wily shouts after him, "You smell like ass!"

"Shower in a can, dickheads!" he calls over his shoulder before disappearing from view.

Tyrell laughs, grabbing a towel and heading for the showers.

I'm about to do the same when my phone starts ringing. Pulling it out of my bag, I check the screen and grin.

Wily notices and nudges me with a laugh while Grady lightly punches my shoulder, obviously happy for me. The guy has always been a romantic.

"Hey, Sparks."

"Zander! He's taken Zoey. Shit! I don't know where she is or what he's doing with her. Shit, shit, shit!" Words punch out of her like sobs, and I'm struggling to register what she's saying.

I blink and press the phone closer to my ear. "Sienna, what? Who's got Zoey?"

"Russell! He picked her up from Mrs. Ward's place before I got there. I tried calling him to ask where she is, and he says he won't give her back to me unless I dump you and be with him. He's fucking psycho!" Sienna lets out another sob while I gape at the wall, trying to comprehend this shit.

A raging hot fury swirls through me like a tornado, and the first thing to pop out is a low growl. I am going to kill that fucker. If he's scared my daughter…

My guts start to boil.

He's fucking scaring my woman, and that's enough for me to issue a "Your Life is Over" warrant.

"I don't know how to find him," Sienna whimpers. "And he said if I call the police, he'll take Zoey away and I'll never see her again."

"Dude, is everything okay?" Grady leans in, catching my eye.

I clench my jaw, shaking my head and gritting out a soft. "Sienna, where are you, baby?"

"Ummm… I'm on, um… the road with the pet store on the corner and that diner that makes the amazing milkshakes. You know the one?"

"Yeah, yeah. Okay. I'm gonna come and get you, and we'll figure this out together. We'll find her, okay? I promise you. We're getting her back."

"He's lost his mind," Sienna's whispering on repeat. "He's lost his fucking mind."

"It's gonna be okay."

Fuck, those words feel so useless and empty.

What I really mean is it *better* be okay, or *I'm* the one who'll be losing his fucking mind!

"Zander?" Grady's right in my grill as I hang up and snatch my bag off the hook. "What the fuck, man?"

"Russell's taken Zoey. Sienna's freaking out, and I've got to go be with her."

"What do you mean, he's taken her?" Wily barks, snatching my arm before I can leave.

I shake him off and growl, "It means he's taken her without Sienna's permission, and he won't fucking tell her where she is!"

My voice cuts across the conversations in the locker room, and soon every head is turned my direction. I don't know if everybody heard me, but I figure, what the fuck... I could use the help.

"My daughter's missing!" I flick my hands up. "She's been taken by Russell Fisher. He's the assistant coach for the hockey team, and I need to find her. Fast."

"Start at the arena," someone suggests.

"We'll start canvassing the campus," someone else shouts. "Have you got a picture?"

I pull out my phone, my hands shaking and making it nearly impossible to upload my latest picture of Zoey to the team group chat.

"We should be calling the cops!"

"No!" I shout. "He said if we do that, he'll disappear with her for good. I'm not taking any chances. Just... help me find my girl, okay!"

There's a rush of activity as football players move into action, and I grab Wily's shirt while Grady moves in to hear me. "The arena's a good idea. I'm gonna go get Sen, then meet you there, okay?"

"Got it."

"I'm gonna let Coach know." Tyrell rushes past me with nothing but a towel wrapped around his waist. He's still dripping from his shower.

I nod and bolt out the door after him, running to my car.

I call Sienna on the way, and she tells me she's okay to drive and will meet me at the arena.

That's my girl.

Squealing away from the stadium, I haul ass to the arena and pull in just before Sienna gets there. I'm opening her door for her as soon as she's parked and pulling her into a fierce hug.

She clings to me, shuddering against my chest.

"It's gonna be okay." I rub her back. "The whole team is out looking for her. We'll find our girl, okay?" Pulling back, I hold her face and make sure she's looking at me. "We'll get her back."

"Yeah." Her head bobs erratically, and I take her hand, pulling her toward the arena and starting to shout when I see two guys walking out with hockey bags slung over their shoulders.

CHAPTER 58
SIENNA

"Hey!" Zander catches the attention of two hockey players.

The taller one turns, brushing floppy hair back off his face and eyeing us with confusion as we run toward him.

"'Sup, Donohue?" He raises his chin, then looks past us and waves.

I whip a look over my shoulder and see Wily racing out of his truck. Grady slams the other door and is bolting our way too.

Thank God.

Wily gives my shoulder a light squeeze as he greets the tall one. "Hey, Ethan."

"Wily Wilson." The guy grins, and I get the impression that he greets the blond football player the same way every time.

But his smile quickly vanishes when he takes in our expressions. "Okay, what's going on?"

Two more hockey players slip out of the arena and

notice us standing there. Obvious curiosity pulls them in our direction.

"My daughter's missing," Zander starts to explain.

Ethan's eyebrows pop high. "Wow, dude... you've got a kid? When did that happen?"

"A while ago."

"How did you not know that?" A stylish-looking guy with dark hair slaps him on the arm. "The rumors have been rife for weeks." His smile grows as he looks from Zander to me. "Congratulations, by the way. I've heard she's a real cutie."

"What?" I snap. "How do you know about Zoey? Do you know where she is right now?" I push around the tall guy and start poking Mr. Slick in the chest. "Did you help him take her?"

"Uh... nope." He raises his hands as two white flags while the guy beside him starts snickering.

"Ash-Man's scared of the little blondie."

"She's yelling in my face, dude. What the fuck is going on!"

"Hey, don't yell at her!" Zander thunders at him. "And don't you fucking touch her "

"I'm not touching her! She's touching me!" Ash-man yells back. "Everybody just needs to calm the fuck down and tell me what's going on!"

"Okay!" The guy who let me into Athletes Hall earlier today steps between me and his teammate, lightly nudging me back. His voice is calm and easy as he looks around us. "We're not accomplishing anything right now." Looking at me with his kind brown eyes, he softly asks, "Is your daughter missing? How can we help?"

Covering my mouth, I nod and fight an onslaught of

tears while Zander steps up and wraps his arm around my shoulders. "Your assistant coach."

"Oh, you mean Fish Sticks?" Mr. Tats crosses his arm and snorts. "That twat didn't even show up to practice today."

"That's because he was busy taking my daughter!" I scream. "He picked her up from the babysitter when I was with Zander, and now he's threatening to disappear with her unless I meet his ridiculous demands!"

Four shocked gazes stare back at me, one of the guys mumbling, "What the actual shit?"

"I know!" My voice cracks before I manage to bring it down an octave and ask, "Do you know where he might be?"

"Uh, no... but"—Ethan points back to the arena— "I'm gonna check in with the coaching staff." He runs toward the glass doors, and I hold my breath while he swipes his card. I then just have to stand there for what feels like an eternity, avoiding gazes from the hockey guys and irate pacing from Wily while he checks with the other coaches.

When the arena doors pop back open and I see two worried staff members running out of there, I let out a shuddering breath.

One of them walks straight toward me, pulling out his phone as he talks. "I'm Coach Bergeron. Ethan's told me the problem. Are you Zoey's mother?"

"Yes." I take his hand and give it a weak shake.

"Russell won't shut up about you guys. I was looking forward to meeting you, but not under these circumstances." He frowns down at his phone. "He came back from lunch and was really off. I mean, he's been off for a few weeks now, but today was next-level. He asked to borrow my truck. He said it was for a personal appointment. He seemed kind of hedgy and anxious, so I passed on my keys without thinking, assuming he was going to see a doctor or specialist. I was waiting for him to come back with news that he had cancer or something. That would explain his slightly erratic behavior, but..." The man shakes his head, muttering a string of curse words under his breath. "He's not answering."

"How are we going to find him?" I look at Zander.

"Does your truck have any kind of tracking device?" Grady steps forward.

The coach shrugs. "I don't know. I'm not a tech guy."

Grady quickly asks for the specs, and Coach Bergeron does at least remember the make and model.

"Those trucks will definitely have something. Is there an app on your phone?"

"Uh... yeah, I think so, but I never use it." Coach Bergeron shrugs and hands his phone to Grady.

I step up beside him, watching his thumbs race across the screen as he quickly finds the app and gets to work hunting down the coach's truck.

"There it is." Tapping the screen, he shows Zander, who nods.

"I know where that is."

Snatching my hand, he starts pulling me toward his car, and we run over together, ignoring the shouts behind us.

We have one focus right now, and it's to get to our girl.

I just pray she's okay.

What the hell has Russell done to her?

I try to remind myself how much he loves her and

that he wouldn't hurt her, but my mind is in chaos, my body convulsing as I try to deal with my worst fear. The one thing I thought I'd never be able to handle as a parent is now happening to me.

But I have to survive it.

I can't fall apart right now, because I have to get my baby girl back.

CHAPTER 59
ZANDER

I drive like a demon and don't slow until we pull into the wooded area on the outskirts of town. We have an army of people looking for Zoey, and I'm grateful to every one of them, but if Russell is where Coach Bergeron's truck is, then we need to go for a quiet approach.

Coming to a stop on the side of the road, I peer into the greenery and think I spot a taillight.

"Do you see anything?" Sienna asks, her voice a shaking, wispy mess. Her eyes are so swollen and red-rimmed she looks like she's had stage makeup applied.

I hate seeing her like this and lightly brush my finger down her cheek, trying to comfort her in even the smallest way.

My insides are raging. It's taking maximum effort not to turn green and start smashing the shit out of everything around me, but I have to stay calm. For her. For Zoey.

So I nod and keep my tone soft and even. "I see the edge of a truck. I'm assuming it belongs to Coach Bergeron. Down that way"—I point into the wooded area—"there's this abandoned greenhouse and a barn and stables and stuff. This is the edge of an old farm, and it's been sold off in sections. I don't know who owns this land, but students have been coming down here ever since I started at Nolan U. It's a quiet place to share a drink or a smoke or... you know."

Sienna whimpers, covering her mouth and sobbing into her hand.

I squeeze her shoulder, running my hand down her arm. "There's a chance he's got her in there."

"I can't breathe." She pushes her hand against her chest. Her face is bunched in agony. This is fucking killing me.

"Hey." Peeling her fingers away from her body, I thread them through mine and kiss her knuckles. "Sparks, we can do this. We can get her back."

"Yeah." Her head bobs, her breath shaky when she finally releases it.

"Come on. Let's go." Slipping out of the car, I close the door quietly and walk around the vehicle, grabbing Sienna's wrist before she bolts across the road and gets hit by the car that's speeding toward us.

The truck pulls to the side, slamming to a stop behind my SUV. Wily and Grady jump out, both looking ready to maim and slaughter for the sake of my family. I'm so fucking grateful right now.

"The police are on their way," Grady informs me. "I tried to say no cops, but Coach B wouldn't have it. He's called anyway. We left while he was still on the phone."

"Okay, well... we have to go and get her before they arrive." Sienna points across the road.

"They'll approach quietly. Coach B was explaining it as we left."

"I don't care. I'm not waiting for the cops." Sienna shakes her head. "Let's sneak up quietly and get her back before he disappears for good." She ends in a squeak, stealing some of the power from her assertive commands.

I squeeze her wrist, then thread my fingers between hers again. "I think he might have her in that greenhouse or the stables maybe. Have you guys been here before?"

"Yeah." Wily nods.

"Teah and I have come out here before." Grady points into the bushes and quickly describes the layout.

"Okay." I visualize what he's saying. "Okay, Wily can you flank the left side, and if you don't seem them in there, head toward the stables, do a systematic search from north to south?"

"Got it."

"Grady, you start on the right and follow through to the barn. Sienna and I will check the car, then head to the front of the greenhouse. Hopefully one of us can catch him somewhere along the way. Be quiet. We don't want to scare him off."

"What if he's not here?" Sienna blurts.

I squeeze her hand. "We'll check this area and deal with that question once we know for sure."

Her head starts to bob again, and I can feel her waves of panic washing over me.

It's tempting to fall apart right alongside her, but like hell that douche is taking my baby girl without a fight. We're getting Zoey back. There's no other option.

Another vehicle pulls up just as we're crossing the road… and four hockey players pile out of it.

"Where do you want us?" Ethan asks.

I point behind me and dish out a few more directions.

Casey pulls out his phone. "I'm gonna record this shit. Any evidence we can get to bury this fuck nugget, right?"

"Thanks, man." I nod and spin to get on with it.

Wily pulls out his phone as well, unlocking it as we split up and quietly form a perimeter around the old greenhouse and surrounding buildings.

We pass Coach Bergeron's truck, and I glance in the windows, making sure it's empty before moving on. I spot Zoey's diaper bag, and it fuels my anger. That fucker is not taking my daughter away from me!

Spotting the edge of the greenhouse, we slow our steps, creeping as carefully as we can through the under-growth. I crouch low and catch my breath when I hear Russell's voice.

"It's okay, sweetie. Mommy's calling back any second now, and then we're going to go on an adventure together."

"Like hell," Sienna hisses, letting go of my hand and bolting into the greenhouse.

"Mommy!" Zoey's sweet enthusiasm pierces me right in the center of my chest. I want to run in and grab her, but I force myself to use a little self-control and hang back, wondering if Sienna can talk Russell down and we won't have to traumatize Zoey with a fight.

If she can get her close and make a run for it, then I'll step in to stop Russell giving chase.

Crouching near the entrance, I steal a peek through the broken window and form a tight fist when Zoey tries to run to Sienna and Russell grabs her by the back of the jacket, pulling her to a stop.

"Stay with Daddy, sweetheart."

"You're not her daddy," Sienna warns him. "Now, you let her go."

"Mommy?" Sienna's expression buckles, and she points to the plastic cups and saucers on the picnic blanket behind her. "Tea pawty!" She smiles, so obviously trying to break the tension.

Sienna's shoulders shake, and I can sense her body convulsing as she crouches down to get eye level with Zoey. "That looks so fun."

"Wanna pay?"

"I do." Sienna nods. "But first I want you to come with me, and then we can play with Football and Wily. They'll play with you."

"Foobawl!" Zoey jumps on her toes, and it takes everything in me not to bolt through the door, punch Russell in the throat, and carry Zoey out of there.

But I won't scare her like that, and I have no idea how Russell will react if I make an appearance. Even just my name is causing his face to mottle into an angry shade of red.

"Zoey, come here," he snaps.

My little girl flinches, and she turns to look at her Uncle Rusty with a confused pout.

"We're having fun." He softens his voice. "You want to play with *me*, don't you?"

She looks back at Sienna, her sweet little face the picture of uncertainty.

"I know it's confusing, lil' bug." Sienna's voice is wobbling with unshed tears. "But you really need to come with Mommy now. Uncle Rusty wasn't supposed to take you on an adventure today. I was going to pick you up from Mrs. Ward's house." She's doing an amazing job at keeping her tone light and fun. I can only imagine how much effort that's taking. "So, you ask Uncle Rusty to let you go and you come with me, okay?"

Sienna holds out her arms just as Russell snatches Zoey back against his chest.

Zoey lets out a frightened wail, but it's drowned out by Russell's shouting. "I have every right to pick her up. She's mine! I've practically been raising her ever since she was born! You're just too blind to see reason!"

"Russell, don't do this," Sienna begs. "Please, just... don't hurt her."

"I'm not going to hurt her! I love her!"

"You're scaring her."

"She's the best part of my life, and you're trying to take her away from me. I thought when you moved to Nolan, we could finally be a family, but you're being such a stubborn bitch about it!"

Sienna jolts back like he's just slapped her, and I can't fucking do this anymore.

Standing tall, I storm into the greenhouse with a growl and point my finger at Russell "Let my daughter go. Right now!"

Russell sneers, his eyes wild as he clutches Zoey, who's now squirming like a trapped animal. "I've been the closest thing she's ever had to a father, and then this douche comes along and just takes over?" His voice pitches with incredulity. "That's not right, Sienna!"

"Zander *is* her father, and he's a good one. I'm sorry it hasn't worked out the way you wanted, but I've never loved you like a wife. We were never going to get married and raise Zoey together. That wasn't in the cards for me."

Russell's expression buckles, his chest starting to heave.

Zoey whimpers, her bottom lip forming a deep pout just before her tears bubble out in a loud wail.

This is killing me, but I'm trying my best to stay calm. I don't want to scare Zoey even more, so I hold up my hands and take a slow step toward them. "Look, man. I get that this situation sucks, and I'm sorry it's turned out this way for you, but you need to let Zoey go. She wants her mom. Just let her go. Please. Let her go."

"Shut up!" he bellows. "You shut the fuck up. You have no say here!"

Zoey covers her ears and cries even louder.

"You're scaring her!" Sienna steps forward. "Please, just let me hold her."

"No. She's mine!"

Shit. This arrogant fuck just won't see reason.

I'm just trying to calculate my next best move when I spot two blurry shadows moving past the back of the greenhouse. I dart my eyes back to Russell, making sure to distract him. "It's obvious you're not in a good headspace, but let me just say this... You took Zoey without Sienna's permission. That's kidnapping, man. The police are already on their way, and I'm not letting you disappear, so just make things easier for yourself and let Zoey go."

Russell's shaking his head, his jaw clenching as he tightens his hold on my daughter. Her wails increase to an earsplitting scream followed by a shattering of a glass.

Two bodies jump through the broken window, launching themselves at Russell and Zoey.

I run forward, worried for my little girl's safety, as

Wily snatches Russell's arm and Ethan clamps his fingers around the back of his neck.

Zoey starts to slip from his grasp, and I lunge, catching her just before she hits the ground. Hauling her into my arms, I cradle the back of her head. She's still crying, whimpering against my shoulder as I turn back to Sienna, who's running toward us with arms outstretched.

I walk into her embrace, wrapping my free arm around her and forming a tight huddle with my girls.

"Shhh, it's okay, baby girl." I kiss Zoey's chubby little cheek, then press my lips into Sienna's golden hair.

Thank fuck they're both okay.

"Get your fucking hands off me!" Russell is yelling up a storm, and I have to get Zoey out of here.

"Take her." I pass her to Sienna, who holds her close, shielding her from the chaos behind my back as she runs outside.

As soon as the girls are gone, I spin back, stalking toward Russell with a growl. Fisting the front of his sweater, I walk him backward and slam him against the greenhouse wall. "You fucker!" I roar in his face.

Wily and Ethan stand on either side of me, their glares lethal as they snatch his flailing fists and pin them to his sides.

Russell's eyes flash with a manic look. "Careful, you three. I'll press assault charges. I'm paid staff at this school. You can't treat me this way."

"I don't give a fuck what you are," I seethe. "If you ever scare Zoey or Sienna like that again, I will end you. I don't give a shit what it does to my career. You stay away from my family!"

I give him one more shove before walking through

the plastic tea set. Tiny cups and saucers go flying just as the faint sound of police sirens fills the air.

"Paid staff. You think that fucking matters when you've just kidnapped his kid?" Ethan mocks him.

"You're done, dude." Wily's hard voice is music to my ears.

It matches the sweet harmony of Grady shouting, "I got it! I recorded the whole thing."

"Me too!" Asher shouts.

"Ha! Suck it, Fish Sticks!" Casey lets out a raucous laugh, and my lips start to twitch as I barrel outside and find Sienna and Zoey cuddled up on a tree stump—safe and together.

CHAPTER 60
SIENNA

Zoey's whimpering against my chest as I rock her back and forth, trying to soothe her. The poor little thing is so confused. She doesn't understand how Uncle Rusty could go from playing tea parties with her to shouting and squeezing her too tight.

She's terrified, and I hate the way she's quivering against me.

But then two strong arms are sliding around us, securing us against his chest, and I close my eyes, relief pulsing through me.

"It's over," Zander murmurs against my hair. "The police are on their way."

I sniff and nod, trying to bolster a smile, but I'm a wreck. All I can do is cry and hold my baby girl.

"She's safe," Zander reminds me. "She's with us, and no one's going to take her away again, okay?"

Sucking in a dry sob, I nod. "Yeah. She's safe."

"I've got you." His husky voice whispers against my cheek. "I've got you both."

Zoey pulls away from me, glancing up at Zander with her tear-streaked face. Her eyes are so big and blue and round.

"Foobawl," she whimpers, her lips puckering.

"Hey, baby girl. You doing okay?" Zander's voice when he talks to her is so gentle and sweet. My insides instantly melt, a smile tugging at my lips as I brush Zoey's curls off her face.

She nods and touches my chest. "Mommy."

"That's right." Zander's smile is warm with affection. "That's your amazing mommy."

Zoey nods again, then looks at Zander, studying his expression before quietly asking, "Daddy?"

"That's me." Zander pats his chest. "I'm your daddy, and I love you so much." His voice breaks, and he has to clear his throat. "But you can keep calling me Football if you want to. Whatever works, okay? Because no matter what name you use, I'll always be your daddy, and I'll always come when you need me."

Her cheeks tinge a soft pink, her nose wrinkling as she smiles up at him. "Daddy pay?"

Aw, bleoo. Zander looks like he's about to start sobbing like a baby.

His eyes glisten, his voice husky and raw when he replies, "Yeah. I'd love to play with you. Should we go now? Let's go play right now."

Standing us up, he walks us around the back of Coach Bergeron's truck, avoiding the rush of police officers who are storming into the greenhouse. We, of course, get stopped and questioned. Two officers check that Zoey is with her rightful parents, and it's a relief to assure them that she is.

It takes way longer than it should, and Zoey's fussing by the time we finally get to walk away from the greenhouse. I don't want her seeing her Uncle Rusty being marched out of there in cuffs, and thankfully the policewoman gives me a nod of understanding when I mention it.

"We'll call if we have any more questions."

"Thank you, Officer." Zander gives her a grateful smile, then leads us out to the road. He keeps us in a protective bubble until we've crossed to his car.

I buckle Zoey into her new car seat and brush her hair back with a smile. "Love you, lil' bug."

"Lalu, Mommy."

Kissing her forehead, I slip in the back next to her, needing to hold her little hand the entire way home. Zander grins at me in the rearview mirror. As soon as he catches my eye, I get the pleasure of his sexy little wink, and my flailing insides simmer down with a soft sigh.

It's over.

Zoey's safe, and finally she can grow up with the father she was meant to have all along.

CHAPTER 61
ZANDER

The house is in chaos. You'd think we were throwing a major party with the amount of noise in here, but I guess that's what happens when your woman insists that we invite the entire crew from Hockey House over as a thank-you for helping us get Zoey back.

It's kind of a miracle that they were all free. Even Lani walked through the door with a determined look on her face. I patted her arm, a silent show of support as her eyes darted down the hallway and then quickly shifted to Asher.

"We can bail if you need to, Boo."

"No, I'm okay." She nodded, pulling in a breath. "I'm not going to let him touch me anymore. Even metaphorically."

"Never again," Asher promised her, and I sent her a silent promise of my own.

The fact that she got raped in this house during one of our parties still makes me see red. I fought sleepless nights for weeks after I found out, but my angst faded over the summer, and when the school year started, I made the guys promise that we wouldn't slip up like that again. Any parties we throw this year are going to be invite-only.

We've actually been so busy this season, we haven't even had the time or energy to organize a party.

Until today.

As soon as Wily got in touch with Ethan, he made sure everyone could make it. So here we are at Football Frat, drinking beers, waiting for the meat to finish cooking on the grill, and watching a four-year-old Kai chase after my screaming two-year-old.

"They are so adorable." A short Asian woman whose name I keep forgetting laughs with Sienna as she watches her son leap around the couch and roar like a lion.

Zoey lets out another gleeful scream and takes off running, using Wily's legs like tree trunks and hiding behind one of them before darting between them and shooting past Casey. He's taken over the biggest beanbag and is sitting on it with his redheaded girlfriend whose name I can't remember either.

Shit, we need fucking name tags in this place.

I know all the guys, but I'm struggling to remember the girls. I think that's Mikayla—or is it Michelle?—talking to Teah. They both look kind of nervous for some reason. Grady's standing nearby, his arm around Teah's waist, and Rachel is on the other side of Mikayla, looking kind of protective. I have no idea what that's about, but at least I remember her name, right?

I only know it because she used to work at Eat Your Faves diner, and they serve the best milkshakes in Nolan. She wore a name tag, and I'd say hi and smile at her every time she served me. See? Name tags, people. They fucking work.

"Oh, you wanna bet?" Mikayla's head jolts back, her voice rising by a few decibels as she looks up at her boyfriend.

He gives her an incredulous frown. "I'm smart enough to never make a bet with you, lil' mouse. I don't want to end up getting my left nut tattooed because I can't win whatever ridiculousness you're about to throw at me."

She snorts and starts laughing, tipping her head back before leaning against him and patting his stomach. "A tattoo on your left nut. That's funny. What would you even get down there?"

"Dude! Nothing! You don't put needles near the love cannon and ammunition, are you crazy?" Casey calls from the beanbag. "What's this bet anyway?"

Teah giggles. "Ethan doesn't think Mikayla can handle the Sig Be party I'm inviting everyone to without getting completely wasted."

Rachel grins. "And now we're just waiting to hear if Mick has a counter bet for her man."

"How about we just hold all bets and get through one meal together without anybody losing anything?" Lani raises her glass. "To acting like normal human beings when we're guests in someone else's home."

"Are we even capable of that?" Mick raises her glass with a dubious frown.

Ethan laughs while Casey yells, "Puck yeah, we are!"

Everyone cheers and takes a drink except Mikayla, who bulges her eyes and mutters, "Just proving my point here, guys. Nobody normal says, 'puck yeah.'"

I can't help laughing as I shake my head and share a

quick look with Grady. These hockey guys are entertaining if nothing else. As are the two little squirts jumping over outstretched legs and giggling up a storm.

"You know, if you ever want to hang out, we could do a playdate for Kai and Zoey. I'm sure he'd love that."

Sienna spins to look at Tara. No. Tyler?

"Tammy, that would be amazing."

Tammy! Got it.

Stop forgetting, you douche. Especially if your daughter is going to be hanging with her son.

"Yay." Tammy grins, her dimples popping into place. "We live out at the Ponderosa Villa now. I can give you directions. It only takes like twenty minutes to get there, and there's a big backyard, and Baxter's building a playground castle thing for Kai. Plus, Rachel bakes the best muffins. You should totally come hang with us. We'd love it."

"Oh my gosh." Sienna wraps her arm around Tammy's shoulders. "You just made my day. Seriously. Thank you. I've been trying to find some little buddies for Zoey, and I've gone to one playgroup, but it's kind of awkward, and I know it'll probably get easier and I should keeping trying, but..." She winces. "I'm like the youngest mom there by so much, and it just feels—"

"Weird. I totally get it. I had Kai when I was eighteen, and people don't always understand what it's like being a teenage mom. They look at you like the babysitter, and then when they find out you're the mom, they treat you like you don't know what you're doing or you're a complete screwup for getting pregnant in the first place."

"I know, right?" Sienna's blue eyes glisten with relief. "Oh my gosh, it's so good to talk to someone who gets it.

I'm so glad you made it today. It's seriously so nice to meet you."

"You too." Tammy's smile is golden, and I'm so fucking grateful for her right now.

"Hey, Zan-Man?" Wily calls across the room. "Got any more drinks, or should I make a quick run to the store?"

"Let me check the fridge first." I head toward the kitchen, checking our stock and getting out a few more beers and sodas to pass around.

The grill is fired up outside, and I poke my head through the window, grinning at Liam, Baxter, and Tyrell, who are manning the barbecue.

"Smells good, guys."

"Brats will be ready in about five."

"Sounds good." I'm about to walk back through the kitchen and play best host when I'm stopped by a sexy-ass smile on the most gorgeous blonde I've ever seen. "Hey, you." I put the drinks down on the table so I can wrap my arms around her waist.

Pulling her close, I nuzzle her neck.

She lets out a sweet little moan, so I do it some more until she's giggling against my shoulder.

Damn, I love this woman so fucking much.

Considering the shit we went through a week ago and then the pending visit from my parents, she still manages to find a way to laugh and smile through it all.

Russell was immediately fired from Nolan U and is dealing with kidnapping charges. I haven't heard the latest, but I think his lawyer is trying to plea some kind of insanity-type deal. He lost his mind for a minute. I don't know if that's just a rumor. All I care about is that he stays away from my family.

Sienna never wants to see him again, and it's been hella awkward considering her dad is best friends with Russell's father. I have no idea how things will unfold, but I'll be protecting my girls at every turn.

A squeal bounces off the walls as Zoey darts into the dining room. I can't see her from this angle, but her laughter is my favorite song, and I smile down at Sienna, who is obviously enjoying the sound just as much as I am.

"It's so cute watching her play." Sienna looks toward the doorway. "It makes me want another one."

"I want another three."

"What?" She whips her head back to gape at me, and I can't help grinning at her shocked expression.

"I want a big family with you, Sparks." I squeeze her hip. "But I know you had a really shitty pregnancy, so I'd never ask that of you. Unless, of course, you wanted to."

She keeps gaping at me, like she's still trying to process my first comment.

I lightly pinch her earlobe, brushing my fingers down her face. "When I picture our future together, we're surrounded by kids. Our house is buzzing with laughter and Taylor Swift."

She laughs. "There'll be football on the TV and Nerds scattered on the coffee table."

I wrinkle my nose and tease her right back. "We'll be serving hot dogs for dinner."

She sticks out her tongue and dry retches. I laugh and kiss her lips, then lean back and soften my voice. "I know our future is kinda uncertain. If I get drafted, who knows where we'll end up. Going pro will be a busy life for me, and I'll be away. It's asking a lot of you, but—"

"I've always imagined us having a bunch of kids," she interrupts me with a grin. "And I know you'll be away and traveling, but I can do this. My parents will support me, and I'll make it work. I have to make it work, because I want to be with you, and I want Zoey to have siblings. I love being a mom." She wraps her arms around me, rising to her tiptoes. "And I love making babies with you."

My laughter is low and husky as I pull her tighter against me and kiss her deep. "I love that part too."

Her breath whistles across my chin, and I peck the tip of her nose. "So, you'll get me pregnant again?"

"When you're ready, yeah. I'd love to do that... on one condition."

"Oh yeah, what's that?" Her eyes twinkle with that playful sparkle I love so much.

"Marry me."

She gasps. "Are you proposing right now?"

I shake my head. "No, I want to come up with something way more romantic, but I just... I'd love you to be my wife before we have any more kids. I know that's old-fashioned, but I've wanted to marry you since..." I tip my head, memories flooding me, but the truth is... "Our first date. Watching you devour that insanely sweet dessert, teaching you how to play mini golf. I knew then that I wanted you forever. I just..." I wince. "I lost my way in the middle there for a little minute. But I promise, I am never letting you go again."

"I know." She jumps up, wrapping her legs around me and kissing me until I can't see straight.

I groan, palming her ass and giving it a light squeeze while gliding my tongue across hers and forgetting that we're in a house full of people.

"Food's ready!" Tyrell hollers, walking through the kitchen with a steaming tray of brats.

I take my time, finishing up my kiss before pulling away and smiling at Sienna.

Baxter eases past us, and I barely notice him until he lets out a "Whoa" and catches a missile with blonde curls as she races through the kitchen.

"No running in the kitchen," Sienna reminds her.

I reluctantly lower my woman to the floor. We'll pick this up later, and I seriously need to come up with a decent proposal. And a ring. Shit, I need to find the perfect ring. I'll get Monica to help me with that.

My mind is ticking over while the bustle of activity in the dining room grows. Sienna gathers up the drinks and is about to take them through when she's stopped by Carson. He frowns down at her, and I give him a warning glare, which he doesn't notice because he's too busy taking in Sienna's unimpressed scowl.

Okay, so we still have a few kinks to work out with our living situation.

But I've yet to think of a decent solution. I wanted to get the girls settled after that clusterfuck with Russell.

"Ah!" Zoey lets out another scream, diving in front of Carson to hide from Kai.

Carson winces at her earsplitting volume and tries to move away from her, but she wraps her little arms and legs around him, sitting on his foot when Kai makes a move to tickle her.

Carson darts his foot away so Kai can't reach, and Zoey laughs.

"Again! Again!"

"No! Get off me, kid."

Kai stiffens at Carson's grumpy voice, shrinking away from the guy and darting out of the room.

Sienna tuts. "Carson, be nice. You tone is too harsh. You just scared him."

"I don't give a shit," he grumbles.

"He don't give tit."

"Zoey!" Sienna frowns. "Do not talk like Carson. He uses bad words."

Confused, Zoey stares up at Carson like she's thinking, *He wouldn't do something bad, would he?*

I fight my grin as he stares right back at my adoring daughter.

"Get off my foot. I'm leaving."

"No." Zoey shakes her head. "Stay. Pay."

"I don't want to play." Carson lifts his leg and gives it a shake, but Zoey holds on tight, giggling like this is a fun ride. "Seriously, would you get her off me?"

His exasperation is hilarious, but I don't want him accidentally hurting my little girl, so I grab her around the waist and help my buddy out. Pulling her against my chest, I give him a smile, but all he can do is narrow his eyes at me and growl, "This isn't working, Donohue. Either you find some new digs or I will."

I wince, hating that idea. Carson can't leave. He's too unpredictable, and he needs us to keep an eye on him.

But I don't want to go either.

Unfortunately, that's the better choice. Sienna and I will need to figure this out sooner or later.

"Sorry, man," I mutter. "I'll try and come up with something soon."

"I still say we convert that garage out back into a studio apartment." Wily walks in on our conversation.

"You know Baxter's thinking about starting up a reno business. Maybe we could give him some work."

I hiss. "Not sure I can afford that, man." Especially now that I have a ring to save for. I still have some funds left in my college account, but it won't be enough for both.

"We can try pitching it to the landlord. Maybe he can cover the cost, or we can go halves with him. I've got the money."

"Your *family* has the money," I counter.

Wily rolls his eyes and ignores my comment. "It'll definitely up the resale value of the house. Right now, it's just an empty, wasted space filled with junk. I'll help empty it out and prep it."

Wily's getting all excited, and I look across the room at Sienna, who's nodding with a little grin.

Yeah, that could be a fun project.

I move out of the kitchen with Zoey and start hunting for Baxter while Carson mutters, "Thank fuck," behind me and heads for the front door.

It slams a few moments later, and then Zoey and I watch him rev his motorcycle and shoot out of the driveway.

Shit, I have no idea where he's going right now, but I hope he doesn't do anything reckless.

He's been off for a few weeks now, and I put it down to Sienna and Zoey being here.

The problem is, when Carson's off... trouble always follows in his wake.

"You okay?" Sienna's arms wrap around me from behind. Leaning her cheek against my arm, she stares out the window with me.

"Yeah." I nod, turning so I can put my arm around her. Giving her a reassuring smile, I kiss her head. "Come on. Let's go talk to Baxter and see if we can't make ourselves a little studio apartment out back."

She gives me a happy grin, kissing Zoey's chubby little hands before heading into the dining room. I trail after her while Zoey pokes my cheek with her little finger and asks, "Daddy pay?"

"Yeah, of course I'll play with you. Let's just have some food first. Hey, how about a hot dog. I bet you've never had one of those before."

I grin, walking into the dining room while Zoey cheerfully shouts, "Ho dogs! Ho dogs!" making everyone in the room but her mother laugh.

Giving Sienna a little wink, I prepare lunch for our daughter and see how easy it's gonna be to get used to this.

Marrying Sienna. Making babies with that beauty. Raising Zoey and however many other kids we have.

Damn, if that idea doesn't make me the happiest man on this planet.

CHAPTER 62
CARSON

I shoot down the road, shaking off the happy family vibes radiating out of Football Frat right now. I mean, what the actual fuck?

Hockey guys and their girlfriends? Kids running around like it's a fucking Christmas movie?

As if Thanksgiving coming up isn't bad enough. Zander's taking over our fucking house with his daddy bullshit, and I'm done.

I don't want to live with a toddler. Yes, she's damn cute. And yes, when I found out what that prick Fisher did to her, I wanted to smash the guy's head in. How dare he scare her that way? That fucker!

I didn't even find out about it until the early hours of the morning. I got home at like two and Zander was still up, sitting in the darkness and stewing. He told me everything, and I wanted to ask him why he hadn't called me. I would have been there in a heartbeat. I could have helped.

But he probably thinks I hate his little squirt.

I don't. She's fucking adorable, okay?

She just doesn't belong at Football Frat, and no one seems to understand that.

I am a junior in college, and I should be partying it up and having a good time, not living with a kid who still shits their own pants.

Shaking my head, I drive a little faster, heading for the one place I know I shouldn't go. But the reminder text came through twenty minutes ago, and I could only respond with an "I'll be there."

I can't seem to stay away, even though I know I should.

If I get caught, there's a strong chance I'll get kicked off the team. Coach doesn't care that I'm one of the best wide receivers Nolan U has ever had. He cares more about character and shit, the type of men he's training in his football program. It's not about results; it's about integrity and all the other horseshit he won't shut up about.

Despite all that, football has been a lifeline for me. I really shouldn't risk losing it.

But as I pull up next to the curb and spot her waiting on the sidewalk, I know I'm gonna go. I'm gonna cross that street, because she's a fucking tractor beam.

She has been ever since I met her three and half weeks ago...

I turned up to practice a little hungover.

Anyone would think that was a crime against humanity the way Coach was acting.

"If you can't be here ready to give it your all, then you shouldn't bother coming!" he barked at me.

I resisted the urge to give him the finger and then tried to prove that I was fucking capable of being slightly buzzed and still giving it my all.

He saw straight through my bullshit and made me stick around after practice.

"I wanted your best, and you gave me barely half of what you're capable of. So you can stay behind and run a few more drills, sweat that stuff right out of your body."

"What? That's bullshit!" I'd snapped at him, my insides raging as my roommates tried to signal me to shut the hell up and just take it.

"You're gonna give me five minutes of up-downs, then you're gonna give me five on the ladder, then five around the cones. I'll set up a course for you."

"No," I barked like an idiot.

"Okay." Coach nodded, his calm smile riling me up another notch. "Let's make it ten minutes of each, then."

"I don't want to do that shit!"

"Then turn up to my practices sober!" Coach yelled. "Now, you get your butt on that field, and you give thirty minutes of your best."

I stood my ground, my upper lip curling as I threw my helmet down with a smack.

"Forty-five minutes, then." Coach crossed his arms. "Are we gonna make it a full hour, or do you just want me to pull you from the game this weekend?"

"Fuck," I whispered under my breath, my pulse hammering as I ran a hand through my sweaty hair. I couldn't be benched again. I fucking hated that.

Spinning with a growl, I stalked over to the cones.

"Sorry, man." Grady winced as I passed him, but he didn't stick around to run the drill with me. Fuckwit!

Even Zander bailed. He usually would have stayed for moral support, but he'd been stupidly distracted with this whole ex-girlfriend/new daughter shit.

So there I was, stuck on the field by myself.

Coach popped out to check on me once, hollering some new instructions at me, then punching me directly in the nutsack when he ended with "And when you're done, pick up all the gear. Once it's stored away properly, you can go."

It pissed me off, but I got through my fucking drills. My head was pounding, and I couldn't fucking wait to get out of there. All I had left was the cleanup, which was damn unfair. So I was a little hungover. Give me a fucking break!

Snatching one of the balls off the ground, I hurled it down to the other end of the field.

My chest was heaving as I watched it bounce off the grass and ping toward a Black girl who was standing on the sidelines watching me.

Fuck, how long has she been standing there?

I frowned at her, ready to bark her off the field and tell her she was trespassing. But I figured I may as well check her out first. She was pretty hot. Long black hair with a wave to it, lean body with a decent rack. She had a sweet curve to her ass, which was obvious in those tight jeans she was wearing.

Shouting at her was possibly the wrong move. What would actually make me feel better was getting in those pants. If anything can put you in a better mood, it's a quick fuck to release some of the tension, right?

Sauntering toward her, I was about to smirk and do my chin-raising gesture, but she looked away from me, walking over to the ball I'd just thrown.

Her gait was a little weird. Was she limping?

I frowned, studying the way she awkwardly leaned down to grab the ball, but then she was pinging back up straight, pointing at me and yelling, "Go long!"

Yeah, right.

Those skinny arms?

I ignored her, moving forward to collect the ball, then unhinging my jaw when she sent a perfect spiral down the field.

With a surprised blink, I spun and sprinted after it but missed, the ball bouncing wildly near my feet before I picked it up and threw it back.

She hobbled to the side, getting herself in position and catching the ball before giving me a pointed look and saying again, "Go long."

This time, I did as she told me, watching the ball like a hawk and making a perfect catch.

Damn, what an arm.

Spinning back with a curious frown, I jogged toward her, throwing the ball back as I went.

She caught it and passed it back to me when I ran forward.

Cradling the ball against my side, I stopped a few feet away from her. "Who are you?"

Her smile was slow and beautiful, stretching over her face and sending this weird spark through my chest.

"The name's Nylah." Her brown eyes glinted. "And you are?"

"Carson." I pointed at myself. "What are you doing here?"

"Just waiting." She shrugged, her smile kind of cryptic.

"For what?"

"Nylah!" Coach Jones shouted from the other side of the field. "That boy doesn't have time to chat!"

I glanced over my shoulder, wondering how Coach knew this chick's name, until she went and made everything worse by saying...

"Hey, Dad."

"Dad?" I whipped back around to look at her. "Are you fucking kidding me?"

She snickered and shook her head. "I'll see you around, Mr. Attitude."

"That's the lamest insult ever." I shot her a dry look. "You know that, right?"

She laughed. "I'll keep working on it, then." With a playful wink, she waved goodbye and then walked across the field toward her father.

Her father.

Fuck.

So not worth going there.

Gripping the back of my neck, I raised my hand to acknowledge Coach when he barked a few more orders, then got back to collecting all the gear, but not before pausing to watch the hottie walk across the field and give her father a hug.

Coach caught me watching, and I quickly averted my gaze.

You stay away from that chick, Carson. Stay the fuck away.

. . .

But have I listened to my own advice?

That would be a big fat nope.

Getting off my motorcycle, I check the road, then run across it, coming to a stop next to the girl with the sexy smile and glinting brown eyes.

"Hey, Trouble." I smirk down at her.

She grins up at me. "Lame."

I can't help a short laugh. This chick is a piece of work.

"How's it going, Douche Nugget?" Her flirty smile makes my chest tight.

I try to hide how much she affects me and manage a soft "Lame" before shrugging and tipping my head toward the movie theater behind me. "So, are we doing this or what?"

"Let's go." She turns and walks toward the building.

I trail after her, trying not to notice how fucking hot she looks in those pants. The little tank top she's wearing under her jacket shows off a strip of her stomach, and I want to trail my fingers over that smooth skin so fucking badly.

But we haven't gone there yet.

It's bad enough that I'm going to the movies with her.

If Coach finds out, I'm dead.

But since when has the threat of death ever stopped me from doing what I want?

Dude, you are so fucked.

Yeah, I'm well aware.

But like hell I'm walking away now.

Nylah Jones is something else.

A forbidden fruit I have to taste... but also so much more.

She's fire, and I will turn myself to fucking ash if it means I get to spend more time with her.

Carson and Nylah's sizzling, forbidden romance will be available in June 2025.

Get ready for witty banter as this good girl and bad boy clash and flirt and fall in love. This steamy romance will send you on a roller coaster of emotion.

Available on Amazon: June 10, 2025

NOTE FROM KATY

Dear reader,

Thank you so much for reading Zander and Sienna's second-chance romance. I hope it filled your chest with warm fuzzies and love bubbles. I had so much fun writing it and watching these star-crossed lovers finally find their way back to each other. And Zoey is all things cute. I love how much she adores the big football boys... and the way she keeps interacting with Carson even though he doesn't want her around. It's like she can sense something in him that no one else can see... except maybe a certain Coach's daughter...

Eeeepppp! I'm so excited to write this bad boy/good girl forbidden romance. So many of my favorite elements are involved in THE OFF-LIMITS PLAY—grumpy x sunshine, forbidden romance, and family angst and drama. I adore forbidden romance. There's something so enticing about the whole sneaking around/secret affair thing and I love a good bad boy. Nylah is going to change Carson's life and I can't wait to see it unfold. Bring on the sizzle and the banter and the heartache... and those sweet moments that turn our hearts to mush 🫠 🤍

If you enjoyed *The Forever Play*, I would so appreciate you leaving an honest review on Amazon and/or Goodreads. Even just a star rating is helpful. You don't have to write anything if you don't want to. But star ratings and even short reviews really help validate the book, letting readers know it's worth a shot. It also tells Amazon and Goodreads that this book is worth shining a spotlight on. I know there are a bunch of readers out there who love college sports romance just as much as we do. If you can help me reach them, then that would be freaking fantastic.
Thanks for the assist!

I'd also like to thank a few key people who have been instrumental in helping me get this book off the ground —Megan, Kristin, Beth and Rachael. You are such a great team to work with and I appreciate each and everyone of you so much.

Maggie and Trudi—my writing buddies and total inspirations. Thank you for always cheering me on.

My review team—you are seriously the best! Thank you so much for the constant support and promoting of my books. I'm so incredibly grateful.

My readers—Nolan U wouldn't be out there without your

support. Thank you for loving this world and the characters so much. I appreciate you more than I can say.

My fellas—thanks for making me laugh on the daily. Thanks for loving me and looking after me and giving me a reason to get up in the morning. I love you all so much.

My heart and soul—thank you for being my forever love, the one I can always rely on. You're my safety, my harbor, my home and I wouldn't want to live a single day without you. Thank you that I never have to 🤍

xoxo
Katy

BOOKS BY KATY ARCHER

NOLAN U HOCKEY
Hockey House V-cards (prequel)
The Forbidden Freshman
The Heart Stealer
The Game Changer
The Love Penalty
The Only Goal
The Forever Game

NOLAN U FOOTBALL
Releasing in 2025
The First Play (prequel)
The Forever Play
The Off-Limits Play
The Surprise Play
The Illicit Play
The Perfect Play
The Christmas Play

NOLAN U BASKETBALL

Releasing in 2026

NOLAN U - GEN 2

Starting in 2027

CONTACT KATY

I love to hear from my readers, so feel free to email me anytime. You can also find out more on my website.

EMAIL: katy@katyarcher.com

WEBSITE: www.katyarcher.com

And if you want to connect with me on social media, you can find me Addicted to College Sports Romance on...

INSTAGRAM:
www.instagram.com/addictedtocollegesportsromance/

FACEBOOK:
www.facebook.com/people/College-Sports-Romance-Books/61553919569131/

TIKTOK:
www.tiktok.com/@katyarcherbooks